OBSESSIONS

OBSESSIONS

SEARCHING ARCANIA 2

Anthony R Galetti

Contents

To all those who read and enjoyed Searching Arcania; you inspired me to keep writing.

To the donators who helped make publishing this book possible;
my sincerest thank you.

Prologue

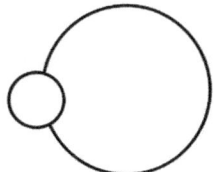

My walker makes its steady clicking sounds as I shuffle my way slowly down the short hall to the front room of my cabin. My legs have little strength left. The doctors have only recently figured out that I have ALS. They find it odd that, so far, it has attacked only my legs. In the last few years, I've gone from a cane to crutches, then to the walker I now use. They think I'll need a wheelchair before this year's end.

Reaching my recliner, I find Sada, my white cat, curled up on her cushion nearby. I sit and loosen the straps on my leg braces. The noise wakes Sada, and after a couple of stretches and a yawn, she moves to my lap only to lie back down. I gently scrub her neck and look out the windows to see a familiar car come up the long driveway.

I turn to watch the deer graze in the nearby meadow while waiting for my visitor to arrive. I notice that, even with my glasses, the deer aren't as clear as they once were.

It's progressing, starting to take my eyesight from me.

Hearing a car door close, I look to see Alicia, my home care nurse, come up to the door. "Morning," she calls as she comes in.

"Morning."

Sada slowly rolls onto her back, purring, wanting a belly rub. Alicia chuckles and gives her a quick one. "How are you feeling?"

"I'm getting worse," I sadly admit, "I can't see the deer clearly anymore."

She sits on a stool next to me, looking at me with a concerned expression. "Is there anything else?"

I hesitate, not wanting to tell her, but honesty gets the better of me. "Yeah, I had an 'accident' this morning."

She makes a few notes and gives me a curious look. "Do I need to change the bedding?"

I smile, only slightly embarrassed. "No, I got it."

"You should start wearing the diapers, at least at night."

I give her a sour look. "I'm not losing control. It was just an accident."

She looks at me skeptically but concedes. "Alright."

She then starts with my checkup, checking the usual things, like my temperature, blood pressure, then listening to my heart and lungs. Then she moves on to the more specific tests like reflexes and strength, making her notes after each one. Afterward, I gently rub my left arm as a muscle there starts twitching.

She looks up and apparently sees it twitching. "How often has that been happening?"

Sighing again, I give up. "The first was a few days ago. Yesterday I must have had more than a dozen in that arm. I also had some trouble swallowing this morning." I look sadly over at her. "I'm running out of time, aren't I?"

She hesitates, not wanting to answer the question. "Are you sure you want to stay out here? You could get much better care at a nursing home, or assisted living."

"I don't want to sound like a grumpy old man but, I'm not going to die somewhere I don't feel comfortable." I gently rub Sada's head. "Besides, they wouldn't let me keep her with me."

She sighs, knowing I'm right, also knowing that either of us would probably die without the other. "How old is she now? Fifteen? Sixteen?"

"Seventeen, Meagan picked her up when Michael was six months old. I've had her ever since."

Alicia sighs, looking at Sada, then the floor, I see a tear run down her cheek as she looks back up at me. "Is there anything you need me to pick up?"

I sigh, fighting the urge to cry myself. "I'd like... some mint chocolate chip ice cream."

She smiles as another tear rolls down her cheek. "I can do that." She gives Sada a gentle rub on her head and me a kiss on the forehead. "I'll see you tomorrow morning."

"I'll be here."

I watch as she picks up her bag and heads for her car. As she sits in her car wiping her eyes, I realize that I'm taking my impending death better than she is. After a few moments, she starts her car and slowly drives away.

After she's out of sight, I pick up my phone and press the redial button.

"Hello?"

"Tom, it's Kyle."

"Kyle, I was about to call you, the paperwork you wanted is ready."

"Good, how soon can you come out so I can sign it?"

I hear him shuffle some papers. "How about, tomorrow at, uhm, one?"

"That'd be good, thanks, Tom. See you tomorrow."

I set the phone down, lean back in my recliner, and watch the deer graze in the field.

As I watch the sky darken, Sada shifts positions, trying to get comfortable again. I gently scrub her cheek and she stretches. After a while, she hops down and I tighten the straps on my braces. After moving my walker into position, I lift myself out of the chair and onto it.

I make my way to the bathroom and eye the adult diapers that Alicia brought me last week. I breathe a heavy sigh while contemplating what happened this morning; waking up in bed to find I needed to change not only myself but the bedding too. Swallowing my pride, I grab a couple diapers and make my way to my bedroom. Sitting on the edge of the bed, I change, putting one on under my pajamas.

Sada comes in and walks up her steps to get onto the bed. I had them made for her when she started having trouble jumping. She walks up to me, purring as I pull the covers up. After I get comfortable, she lies down on my chest. I gently rub her back, keeping her purring as I let myself drift off to sleep.

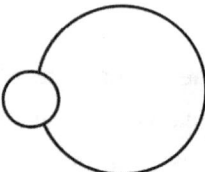

"Hey, sleepyhead, did you spend the night in your recliner?"

I open my eyes to see Alicia leaning over me, smiling. I smile back. "Just a nap. I woke up too early this morning."

She sighs. "You're losing bowel control aren't you?"

I nod my head sadly. "Yeah, thanks for the diapers."

"Not so embarrassed now are you."

As I shake my head, she reaches into her bag and pulls out a small, paper-wrapped container. She then heads to the kitchen and I hear her get a bowl. She comes back with the bowl and a spoon. "Your ice cream."

I take the bowl and gently sniff its mint chocolate aroma. "Mmm, thank you."

She pulls out her stethoscope and starts listening to my heart as I savor the first spoonful of ice cream. I set the bowl aside for a moment as she checks my lungs. When I pick it up again, Sada is licking at the ice cream. "Hey, no chocolate. I'll give you some ice cream in a minute."

She looks up at me, purring, as Alicia chuckles. "I brought a saucer, too." She sets it down on the table as I scrape up some of the mint ice cream, carefully avoiding the chocolate chips. Sada slowly follows my spoon over to the saucer as I drop the small scoop on it, then happily dives into it.

Alicia gets out some things, and I sigh. "Do we really need to run *those* tests today, I'm really not feeling up for them right now."

She frowns slightly but concedes. "Tomorrow then, but I will not put it off another day. I need to do these if you're to stay on the new meds."

"I know." I set my ice cream aside and pull myself up in the chair, trying to get more comfortable.

She looks sadly at me for a moment. "Pains?"

"Yeah, a few."

"New ones?"

"No, old ones, reminding me that they're there."

She sighs as she makes some more notes. "With tomorrow Friday, I have to do the tests. Trish is covering this weekend. I'll bring her up to speed after I see you tomorrow."

"Any plans?"

She smiles. "Seeing my family."

"No boyfriend yet, huh?"

She smiles and blushes. "That obvious?"

I smile back. "You haven't talked about a man since you dumped the last one nearly two years ago. You would've said something if you had a new one."

She blushes again, nearly laughing. "You're right, I would've."

"No offense, but you need to find a man who'll respect you."

"I know." She starts repacking her equipment, trying to hide her mild frustration. "I'm just too busy lately."

"You need to make some time for yourself, and have a life."

As she closes her bag, I can tell that something is bothering her. Not wanting to pry, I let her finish in silence. After a moment, she sighs sadly but doesn't look up at me. "You're all I have left, you know."

Puzzled at her sorrow-filled statement, I ask, "What do you mean?"

She turns to look at me, a tear in her eye. "Mr. Turnkle passed last week, and my other was moved to a home. You're my last."

Seeing the sadness in her eyes. I lower my gaze, "I'm sorry." She starts to say something but stops, and instead, she sits quietly for a moment.

When her phone chimes, she checks it. With a heavy sigh, she says "I need to go."

"See you tomorrow, then." I watch her slowly leave, wondering what she's going to do after I pass. As her car disappears down the drive, I realize that Sada's eating my ice cream.

"Oh no you don't, that much will make you sick," I gently scold, as I take the bowl. She curiously looks up at me, licking her lips. I chuckle at how the fur around her mouth is tinted green with ice cream. I gently wipe her chin with a napkin, then turn my attention to the hummingbirds just outside the window and finish what little is left of my ice cream.

Tom arrives and finds me waiting for him. He pulls out a large packet and sets it in front of me on the kitchen table. "I take it, your sister is aware of this?"

"Yeah, I spoke with her and she agrees, it's still mine to do with as I please." I quickly review the first page, making sure that it's what I want. "This takes effect as soon as I sign it, right?"

"Yes, though I would need some signatures from her, however, per your stipulations, that can happen at any time, even after…"

"Good."

Tom starts giving me a summary as I skim through the documents, signing my name or initials where needed. After over an hour, we finally finish.

He puts the packet up, pulls out a smaller packet, and sets it on the table. "These are what she'll need to sign and she can present them to my office anytime. My card's inside if she has any questions."

"Thanks, Tom."

"It's been my pleasure." He shakes my hand and heads out the door.

I grab my notepad and pen and start writing a letter.

Dear Alicia,

You have shown me a kindness that has brought back memories of happier days, and have made these last few years of life worth living. For that, I am eternally grateful. I know that I have made some unusual requests of you these last few years, and I greatly appreciate that you have humored me.

I know you did not expect this, but I've come to think of you like family, and as my thanks, I have a gift for you. You don't need to accept, but I ask that you do. You can do what you want with it, but I ask that you take some time for yourself, and live, enjoy life while you're still young.

If you have any questions about what's inside, Tom will be glad to help you with them.

Sincerely yours,

Kyle

I put the letter in an envelope, write her name on it and set it on top of the packet, then push them to the center of the table. After grabbing my walker, I slowly make my way to the bedroom and lie down for a nap. Sada follows me onto the bed and stretches out alongside me, purring.

1

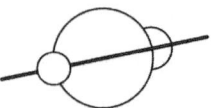

"Kyle, Railu needs you. She's in her room."

"Tell her I'll be right there, Ziggy." I slide out from between the converter's housing and wall of the cold storage room and then push it up against the wall. Its lights come on indicating that it has power and should be working. That's the fourth converter, and currently the largest, I've salvaged from the facility and installed in my home.

"Link complete, diagnostic check complete. Unit operational," Ziggy reports.

I smile at Zoe. "There you go. One, oversized converter."

The humanoid grey squirrel excitedly bounces and wraps me in a hug. "Thank you, thank you, thank you!"

I chuckle at her exuberance and hug her back. "You're welcome."

As I turn to leave, I see her grab her tablet and ask, "What to make for lunch..."

I walk down the main hall and marvel at how quickly we've turned the near-empty house into our home. Within the first two months, I sprayed a liquid nano-matrix to the inside and outside of the entire house. Into that Aime programmed the house AI, Ziggy as we've all come to call him. Through the matrix, he can connect to and control the converters, solar panels, lights and any other devices I install.

The converter I just installed in cold storage is over three times larger than the rest. It's large enough to lie down in. I decided to put it in cold storage so Zoe could use it to make large meals, but it has other uses as well.

As I enter Railu's bedroom, I find Railu, a humanoid red fox, and my adopted sister, lying on her back. Putting my hands on her swollen belly, I state, "You know you can't be on your back. You might suffocate the kit."

"I know, but it's the only position that's comfortable right now."

As she rolls onto her side, I frown slightly. Without the few restricted raw materials, that the normal converters can't make, Aime can't finish her medical upgrades. Because of that, Railu is still having a difficult pregnancy and I haven't brought Cayla out of cryo yet.

I've been spending a good deal of my time searching the facility for a working industrial converter, or nanite class converter. While I have found a few nanite class units, none have worked. I've saved them though, to see if I can put together a working unit. Unfortunately, they all seem to have the same problem.

"Ahh. That's better, thanks," Railu states, bringing me back to the task at hand.

"I know you hate to be bedridden, but if you continue to get up and walk around, this'll keep happening."

She sighs heavily, showing her frustration. "I know. I just get so...bored."

I sit on the edge of her bed and rub the fur between her ears. "I know." When she closes her eyes, I quietly leave the room.

Passing Roen in the hall, I sigh and softly say to him, "She's been walking around again."

He nods, sighing heavily. "I thought so. I'll take care of her, even if I have to tie her to the bed."

I can't help but chuckle as he disappears into their room. I continue down the hall to the garage. After checking the charge on the three scout bikes that I've salvaged from the rescue ship, I head out to the shuttle to unpack more salvaged converters and other equipment. I unload them directly into the garage, making use of the large room to store them.

Hearing the lunch bell, I quickly wash and head to the dining room. I find Zoe waiting, with her two servers, Nanai, a red panda, and Kosh, a sable, standing behind her. Before I can get to my seat, Tayla slowly comes in the nearer door. With the twins due in just over a month, she has become quite large, and I dart over to help her to her chair.

I gently run my hand over her belly, feeling the cubs kick. "How ya feeling?"

She bumps her head to mine. "I don't know if I'll be able to move by the time they're due."

I give her a kiss. "That's at least another month. I'll help you."

"You're busy enough, helping at Garrent, scrounging things from the facility, and working on the house."

Megai gives her a hug from behind. "Then I'll help you."

"You already do, and you're busy with Amela too."

"I get her up in the morning and put her to bed at night. She has her lessons during the day and usually plays with Fey or Oana after that. I have time if you need me."

"And I can make time, all you need to do is ask," I add.

A nose pokes between us. "Oana help, Oana like help."

"I'm feeling outnumbered."

'You are,' Sada signs as she sits next to her. 'I'll help too.'

"There you have it, four willing helpers. All you need is to ask."

She sighs heavily. "All right, I will start asking for help, but only if I need it. I will not be a burden."

"Does that make me a burden?" We all turn to see Railu, in her wheelchair, being pushed to the table by Roen.

"No, that does not make you a burden," I lightly chide. "But your refusing to follow directions certainly doesn't help."

She rolls her eyes and sighs.

I kneel down next to her. "You're strong-willed, and that's helped you with other things, but you do need to learn to relax and follow instructions too."

She nods slightly, as Roen chuckles and sits next to her. She gives him a stern look. "Why are you laughing?"

"He's right, you know. You *do* need to relax a little." He gives her a nuzzle as I find my place between Megai and Tayla.

After everyone is seated, the servers pass out drinks. Zoe rings a small bell and then clears her throat. "I'd like to have everyone's attention. As you know today is the First of Duodemense. It was a year ago today that something very special happened that would change all our lives."

I find myself trying to hide my embarrassment as she continues. "Kyle, this is your day, it's been one year since you woke up. I know I speak for everyone here when I say, thank you for coming into our lives. Thank you, for everything you've done for us." As she lifts her own drink, several others agree and everyone takes a drink, toasting me.

Zoe then nods to the servers, and they rush through the kitchen door, only to come back pushing serving carts.

They quickly start placing various dishes around, and a pair of large ones down the middle of the table. They then start pulling off the covers. The two large dishes are baked nakku, and there are several bowls of stuffing, various vegetables, breads, and other sides.

Looking across the table at all the food, I smile and turn to Zoe. "I think you've finally outdone yourself."

She giggles and bows slightly. "Nonsense. Just be sure to leave room for dessert." As she heads back into the kitchen, I start carving a chunk of breast meat from the closest nakku for Tayla.

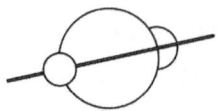

As evening approaches, I find myself on the couch between my mates. Tayla has leaned against me and is purring as she rubs her very pregnant belly. Megai watches Sada as she watches the fish in the spring.

I put my arms around both and close my eyes. I find myself drifting off when someone climbs on my lap.

I look to see Amela curling up against me. "Happy birthday, dad," she says, smiling up at me.

"Thank you, hun."

She tilts her head curiously and asks, "How old are you?"

Unable to help myself, I chuckle. "Well, let's see. I was 43 when I was frozen, so I should be 44."

"Are you sure?"

"I'm positive. Despite what I've been through, I feel like I'm 20 again."

"Okay." She stands on my lap and gives me a hug and a kiss. "Love you."

I return her hug. "I love you, too."

She then leans to Megai, and then to Tayla, giving them both a hug and a kiss, then to Tayla's belly, and kisses it. "Love you, Tashi, love you, Kuma."

Amela hops down and goes to play, Tayla gently rubs her belly and sighs. "Every time she does that they start kicking."

I put my hand on her belly. "Shh, quiet down my cubs. You're making mommy feel queasy."

She gives me an odd look. "They stopped. How do you do that?"

I give her a kiss and lightly joke. "They know their father's voice."

She leans back into me as I put my arm around her. Megai though, turns to me, and asks, "You're really 44?"

"Yeah, but like I said, I don't feel any older than twenty."

She gives me a look of disbelief. "I remember you saying that Aime thought you were about 30. How's that possible? Was she wrong?"

I lean back, planning my answer carefully. "I feel 20. Physically, I'm closer to 30. Technically, I'm 44. I think it's about time I let you all in on why that is and how Sada got like she is. Ziggy, tell everyone that I'd like them in here, please."

"Certainly."

As the others gather, we rearrange some of the couches forming a loose circle. Fey, Amela, and Oana sit together on floor cushions in the middle. As everyone else settles into seats, I walk around the outside of the circle, looking around at my family, and staff, making sure that they're all here.

"As you all know, Sada and I were both frozen for well over a thousand years. What a lot of you don't know is that before that, when we were last on Earth, I was dying, and Sada looked like this." I gesture to a larger screen on the wall, and Aime changes its display to show a white cat curled on a pillow, the image that Sada looked at in the facility.

I fall silent for a moment, to let everyone get a look at the picture, Tayla though, says, "The myth of our ancestors, my grandmother told me, but I didn't believe."

"How big was she?" Railu asks.

The screen changes to show a scale of me against one of a house cat. I look at Sada and she's now sitting between Tayla and Megai, watching the screen happily.

Megai looks for a moment and then turns to me with a worried look on her face. "You were dying?"

Feeling a little embarrassed. "Yeah, when I was 30, I started having problems with my legs, I'd occasionally stumble for no reason, have muscle spasms, numbness, and random pains. The doctors couldn't figure out what was wrong."

"They started me on an exercise program, coupled with medications. It worked for a few years but it all returned and started getting worse. By my mid-thirties, I couldn't walk without a cane. After another couple more years, I couldn't even get out of a wheelchair."

I see Railu look down at her own wheelchair. An odd look of regret crosses her face and tears come to her eyes. I gently put a hand on her shoulder as I walk behind her, letting her know I understand.

"Nearly ten years after I was stricken with the illness, they finally figured out I had something called ALS. Amyotrophic Lateral Sclerosis;

it's a motor neuron disease. Basically, my body was breaking down. I was dying.

"At that point, my legs were useless, my arms were showing signs that it was progressing. When I started having trouble breathing and eating, I realized that I didn't have a lot of time left. I made peace with who I needed to, and prepared for my end."

"What did Sada do that whole time?" Fey asks as a tear rolls down her muzzle.

"She stayed with me, usually on my lap, as I spent many days seated in a chair. I would watch the animals graze in the fields and she would watch the hummingbirds at the flowers." The screen changes to show a likeness of the view I had when I lived at the cabin. I hear Tayla gasp a little; she always did want to see what Earth was like.

"We spent almost 17 years at that cabin together. That's part of the reason she's so attached to me. She was small then, yet she was an important part of my life."

"That's why you have so much trouble describing your relationship with her, isn't it?" Tayla asks.

"Yes, it is. Meagan and I raised her from a kitten, she curled up with me wherever I've slept. I've shared my meals with her, played with her, and cried with her. Almost everything I did, she was there."

"She's a part of you. I think I understand the bond you share with her," Megai states. Her long ears seem to droop a little more than usual.

I step over behind her and rub her shoulders as I continue. "After I had my affairs in order, and having resigned myself to my perceived fate, something happened that would change everything."

2

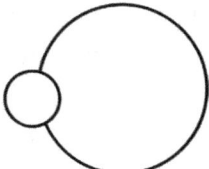

I gently reposition Sada, and her cushion, on my lap and drive my power chair to the kitchen. With the ALS affecting my arms, I no longer have the strength to use a regular wheelchair, let alone a walker. The weekend is here, I have a feeling my time's almost up.

Reaching into the pouch on the chair, I pull out the packet I had Tom make for me last year. I place it and my letter to Alicia on the table, as I have done every night, knowing she'll find it easily if I don't wake to hide it again.

Once in my bedroom, I move Sada to the bed and pull back the blankets. With practiced ease, I move from the chair to the bed and use my arms to position my legs. I set my glasses and false teeth on the nightstand before grabbing my BPAP mask and staring at it for a moment.

"What do you think Sada? Is tonight the night?"

Sada slowly walks up to me, stretches, and purrs, so I sigh and rub her head. "Maybe tomorrow's the night."

I put the mask on and adjust it for comfort. After turning the machine on, I cover myself and get comfortable. Sada curls up to my left side, resting her head on my arm. Despite the noise from the machine, I can still hear her purring. Comforted by the sound, I close my eyes and fall asleep.

I awaken to find myself floating in a warm liquid. There's a mask on my face providing air, and the lights shine purple through the liquid. Taking a few moments to orient myself, I realize that I can feel my legs and feet, something I haven't been able to do for a few years. I also realize that there are teeth in my mouth, real teeth, not the dentures I'm used to. Whatever is happening to me, I really don't care. I feel better than I have in years.

After a while, I start to get curious about my surroundings. I try to look around, but through the tinted liquid, all I see are the hoses and things attached to me and purple lights from outside. I reach out and find the walls curved around me, I must be in some type of tank.

Suddenly the liquid starts to drain, and I settle to the bottom of the tank. The light changes to white as the liquid drains away. The air is thankfully warm on my wet skin.

I blink my eyes, trying to clear my vision, as someone removes the mask from my face.

"Just relax, you're all right, now." The voice is female, and it sounds like she cares.

"Where am I?" I manage to ask, still trying to get my eyes to focus.

"You're in the med bay. You just finished with rejuvenation."

Feeling a towel get placed on my chest, I reflexively use it to wipe my face. My eyes start to focus and I get to see the woman. She has light blond hair, light skin, and she's wearing a light blue smock.

I blink a few more times, amazed I don't need my glasses anymore. "Who are you?"

"My name's Carrie, I'm a med tech." She gives me a curiously sad look. "What's the last thing you remember?"

"Going to bed, in my home. Where am I?"

I hear her pull something across the floor and then see her do something, the walls of the tank lower, leaving me lying on an elevated table. She then sits next to me. "You were picked up two days ago. Both you and your cat were brought to me for treatment. How do you feel?"

"I feel surprisingly great, considering I'm dying," I find myself admitting.

"Your ALS is gone," she states, smiling. "You're completely healed, and you're about 14 years younger."

Shocked, I sit up, and almost fall off the table. "What? How?"

"To remove your ALS, we had to regenerate you on a cellular level."

Not understanding what she just said, I test my legs, getting used to them again. "Where am I?"

She sighs heavily, looking somewhat ashamed. "I suppose it doesn't matter if you know. You're onboard the Obsession."

"The Obsession, what's that?"

She looks at my face, realizing that I truly don't know what she's talking about. "The Obsession is a star cruiser. We were with the third fleet, but now..." she sighs heavily as if regretting her next words. "Now we're pretty much a pirate ship."

I find myself unable to believe her, but knowing she's telling the truth at the same time. "What ocean?"

"Not an ocean, space."

"Space? As in outer space?"

She nods.

I look around the room again, realizing that it looks just like many of the hospital rooms I've been in. "How? I mean, this looks just like a normal hospital room, not any spaceship or station I've heard of."

She looks curiously at me. "This room is the whole med bay, and yes you are in space. The techs took a shuttle down to Earth to pick up you and your pet."

I look at her carefully. "Wait, how, we don't have the ability to land a shuttle, and then take back off like it was a helicopter."

She gives me an odd look. "What'd you mean? Of course, we do. We've had the tech for nearly five hundred years." Her expression drops. "What year do you think it is?"

I give her a skeptical look, and slowly answer, "2019."

"Well, here it's 3047." Her eyes suddenly go wide. "Wait...What's your name?"

"Kyle. Kyle Andolina."

Still in shock, she walks over to her desk and looks at a screen. After a few moments, she absently says, "The crazy bastard finally did it."

"Who did what?"

She suddenly gets a determined look on her face and hands me a bundle of clothes. She then starts removing the various leads stuck to me. "Get dressed. I need to get you out of here."

I quickly start pulling on the clothes, realizing that it's some kind of uniform. "What about Sada?"

She stops for a moment. "Your cat? She's...in the middle of something. I'll bring her to you as soon as I can."

"What's happening to her?"

She looks apologetically at me. "I really don't know. I know she went through a rejuve like you did, but Barker took her after that."

"Barker?" I ask, taking my first couple steps from the table. I find readjusting to walking easier than I expected.

"Science tech, not a pleasant guy."

"Will they hurt her?"

She opens the door and checks for anyone outside. "No, not if I can talk to Maurice first. Come on."

Seeing how nervous she is, I decide to wait on further questions. Still barefoot, I follow her out into the corridor. I suddenly see that the ship looks more like an ocean-going vessel, at least from the inside. We walk through several bulkheads, and into another room.

"Mike, good, you're here. This is the captain's latest catch." She motions to me and stops abruptly. "Kyle Andolina."

"Andolina?" he asks skeptically.

"Yeah."

He looks at Carrie, who nods. "He's finally done it."

Mike sits up and sighs. "What year?"

"2019."

Mike's expression turns serious. "We'll have to send him back."

"He's already been through rejuve."

"Oh." His expression suddenly drops.

"What's going on?" I ask, not following their conversation.

Mike walks over to a wall terminal. "Julie, show him the founding history of Andolina Neurological."

The screen lights up showing a stone and brick two-story building, and a female voice says, "Andolina Neurological Research was founded in twenty thirty-nine by Dr. Alicia Belanger and Kayley Reynolds. Its original purpose was to find a working treatment and cure for ALS, but that soon expanded to include other neurological diseases, and then into nano-tech research."

"Way to go, Alicia."

"You know her?" Mike asks as the screen fades.

"She's my nurse, and Kayley's my sister."

"Your nurse and sister?" Carrie asks, shocked.

"Yeah, I left them my estate."

"How'd you do that?" Mike asks.

"For the last few years, I've been leaving a packet with everything pre-signed over to them on the table, in case I don't wake up. I had my attorney set it up so it could happen whether I'm dead or missing."

Both look at me surprised. "Why that way?" Mike asks.

"Well, I'd planned on either letting myself go in my sleep, wandering off, or something. So..." I shrug leaving the rest unsaid.

Carrie looks worried, but Mike frowns and shakes his head. "I'll take care of him, get back to the med bay and report him disposed."

She nods and heads out. He waits until she's gone before turning back to me. "Kyle, we need to get you to a safe area."

"Disposed of?"

He sighs as he opens a secondary door, and begins to lead me through some maintenance corridors. "Captain Nabire is crazy. He has us do things to see if they work and he has us dispose of the results. The few people that he's pickup have usually been criminals. You're the first who's been...famously innocent."

"What? Why me?"

"Not sure. Did anything big just happen?"

"Not really, got diagnosed with ALS several years ago. I was actually getting pretty close to dying. Could that have been it?"

He turns a corner, then stops at a ladder and waits for me. "Possibly, were you alone?"

"Sort of. It was just me and my cat, and Carrie said that a science tech still has her."

He starts up the ladder. "Did she say who that was?"

I continue to follow. "Uhm, all I remember now is it started with a B, and they're not a nice person."

"That sounds like what he was after then."

"Then why heal me?"

"I wish I had an answer for that. He's had us heal everyone he's picked up. Then he kicks them out in an escape pod. Nothing he has us do makes much sense anymore."

"Why is he still in command?"

"He has the whole command crew behind him, so a mutiny's out of the question."

After descending another ladder, we exit into a large room with several sealed metal crates. "Where are we?"

"Cargo bay seven, because of some damage, it's mostly cut off from the rest of the ship. It still has power and life support though. You'll be safe here." He leads me to a larger crate and opens a hidden door. "This crate has a converter, bed, and bath. You can sleep here until we can find a way to get you back to Earth."

"What about Sada?"

"Carrie will speak with Maurice, he'll bring her to me, and I'll get her to you." He looks at me for a moment, then asks, "She means that much to you?"

"She's the only family I have left."

He nods. "That, I understand." He turns to look at the other crates. "Don't worry about anyone coming for the crates. We can't get in here with anything to get them." He turns to point at various doors as he continues, "That door leads to a corridor that's exposed to a vacuum, that one's collapsed, and those are the main loading doors, they lead directly to open space."

"The doors all have a safety that won't let them open if there's a vacuum on the other side, so don't worry." He pauses for a moment before continuing, "I've got to go, someone in my group will check on you after a while."

"How will I know if they're friendly?"

"We're the only ones that can find our way here right now." He takes off, back through the service corridor that we came through, leaving me alone in the bay. I walk around for a little while, looking at the shipping crates, then head into the larger one and lay down. The bed is surprisingly comfortable and I find myself drifting off to sleep rather quickly.

Hearing a hatch open, I sit up and look out through a crack in the door to see a woman approach. As she gets closer, I see she's wearing a uniform, apparently of some rank, and wearing a sidearm of some kind. She comes right to the door of the crate I'm in and knocks.

"Mr. Andolina, are you inside?"

Out of nervous fear, I don't answer.

"Kyle?"

Figuring if she knows my whole name, she's talked with Carrie and Mike, I nervously open the door. "Who are you?"

"I'm Lieutenant Commander Ariel Takana. I need you to come with me."

Curious, I scratch my head. "Why?"

"I need to take you to your cat."

As I start to follow her, I ask, "Why can't she be brought here?"

She stops at a corner, giving me a hesitant look. "I couldn't carry her through the corridors."

Suddenly puzzled, I ask, "What do you mean you can't carry her? What happened?"

She continues leading me through the corridors. "She's still your cat, but she's not just a cat anymore."

Getting to a hatch, I stop her and ask, "What's that supposed to mean?"

She turns, reluctantly facing me. "It means, she's...different." She opens a door and we exit the corridor to a room, not the same one that I met Mike in, but similar. Opening the outer door to the main corridor she steps out, checks for others, then motions for me to follow.

Still confused, but wanting Sada, I follow her out. I try to walk casually like she does, but feeling both nervous and scared makes that difficult. Thankfully we don't come across anyone as we walk down the corridor.

She takes a sudden turn, only to come face to face with three men, one is Mike, the other two I don't recognize. They nod as Mike opens a door. "Inside, please."

Walking through the door, I enter a rather stark room. There's a door to my left and a desk beyond that. Along the far wall, there's some equipment, and then I see Carrie sitting by a bed to my right. There's someone lying in the bed, completely covered, apparently asleep. The others follow me inside making it rather crowded in the small room.

"Kyle, this is Maurice and Kevin. You already know Mike and Carrie."

"What's going on?" I ask, confused.

The other four look to Ariel, and she clears her throat. "You and your cat were picked up from your house because the captain wanted to test a few procedures. He has never told anyone why he does this, but with you, he did something he's never done before, he went back in time and took an innocent."

"Only the senior officers know how he pulled that off, but he most likely stole it from a research colony just like everything else. He had us put you and your cat through a rejuve, to make both of you healthy, and younger. Your cat, however, was taken to the lab for another process." She looks to Maurice.

He nods, and continues. "The captain had us...evolve her." Seeing the sudden concern and anger in my eyes, he adds, "We kept her sedated for the whole thing, she wasn't in any pain, but she's not physically all cat anymore." He turns to the bed and Carrie moves the covers, revealing Sada's head, now larger, almost the same size as Carrie's, but mostly unchanged aside from a slight forehead and some longer fur on top of her head.

I find myself unable to take my eyes off Sada's face. Seeing it that large, I find myself confused and amazed. Feeling weak in the knees, I sit in the nearest chair.

"The captain wanted us to wipe her memory, too, but I couldn't bring myself to do that, not after Carrie and Mike told me about you and your attachment to her."

Carrie flips the sheet from Sada, revealing the rest of her. The first thing that I notice is that she is still covered with white fur, but her body is shaped like a human's, aside from her knees down, which look very much like they did when she was still a normal cat, and she also still has her tail, and it's longer than her legs.

"She's...?"

Carrie hands me Sada's collar as she continues, "She's still your friend, and she can understand a lot more now. She'll need someone to teach her how to be...human. Can you do that?"

"Why'd he do this to her?"

Ariel sighs. "We don't know. Most of the time, we're better off not knowing. All I can offer is to try to protect you, and her, from him, by hiding you both."

I try to let that soak in as I look at Sada, and find myself asking, "What am I supposed to do?"

Carrie looks at me. "Care for her, teach her. She needs your help."

I sigh, still taking the sight of the new Sada, I swallow hard. "Alright."

Carrie nods. "She's sedated, but it should wear off soon."

Ariel points to a small light near the door. "When one of us comes to check on you, this light will come, we won't knock. Safety."

I nod and my stomach growls, reminding me of just how hungry I am. "Can I get something to eat?"

Carrie walks over to an opening in the wall as a plate of food appears in it. "Sorry, we forgot you didn't know how to use these." She picks up the plate and hands it to me. "To use the converter, you can press here, then say what you want, or just select something from the list on the screen."

I shake my head. "I feel like I'm in a sci-fi movie."

Puzzled, Maurice asks, "What's a movie?"

Mike answers him. "Video, like security feed, but it's usually made up."

Kevin rolls his eyes and groans, "Historians."

"Come on, we're all on duty in an hour," Ariel states, opening the door. "If you need anything press this button. One of us will try to check in on you."

As they all step out, Mike turns to me and whispers, "Do try to stay inside." He then winks and pulls the door shut. I walk over and turn the lock bar, securing the door, then sit and look at Sada. As I start to eat, I find myself at a loss at to what to do, but unable to take my eyes off her. I find the new her odd, but beautiful.

She suddenly rolls over, trying to get more comfortable, then opens her eyes and looks around. When she sees me, her face lights up and her ears perk forward. She then tries to get up, only to have her arms slide out from under her.

I set the plate aside and sit on the bed next to her. She reaches out to me and touches my hand. She starts purring and nuzzles into my hand as I cautiously rub her cheek fur.

Suddenly her eyes widen, and she starts clumsily trying to back away. As she does, she falls from the bed to the floor. She continues to try to scramble away, but not being able to coordinate her arms and legs like she did when she was a cat, she ends up flailing clumsily on the floor.

She keeps looking at herself like she's afraid of something on her. I realize that she's noticed that she's different, and it scares her.

I scoop her up in my arms and sit on the bed, gently trying to calm and comfort her. After a while, she settles, finding comfort in my arms. I continue to hold her close, and she eventually falls asleep. I lie down with her and wrap my arms around her, both for her comfort, and my own.

3

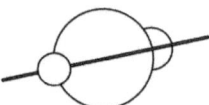

I look around at my family and friends. Everyone seems stunned except for Sada, who's sitting happily between Megai and Tayla, purring.

Tayla looks at Sada, then at me. "That's the ship you mentioned, isn't it."

"Yes, it is," I admit, remembering having spoken of it when my memories returned.

"Why tell us this now?"

I look curiously at Railu. "Because it's something I feel you should know, and I want you to understand her like I do."

"So you had to teach her everything?" Fey asks.

"Yes, everything, just like she was a baby."

This makes Fey giggle. "A full-grown baby."

We all chuckle. Sada though, buries her face in her hands, embarrassed, so I gently wrap her in a hug. "You've come a long way since then, my love."

She purrs as she rubs her head against mine. Tayla and Megai both lean into her, also purring.

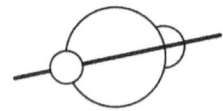

Barefoot, as usual, I walk down the hall to Oana's room to check on her plants. Finding the door open is no surprise, but once I step in, I find that several of her plants have been knocked over. As I start to stand them up, I find that some are actually broken over or cut off.

Puzzled and concerned, I softly call out, "Oana?"

"Kyle out. Oana hurt plants."

I find her cowering on her belly in a corner, behind some untouched plants. "What happened?"

"Tail."

I sit down on the floor beside her, knowing what she means. "Your tail did this?"

She nods but doesn't say anything.

Sighing, I ask, "Is your tail too long?"

"No. Oana bite tail. Tail behave now."

"Is it bleeding? Oana, give me your tail."

She slowly curls her tail around, placing the end in my lap. I pick it up and find that she has indeed bit the end off and it's oozing. I slowly run my hand over the end, letting Aime heal it.

"Oana, if your tail's a problem, let me know."

It's taken a few months for her tail to grow back. With it longer than the rest of her now, she's having trouble remembering it's there and that she needs to control it.

"Kyle fix tail?"

"Yes, I fixed your tail. Stop biting it."

"Oana sorry."

With her tail not bleeding anymore, I let it go. Still sitting on the floor, I turn around and lean back against her. She rests her head on my lap. "Kyle tired."

"It's been a busy day." I absently start rubbing her neck, getting her to let out a gentle coo.

"Oana hurt plants."

"They'll grow back."

"Oana tail grow back?"

"Yeah, tail grow back too."

We stay like that for a little while, until I get a sudden urge to laugh. Ziggy softly interrupts, "Kyle, Tayla would like to see you. She is in the master bedroom."

"I'll be there in a minute." As I get up to leave the room, Oana sighs heavily and starts to pick up the rest of her plants.

Walking into my bedroom, I find both Tayla and Sada sitting on the bed. Sada has a scowl on her face and is covering her chest with a towel, while Tayla's trying not to laugh.

"What's going on?" I ask curiously.

"It appears, I may have help feeding the cubs after they're born."

I look between the two. "What do you mean?"

"She's lactating."

Sada pulls the towel off of her chest, showing me her breasts. I notice right away that they're slightly swollen, and the fur around her nipples is wet. 'They're tender, and leak.'

Trying not to laugh, I sit next to her and give her a hug. "Well, I suppose we should have expected something like this." I gently hold my hand over her breast without touching it.

"She is indeed ready to start breastfeeding," Aime confirms.

Sada gets a sheepish look on her face and covers herself with the towel again.

Suddenly Megai comes in, and seeing the looks on our faces, asks, "What's going on?"

Unable to hold back any more, Tayla chuckles. "Sada's lactating."

Sada scowls at Tayla, but Megai tilts her head curiously and gives Tayla a meaningful look. "Well, since you're having twins, this may be a good thing." She walks over to us and sits next to Sada. "Do you want to help nurse the cubs?"

She looks solemn for a moment, then scratches her head. 'I'm...not sure.'

"I'm nervous about it," Tayla comments, "but I'm going to. It's good for the cubs."

'I'll think about it.'

"All right, but in the meantime." I walk over to the converter, picking up the two small, slightly cupped disks that just appeared. "You'll want to put these over them to keep the milk from soaking through your tops."

She takes them and nods, and I look at Tayla. "Will you need a set?"

"Not yet, but I should have a couple ready."

I retrieve a second pair from the converter and hand them to her. She puts them aside, and turns her attention back to Sada, bumping her nose to her cheek. "Take your time." She then does her best to crawl up on the bed and lies down on her side, and sighs heavily. "I don't know how mother did this, and she carried my two brothers *and* me."

I step over and gently rub her belly. "Need anything?"

"To give birth."

I chuckle lightly and give her a kiss. "When they're ready, love." Realizing that she's already asleep, I pull the sheet up to her shoulders.

"Come on, let her rest," Megai prompts, taking my hand. We walk from the bedroom as Sada gets a fresh outfit from her dresser.

As she leads me back to the great hall, I ask, "What are you doing?"

"I want a moment with you, is that too much to ask?"

"Well, you don't have to drag me off to do it."

"I know. I just..." she sighs, unable to find the words.

I stop walking and gently pull her to me. "What's bothering you?"

She suddenly gets upset and pulls back. "How do you do that? How do you see through someone's façade and see that something's bothering them."

I sigh as I sit on a couch. "It's been with you since I told you about Sada's evolution. You're jealous, aren't you?"

She sits sideways on my lap and sighs heavily. "You and Tayla have your 'link.' Sada has history, a lot of it. What is it that you and I have?"

I smile and pull her close to me. "Is it not enough that we love each other?"

"Sometimes I don't know." She leans into me. "Why did you fall in love with me?"

I sigh heavily, hearing the doubt in her voice. "That's a difficult question to answer, but I'll tell you this; before we first met, I felt alone. When you came on to me, I realized that I'd been overlooking something important, I was surrounded by people. You cracked my world wide open with one gesture."

I feel her relax a little. "Why do you still love me?"

Burying my nose in her cheek fur, I think for a moment before saying, "I love your openness, your honesty, how you think practically, and the way you sometimes tease me. I love your spots, fluffy tail, and how soft your fur feels." As she nuzzles under my chin, purring, I add, "And I really love the way it feels when you do what you're doing right now."

"How do you do it?" she softly asks, "How do you have enough love for us all?"

"My heart has a lot of room, and like this house, all I have to do is let someone in."

"You make it sound so easy."

"For me it is, but I've also lost a lot too, both parents, my first mate, my son. That may have something to do with it." I gently kiss her on the head. "Why do you love me?"

I feel her sigh and lift her head a little. "You made me feel like no other male has, you trusted me, believed me, you let me be myself, even after I found out about who you really were."

"It took me a while to realize it, but when you came back, you did it again. I knew then that you were for me." She wraps her arms around me and nibbles my cheek, a sensation she knows I'm fond of. "Now that I've said it, I feel better."

"I have something for you."

She looks up at me. "What's that?"

I reach in my pocket and pull out a small, velvet-covered box. "Here, open it."

She sits up as she takes the box. As she slowly opens it, I see her eyes start to water. "I can't..." She closes the lid. "I...I won't wear another shackle."

"Hun, it's not a shackle, it's a union ring, and you'll be able to take it off whenever you like. I'll be wearing one too."

"A ring?"

"Among humans, it's a way of saying we love each other and choose to stay together."

She slowly takes the ring out of the box. "Will Tayla and Sada get one too?"

"Do you want them to?"

"They are your mates, and they are my mate-kin...so, yes. I would like you to offer them rings too."

"As you wish, my love." I smile and give her a kiss. I then take the gold and silver band from her and put it on her left ring finger.

She watches curiously as the ring sizes itself, then she smiles as I hand her mine. She puts it on my left ring finger and then nuzzles into me, purring.

I wrap my arms around her. "I love you."

"I love you too."

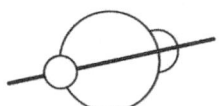

While flying the shuttle to the facility to look for more usable equipment, I change my mind and decide to stop at the rescue ship. I land the shuttle on top of it, aligning the airlocks and lift port, docking the two together. As I check the readouts, I see that their systems are linked with the shuttle providing additional power to the other.

Heading to the rear of the shuttle, I find Tareth, my ever-present shadow, and the lift waiting for me. A quick glance down shows that the lift is extended up from the ship below, through an open floor hatch.

"Nice." The doors open automatically as I approach and we step inside. Not seeing any controls, I ask, "Uhm, Aime?"

"Voice command or I can override."

"Bridge." The doors close and I barely feel the lift move before the doors open again. I step out and walk to the bridge. Tareth follows quietly behind me.

"Aime, give me a status report."

Aime's voice comes over the ship's speakers, more for Tareth's benefit than mine.

"Main power: seventy percent, engines: offline, structural integrity: ninety-eight percent, repulsors: twenty-eight percent, flight control systems: offline, maneuvering thrusters: twelve percent...Shall I continue?"

"No, I get the idea." I drop into the pilot's seat and lean back. Looking up at the sky through the windows, I see the nose of the shuttle overhead. "Can they fly while attached?"

"Yes."

I think for a moment. "Can the shuttle fly this back home?"

"No, the shuttle lacks the lifting power."

After another moment's thought, I ask, "Can we use the shuttle's flight systems and this ship's repulsors?"

"Simulating."

Figuring that could take a moment, I head back to the lounge and get a couple of drinks from the converter. Returning to the bridge, I hand one to Tareth. He nods his thanks, as I sit and put my feet up in another chair and look at the metal skeleton still sitting in the captain's chair.

"Simulations complete. While I would not advise it, it is possible to fly back in the way you are suggesting. There are limitations though, due to the Wanderer's crippled systems, you will not be able to fly over fifty meters from the ground, and with its flight control systems offline, responsiveness will be sluggish at best."

"Wanderer?"

"That is the name of the rescue ship."

I nod, still looking at the metal skeleton. "Aime, does...does that, have what you need?"

"Yes."

"How could we get it?"

"You could simply swallow the micro pods. There is no chance of biological contamination, the nano-virus made sure of that. There is also no chance of infection from the virus. It was carried by the nanites and the pods do not contain nanites."

I sigh. "Not really what I want to do." I glance at Tareth, he wrinkles his nose, realizing what's going to happen.

"We have yet to find a source of the needed materials."

"I know." I reluctantly lean forward, looking at the smaller pieces scattered both around, and in the chair. "Which ones?"

Several circles appear in my vision, indicating what pieces contain the needed materials. I start sifting through the tiny pieces, picking out the ones indicated. Tareth turns and walks out of the bridge, apparently not wanting to witness what comes next.

"How many?"

"I will need all of them."

I look at the assortment of pieces in my hand. There are dozens, and range in size from fine gravel to sand. I take a breath, steal my nerves, and lick my hand, letting my tongue pick up the pieces. I take a drink to wash them down. I take another drink to make sure they go down.

"How long?"

"Nearly a day, I'll need to dissect the pods to extract the needed materials before I can finish the upgrades."

"Alright." I turn my attention back to the Wanderer. "Aime, let's start her up."

"Initiating main power. Running diagnostics on flight systems: maneuvering thruster ducts overgrown, purging maneuvering thrusters...purge complete. Maneuvering thrusters: ten percent function. I would recommend removing the rest of the wire vine from the exterior, before trying to lift off."

"Cutting tool?"

"Waiting in the shuttle's converter."

We head back up the lift into the shuttle and I grab the tool. Opening its side hatch, the lower half of the door lowers to the hull below and then alters its surface to be steps instead of a ramp. I step out onto the hull and start cutting off the wire vines. Letting them fall to the ground. Tareth watches over me, standing guard. I don't expect him to help, that's not his job.

When I'm done, we head back in. I drop the tool in the converter as I proceed into the Wanderer's cockpit. "Okay. Where were we?"

"Linking flight systems, slaving shuttle, calibrating link, one moment please...calibration complete. I again stress to go slow, your altitude is limited and control is sluggish."

"All right, let's close up and lift off." Suddenly a loud screeching, groaning sound fills the ship.

"Loading ramp," Aime states.

Remembering how it opened over a year ago, I find myself glad it still works. When the screeching stops, she announces, "All exterior hatches closed."

As I slowly dial up the power to the repulsors, the ship starts to creak and groan.

"Structural integrity holding."

"Good, let me know if it changes."

Adding some more power, the ground starts to slowly fall away. I decide against retracting the landing gear, as I may need to land quickly.

"Plot a course between Pridewyn and Arroketh, then north to home."

"Plotting course, terrain mapping engaged, applying a mammalian filter to life scans, avoiding populated areas."

"And tall trees."

"Of course."

I apply some thrust and we barely start to creep forward. "Sluggish is an understatement."

It takes over an hour to get to the road between Pridewyn and Arroketh. During the slow turn towards Arindell, I get to see the branch of Pridewyn River that waterfalls into a crevasse. The sight reminds me of Niagara Falls, just by the sheer volume of falling water.

Tareth, taking in a moment of curiosity, steps up and looks out the window. "It looks very different, from up here."

"Sure does."

"I've been down there, you know."

"Really?"

"Yeah, it was a long time ago, I wasn't much older than Kotu."

I smile, expecting to hear more of the story, but he just watches in silence for a while, then returns to his seat when the falls disappear from sight.

After two long, boring hours, I see home. "Ziggy, we're coming in."

As I slowly approach the house, I see the landing lights flashing. I also notice that there are a few people standing by the garage, watching our approach.

Setting the Wanderer down, nose toward the garages, I get to see that one of the watchers is Sada, and she's bouncing happily. Everyone else though is in mild shock.

After powering down, I transfer to the shuttle and land it alongside the garage, in its usual place.

Walking down the side ramp, I see Sada excitedly sign, 'It works.'

"No, not completely," I correct as I approach, dampening her spirits.

"W–w–why, uh, why bring it here then?" Roen stutters, unable to take his eyes off the Wanderer.

"Well, I want to fix it up. It'll be easier to do here."

"It's huge."

"It's larger than the planes that I'm used to, but there are larger ships out there."

"Like the Obsession?" Larrah asks, also staring at the Wanderer.

"Yeah, it's so large it'd make this look like a shuttle."

I see Roen's eye go wider in shock, but he says nothing. Larrah, on the other hand, looks down the length of the ship. "How much longer is it?"

"I think the Obsession was about a kilometer long."

"Can it land, too?"

"I don't know. It had a lot of damage."

4

With Sada coming to terms with the fact she has a new body shape, I've been able to start teaching her how to use her new form. This has not been easy as she tries to act and do things as if she was still a normal cat.

Her coordination is like that of a newborn, mixed with a cat. She tries to grab things but has no idea how to use her thumb, so she curls her hand like a paw. Most of the time, she can get by like this, but if she needs to go anywhere (like the bathroom), I need to carry her.

She lies across my stomach as I lounge on the bed. I've been trying to teach her how to do things and have slowly come to realize that I may be trying too hard. So I've started over, letting her learn by example.

Right now, she's playing with my hand, comparing it to hers. As she does, I slowly scrub the fur between her ears, trying to get myself used to the new her.

Unexpectedly, she looks up at me and smiles. Not a toothy smile, but with her eyes and ears.

I gently pull her up to me, and she immediately starts purring. "You still like that, huh."

She nods happily and clumsily tries to scoot closer to me.

As I help her to me, I see that she's having difficulty pulling her legs under her, so I sit up. "Here, let me help you learn how your legs move."

I gently roll her onto her back and take her foot-paw in hand. "Now relax and let me move your leg. Feel how it moves."

She watches intently as I start to manipulate her leg, and I find myself learning as she does. From her hip to her knee, her leg is much like mine. Below the knee, it's almost unchanged, retaining its original-if oversized-form.

After a few repetitions, I ask, "Think you can repeat that motion?"

She tilts her head, then nods, so I keep my hand against her foot-paw as she tries flexing her leg, giving her something to push against. She does a few reps, and then we switch legs.

After a few minutes of this, she abruptly stops, apparently bored. She lets out a huff and manages to roll over on her own.

I lie down next to her and gently take her tail in hand and start idly playing with it. As always, I feel it gently twitch until Sada eventually pulls it from my fingers. She quietly sighs and rolls against me.

I find myself hoping that she learns how to use her body quicker than Michael did.

While sitting at the desk, reading, the ship suddenly lurches. Then, an eerie rumbling echoes through the corridors. I look around the cabin and notice that the ship's calling for battle stations.

"Here we go again." I jump to the bed and wrap Sada in a hug as the ship lurches again. In the short time, I've been on board, this is the second fight that the ship's been in. I pull a mesh of crash webbing down over us, effectively holding us down on the bed as the ship shakes again.

Sada starts to tremble as I hold her, so I start gently scrubbing her cheek, trying to reassure her. "We'll be all right. We're together, that's what matters."

She nods, letting me know she understands, but the tears she cries, show me how scared she is. I can't blame her, I'm scared too.

In the moments between tremors, I can hear the Obsession's own guns firing, trying to fend off our attacker. Another hard lurch signals a hit to our hull, the shields are down somewhere. I begin to wonder how bad the damage is when the ship's massive engines engage.

I feel the ship vibrate as the engine powers up, gravity seems to change direction as the ship accelerates.

Something's wrong, we didn't feel the last jump.

We slide to the edge of the bed, but not off. The webbing holds as Sada gets pressed into me. I find that the sensation is similar to a carnival ride. Fortunately, the effect starts to lessen, allowing me to help Sada slide back to the center of the bed.

The ship suddenly shudders and groans, then everything falls silent and dark. It occurs to me that main power just failed. Suddenly surrounded by darkness, Sada squirms in as close to me as she can get. From her trembling, I can feel how scared she is.

Doing my best to comfort her, I softly say, "Calm down, it's okay. They'll get the power back on soon enough." I hold her to me, hoping she finds some solace in my arms.

We stay like this for a while, and I realize that the air's starting to get cold. Life support must be out too. Releasing the mesh, I quickly get up and grab another blanket. After covering the bed with it, I crawl back under the covers and pull the webbing back down. I snuggle back up to Sada and her shivering starts to slow.

With it pitch dark, and silent, I begin to think about the things that have happened. Taken from my home, healed of my illness, *and* made physically younger. My best friend of almost twenty years turned *nearly* human and then spent the following month trying to learn how to use her new body.

I can't argue the fact I still love her, but it's a different kind of love. It's changed, just like she has. Before, she was my friend--my companion, now, though, it's more than that, and I don't know how to define it.

I lie there, holding her, feeling the cold close in, when suddenly the lights come back on and the engines roar to life. As my eyes adjust to the light, I hear the guns open up, firing faster than they usually do.

That continues for nearly a minute, and then the ship suddenly lurches hard, the deck plates rattle as the ship vibrates. A different sound suddenly echoes through the ship, an eerie kind of moan. I feel my skin crawl at the sound, and then I feel Sada's claws sink into my arm, letting me know that she had a similar reaction.

I grimace at the pain. "Retract your claws!"

She lets go of my arm, and the pain subsides, but I know I'm now bleeding. I stick my arm out from under the covers, and straight-up, exposing my arm to the cold air. The combination of elevation and cold quickly slows the bleeding.

Sada rolls over and gives me an apologetic look. I give her a kiss on her nose. "I know you didn't mean to. You were scared."

Hearing that the guns have silenced, and with the room slowly getting warmer, I get up and press the call button on the intercom. Still holding my arm up above my head, I wait for a response.

Suddenly the com pops and Mike responds, "You okay?"

I nearly laugh. "Uhm, we're cold, wondering what just happened, and, oh yeah, I bleeding from some puncture wounds and need a dressing."

I hear Mike laugh. "I'll be right there."

When the light comes on, I let him in. He smiles, but when he sees my arm in the air, he asks, "What, not healed yet?"

"No, but thanks to the cold, it hasn't bled much."

Suddenly his expression changes and he scolds himself. "What was I thinking, you don't have one. Sorry." Before I can ask, he turns and steps back out. When he comes back, he's carrying a small first aid kit. "I thought for a moment you were just kidding."

Taking the opportunity, I ask, "I don't have one what?"

"An AI." He takes a small packet out of the kit, and I lower my arm to him. He opens the packet, pulls out a cloth, and begins to wipe my arm down, cleaning the blood away, and explains, "Some 700 years ago, we figured out how to use nanites to build computers inside ourselves. Now, almost everyone has an AI of some sort. Julie's mine. Among other things, they speed up our healing process."

"Do I get one?"

"Well, Carrie could set you up with one, but if we're able to take you back, that'd be a problem." He puts the cloth away and gets out a roll dressing and wraps my arm.

"Yeah, I guess it would, but wouldn't my health be a problem, too?"

He sighs again as he finishes. "How close were you to dying?"

I sit on the bed, and Sada crawls up against me. "I was in the final stages, it was hard to breathe at night without the BPAP machine, I drank all my meals cause it was too hard to swallow solid food, I couldn't walk, and I could hardly pick up anything."

I think for a moment, then add, "I was strongly considering just driving my chair out into the woods to die."

Seeing the sincerity in my eyes, he nods. "Can't say I know how you felt, but I do understand the helpless feeling." He stops for a moment, then says, "I looked you up as best I could, but not a lot of records survived the Gene War. You were a paramedic, right?"

"Yeah, for nearly ten years."

He nods and hands me the kit. "When your arm's healed, just re-roll that and put it back in here. Probably take an hour."

"Thanks."

"No problem. Did you really want to know what happened out there?"

I nod. "Obviously, we're still here, but what was that last big lurch?"

He sighs, hanging his head slightly. "The picket ship exploded."

I frown but nod.

He taps on the door, obviously thinking of what to say. "Never really get used to it." He tries to smile, but it's weak and fades fast as he steps out.

I lock the door behind him and slowly sit back down on the bed. Sada slides onto my lap, trying to get comfortable, but quickly finds she doesn't fit like she did as a cat. I set the kit aside and lie back. She squirms up to my left side and lies against me, putting her nose under my chin.

Hearing her sigh heavily, I wrap my arm around her and gently start rubbing her back. As I lie awake, I can't help but wonder what this future holds for us.

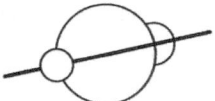

5

Stepping into the nursery, I see that Tayla has been rearranging things again. Her nesting instinct has been getting very strong lately, and this is the seventh time she's rearranged the nursery in the last month and a half. I notice that this time, she's added a second rocking chair. Sada must have decided on helping with the nursing.

I smile and head through the door to our adjoining bedroom to find Tayla sitting on the edge of the bed.

"Hey, see what I did with the room?" she asks.

"Yeah. Hope you had someone help you."

"Two, actually. Good thing too, I couldn't make up my mind on a few things till Sada came in."

"I see she's made her decision."

"Yeah, and I'm glad she wants to help. I also saw that Megai loves the ring you gave her."

I sit next to her. "Yeah, and she wanted me to do this." I hand her a small felt box, matching the one I gave Megai.

She gives me an odd look. "I thought that this was supposed to be a bond between you and her. Why give me one too?"

"She insisted, said you are her mate-kin and wanted to include you and Sada in this too."

Tayla slowly takes the ring from the box. "As you did with her, you should put this on me."

"You saw?"

She nods. "Only when you put it on her finger."

I slowly put the ring on her finger and let it adjust to fit her finger as she leans into me, purring. Having a thought, I softly say, "Ziggy, ask Sada and Megai to come here when they have a moment."

"Certainly."

Tayla gives me an odd look. "What are you going to do?"

"Something we should have done already."

"We?"

I nod, and both Sada and Megai come in.

Catching Sada before she sits, I gently slide a ring on her finger. "I know we're not technically mates, but you're just as important to me."

She nods and sits next to Tayla, then starts to fidget with the ring.

As I sit back down, I smile at my mates. "I would like us to be more open with each other. You're all important to me, and I don't want anyone feeling like I'm playing favorites or leaving someone out."

"Why would we think that?" Tayla asks.

Megai sighs lightly, then says, "Because I felt that way. You have your bond, and you have years of history. What do I have? Nothing, I couldn't help but feel a little left out."

'You had him first,' Sada signs.

Megai smirks then smiles. "I did, but it really didn't establish the kind of connection that you two have." She holds up her hand, stopping further comment. "He helped me see that we also have a connection, a different kind of connection, but one that's strong and no less meaningful than yours."

"So when he offered me the ring, I insisted that he give one to both of you too, because we are mate-kin, we are a family. These rings are a tangible symbol of that."

Tayla nods, and Sada gives Megai a nose bump, making her smile.

"Now that that's been said, anyone else have anything they want to say?" I ask.

Sada huffs then signs, 'I envy the intimacy you can share with him.'

Tayla takes Sada's hand and asks, "Isn't there anything you can do about that?"

Saddened by her dilemma, I admit, "I've been searching the records from the facility, but there's a lot of data to go through."

Seeing her posture slump, I kiss her and say, "As soon as I find something, you will be the first to know."

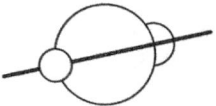

Planning a surprise for Sada, I slip out of the bed early in the morning. Once I'm out of my room, I head to the kitchen. "Ziggy, is Zoe up yet?"

"Yes, she's in the kitchen, planning out breakfast."

I pick up my pace, nearly running there. Despite the early morning, the floor is warm and comfortable under my bare feet as I enter the kitchen.

"Zoe, have you got anything planned for Sada's day?"

She looks at me for a moment, surprised. "No, not really."

"Well, if my birthday's going to be on the first, then hers should be today."

She tilts her head curiously. "What do you have in mind."

I chuckle as I fill her in on what I'd like her to fix. I then rush back to my room and find my place between Megai and Sada. Thankfully Sada has rolled against Tayla, giving me room to lie back down.

With a little help from Aime, I calm myself down and pretend to be asleep. While I wait for someone else to wake up, I mentally review what I have planned for today.

After a short while, Sada rolls back onto me, purring. I wrap my arm around her and give her a kiss. "Morning," I whisper.

Not opening her eyes, she sighs heavily and then licks my cheek.

"Come on, sleepyheads. Let's get up," Megai mumbles.

Sada sits up slightly and licks Megai's cheek.

"Ugh, morning breath."

Tayla chuckles at Megai's retort and then grunts, "A little help here."

I give Megai a morning kiss as I roll out from under her and get up. After helping Tayla sit up, I then hand her the clothes she set out last night.

She smiles sleepily. "Thanks."

I give her a kiss, and then kneel down and gently rub her belly. "How are the twins this morning?"

"Quiet, thankfully. Help me up."

I give her belly a gentle kiss, and then help her to her feet. She waddles over to the grooming room and disappears inside as I turn my attention to Megai, who's still lying in bed.

Starting at her toes, I start lightly tickling and ruffling the fur on her toes. She starts to giggle as she tries to keep away from me. When I get to her knees, I see tears in her eyes, so I stop and sit next to her.

She reaches up, pulls me down to her, and nibbles on my ear. "I'll get you for that."

This time I giggle. "I can't wait." After a kiss, she playfully pushes me up, and I pull her with me. "Come on, breakfast will be ready soon."

She slowly gets up, grabs her clothes, and heads for the grooming room as Tayla comes out.

With Sada still in bed, I jump up and land on the edge of the bed, launching her into the air. She doesn't fly high, but she does flail about before landing next to me.

Apparently not happy with my action, she hisses and glares at me. I smile and give her another kiss. Then I grab my clothes and change as I hum a few lines of 'Happy Birthday.'

She climbs off the bed, still glaring at me, but grabs her clothes and changes.

As I take Tayla's hand and start walking her to the dining room, she gives me a stern look. "If you ever do that to me, Aime won't be able to save you."

I smile and give her a kiss. "Yes, love."

She gives me an odd look but then smiles. "Her look was for show, you know."

"Yeah, I know. She's been through worse, besides, it's a glimpse of her birthday present."

"Today's her birthday?"

"Well, not really, but if we're going to say the first is mine, then today is hers."

"Will we be celebrating everyone's birthdays?"

"Of course."

Megai comes up on the other side of Tayla. "Great, I wonder what you'll get me."

I chuckle. "Nothing you won't like." She looks at me suspiciously but says nothing further about it.

Breakfast is light, just as I requested, and we eat slowly, enjoying the morning. I find myself pleased that Railu's in a better mood, and more cooperative, since my birthday. Apparently finding out that I was stuck in a wheelchair for a few years changed her outlook on being in one for just a few months.

As everyone finishes, I stand, getting everyone's attention. "As many of you know, Sada woke eight days after me, so, this will be her birthday." Sada buries her face in her hands, apparently embarrassed. "I wanted to give her something special today, something she found very fun in the past, but I realized that she would want to share that with those she cares about, so, I would like you to come to the shuttle in three hours. Ziggy, will you please remind everyone?"

"Of course. Would that include the staff?"

"Yes, it would. I would ask that you please not eat anything between now and then, and to use the restroom before you show up."

Sada looks at me curiously, apparently trying to figure out what I have planned for her. I notice several others all looking between her and I, also trying to figure out what her surprise could be.

Having already removed the unneeded seats, I stand by the shuttle door, waiting for the others to come out.

Nanai is the first, and she nervously looks at the shuttle, then at me. "Are we going somewhere?"

Knowing how she doesn't like to travel much, I find myself suddenly wondering why she accepted Megai and Zoe's job offer. "Just a short trip, we won't even leave the shuttle."

She gives me a curious look, but steps in and asks, "Why are half the seats gone?"

"We won't need them, and they'll just be in the way."

She gives me another curious look but disappears inside.

Roen soon comes out pushing Railu. I help him move her to a seat in the shuttle and put the wheelchair out in the garage. When Sada finally shows, most of the others are already aboard. I have her sit with the others, so she can't see where we're going.

With everyone aboard, I close the door and stand in the cockpit doorway. I look at Kotu as I ask, "Has anyone eaten since breakfast?"

"No, I haven't," he retorts as others shake their heads.

Seeing one of the seats available, I turn and see Tayla smiling at me from the copilot's seat, so I call out, "Please, buckle up." I hear several clicks as I sit in the pilot's chair. I look over at Tayla. "Are you sure you want to be upfront for this?"

She nods. "Where are we going?"

I smile. "Up." I start the engines and apply some power. Lifting off is easy, and within a few moments, we're well on our way. I look at Tayla; her eyes seem to be getting bigger and bigger the further up we go.

Soon the blue sky starts to darken, losing its color. Tayla gives me a curious look, but with me still smiling, she stays quiet. As she turns back to the window, I let her wonder fill me. I find myself chuckling softly as park the shuttle in a very high orbit above Arcania, rolling it so the planet is above us.

"Aime, hold the shuttle here, please."

"Understood." I exit the cockpit and look at the others.

"Where are we?" Nanai asks.

"We are," I wave my arm to the ceiling and it appears to turn clear, "in space."

I look up with them and we see the world—Arcania, our home—appear above us. The rings are clearly visible, lit by the sun, and the moons are casting their shadows across the planet and rings on the far side. Several gasp at the view, and I let them look.

Tayla steps up beside me, looking up. "It's so beautiful."

I look at her, seeing the reflection of Arcania in her eyes, feeling the wonder flow from her, and agree, "Yes it is, isn't it."

I look back at everyone, suddenly remembering why we're here. "What do you think?"

"That's what we live on?" Roen manages to ask.

"Yep, that's Arcania, and those are Nai and Terr, our moons."

"Rings bee-tu-ful."

"It's 'beau-ti-ful,' Oana," Tria corrects.

"Rings beau-ti-ful."

"I feel dizzy," Fey comments.

I smile at her. "Don't look off into the empty space, focus instead on the planet, the rings, or a moon."

"Is this her present?" Tayla asks.

"No, this is just so you know where we are." I look around again, smiling. "Sada, I know how much fun we had when it happened, so, as your present, we are going to be weightless for a while." The roof slowly opaques as I look at everyone and continue, "I'll ease you into it, but it'll still feel strange. Please relax and enjoy."

Getting several nods, I say, "Aime, thirty seconds to zero-G." As she steadily dials the gravity back, I see faces of confusion and wonder amongst my family as they express concerns and comments.

"Please, stay calm. Let me know if you start to feel sick."

From beside me, I hear Tayla start to purr. "This feels wonderful."

"I thought you might like it." I turn and look at Railu. "How do you feel?"

"Strange. Better, but strange."

With no gravity, I find out who wasn't buckled. "Oana fly?"

"Watch your tail!" Niku calls.

Tayla suddenly grabs my arm and pulls herself back to me. "Why aren't you floating?"

Since I'm wearing my armor's boots, and I've had Aime keep me on the floor. "I will when everyone's adjusted."

Sada suddenly comes flying at me and wraps me in a tackle-hug, purring. I don't move much, but she starts to happily nuzzle my face.

Laughing, I hug her back. "Having fun?"

She gently pulls back, 'I love this.'

"Happy birthday, love."

She gives me a lick, then bumps noses with Tayla and slowly spins away. With a touch to the ceiling, she heads to Megai and releases her seatbelt.

"Oh no, I'm not ready, Sada don't—." Her protests are too late, she's already drifting away from her seat. I hear several clicks as others start to release their seatbelts.

"Gentle pushes, be careful of others," I call. Noticing Fey still in her seat, I walk over to her. "You feeling okay?"

She shakes her head, so I put my hand on her belly.

"Upset stomach?"

She weakly smiles and nods.

"Is that any better?" I ask, knowing that Aime has given her something for nausea.

She sighs. "Thanks."

I give her a kiss. "You're welcome, hun. If you want, there's still a little gravity in the front. Just make sure your hooves are on the floor before you try to go in."

She nods but doesn't unbuckle yet, so I turn my attention to Railu. "How are you doing?"

Still buckled in, I see a tear in her eye as she looks at me. "I'm sorry."

I give her a puzzled look. "Sorry for what?"

"You spent years in a chair, and I've been fighting you about spending a few months in one."

"Hey, forget it. We all have things we can and can't tolerate, being trapped is yours. Now that Aime has her updates finished, let's see what we can do for you." I put my hands on her belly as I feel someone grab my clothes. I see Tayla float into the chair next to Railu as Aime starts showing me what's wrong.

With her expanded medical library and physical upgrades completed, I can finally start to address her two major persistent problems, cervical insufficiency, and placental abruption. The new upgrades allow Aime to strengthen her cervix, correcting the insufficiency, and then strengthen the bond of the placenta, hopefully preventing the reoccurring abruption.

After several minutes, Aime signals that she's done, and I let myself float away. Railu sighs heavily, obviously feeling better. I chuckle to myself at the sight of Railu drifting off to sleep when I was so sure that she would literally jump at the chance to get out of a chair.

Regardless of her wanting to rest, Sada eventually pulls her into a 'dance,' gently spinning through the air, carefully touching a wall or another person to keep from bumping into them. After she lets Railu go, she plucks Fey from her chair. She then repeats her dance, taking turns with each person in the cabin.

She makes sure to save me for last, pulling me into a hug while she purrs loudly. We drift around in a slow spin, and I notice a tear in her eye. Without gravity to make it run down her cheek, it just sits where it formed, gently jiggling as we move.

I touch a wall to stop our spin before gently wiping the tear away. "What's this for?"

'I remember our first dance.'

6

Sada sits leaning back against me as I lean against the headboard. I've been teaching her how her hands and arms can move by using my own to show her. It hasn't been easy as she keeps trying to use her hands like paws, but my feelings for her keep me trying.

Having reviewed some of the simple motions, we move on to some, more different ones. I put my hands together and start interlacing my fingers, a pair at a time. She watches intently as I repeat the movements, and then tries for herself. I watch as she begins to interlace her fingers, gently helping or correcting her when needed and complementing when she gets it right.

After a while, I have her try using one of my hands instead of hers. She tries awkwardly a few times but doesn't get it right. She takes my right hand in hers and puts her left palm to my palm. She watches intently as I start moving my hand, and she lets her fingers move with mine.

"Now you lead."

She tries to mimic the moves but soon gets frustrated.

"All right, calm down. We can take a break."

She turns and lies down on the bed, trying to relax. A weird sound suddenly echoes from the floor and an odd sensation washes over us. I quickly suppress a wave of nausea as I realize that we're floating up from the bed.

Sada though reaches out to me and pulls herself close. Seeing the fear and confusion in her eyes, I pull her close to me in a hug.

"It's all right. We're just floating. The ship's lost gravity for a bit."

She nods but continues to hold me tightly. As we drift, I try to direct us to the com by gently pushing off of various things. When I finally get us there, I press the call button and the light comes on. Kevin's concerned voice comes from the speaker. "Kyle, need something?"

"Yeah. We're weightless. What's going on?"

"Sorry, should've warned you. We're moving some heavy equipment through your section right now, so we had to turn off the gravity in your area. It may take an hour or two, so just relax and have some fun, I'll be sure to let you know before we turn it back on."

I watch the light go out and look at Sada. "See, we're fine."

She relaxes and her curiosity gets the better of her. She nervously lets go of me for a few moments, but she keeps her close to me. She begins to relax and her eyes start filling with wonder.

As we slowly drift apart she suddenly reaches out to me. Seeing her claws out, I reflexively pull away. "No claws." I quickly realize that I moved too fast as I start to spin away from her.

I find myself laughing as I bump into a wall. Back in control, I turn around to face her and gently push off the wall to her. "Here I come," I laugh. She starts scrambling, trying to move out of my way, but not being close to anything, she just flails helplessly in the air. I catch her and we drift to the other end of the room.

I grab hold of a conduit and turn us around. "Let me show you how. Watch me."

She nods and looks at how I'm positioned. It takes her a moment, but she manages to mirror my stance as she takes hold of the conduit. I let go and use just my toes to push gently from the wall, I drift slowly to the other side and catch another conduit.

"Gently now, just a little push."

She looks at her toes, then at her hand. As she lets go of the conduit, she kicks off the wall a little too hard. She comes at me fast and I quickly reposition myself to catch her. She collides with me harder than I expected, bouncing me off the wall.

As we drift out into the room again, she holds me close, purring in my ear.

I sigh lightly, enjoying the sound. "It's been a while since you've purred."

I touch the wall, keeping us from it. She buries her nose in my neck, nuzzling me while she purrs.

We slowly spin into the middle of the room like this, drifting slowly above the floor.

Suddenly the com clicks. "Gravity coming back in ten seconds."

I reach up and touch the ceiling, gently pushing us to the floor. We land on our feet in time with the zero count. I hold her to me to keep her from falling as gravity returns.

The com pops once again and Kevin explains, "Sorry about that, it was an easier move than expected."

The light goes out before I can respond, so I look at Sada. "Well, that was fun."

She nods and nuzzles into me again, still purring.

Having only used the converter to make food, I find myself trying to figure out its *other* uses.

"All right, she said it was just like making food." I pause for a moment, thinking of what to make. After a quick look at Sada, I realize what I need to make first.

I put my finger to the black square. "Black ribbon."

Nothing happens.

"Black ribbon."

Again, nothing happens.

Puzzled, I step over to the door and press the call button.

"What's up?" It's Mike.

"I can use the converter to make stuff that isn't food, right?"

"Yeah."

"How?"

"Just touch the activator and tell it what you want."

"I did. Nothing happened."

"What're you trying to make?"

"A new ribbon for Sada's tag."

"What'd you say to it?"

"Black ribbon."

"Okay. For something like that, you'll need to be very specific. So, you'll need to tell it the color, width, length, material, and style."

"Why doesn't it need to be that specific for food?"

"For food, it uses standard portions and most common recipes. There are some other things that you won't need to specify because they're standardized."

"Thanks, Mike. I'll give it another try."

"Don't make too much stuff. The ship's rationing energy right now."

"Got it." The light goes off and I return to the converter.

I give Sada another look, deciding on the features of the ribbon. "Black ribbon. Uhm, silk. Twelve inches by a half-inch. Basic design."

This time, I notice that what I'm saying appears on the selection screen, but nothing happens. Rereading the command, I notice a question mark by the dimensions. Puzzled, I remove my finger from the activator and the screen fades. I return to the door and press the call button.

Mike answers again. "Did you get it?"

"Not yet. It showed me some question marks by the length."

"What'd you say for the length?"

"Twelve inches."

There's a moment of silence before he answers. "What's an inch?"

His answer surprises me, so I try my best to explain. "Uh. It's used to measure length. You know, inch, foot, yard, mile. Don't tell me you don't know what those are."

"I'll look them up. Do you know what a meter is?"

"Metric system? Yeah. Don't know it too well, but I'll manage. Thanks, Mike."

Before the light clears, I hear him mutter, "Julie, start researching..."

With a heavy sigh, I turn back to the converter. "One-meter long fabric measuring tape." The neatly rolled, soft measuring tape appears, and I scoop it up.

As I start to measure Sada's neck, she starts to play with the loose end, batting at it. This makes me happy, but I want to finish this before I play with her. "Hold on, hun."

I return to the converter and have it make both the silk ribbon and a meter length of small nylon cord.

I put her tag on the ribbon, and as I start to tie it around her neck, she licks me gently on my lips. Smiling, I finish the bow and return her kiss.

"I want you to know that I still love you. We are family."

She tilts her head curiously and then notices the cord. Her eyes dilate quickly, telling me she wants to play.

I chuckle and grab the cord. "All right, let's play for a bit."

While I sit at the desk, reading a book on the computer, Sada crawls off the bed to me. It's not a normal crawl, not for a person or a cat. Her legs are now much longer than her arms, and she doesn't put her weight on her knees. Instead, her behind sticks up in the air.

I find myself chuckling as she approaches, drawing an odd look from her. "I think it's time you learned to walk upright."

She shakes her head no, but I take her hands and help her stand up. She gives me a frightened look, so I put an arm around her and hold her up.

"All right, your feet are still paws, just like when you were small, so you'll need to use your tail to help balance."

She nervously nods and looks down at our feet and takes a tentative step forward, leaning heavily on me.

"If you want to take small steps, that's fine."

She looks curiously at my bare feet and then back to hers. When she tilts her head, I take the hint and state, "I have feet. I walk from heel to toe. You have paws so you walk on your pads."

She nods and takes another tentative step forward. Her tail flicks violently behind her and I feel her weight shift frequently in my arms as she tries to keep herself up.

"Take your time, it's a lot to adjust to, but I know you can do it," I gently coach.

She bumps my nose and starts to purr as she looks back down. After positioning her foot-paws, she starts trying to take her hands off me. I brace myself, in case I need to catch her, but let her try.

When she takes her hands off me for a moment, she teeters slightly and grabs my arm firmly to keep from falling, thankfully not using her claws. After a moment, she tries again. This time, she's able to stand on her own longer. She smiles at her small victory and takes a step towards me. Before she can put her foot back down, she falls forward.

I hear her gasp as I catch her, and find myself giggling. "I've got you. I won't let you fall."

Still hanging on me, she pulls her foot-paws under her. After straightening herself up, she wraps me in a hug.

"That was great," I tell her as I return her hug.

After a moment, she pulls back from me, stopping at arm's length, and tries to stand again. I keep ready to catch her as I take a step back. She takes one of my hands and holds it as she takes a short step. This time she manages to move her foot-paw fast enough to keep her balance.

She smiles, as do I, and I take another step back, giving her room to take another step. She nods and carefully shifts her weight to her lead foot. After a moment, she takes a half step, bringing her feet together. Unexpectedly, she takes another half step with the same foot, completing her stride.

"Good! You're getting it."

She smiles again and then looks back down at her feet again. She shifts her weight again and then quickly takes a full step. I feel her pull on my hand, trying to keep her balance. Staggering for a moment, she nearly grabs my other hand, but stops with a flick of her tail, apparently catching her balance that way.

She smiles and exhales sharply. I realize that she just tried to laugh and find myself doing the same. She takes another step and wraps me in a hug.

"That was great!" I return her hug, picking her up in the process. When I gently set her down, she gives me a lick on the cheek and purrs softly into my ear.

Awakening in the middle of the night, I stretch and realize that I'm alone. Without sitting up, I look around in the dim light and see Sada sitting in the desk chair. As I watch, she slowly paws at the floor with her feet, flexing her toes and claws. After a few moments, she scoots to the edge of the chair and leans forward. She moves her feet around, trying to find a comfortable position. Every now and then, she shifts her weight forward, apparently testing her balance.

Not wanting to disturb her, I stay quiet. I already know what she's doing. She's trying to stand on her own, learning the best position for balance.

Suddenly she rocks forward onto her feet. She stays squatted for a moment, then starts to slowly rise. Without touching the desk or table, she stands straight up. She stays still for a moment, then slowly takes a step forward.

She smiles and takes another slow step. After a few moments, she relaxes and starts to slowly walk by the foot of the bed. When she gets to the bathroom door, she steadies herself against the wall as she stops and turns around. After a moment, she starts to walk to the other end of the room.

Her pace, this time, is a little quicker, a little more fluid. When she turns back to face me, I sit up slightly and pat on the bed. "You're doing great, but come back to bed. Let's get some sleep."

She walks over to me and looks at the bed. She thinks for a moment and then simply flops onto it, landing next to me. She wiggles around, getting comfortable.

I chuckle lightly. "You meant to do that, right?"

She looks at me, thinking for a moment, then nods, taking my offered excuse.

I chuckle as I pull her close. She snuggles into me as I flip the blankets over us.

7

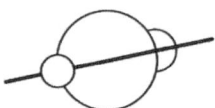

Having just returned from Garrent, I have a seat in my favored chair to relax. It's not long before Fey sits in the chair next to me. She doesn't say anything, but leans into me and sighs heavily.

This gets my attention. "What's the matter, hun?"

She sighs again, then asks, "Dad, what'll happen after the cubs are born?"

"What do you mean?"

"With me and Amela. What'll happen to us?"

"Hun, the only things that will change is that I and your moms will be a lot busier, and you two will have a little brother and sister."

"Oh." She leans into me and sighs again.

"You remember how it was with you and Amela?"

She nods.

"There's no need to get jealous."

"I know. I was used to it being just me and Kotu, I thought that, well..."

I softly chuckle. "Hun, why would you ever think that someone could replace you in my heart?" I pull her onto my lap, hugging her tightly. "I love you as if you were my own."

She quickly giggles and returns my hug. "Thanks, dad."

"What about me?" Amela asks as she climbs up in the chair with us.

I pull her into the hug. "Same goes for you, sweetie."

She starts to purr, and I recline us back in my chair.

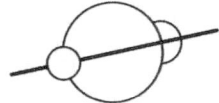

Sada stands beside me as we look at the cryo-tube. It's been one local year since we've been in the room. With the recent events, it seemed only appropriate that we wait till today to do this. Sada sees my hesitation and gently touches my shoulder.

I nod, and double-check the med-kits and nano injector, making sure they're in reach if I need them. I press the release and wait for the cryo-tube to drain. Sada grabs a towel, knowing what comes next.

When the door opens, I reach in and release the breathing tube. As it falls away, Sada dries Cayla off. I step in again and lift her up and unhook the straps from her shoulders. I quickly lie her down on the bed and start holding my hands to her chest and belly, moving them as Aime indicates.

Sada though, removes Cayla's mask, hood, and earplugs. After wiping down her face, Sada then looks curiously at me, waiting in case I need her to do something. I spend several minutes standing there, not appearing to move, one hand on her sternum, above her heart, the other just underneath, over her diaphragm.

"She's starting to come to," Aime states.

As she begins to open her eyes, Aime directs me to move my hands again. "Hi again," I state, hoping she remembers me.

She smiles weakly and nods, I quickly realize that her memories are intact and she knows that her larynx is too soft to speak.

"Just relax, almost done."

She takes a deep breath and sighs, letting herself relax and fall asleep.

"Marc would like to express his gratitude, and reports that she is now stable."

"Good, let's do a little more, and then we'll take a rest."

Sada grabs a blanket and covers her as I finish. We let her sleep, knowing that Marc, her AI, will continue healing her.

Returning to the anterior room, I find my family waiting. They had insisted on coming with me, wanting to see the place where I woke up. Thanks to my previous trips looking for working equipment to salvage, I had already set up lights, cleared the karnesh skeleton, and removed a lot of debris, making it easy for everyone to walk in.

I have a seat between my mates, on a longer sofa. Tayla quickly leans from the arm to me, so I put my arm around her. Sada had shown everyone around when we first arrived, so now she joins the children in a board game. Railu and Roen both sit on a couch opposite us. Thankfully, Railu's pregnancy has been nearly trouble-free for a week, though she still takes it easy.

The conversation is light as we wait. Arru sits at a desk, looking through information on human culture. I find her curiosity about my people interesting, at times I think she wants to go to Garrent to interview some of the people there, but other times she seems uninterested and works on the trade agreements that Arindell needs to reestablish. Tria, Niku, and Zoe are also busy looking through the records, occasionally downloading files to their tablets.

With Tareth and Skye, our guards, standing at the door, Larrah stands at the opposite end of the room. Though none are actually on duty, they all chose to consider this an official function and keep their vigil. Nanai and Kosh, however, wander around, occasionally watching the children play, but keeping available if someone wants something.

After nearly an hour, Megai turns suddenly, looking at the door to Cayla's room. "I think she's awake."

Tayla sits up and I head to the door. Before I can knock, Aime speaks, "Marc indicates that she's changing. I have advised him of our presence and intent."

Now having no need of knocking, I lower my hand and wait.

After a minute, the door opens, revealing a dressed and ready-to-go Cayla. "Hi. Marc says we have a lot to talk about."

"Yes, we do, but I'd first like to introduce you to my family." I move aside as she steps out into the room.

She stops abruptly, seeing all the different people in the room. "They're...evolved!"

"Yes. You've already met Sada."

She happily comes over and signs, 'Nice to see you healthy.'

"Thank you."

I give Cayla a curious look. "You understand sign language?"

"Marc translated."

"Ah." I nod. "I should tell you that it's been a year since I last woke you. In that time, I've walked far to find the humans, making several...friends, in the process."

"Walked, why not fly the other shuttle?"

"The shuttle that was here, didn't survive the 223 years."

Her mouth drops slightly, and her posture slumps as she looks around again. "Where's John and Dan?"

I shake my head. "I'm not sure, but I think they may have been in there when the room collapsed. None of the other pods were used."

She sighs and nods. "Marc was wondering why he couldn't contact their AIs"

"How well did you know them?"

"Not too well, they transferred in about a month ago." She frowns, and then corrects herself, "Before the accident."

"Do you want a moment?"

She sighs heavily and then shakes her head. "No."

"Well then, let me introduce you to my family and friends."

"Family?" she looks around the room, slightly awed by the mix of people waiting.

I smile. "Yes, some I've adopted, like Fey and Amela here, Kotu's my ward." They come over as I introduce them.

Cayla's eyes fill with wonder as she looks at them. "I never really got to meet any of the evolved. You're beautiful."

Fey smiles. "Thank you."

"You're welcome."

"Am I boo-full too?"

Cayla bends down to Amela. "Of course you are." In response, she reaches up, so Cayla picks her up, and sets her on her hip. "And your fur is so soft."

Amela giggles and snuggles up to her as she turns her attention to Kotu. He bows slightly. "Nice to meet you."

Cayla gives him a curious look, and bows back in kind. "Nice to meet you too."

I pat him on the back and then gesture to the larger couch. "These are my mates."

"Mates?"

I smile. "Yeah, I've adopted many of their ways as my own. It felt...right." We step around the couch. "This is Tayla and Megai."

Tayla reaches out her hand. "Nice to finally meet you."

As Cayla shakes her hand, she notices Tayla's belly. "You're...pregnant."

Tayla nods. "Twins, and yes, they're his."

She turns to me. "How?"

"Marc can fill you in on the details, but let's just say thanks for the DDE."

She sets Amela on the couch and puts her hands on Tayla's belly. "Are they stable?"

"Yep, Aime made sure before we tried for real."

"They're beautiful. When are you due?"

"About two weeks," Tayla states.

"Do you know what they are?"

"One of each, and we have already named them, Tashi and Kuma."

She looks curiously at Tayla then asks, "How'd you pick the names?"

"It's my family's tradition to name the male, based on the father's name, and the female, based on the mother's. His name begins with a K, mine with a T, our cubs follow that."

She smiles and blushes slightly. "Well, congratulations."

Tayla nods. "Thank you."

Megai extends her hand. "And, thank you for sending him after the other humans."

Cayla takes her hand, "You're welcome." She then notices her spots, "Are you her mother?"

"Amela is my twin sister's daughter. Both she and her mate have passed, so she is now ours."

"I see. So, how does this work, are you both mom to the children?"

Megai explains, "Fey and Amela call us both mom, and Kyle, dad. Kotu however, has continued to call us by name."

"Why?"

This time I explain, "After I rescued Fey, I adopted her and she decided to start calling me dad within about a week. When Tayla became my mate, she started calling her mom. Kotu, however, being my ward, always called us by name. I don't mind. They both respect us as their guardians. Amela, being adopted by Megai, followed Fey's example."

"How's Sada fit into this?"

"She remembers her life as a house cat, so she's still much like that. She's not a mom to the kids, more like a friend. Still sleeps with us, but sometimes she'll sleep with Fey or Amela. Usually plays games with them."

"Oh, is this how life is in the villages?"

"Close, I've carried in some of my influence too." I turn to Railu and Roen. "This is my surrogate sister, Railu, and her mate, Roen."

"Nice to meet you both." She then notices Railu's belly. "You too?"

"Only one, and we don't want to know. We want to be surprised," Railu explains.

She puts her hand on Railu's belly. "You've had some problems, haven't you?"

"Yeah, I was in false estrus, and it took. Kyle's kept us from harm."

"You're due in, what a month?"

"A little longer, but close."

"Well, congratulations to you both."

Roen smiles, as he nods. "Thank you."

I step over to where the others are. "This is Arru, my advisor. Zoe, cook. Tria, teacher. Niku, shaman."

"Shaman?"

"Healer, I specialize in herbal medicine."

"Wow, that sounds like a lot."

"Yeah, she saved my life once, and helped save Roen's too."

She nods, then looks at Tria. "Teacher?"

"Yep, I hold classes for the children, and occasionally work with the others when they need help with research or something."

"Looks like you'll be busier in a few years."

Tria smiles. "I look forward to it."

With a nod, she looks at Zoe. "You cook for everyone?"

"Oh yes, I have help from Nanai and Kosh over there. Kyle recently installed a large converter so I can make almost anything now."

"So, you don't actually cook?"

"Oh, yes I do. It makes the raw ingredients, then I season and cook it. Converter seems to lose something when you make the cooked meal."

"Sounds like you love it."

She smiles happily. "It's a dream."

Cayla then turns to Arru. "Advisor?"

"I counsel the family and guests if they need to talk. I also help negotiate trade agreements or mediate a dispute between the villages. Kyle has set up several communication relays between villages, so the Sages can talk directly to each other, and to Ziggy if they need to."

"Ziggy?"

"My house AI. I've been busy these last few months."

She raises her eyebrows. "I guess."

I gesture to the far wall. "That's Larrah." Then to the huskies. "Skye and Tareth. My family guards."

"You need guards?"

I sigh. "Let me formally introduce myself." I bow slightly as I state, "I am, Pendekar Kyle Andolina, Sovereign of Arindell."

"Sovereign?"

"Misunderstanding really, when Sage Arindell explained his reason for responding to me, the council took him literally." I shrug. "I really don't do much right now but remind the council to ask Sage for help when they need it."

"Sounds like I need to hear about your adventure."

"Aime sent it to Marc, so he can fill you in." I smile, "There is one more member of my family you should meet. Oana."

Oana hesitantly steps out from behind me, where she's been hiding. Cayla gasps and backs up a step.

"It's okay, she's harmless."

"Oana, friend. Cayla, friend?"

"Yes, Cayla friend."

"She speaks?" Cayla gasps.

"Yeah, she's been learning our language. We can't quite get her to use pronouns yet, and she still thinks I own her."

Cayla gives me an odd look but quickly turns her attention back to Oana. "Why does she think you own her?"

I sigh. "It's in the Ootuku culture for the males to own the females." I pause for a moment, then get an idea. "Put your hand out."

Cayla nervously puts her hand out and Oana sniffs it, then presses her nose to it, cooing.

I chuckle. "She likes you."

"She's not evolved." She gasps, gently feeling her scales.

"Nope, she's a product of natural evolution."

"Where'd you find her?"

"Far to the east, near the dig. The humans there had some run-ins with another tribe of Ootuku."

"You found them?"

"Yeah, doing surprisingly well, too. We relocated them to Garrent, it's their home now."

Her expression lightens, and then quickly saddens. "The Moku?"

Now my expression saddens. "They're...dying off. I did an aerial survey, looking for their mammal type. I only found about twenty of them. I've tried to get them together, telling them that their race's survival depends on it. They know they're dying, and they accept that."

Her posture reflects her disappointment. "Oh."

"I've given them all a standing invite, and some stop by from time to time. They'll teach us some of what they know in trade for the room and board." At least their knowledge won't die with them."

She looks around, then back at me. I can see the lost look in her eyes. "Will you be taking me to Garrent, then?"

Remembering how alone I felt when I first awoke, I make her an offer. "I can if you like. If you prefer, you could use a room at my home while you get adjusted."

She smiles. "I wouldn't be imposing at your place?"

Megai steps up beside me. "Not at all, we have plenty of extra rooms."

Tayla manages to waddle up as well. "And we would be honored to have you as a guest."

"How could I refuse an invitation from the Sovereign?" She bows slightly. "Let me pack my things."

I smile as I bow back, and she disappears into her pod room. It doesn't take her long, and we take our time walking out.

When we emerge from the facility, I get an odd look. "You have a shuttle? I thought you said you walked."

I chuckle. "I walked to find the humans. They had this shuttle, and gave it to me."

She's quiet for a moment, seemingly in thought, as we climb inside. She follows me into the cockpit and asks, "What'd they find?"

I sit in the pilot's seat and sigh. "Natural formations."

She sits in the navigator's seat next to me. "WHAT?"

"Yeah." I start up the shuttle, check to see that all are seated, and apply some power to the engines. "Think of Earth's Giant's Causeway."

She slumps in the seat. "That's disappointing."

"It saved their lives."

She nods and solemnly answers, "Yeah, I guess it did." She sits quietly, turning her attention out the windows as she watches the scenery go by.

I fly slowly, giving her a chance to actually see some sights. Hoping to cheer her a little, I fly over Pride River Falls. When she sees them, she smiles and watches them intently. I circle around it once, letting her watch a little longer, before heading home.

As we approach the house, Cayla stands and looks out the front window. "That's your house?"

"Yep, that's Ziggy."

"Why Ziggy?"

I chuckle. "When we first looked at the place, Aime stated that it looked like a ziggurat. It stuck."

"Is that a Black Hole class?"

"Yep, it's the Wanderer, showed up sometime after the accident. Unfortunately, the virus was still here, and the crew perished."

"I couldn't stop the automated mayday. It's a standard part of the decontamination process."

As I start landing the shuttle, I state, "Well, they launched a quarantine buoy, so no one else showed up. Planet's off-limits."

She sighs as she sits back down. "How many people are left?"

"Humans?"

She nods as I power down the shuttle.

"Five from the original team and about forty others."

"Forty?"

"Yeah, their descendants." After the door opens, she follows me out. "Welcome to my home."

8

I cautiously open the door and, using a small mirror, I check the corridor for people. Finding none, I take Sada's hand and lead her across the hall to an access hatch. After she's in, I follow, closing the door behind us. Having been cooped up in my room for over a month, I started sneaking out, exploring the service corridors. Since Sada can now walk, we've been doing this together.

Following the service corridor through several doors and turns, we eventually come out in a garden. It had taken me a while to find this place but found it worth the effort. The room is long and narrow, apparently down the spine of the ship, as it's well protected. The floor is covered with grass, laid out like a park. Stone paths wander throughout, and there's a mix of shrubs, flowers, and small trees breaking it into sections.

Sada and I stretch and start slowly walking barefoot through the grass. We remain quiet, unsure if we are alone. She occasionally stops to smell various flowers, I find myself smiling at her curiosity, being glad she can explore again. We meander slowly, working our way to the far end of the garden. It takes us nearly an hour to get there, and when we do, we settle into a corner to relax for a while.

I watch Sada curiously for a bit. Seeing her try to pick individual blades of grass makes me smile. She clumsily tries to grab one in her fist, but it slides right out between her fingers when she tries to pull it. I chuckle lightly as I watch her getting used to the fact that she now has an opposable thumb.

"Here, let me show you how."

She watches intently as I demonstrate how to use the thumb and a finger to pick a single blade. She mimes the motion a few times, getting the hang of it, then tries on a piece of grass. She quickly plucks the blade from the dirt and smiles. She then starts repeating the action, plucking individual blades with both hands, changing fingers often.

Lying back on the grass, I start to watch the artificial sky. Clouds seem to drift through and I find myself wondering how they are simulated.

A poke from Sada gets my attention and I watch her crawl over to some bushes, her tail held low. Realizing that I hear voices, I follow as quietly as possible.

As they approach, I can tell they're both males. One sounds older and gravely, but the other is full of confidence and has a slight accent. Still getting closer, I begin to understand the conversation.

"...be ready in three days."

"Good, make the calculations for the jump and make sure the drones are prepared."

"Certainly sir."

"Dismissed."

Through the bushes, I can barely see the two men, the older leaves the garden, having been dismissed. The other stays for a moment, looking slowly around, then turns and walks purposefully towards the far end. Seeing Sada's ears still focused in the man's direction, I wait.

After she relaxes, I roll to my back and let out a long quiet sigh. We wait for a few minutes before making our way back to the service corridor and then to our room.

After locking the door, I find myself laughing. Sada looks at me curiously, apparently wondering what's wrong with me.

As I start calming down, I look at her. "We almost got busted. That was the captain."

A look of shock crosses her face and her jaw drops. She shakes her head a couple of times, but seeing me nod in silent argument, she relents. With a heavy sigh, she lies down on the bed and stares blankly at the ceiling.

I sit in the desk chair and put my feet up, leaning back. "What's going to happen in three days?" I see Sada look at me curiously, still doing her finger exercises.

"Sorry, just thinking aloud."

She frowns a little and then gets comfortable on the bed.

Curiosity getting the better of me, I sit up and turn my attention to the terminal on the desk. After touching the screen to wake it up, I log in using the key that Mike gave me. While sorting through the recent activities, I find a course correction and quickly locate the destination.

"Aquia?"

Sada looks at me again, as if expecting me to continue, so I do a search. What comes up is initially disappointing. I find creeks, harbors, and a company, all on Earth. Looking further down the list, there are more places, scattered all around Earth, and some apparently on other planets, but none seem to stand out.

Several entries in, I find a 'See also' listing, followed with the word 'Aquellia." I tap that entry. Up comes an entry for a planet. From the spinning globe view, I can see that it's almost entirely water-covered. The few landmasses I see, all appear to be smaller than Iceland.

As I watch the graphic slowly spin, I see a flag on one of the islands. I touch it and it zooms into a rather elaborately constructed building. It has elevated walkways and a landing pad with several towers scattered around, all on an island surrounded by beaches.

I notice that the entry changed to show 'Aquellia Research Labs.' The rest of the entry, however, is blank.

I cancel the search and sit back in the chair and turn to watch Sada, who's now asleep. As I look at her, I find myself wondering what kind of research they do, and what business the captain has there.

The com pops and Kevin's voice comes through slightly panicked. "Better strap in, we're in for a bumpy ride. We're passing through the planet's magnet field. It's a lot stronger than most, and the dampeners aren't strong enough to compensate."

I abandon the book I was reading and dive into the bed, waking Sada in the process. She gives me an odd look as I pull the webbing down over us. "It's gonna get bumpy."

She huffs as she slides closer to me. I can't blame her for being upset. It seems like we spend more time under this webbing than out.

The ship groans as it enters the field and the floor and walls start to vibrate, making the furniture rattle. I soon realize that Sada shaking as hard as the furniture, so I pull her close to me, trying to comfort her. As the shaking increases, I soon realize that I need her for comfort as much as she needs mine.

The ship continues to groan and rattle as the planet's magnetic field tries to distort the ship's frame. Through all the ship's noises, I manage to hear the engines fire. Everything suddenly quiets.

The intercom pops, startling us both. "The worst is over, we're in orbit. The ship'll still make some noise, but it should be minimal."

I slowly release the webbing and Sada takes the moment to try to smooth her ruffled fur.

I quickly grab a brush and sit behind her on the bed. "This ship's in worse shape than they let on." She nods as I start brushing her, helping her smooth it down. She starts to purr, letting me know she likes the attention, but her tail keeps twitching, telling me something's bothering her.

As I work my way down her back, her tail starts flicking harder. Unable to ignore it, I ask, "What's bothering you?"

She huffs, looking down at her lap as she stops purring.

"That bad huh?"

She nods, and her tail calms noticeably.

Unsure what else to do, I gently prod, hoping to find an answer, "Is it, me?"

She shakes her head and leans back onto me, purring as she gently rubs her cheek to mine.

I put my arms around her and hold her for a moment. "Okay, not me. How about, is it the ship?"

She shakes her head again.

"Hmm, not the ship. Something in the ship?"

She frowns as she shakes her head.

"Nothing in the ship. okay, well—"

She nods, interrupting my thoughts.

"Nothing in the ship?"

She nods again, then makes a gesture, like she wants more.

I think for a moment. "Nothing...to do, in the ship?"

She nods happily, confirming my guess as correct.

I sigh, as I look at the rough map stuck to the wall, that I've been drawing of the ship as I've explored. "We could go to the garden again."

She turns to me and rolls her eyes.

"Okay, not the garden. What about, the gym?"

She shakes her head again.

I sigh, wondering what else we could do onboard. With her finally getting used to her new body, she has more time to get bored, and I beginning to realize that I do too. We need something new to do together.

"I have an idea." I go to the converter. I'd learned long ago that it can make more than food, that's how I got the paper for the maps. I shuffle through the list of games and find a couple of simple things with a lot of uses. I have the converter make both and sit back down with Sada.

"Cards or dice?"

With her curiosity peaked, she looks at both for a moment, then points to the cards. I set the dice aside and open the deck. After fanning out the cards, I start to teach her one of my favorite games.

Lying in bed, I'm awakened by the sounds of the ship rattling. I reach up and pull the webbing down over us as Sada snuggles in closer to me. She lets out a huff as I wrap my arms around her.

"This is getting old," I groan.

Sada lets out a heavy sigh, apparently agreeing with me.

The ship's vibration is not that pronounced, so I'm unable to tell if we're in another fight, or just near a source of gravity. This seems to go on for hours, preventing us from getting any sleep.

Too tired to get up, I lie there and focus on Sada. I can feel her fur against my bare arms, her tail twitching by my legs. I can feel her ear twitch each time there's a loud pop or bang from the ship.

Comforted by her presence, I begin to think of the only other person I've been this close to.

Meagan slowly rolls over to face me. "Kyle? You still awake?"

I drowsily open an eye. "Mmm-hmm."

She smiles. "What do you think about having another?"

"Another?"

"Baby."

I slowly prop myself up on my elbow. "So soon? Michael's not even out of diapers yet."

"I don't mind waiting a couple of years. I was thinking though, once he's potty trained..."

I lean over her and kiss her. "Hun, sometimes you talk too much."

She reaches around me and licks my cheek, purring.

I snap awake and realize that I'm laying on Sada, who's giving me a very happy, if puzzled, look.

Realizing that I probably just kissed her while I was dreaming, I slowly roll off her and sigh.

She rolls over onto me and gently licks my cheek again.

"Sada..."

She put her finger to my lips, hushing me, so I wrap my arms around her and hold her to me. She nuzzles into my neck, and her purring drowns out the sounds of the ship vibrating.

9

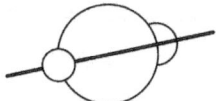

It's time.

I pace nervously outside Niku's office while waiting anxiously for her to allow me in. I can feel Tayla's fear jump with each contraction. I glance occasionally at Sada, who now lies sedated on a couch. She was having sympathetic contractions and they were making her very sick. The children and Oana are upstairs in class with Tria.

Megai is inside with Tayla, as are Niku, Zoe, Nanai, and Cayla. Despite everyone else being in this room, I feel alone, trapped. I just want to be in with my mates, waiting for the twins to be born.

Arru comes up next to me. "Calm yourself, Niku will let you in when they're ready."

"I know, it's just..." I sigh, trying to find the words. "I felt her excitement when she had her first real contractions. Then she was serious for a while, but now, she's in doubt, I need to be in there with her, encouraging her."

Suddenly, the door opens, startling me. Zoe stands just inside, wearing the simple gown that she and Niku wear when they work. Smiling, she looks at me. "Come on."

Tayla sits in a birthing chair, knees up nearly to her chin, breathing heavily. Megai sits behind her, holding her. She sees me and motions me over. "You should be the one sitting here."

I slide in as Megai slides out. As I wrap my arms around Tayla, she grabs them firmly. "I don't know if I can do this."

I do my best to suppress the doubt I feel from her, and try to fill myself with confidence and love. "You're doing wonderfully."

"Easy for you to say, you're not the one that's going to be pushing out two cubs."

I gently kiss the back of her head, waiting for a contraction to pass. "I know love, but I have faith in you. You can do this."

Another contraction hits Tayla, and I feel her hands clamp onto mine as she blurts, "I WANT TO PUSH!"

Niku quickly washes her hands again and sits on a low stool in front of us. "With your next contraction, go on ahead and push."

"Sorry if I claw you."

"I'll heal."

Feeling another contraction coming, she suddenly takes a few rapid breaths. I brace myself as she grunts and begins to push.

"Good, now relax." Niku coaches, as the contraction fades. "Breathe."

Tayla takes a few rapid breaths. I try to keep my focus, holding on to the confidence, hoping she feels it. She nods quickly as she again squeezes my hands. This time she screams as she pushes.

After nearly an hour, the first cub is finally born. As Cayla, holds the cub, Niku takes care of the cord and swabs its mouth and nose, then Cayla quickly checks it over. "This one's the girl. She's in good health."

"Tashi," Tayla states, gasping.

Niku does something to the cub and she starts to make chirping sounds. Zoe then takes her for her first bath.

"One more, Tayla," Niku coaches, bringing my attention back to my mate.

"I know," Tayla pants. "HRRRAARRR"

Pain rips through my arms as her claws sink in. I grit my teeth and endure it.

As the contraction passes, she pulls her claws out. To my relief, Aime was ready for this and the wounds heal almost immediately.

Her contractions seem to intensify over the next few minutes, and I see her exhaustion quickly build.

"Just a little more," Niku coaches. "I can see the head."

"Come on, love, you can do this," I gently encourage.

She pants a few times. "I'm *TRYING!*"

"I have him!"

After a moment, I see Cayla take the cub. "It's the boy! He's healthy, and he has white fur."

"Kuma." Tayla gasps, between pants.

When he starts chirping, Nanai takes him off for his first bath and we hear a splat. "Placenta," Niku states.

Cayla and Niku start tending to Tayla as Zoe washes Kuma.

Tayla turns to me, and pants, "Go...get her. She...should be...okay now."

Megai slides a thick cushion in while I slide out. I get to Sada quickly and put my hand on her head so Aime can wake her.

Seeing her eyes open, I softly say, "Come on." She gets up and follows me back in. I find Tayla reclined slightly, holding Tashi as she suckles.

Megai is standing, holding a swathed Kuma, but seeing Sada with me, she comes over and hands Kuma to her. She smiles and nods. "You wanted to help nurse."

Sada nods as she takes the cub and looks at him curiously. She gently rubs his freshly cleaned fur, and the cub starts to chirp, trying to use his little shaky hands to grab her fingers.

"Just put him to your breast, he knows what to do," Niku states.

Sada nervously moves her top aside, revealing a breast and Niku helps her position Kuma. "Hold him like this, and he'll..." As she speaks, the cub latches on and starts to suckle. This startles Sada and she gasps at the sensation.

I find myself looking between my cubs. Now that they're clean, I can clearly see their markings. Tashi's patterned much like her mother, with a yellow honey badger coat and gold eyes, while Kuma's fur is white, with dark blue-grey spots and blue eyes. "They're beautiful," I admit.

Sada finds a spot to sit next to Tayla. I see her eyes fill with wonder as she watches the cubs purr and suckle. I find that I can't help but feel the same way as I put my arm around Megai and hold her close.

Tayla weakly looks at me and smiles. "Thank you."

I give her a loving kiss. "Love, you did all the work."

"For the boost to my confidence."

I give her another kiss. "I never had any doubt."

The room soon fills with the others as Zoe lets them in.

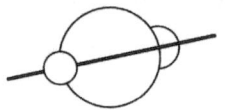

While Tayla naps, catching up on some needed sleep, I recline in the nursery, gently rocking the newborn cubs to sleep. Kuma's on my right arm, Tashi's on my left. Both are swathed in their own blankets, Tashi's is yellow while Kuma's is grey. As I rock them, Tashi makes a squeak as she lets out a big yawn.

I see Oana's head appear alongside me and realize that class is out. She looks at the cubs for a moment, then back at me and softly asks, "What they?"

"Oana, meet Tashi, and Kuma," I nod to each as I say their names.

She makes a couple of clicks as she looks curiously at them. "Tashi. Kuma." She looks at me, then again at the cubs. "Sada, Kuma? Tayla, Tashi?"

Understanding her clipped version of English, I gently correct. "Tayla, Tashi, and Kuma."

She tilts her head in thought, then rapidly, but softly says, "Kyle, Tayla, Tashi, Kuma?"

"Yes, Kyle and Tayla's."

"Little."

"They were just born."

"Babies?"

"Yes, they're babies."

Suddenly, Amela comes running in and loudly asks, "Can I see?"

Oana ducks, trying to cover her ears as Kuma, startled, starts chirping. This in turn wakes Tashi and she joins him, also chirping.

Keeping my tone soft, I say, "Amela, you need to be quieter, they were sleeping."

Oana starts to coo, trying to sound comforting as Amela climbs up in the chair next to me. "Sorry," she whispers.

"Honey, you need to be quiet when you come up to little ones."

"Like me," Fey announces quietly from behind me. "Hi, dad. Hello, my new brother and sister." She reaches around me and gently rubs their chins. "Shh, go back to sleep."

I smile and lightly chuckle, the combination of Fey's touch and Oana's cooing works. The cubs stop their chirping, but instead of going back to sleep, they look curiously at me.

"Hello, my cubs, I'm your father." I gently move Kuma to my left, alongside his sister, and gently rub their noses. They both sniff my fingers, learning my scent. Tashi lets out another yawn and closes her eyes. Kuma, though, keeps looking around.

Megai comes in from the bedroom, and softly asks, "Everything okay? I heard them calling."

"Amela startled them." I softly say, and then look to Amela. "It won't happen again, will it?"

She nervously chews on her finger as she apologizes. "Sowwy."

"Did you mean to?" Megai asks her.

"No."

"All right. Be careful around them."

"I will."

Suddenly Kuma chirps, getting our attention. I see his blue eyes look at me, then at Megai. I smile at this. "I think he's jealous."

"Why?" Amela asks, trying to sit up to see him.

"You were getting looked at, and he wasn't," I tell her.

"He can see us?"

"Of course he can."

Fey moves around Oana to sit by me, opposite Amela, when she sees Kuma's eyes follow her, she giggles. "He's watching me."

Still looking at her, he chirps curiously.

"That's Fey, your big sister."

Unexpectedly, Oana makes a similar chirp and Kuma does his best to try to look at her. Knowing that wouldn't be a good thing for her to keep doing, I softly say, "Oana, please don't mimic that sound."

"Oana sorry."

With a rather large yawn, Kuma announces his want to sleep and closes his eyes. "All right, time for the cubs to sleep."

As I place them in their cribs, Megai shoos the others out and closes the door behind her. I exit through the bedroom, and quietly check on Tayla.

As I enter, she rolls over and smiles at me. "Are they asleep?"

"Yep." I lie next to her and wrap her in a hug. "How's mom feeling?"

She smiles and nuzzles into me. "A lot thinner."

I chuckle as a third person joins us. I roll to see Sada crawling up the bed. "Want in on this?"

She nods happily and quickly lies next to me.

I take both in my arms and hold them. A sudden feeling of happiness invades my thoughts, and I let it fill me. It doesn't take too long before I hear someone softly crying.

Feeling someone sit at the foot of the bed, I quickly sit up and drag Megai up with us.

"Why the tears?" Tayla asks.

"They're happy tears," she softly states. "Pay them no mind."

She quickly snuggles between Sada and me. I hear Sada let out a silent laugh and start to purr. The others quickly join in.

10

Sada follows me through the service corridor as we make our way to cargo hold four. In an attempt to help allay our boredom and knowing that we've already been out and about, Ariel had suggested that I might find what's in there interesting, so Sada and I decided to check it out. I slowly open the door, carefully checking for anyone inside. Not finding anyone, we step out into the cargo bay.

The first thing I notice is that most of the smaller crates have been stacked along the far wall. What now sits in the middle are several odd-looking racks of metal cylinders. There are ten cylinders on the closest rack, and I see ten racks in the hold.

"So, this is what we picked up from Aquia."

Sada and I approach the closest set, wanting to get a closer look. The cylinders are large enough around to fit in, and about half again my height. Unfortunately, there aren't any windows on them, so we can't see inside. I slowly circle around one of the racks. On the far end, I find a small sign, with only one word on it.

"Aquanatum."

Sada gives me a curious look, shrugging her shoulders.

"It's Latin, 'aqua' means water, 'natum' means…born. Water born?"

She tilts her head curiously, then puts an ear to one of the cylinders and gently knocks on it. The sound it makes means only one thing.

"Well, it's full of liquid." I look at the cylinder more closely. It's nearly one piece, no noticeable seems, except at the top, which is just out of my reach. I put my hand to the side of it and find the metal cool to the touch. I look between the two rows and see some piping joining all the tanks to a central, smaller tank hidden between the rows.

"Looks like some kind of circulation system."

Suddenly Sada starts tapping on something at the other end. I walk around to where she's at and she points to another sign.

Not having yet taught her enough words to read it for herself, I read it aloud. "Warning, cryo system backup. Do not alter settings."

I lift the cover, revealing a display and control panel. I look at the readout on the display and notice that this one's working off of the backup.

"This can't be good," I mutter. A quick check of the other racks reveals that they're all working off of their backups.

"I should probably tell someone about this. I don't think the captain would take it well if the things failed."

Sada nods her head, agreeing with me.

With no other markings or things noted on it, we head back to our room. I press the call button and wait for a response.

When the com finally pops, a new, female voice comes across. "Can I help you?"

Surprised, I give the speaker an odd look. "Who are you?"

"Apologies, I am Julie, Mike's AI. He cannot talk right now, and asked me to check on you."

"Oh, uh, okay. You're aware of those Aquanatum cylinders in cargo bay four, right?"

"I am."

"They're all working on their backup cryo systems."

"Why is this a concern?"

"Well, it the captain thinks they're important enough to take, I don't want anyone getting in trouble if the backups fail."

After a moment's pause, she says, "I see your point. Were there any cables connected?"

"No, none."

"I will relay your concerns as soon as possible. Thank you."

The light goes out, so I turn my attention to Sada. She sits at the desk, trying to shuffle the cards. As they slip from her fingers, she manages to keep most of them on the table. She huffs as she looks up at me.

"It's not as easy as I make it look. It took me months to learn to shuffle the cards the way I do."

I help her pick up the cards, and start shuffling.

"What are we playing?"

She looks down the list of card games that I have on the table and then points to one.

"Rummy?"

She nods.

"All right," I offer her the cards. "Do you want to try to deal?"

She tilts her head, then takes the cards, and starts to deal. We spend a few hours playing, with her winning most of the games.

I begin to feel like conceding when the door light comes on. I quickly unlock the door and open it. Carrie and Maurice hurry in and close the door behind them.

"Thanks for the save," Maurice states.

"For what?"

"The Aquanatum, you saved their lives," Carrie adds.

"There are people in those cylinders?"

"Of sorts. " Maurice states, as he sits in the chair by the desk and the display comes on, showing a picture resembling something like a human crossed with a dolphin. He turns the monitor so Sada and I can see better. "These are the Aquanatum.

"Are they like Sada?"

"No, they're not evolved, they were created."

Sada tilts her head, and I look at him curiously. "What'd you mean?"

He sighs. "Each of us in this room evolved. In our lineage, or in Sada's case, life, we started as something else and became what we are today."

"I know what evolved means."

"The Aquanatum have no past, no ancestors. Those cylinders contain the very first generation of them. The labs on Aquia created them."

I sit for a moment, trying to wrap my head around the concept of creating a species. I find myself wanting to ask a question, but having trouble forming the words. "W-wh-wh, uhm...How?"

"The techs wrote the DNA from scratch, and from what I learned, it took 'em nearly a century to do it."

"I can't even begin to imagine how difficult that was."

He smiles. "I don't even want to try."

Carrie picks up the explanation, "Those cryo-tubes were almost out of power, but, thanks to you, they're now working off the ship's grid. When you told Julie, she had Mike tell Kevin. He had to adjust some of the rounds, but managed to fit a 'maintenance check' into a tech's schedule and got them hooked up. As a precaution, I then did a med check. All one hundred and fifty of them are still good."

"Hundred and fifty? We only saw a hundred cylinders."

"There's more in cargo bay two. Anyway, we wanted to thank you personally. You really saved some of our necks with that."

"I guess you should also thank the lieutenant, she told me about them."

"She's already aware of it."

"I'll leave what we know about them on your terminal, give you some new reading material."

"Thanks."

They leave, and I relock the door. When I turn around, Sada's sitting at the desk looking at the screen. I pull another chair over and join her, and start reading the information on the screen aloud.

Leaving my room as Sada sleeps, I tread lightly down the corridor to a service hatch. Curiosity driving me to explore, I slip silently into the service corridor and make my way to the upper levels. Working my way forward, I pass an access hatch next to the security chief's office, when I hear a sudden loud bang on the wall.

I freeze, even holding my breath, wondering what just happened inside. After waiting silently for only a moment, I suddenly hear someone shout. I quietly lean against the wall and put my ear up to the wall to listen.

"...were you doing?"

"My apologies sir, I was not aware they needed..."

"Shut your mouth. I'm tired of your excuses. First, you lose his cat, and now *this*. You do realize that it was a Petty Officer that caught *your* mistake. It's a good thing he did too. The captain would have your ass personally for that."

"Sir..."

"Shut up, because of your incompetence, the captain's revoked privileges for everyone on that shuttle's crew for a month. You are now on double reactor duty for a week."

"I'm not qualified for that," He protests

"You are now," the other coldly states.

"The radiation..."

"Would you rather have the captain's punishment?"

"N-n-no, sir."

I lean against the opposite wall and wonder who just got in a lot of trouble, though I already know why. That was over the Aquanatum, I saved their lives but apparently got someone in hot water.

Not feeling like exploring now, and having forgotten where I wanted to go, I slowly return to my room.

As I enter, Sada comes up to me. Apparently sensing my melancholy mood, she wraps me in a hug, purring in my ear.

I return her hug. "I got someone in a lot of trouble."

She sighs as she gives me a sad look, then pulls me close and rubs her cheek to mine.

"I know it's not really my fault, but I can't help but feel sorry for the guy. He just forgot to plug the things in."

I flop on the bed and stare at the ceiling. Sada gently crawls up next to me, puts her head on my arm. I give her nose a kiss, making her purr, and let myself drift off.

11

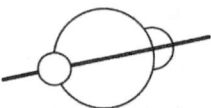

I step out of the shuttle and look across the field to Garrent. I find myself pleased to see a few evolved among the humans that live here. Humans are starting to integrate with the evolved, making friends. This makes me smile as I walk into the village, Tareth follows, keeping pace.

Having been expecting me, Marcus comes walking up. "I got your call. You wanted my help fixing a ship?"

"Yes. There's a Black Hole class ship that needs some repairs. I know it's not what you're used to working on, but you know more about the systems than I do."

He thinks for a moment, then says, "I'd be my pleasure." He then smiles and asks, "May I have a moment, I'd like to check with someone."

"Certainly."

"Thank you."

He heads back as Tareth leans over to me. "What's he doing?"

"I'm not sure."

When he finally returns, he has a younger man with him. "This is Darren, my nephew. I was training him to work on the shuttle so he hasn't had a lot to do lately."

Darren smiles and says, "It would be an honor to help repair your ship."

"Thank you. If you like, I can offer you both rooms, or I can ferry you back here in the afternoons."

They look at each other for a moment. "I'll stay," Darren states.

"I will too, at least for a while."

"Do either of you need to get anything?"

They both think for a moment, and then Marcus shakes his head. "I can use the converters to make what I will need."

Darren nods his agreement, and we board the shuttle. The flight is short and as we approach the house, they both get a look at the Wanderer. The long, sleek ship sits just north of the house, nose towards the garage.

"It's huge," Darren states.

"Not really, it's actually a small ship compared to most others out there."

Marcus looks at me curiously. "Really?"

"Yeah, I was on a cruiser that was several times that length."

"Wow."

Having landed, I lead them up into the Wanderer and start to give them a tour of the ship. After passing through the now empty forward cargo hold, I turn to take them up to the mid-deck.

Marcus stops before boarding the lift and asks. "What's in the aft bay?"

"Over a hundred empty cryo-tubes."

"What are you going to do with them?"

"I'll probably offload them into the facility."

He opens the door and looks inside. With the lights now on, it looks more like a room at the facility than a cargo hold in a starship. After a brief look, he sighs and closes the door. We then take the lift up to mid-deck.

"There are rooms in the fore section. You can use those or the house. I don't mind which."

We turn and head aft. "This is the Science Lab, Med Bay, and here is Engineering."

Marcus immediately walks over to a diagnostic panel and starts working. Darren and I follow, watching him work. After a few moments, the display shows some stats. "This could take a while, there's a lot of components that need to be serviced, just for the engines."

"That's not surprising, it's been sitting outside, unattended for two centuries."

"This converter work?"

"Yeah, but it's not an industrial unit, I'm still trying to find a working one in the facility."

"It's not the unit. It's the programming that makes it industrial." He walks over to the unit and opens the panel under the controls. After a moment, he pulls out a small board and tosses it in the bin with the bad pistols. "Little known fact, without that limiter board, it's now an industrial unit."

I stand in disbelief. "You've got to be kidding me."

He smiles. "Nope."

"I've been looking for an industrial unit for months."

"Should have come to me sooner."

I lean against the wall. "I don't suppose it's that easy for a nanite class converter?"

He smiles and laughs. "No, sorry." He suddenly gets thoughtful, then adds, "But, some of the hardware is interchangeable."

I feel my hopes rise and I smile. "I have a few of them that don't work, and I've found a couple of normal units of the same size."

"I'll take a look, maybe I can get one working."

"That would be great." Before he can respond, we hear a chime. "Ah, lunch. Come on guys, work can wait."

We're the last to enter the dining hall. "Good, everyone's already here. You all remember Marcus, and this is his nephew Darren. They'll be with us for a while, helping repair the Wanderer."

Everyone greets them as Nanai and Kosh quickly add places for them to the table. After they both sit, I find my seat at the head of the table by my mates. Zoe then signals to begin serving lunch.

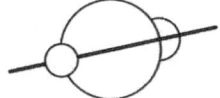

Late in the evening, I sit at my desk reviewing a trade agreement between Lanketh and Garrent. With my office just off the great hall, I have a good view of anyone going through the front doors. Normally this is a good thing, but it makes it hard to see anyone coming from inside the house. Tareth stands, like a statue, in his favored place along the far wall, where he can see both the front doors and into my office.

As I read, Nanai quietly comes in. "May I have a moment, please?"

"Sure." I set the tablet aside and let her have my attention.

Her nervousness is obvious as she sits, and tries not to fidget. She thinks for a moment. "I would like some advice, about, well, uhm...Do you think I'm attractive?" She suddenly covers her mouth, apparently surprised at her own question.

I smile, she's often looked at me curiously, as if wondering what it was like to be without fur. "Nanai, while I'm not looking for another mate, I do think you are attractive. Why the sudden need for my opinion? You're usually quite sure of yourself."

She looks away, embarrassed, and I realize something. "It's Darren, isn't it?"

She looks shocked for a moment, but nods.

I relax a little. "If you are interested in him, just talk to him. Be yourself. If he finds you interesting, you'll know by his actions, not his words. Human males are less direct about their desires than what you're used to."

She nods and then gives me a curious look. "Do you think he'll like me?"

"Nanai, try not to be disappointed if he doesn't. But, if he shows any interest, be patient with him. I'm sure he's not used to people with fur yet. I recommend being his friend first. Let him get used to that, get to know each other before you take it to the next level."

"But you took two mates in your first year."

"I also had the benefit of amnesia and almost a month of being with Sada before walking into Pridewyn. He's still got a lot of preconceptions to work past."

She nods again. "I will try, thank you."

As she stands to leave, I give her a warm smile. "Good luck." She pauses a moment to nod again, then disappears into the hall.

I lean back in my chair and sigh, wondering if he has an open mind when Ziggy interrupts my thoughts. "Your mates are asking for assistance in the nursery."

"I'll be right there."

As I walk, I find myself marveling at how quickly the cubs have developed. Aime had warned me that they would have a slightly accelerated development for the first year. Then it slows to human standard. That would mean that they'll be the equivalent of a two-year-old human by the time they're one. In three and a half weeks, they're already starting to roll over, and they've nearly doubled their weight.

Opening the door, I hear the cubs chirping. Unlike humans, they don't cry, they still use the sounds that they did before they were evolved. Cheetah cubs chirp.

"What's all the fuss about?" The cubs fall silent at the sound of my voice.

"How do you do that?" Tayla gasps. "Even before they were born."

"Maybe it's my deeper voice." I give her a kiss as she tries to put a fresh diaper on Kuma. I let him hold my fingers as she works. He calms as he looks at my hand, letting out an occasional, questioning chirp.

I chuckle, lightly. "You're a curious little one, aren't you?"

He looks back at me, chirps and smiles. He then lets out a long yawn. Tayla picks him up to nurse him, so I turn my attention to my daughter, Tashi. She lying in her crib, holding Megai's fingers as Sada finishes her diaper. When she looks at me, she smiles. I hear her make a couple of short, happy chirps. "They sure do grow fast."

"They've been really hungry lately, too. I've been occasionally getting them some milk from the converter to help feed them," Megai adds as she disposes of diapers in the converter. They disappear with a flash as she turns back to us.

"They'll be starting real food soon enough, so they won't need as much milk," Tayla states as Megai and I start getting the cubs' beds ready.

"I wonder when Railu's is coming?" Tayla asks.

"Any day now," I state.

"I know that it's just, well, she hasn't even had any pre-labor yet," Megai states

"With as much trouble as she's had, she doesn't need to go through a long labor," Tayla counters.

I smile, and add, "Well, Niku's ready and waiting for her when she does. Cayla's even sticking around for it."

As Megai finishes Tashi's bed, she looks at Sada, waiting for the cub. "Well, if she wants to stay after that, she's certainly welcome to."

"She knows it. She's just trying to figure out where she feels she belongs," I add.

As Tayla sets Kuma in the crib, I add a couple of his favored stuffed toys, a giraffe that's almost as large as him and a bear half his size. He grabs the bear and pulls it close into a hug. Tashi's favored stuffed toy is a dragon that's almost twice the size of the real ones. When Sada puts her in her crib, she curls up to its side and lets out a yawn. We all give them their bedtime kisses and retire to our own room.

As we get ourselves ready for bed, Megai turns to me. "Did Nanai talk to you?"

"Yeah."

"Did she tell you who she's interested in?"

"She didn't have to, I could tell."

"What are you going to do?"

"Nothing, really."

She gives me a somewhat shocked look. "What!?"

"It's between her and Darren, I gave her advice, recommending that she proceed slowly, let him get to know her. If he has an open mind, they'll have a chance."

She relaxes considerably. "Oh, she wouldn't tell me who she was interested in, I thought she wanted you."

"If she'd come to me the same way before I picked the guys up, I would have agreed with you, but I saw the way she looked at him at lunch, it reminded me of the way she looked at me when she first started working here. I knew I wasn't the one she was after."

Tayla gives Megai a smile. "She kind of reminds me of someone."

Megai frowns back. "What's that supposed to mean?"

'You're both curious, and attracted to humans,' Sada interjects.

"I didn't know he was a human at the time, besides, you both have no less interest in him than I do."

"All right my loves, no fighting. Nanai has her own way to follow, just like we do. If they can make it work, then good for them." I lie down on the bed and get comfortable on my back. Tayla crawls in alongside and lies on my right while Sada curls up to my left. Both let out a sigh and Sada then moves to be alongside Tayla, letting Megai slide up alongside me. I gently start to scrub their backs, getting them to purr, and let myself drift.

12

Sada and I stroll quietly through the garden, currently the one place on the ship where we don't feel like we're cooped up. Looking up at the sky, we see the stars. It's night, and the best time to come walk the garden. With most of the crew either asleep or on duty, we're alone.

I've come to find the place a little too quiet though, there aren't any bugs or birds. The only background noise is that of the engines. For once though, I find their droning pulse comforting. We're just cruising, holding course and speed, not trying to flee, not being shot at, or passing through something hazardous.

Sada sits in the grass and gestures me to do the same. I join her as she lies back in the grass, and watch the night sky. Before long, I find myself drifting off to sleep, into my own memories.

"Kayley, don't play with that, it's fragile."

"But I wanna see the stars, too."

"Then you should have asked for a telescope for Christmas."

My little sister looks at me, pouting. Her brown eyes are big and sad, her lips are turned down like she's crying.

"All right, but just look, don't touch."

She nods happily as I check the focus. "Look through here, and tell me what you see."

At nine, she's barely tall enough to look into the eyepiece of the telescope, so I place a couple of encyclopedias on the floor for her to stand on.

As she looks, I hear her gasp lightly. "It's the moon. What are all the dark spots?"

"Those are craters, where meteors have hit it."

"Sure is a lot of 'em."

"Yeah, and there's a lot more on the other side."

"When can I see the other side?"

"You'd have to fly there in a spaceship. This side of the moon always faces us."

As she turns to look at me. "How do you know so much?"

"I did a science project on it."

"When do I get to do that?"

"Well, let me think. I did mine last year, school won't have it this year. So, when you're in eighth grade."

"Aww, how come I can't do it when I get to seventh like you did?"

"It depends on when the school holds the science fair."

"Oh." She turns back to the telescope and looks at the moon for a moment. "I'm gonna go there someday."

I smile as I chuckle. "Good luck with that, NASA stopped going to the moon long ago."

"Well, I'm going." She hops down off the books and storms out of the room in a huff.

"You go, girl."

Awakened by Sada shaking me, I see that she's pointing franticly. I roll my head to look, but see nothing through the darkness. She grabs my hand and leads me through a gap in the bushes, back to the service hatch we entered through.

As I pull the hatch shut, I start to hear voices, so I leave the door open just enough to hear what's going on.

"The maintenance bot, indicated a person in here, with the internal sensors offline, we can't be sure if there is or not. Spread out and search the garden." Hearing several sets of boots start walking in, I realize that they're looking for me and close the hatch quietly.

Sada and I sprint back to our room and I lock the door behind us. Sada rolls onto the bed and gives me a dirty look.

I sit down next to her. "I'm sorry, I didn't mean do dose off."

She sits up and presses her nose into my cheek, purring.

I turn slightly and kiss her nose.

She gives me a curious look, then after a moment, lightly licks my lips.

I giggle at the sensation of her rough tongue on my lips.

Her purring stops for a moment, but seeing the smile on my face, it starts again, louder than before.

She leans into me, puts her nose under my chin, and wraps me in a hug. I return her hug, and we sit like that for a while, before I lie down beside her.

As I'm about to drift, the ship suddenly lurches. I reflexively pull the webbing down over us.

As the ship lurches again, I realize that it's not an attack. As I hear a repeated bouncing sound, like something is rolling along the hull of the ship, I conclude that we must be in an asteroid field. After a few more hits, the guns start firing intermittently, apparently shooting the larger ones before they can impact the hull. We listen to the different sounds while we stay under the webbing. The ship shutters every time, whether it be the guns firing, or an asteroid hitting the hull.

When the guns finally fall silent, and all we hear are the engines. I sigh, wondering why the alerts didn't sound when I hear the intercom pop. Sada also stares intently at it while I wait for a moment for some-one to speak, but when no one does I stay quiet. I wonder what's going on when I see the light go out.

Putting my finger to my lips, I tell Sada to stay quiet. I get out of bed and quietly walk to the intercom. The light's out, but I can still hear a gentle hiss coming from the speaker.

I point to the speaker, then to my ear, then put my finger to my lips again. Sada nods, understanding. She steps over to the desk and quietly grabs the cards and dice. I look around, seeing my maps, I quietly stack and scoop them up.

We exit the room and cross the hall to the service corridor. Since I haven't been back there since I arrived on this ship, I shuffle through my hand-drawn maps and find the one with cargo bay seven on it. Sada follows me as I lead the way, retracing steps I haven't done in months.

I slowly open the door and listen for sounds. Hearing nothing, I slowly open the door wider, looking for people. Finding it clear, we step out into the hold. We find that the hold has been rearranged, all the original crates are all against the near wall, and there are now several bundles of containers filling the remaining space. Each bundle is more than twice my height, half that wide and almost as deep.

Sada starts looking at the new containers, walking slowly around to the far end of the bay. I hear her clap her hands, getting my attention.

"What is it?"

She points at her end of a crate. So I jog over to her to look where she's pointing.

Finding a plaque, I read it aloud. "Quantum Teleporter MK VI."

Sada gives me a curious look and shrugs her shoulders.

"A teleporter is a device that moves something from one place to another. Given what year this is, I'd guess that these move things pretty far. I'm not sure what the quantum part means though. Mark Six: there's been five previous versions."

I step back and count the crates. "One, two, three, four, by one, two, three, four, five, six, deep, and eight per. That's almost, 200 units."

Suddenly Sada starts pointing at something else on a different pallet. This one is small, like a milk crate, but has a symbol that matches the ones on the larger crates.

I step over to it and kneel down to read its label. "AI QT Coordination Control Unit MK VI. Well, it definitely goes with the teleporters."

"Yes, I do."

Surprised, Sada and I both jump back away from the box, putting some distance between it and us.

"Apologies, I did not mean to startle you. My name is Charles."

I look at the box, seeing no obvious speaker or sensors. "You're a box?"

"No, I am in the box, I am an AI."

"AI? Wait, you're an artificial intelligence?"

"Correct."

Sada crawls up alongside me. Seeing her fur standing on end, I start smoothing her fur, helping her put it back in place.

"You do not have an AI, were you abducted like I was?"

"Yeah."

"Do you know why?"

"Aside from the captain's nuts, no."

"From what little interaction I had with his AI, I would agree with that assessment. I would surmise that they are both suffering from a mutual breakdown and some of the crew have similar conditions."

"Can they be cured?"

"I do not have that kind of medical knowledge, so I do not know. I could tell that the problem stemmed from exposure to something that affected both the human brain and the AI similarly, creating paranoia and irrational behavior in both."

"That's disturbing. A crazy person with a crazy AI."

"I agree. May I ask you a more personal question?"

"Sure."

"Why are you without an AI?"

I get comfortable, sitting on the floor next to the box, Charles, and start to explain. "As with you, we were taken from our home. We are from the year 2019, my name is Kyle Andolina, this is my cat, Sada."

"That is not possible. It is the year 3710."

"Well, as hard as it is to believe, it's possible. The year onboard this ship is 3047. They went back in time to take me, so I'm not surprised that they went forward in time to take you."

"Time travel is not possible, and she is not a cat."

Seeing Sada give the box a dirty look, I almost chuckle. "Can't you ask the ship what year it is?"

"This ship possesses only a simple computer. Its records can be easily altered."

"Does the name 'Obsession' mean anything to you?"

"Obsession, Star Cruiser, launched 2994, served valiantly until pirated by Captain Abuka Nabire in 3045, presumed lost in 3050."

He pauses for a moment, then continues, "I find it odd that there have been several unconfirmed reports of the ship being sighted all over the galaxy, both before it was commissioned, and after it was presumed lost."

"You're on the Obsession. Captain Abuka Nabire is the crazy one that abducted us."

"That is not possible."

"Let's see, a few weeks ago, he took the Aquanatum from Aquia. He destroyed a picket ship before that. When he picked me up from Earth, I was dying from ALS and he put me and Sada through some process called rejuvenation. Cured me, made us younger. While I got used to my legs again, she was then...evolved. That's why she doesn't look like a cat anymore."

"Your story collaborates the ship's records, but I cannot understand how this is possible. The process of rejuvenation was developed in 3180, the Aquanatum were kidnapped in 3265."

"I would guess he stole the ability to time travel from somewhere, but no one knows for certain."

"That is the only thing that can explain the inconsistencies. I will see if there are any records on how this was done."

"Don't get caught, we're supposed to be 'disposed of,' and I don't want that for real."

"I will be certain to avoid detection."

Fighting back a yawn I concede, "I'll let you do that, we need some sleep."

Sada and I find the large hide-crate under several others. Slipping between two smaller crates, we find the door accessible. Apparently whoever rearranged this hold, knew about its function. I'm pleased to find everything just like I left it, and flop on the bed. Sada quickly crawls alongside me and we drift off to sleep.

Stepping out of the crate, I start to squeeze between the other crates but stop abruptly when I hear voices.

"What do you mean the source of the hack came from in here? There's nothing in here but these." I hear a thump and realize that the woman speaking hit a crate of teleporters.

"I'm sorry sir, but this is where we lost the trace."

As I watch, the two walk back to the far door. She punches a code into the control panel and then the door opens. Through the door, I see a blue light and they step into the corridor. When the door closes, I slowly step out into the bay and head to the door. As I reach it, I hear a hiss and the door handle pulls into the door, preventing me from opening it.

"The hall has been exposed to vacuum."

"How'd they get through?"

"Energy bridge."

"What, like force fields or something?"

"Something. May I ask what you intended to do if you were able to open the door."

I chuckle. "I don't know. Follow them maybe. You weren't supposed to get caught."

"I guarantee that they did not detect my access."

"Then what were they doing here?"

"I do not know, but I will find out."

"Do that."

Not missing a beat, he continues, "I just did. It seems that the hack was done by Lieutenant Barker. He tried routing it through this bay, drawing their attention here. I was able to track it back to his quarters."

"Will the others be able to track him?"

"If they look hard enough, yes."

"What was he after?"

"The captain's medical records."

"What did he find?"

"Nothing, they have been thoroughly deleted."

I sigh, wondering what would happen to him if he's caught. "Can you clean up for him, he's been in enough trouble."

"I do not understand."

"If the captain finds out what he was after, he'll likely be killed."

"The normal punishment for this type of infraction is the brig."

"Well, when he forgot to plug in the Aquanatum, he got a week of double shifts at the reactor, whatever that is."

"I am surprised he is still alive then."

My interest now peaked, I ask, "Why?"

"The reactor in this vessel is damaged. His AI had to work hard to keep him from dying of exposure."

"That sounds like constant pain."

"For both him and his AI."

"You can feel pain?"

"Radiation causes disruptions in an AI's matrix, which can cause damage if the exposure is prolonged."

"Ouch," I sigh, as I sit next to the box. "What'd you find out?"

"I discovered that you are indeed telling the truth. I am still unsure how he is managing the time travel, but I am continuing to search for anything that may be beneficial to our situation."

Sada comes over to us, bearing a plate. She hands it to me as she sits on the floor next to me. Suddenly distracted by the smell, I look at the plate.

Turning my attention to Sada, I ask, "Spaghetti and meatballs, for breakfast?"

She smiles and nods.

"Why does she not talk?"

"As far as I know, she can't. Even when she was a house cat, before she was evolved, she never meowed. She's hissed a few times, purrs a lot, but, no squeaks, mews, or other sounds."

"Then how do you communicate?"

"Body language, pointing, charades. I've taught her a lot these last few months."

"May I ask, what is your relationship with her?"

"Well, she's been my house cat for like 18 years. Now, I find myself thinking of her more like a person, and less like a cat...if that makes sense."

"Considering the year you are from, and that you are one of the first people to see a sentient non-human, I find your acceptance of her quite refreshing."

"Wait, what? First non-human?"

"Correct, while human-kind has explored much of the Milky Way, the only life that has been discovered has been non-sentient."

"We are really alone, huh." I set the plate aside, suddenly uninterested in eating. Sada puts her arm around me and purrs, trying to cheer me up.

Charles remains silent for a moment. "What is wrong?"

"My little sister...she always wanted to go up into space. She was so certain that there was life out there...well, out here. She believed in it, more than she did about anything else."

Sada puts her nose under my chin and nuzzles me. I wrap my arm around her, pulling her close.

"Would you like to go back home?"

"Yes. No. I don't know, I mean, I've been healed of my ALS. Sada's no longer a cat. We've both been given a chance to live new lives. Part of me still wants to go back, but...I've found life worth living again."

"If you like, I can see if the ship has any records of you. It would help you make an informed decision."

"Wouldn't that be cheating or something? I mean, knowing what I'm supposed to do and then trying to do it, that's never really worked out on any TV show I've seen."

"In that case, I could just look to see if you went back."

I think for a moment. "No, I don't want to know, I don't care if you look, but don't tell me. I won't pretend to understand temporal paradoxes, or whatever, but this is a decision that I have to make, free of influence."

"It may not matter if we cannot find a way to send you back."

"Well, if that's true, then the decision will be made for me, no matter what I decide, and I won't need to worry about my future...your past...whatever."

"I will focus my efforts on discovering the method of time travel then. May I suggest that you include her in the decision, since, if you are able to go back, it may require reverting her back."

I look at Sada. "I wouldn't dream of not asking." I grab the plate as I stand. "Come on, we have a lot to consider."

Sada nods and follows me back to the room-crate.

13

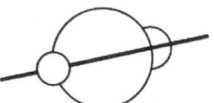

I hang from the ceiling of engineering, held in place by my armor's gloves, boots, and leggings, which are the only parts of it I'm wearing. Fighting the unusual sensation of gravity trying to pull me 'up,' I open an access hatch and start looking inside. Marcus stands below me, on the floor, waiting for me to pull an engine component. I crawl up through the hatch, which is not easy to do in this position, with legs stuck to the ceiling.

I pull myself further up, into place, and find the box. "Main engine sequencer, Found it."

"It should pull straight towards you," he calls back. "I'm still puzzled as to why you didn't just use a tall ladder."

"I need to practice this part of my armor's abilities." I try to get a grip on the edges, but this end is smooth, offering no handholds. I adjust a glove slightly and give the box a slap on the closest side. Feeling my glove stick, I pull. With a little effort, the box slides free, pulling some wire vine with it.

"More vine," I call, slowly letting myself drop out of the hatch. I let gravity help me lower the box to Marcus. When he takes it, I climb back into the hatch and start pulling out more of the vine.

From below me, I hear Darren ask, "How bad does it look?"

Dropping a handful of vine, I adjust my flashlight, getting a good look inside. "Looks like they just got into the box, there are a few more pieces, but they're not attached to anything." After collecting those pieces, I let them drop and exit the hatch again.

I let myself dangle for a moment, relaxing as I hang by my knees from the ceiling.

Darren picks up the vines and nearly hits my head as he stands up. "Are you having fun?" he jokes.

"This feels really weird," I laugh as I watch Marcus remove the top of the box, and pull more vine out.

"They got this good." He grabs a pair of cutters and clips the vine close to a board, then pulls the board, looks at it, then sets it in the converter. "Repair." With a flash that board is replaced, and he puts the new board in the box. He repeats this with a couple more of the boards and then closes the box and hands it back to me.

Climbing back in with the box in hand isn't as easy. I lift the box through the opening and do my best to follow, using my free hand to lift myself into place again.

After pushing the box back into place, I hear Marcus. "Diagnostic says that it's working now. Next is the auxiliary unit. Turn around, it's opposite the main."

I turn my head and see a similar box. "Sure," I grunt. "They didn't make this easy."

I hear them both laugh, but Marcus adds, "With a proper service, they'd normally pull the upper hull off, but we don't have the facility to do that."

I drop out of the hatch, and slowly work my way around it, while still hanging from the ceiling. "Beginning to wish we did. Aime, make a note, I want a crane." I climb back in and pull the box like I did for the main unit. This one has vines in it too, but I can't pull them free.

With my free hand, I grab my own cutters from my belt and clip the vines connected to the box. After passing it down to Marcus, I climb back up, and then pull myself farther into the service hatch, leaving my feet dangling out the hole. Now able to reach the vines easier, I start removing them and dropping them down the hatch for Darren to pick up.

After I've got all I can find, Aime helps me check for damage. Finding none, I carefully work my way back down and out to hang by my knees and find Marcus waiting with the auxiliary unit.

As I'm putting that back in place, I hear Marcus call, "I'll be right back."

Before I can get back out, I hear another voice. "Darren, can I ask you something?" It's Nanai.

"Sure."

"I...do you like me?"

I can't mistake the nervousness in his voice as he speaks. "Uhm, uh, yeah." I manage to get far enough out to see his reddened face as he scratches the back of his head. "Why?"

She gives him a bashful look, then gently gives him a hug, leaning into his chest. "Because I like you too, and I'd like to be more than friends."

"I haven't had a, uhm, girlfriend before."

"So, I've not had a boyfriend either."

"Uhm, uh, I uh, Nan...I uh." Hearing his desperate stutters, I put my hands to the ceiling, letting them grip and then drop my legs down, and then drop to the floor.

"Darren?" Nanai asks.

He looks nervously at me. "Help."

I put my arm around him. "Relax. When you look at her, what do you see?"

"I, uh, what do I see?"

"Right, look at her, and tell me what you see."

"I see, uhm, well, s-s-she has pretty eyes, r-r-really fluffy fur, outgoing, very nice...she's shorter than me ."

Sparing him further embarrassment, I ask, "All right, what do you feel?"

"Nervous." I frown slightly, and she giggles, but he continues, "I feel like I've known her for months, not weeks."

"Okay, so, what's stopping you?"

He looks between me and Nanai. "I...I don't want to hurt her."

"I can understand that, but keep in mind that if you refuse, you might do that anyway, and maybe yourself too."

"No, he won't hurt me," Nanai protests.

Darren sighs, and then shakes his head. "No, he's right, I see now, sorry." He takes her hands. "Nan, I am...interested in you. I would like it, a lot, for us to be...closer."

She smiles at him and I see a tear slowly roll down her muzzle. She then wraps him in a hug. "Thank you."

He hugs her back. "No, thank you."

Smiling, I let them have their moment, and turn my attention to the diagnostic panel, with the aux unit now showing normal, the engines are now operational. Hearing Marcus return, I turn to him and realize that I didn't hear Nanai leave. He looks at the board with me. "Hey, we're almost done."

"Yeah, engines are done. It never fails to amaze me just what those vines can plug, jam, or short out."

"Well, I'm glad that we haven't had to do any major repairs. This is a lot newer than the shuttle."

"Even then, it's over two hundred years old," I retort. "What's next?"

He scrolls through the list, looking through the remaining systems. "Well, looks like we've taken care of all the major systems. The ship's space worthy again."

"Seriously?"

"Yeah, want to take her up?"

I smile. "Ziggy, tell everyone we're gonna lift-off, be back in an hour or two. Sound an all clear."

"I'll stay down here and monitor everything."

"All right, Darren?"

"I'll go up with you."

We quickly head up to the bridge. "Aime, start her up."

"Initializing main power, starting preflight diagnostics."

"Marcus, let me know if you see any problems."

His reply comes through the internal com. "I will."

Darren sits in the captain's chair and starts watching the screens. As I sit in the pilot's seat, the controls light up, ready for use. Tareth steps onto the bridge and sits in the navigator's chair to my right.

Tayla's voice comes over the com. "Kyle, are you sure about this?"

I smile, knowing that message was coming. I fill myself with reassurance and love, letting Tayla know that I feel comfortable with this. I answer more for the other's benefit. "Yes. We'll be careful my loves."

"You better be," Megai states.

"Diagnostic complete, all flight systems ready."

"Here we go."

The ship groans as the weight transfers from the landing gear to the repulsors. As we slowly gain altitude, I retract the gear and set a course due west.

"Terrain mapping and life scans to full."

"I just registered a power fluctuation in the sensor array," Marcus calls.

I check the readouts. "They're still working."

"Probably a bad power regulator, I'll check it after we land."

I apply power to the engines, and the ship starts to move forward. I check the ship's configuration display and see that the wings are swinging out, assuming their position for atmospheric flight. When the wings lock in place, I start running the ship through a few maneuvers, testing the reaction controls, internal dampening, and flight systems. All react within tolerances, so I proceed on to other systems.

"Marcus, setting a new course for space."

"Understood, monitoring internal pressure and structural integrity."

Behind me, I hear Darren gasp. "Space?"

"Yeah, it's a spaceship after all."

As the ship starts climbing, the hull creaks and the wings automatically swing in.

"Don't worry about the sounds. It's just expanding, adjusting to the vacuum of space," I state, trying to ease his nerves.

"Easy for you to say," Darren nervously counters.

"Hey, I wouldn't do anything to hurt Nanai, which means you're safe."

"How do you do it?"

I glance back at him, suddenly curious. "Do what?"

"You know, how do you make it work, you and your mates."

"Are referring to them being an evolved cheetah and rabbit?"

"Well, uhm, yeah."

I chuckle. "Darren, I stopped seeing them that way long ago. I see them for who they are, not what." After making a couple of adjustments to the controls, I continue, "If you truly love someone, what they look like becomes less important. What they think, what they feel, how they make you feel, that's what becomes important. Once you've got that, they'll always be attractive to you."

"How do I do that?"

I quickly check a display. "You've already started."

"What do you mean?"

"When I asked you those questions, what you said told me that you didn't really see her as a red panda, but as a person, a person that you're starting to care about."

I glance back, seeing him in thoughtful awe, I chuckle. "Marcus, how does the tachyon drive look?"

"Ready to go."

"All right, a short jump to the outer belt should be enough."

"Ready down here."

As I press a few buttons, I call out, "Here we go." Planets turn to streaks as the windows darken. Then as quickly, the windows clear and an asteroid field blurs into view. I bring the ship to a stop before we enter it.

"What just happened, why'd the windows do that?" Darren asks.

"Tachyon drive is faster than light. Windows darkened to keep outside light out."

"Why?"

"Well, it's a bit hard to explain. The way I understand it is that the light would be a blue shift, might swirl or make you think you're the one spinning. With some of the research I did into FTL travel's history, some have even reported seeing images going backward, or forward at very high speeds. I'd imagine seeing that for a long trip would probably make someone go crazy trying to make sense of what they were seeing."

"Oh, *that's* comforting."

"Big problem with a simple solution, don't let the outside light in."

I turn the ship to face the closest part of the dense asteroid belt as a bolt of lightning arcs between asteroids.

Marcus suddenly comes in from engineering. "Is that the shell?"

"Shell?"

"That asteroid field is loaded with static, magnetic, and gravimetric anomalies, makes direct travel through difficult at best, even with a safe corridor. This kind of ship has extra shielding, allowing it to pass. Some warships don't even have this level of shielding."

"Well, that would explain why no other ships came," I comment, watching another arc of lightning jump from asteroid to asteroid.

"Yeah, that right there," he points out the window to an arc, "wreaks havoc on a ship's power systems. This type of ship was made to handle that kind of abuse."

"So anyone in a standard starship would have to go around the belt to get into the system?"

"Yep, and the shell's almost a full ten light-minutes tall. Makes this a pretty secure system."

"How do you know this?" Darren asks.

Marcus smiles. "I got a crash course on the system from our elders."

"I haven't had a chance to look at a tenth of what they gave Aime. Been too busy."

He gives me a smile and nods. "Having kids'll do that."

I chuckle my agreement. "We should be getting back. I can feel Tayla getting concerned."

"Way out here?" Darren gasps.

Tayla and I had mutually agreed that we could trust our house guests with knowledge of our unique bond. "Yeah, surprisingly."

"We've gotta be...29, 30 light-minutes from Arcania. Are you sure it's not delayed or something?" Marcus adds.

"One way to find out." I lean back in the pilot's chair and clear my mind. It's taken me some practice, but I've figured out how to meditate and clear my emotions. It's helped Tayla when she's felt overwhelmed, lets her sort out her own feelings without being affected by mine.

As I reach my neutral state, I feel Tayla's concern jump, like she's wondering what happened. I then let my love for her fill me, and her concern quickly gets replaced by calm and then changes to mild anger.

"It's real-time, or at least very close. It felt like she was right next to me."

"Wow, I'd certainly like to know how that works."

"Me too, but she's a little mad at me now. So we're going home." I turn the ship and set a course for home. With another quick jump, we arrive quickly and I pilot the ship into the atmosphere. As we land, I see Tayla waiting.

In an attempt to defuse her anger, I fill myself with love, storm down the ramp as it lowers, and quickly give her a hug and kiss. I hold her for a moment until she relaxes a little.

"Sorry about that, I had to find out."

Still scowling at me, she asks, "Find out what?"

"How quickly you'd react. We were all the way out at the edge of the system."

She tilts her head curiously. "How far is that?"

Aime answers for me. "Roughly five hundred million kilometers."

Her eyes go wide. "That far? I would have thought that you were no farther than another village."

"Apparently distance has no noticeable effect on our link."

"That could be useful if we're separated."

Suddenly, Nanai rushes past and wraps Darren in a hug. To my relief, he hugs her back, holding her close.

Tayla smiles. "I was wondering when they'd get together."

"He's ready, still has some learning to do, but he's curious like she is."

Tayla nuzzles into my neck and I feel her happiness. Sada comes out and seeing Nanai and Darren in a hug, smiles.

Tayla takes my hand. "Come on, let's leave them be."

Sada grabs Marcus's hand as he comes down the ramp, and drags him past the still hugging couple. He gives her, and them, a curious look as we head into the house, into the Great Hall.

"Are they a..."

"Couple? They are now," I chuckle. "Surprised?"

"Yeah. Kid's got an open mind, but he's shy."

"Nanai's got enough drive for the both of them," Tayla states.

Marcus smiles. "She'll have him wrapped around her finger."

I laugh. "I don't think so, she came to him when you stepped out, asked him about how he felt about her, but she didn't push. I had to help him figure it out, because he didn't know what he was feeling, or how to express it."

"Will they be able to have kids, like you two have?"

"Not yet, but I've got Aime working on that."

"Won't that require an AI?"

"Yeah, that's why I wanted the nanite class converter."

"And here I was thinking you just wanted upgrades."

"Just the skeletal reinforcements. Aime's got a lot of ability as it is thanks to your elders. Thankfully she can also delegate some of the work to Ziggy and the ship's computers."

"So are you doing that just for him, or..."

"Everyone hopefully, or at least those who'll want it."

"Why?"

Now in the common area of the hall, we all sit on the couches, as I explain, "I've seen couples that can't have children together, but want to. To me, it's not fair to them that I can."

"So you're going to give them an AI and whatever else they need to do it?"

"Not a full-blown AI, but enough of one to keep them healthy and convert the DNA. Ideally, both parents would have one, that way they could have either species, instead of just the mother's."

"The AI's aren't made for non-humans."

"That's what's been taking so long." I see Sada's and Tayla's ears twitch and they both stand.

"We hear them, Ziggy," Tayla states as they head to the nursery, leaving me with Marcus.

He watches them walk for a moment, before looking back at me. "Have you had any volunteers?"

"Well, Tayla's expressed interest, so has Roen. Larrah would like one, just to have a better way to regulate her estrus. I don't mind their reasons. Are you interested?"

He smiles. "I'm a little old to care about the children part, but I've always wondered what it'd be like to have an AI."

Now I smile. "Well, at first you think that you have no privacy, but after a while, you realize that you still do. You also begin to think of her as a part of yourself, and that you don't always need to say or think what you want her to do, they know by what your actions imply."

"Sounds like you enjoy it."

"Sometimes. Other times, it's like being permanently married, and they're attached to you. Aime will remind me of things, which I appreciate, but there are times when I go to do something and she'll tell me the dangers involved. Spoils the fun."

He chuckles, apparently familiar with the analogy.

Railu comes out of the hall from her room, sitting in her wheelchair again, pushed by Roen. She's a week past due, and still hasn't entered labor. "What're you talking about?"

"Usual, how're you feeling?"

She sighs heavily. "I'm past ready, beginning to wonder if I'll want a second kit."

I put my hands on her belly, getting an idea of how ready she is. "Well, the kit's finally dropped. Should be any day now."

She lets out another sigh. "Won't be soon enough."

"Relax, it'll be here before you want it to be," Maurice adds.

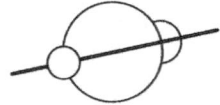

"Kyle, wake up!"

I sleepily answer, "Aime? What?"

"Railu's in labor, in her room. Niku and Cayla need your help."

I quickly slide out from under my mates, waking them in the process.

"What?" Megai groggily asks.

"Railu's in labor," I stammer, trying to get my pants on.

"Go. Go help. We'll be along."

"Eventually," Tayla mumbles.

Having finally got my pants on, I dart, barefoot, down the hall to Railu's room. I find Zoe waiting, holding a smock for me. She helps me put it on, and we go in, I'm immediately greeted with a weak cry from Railu as Roen sits behind her on the bed, holding her knees up as if he was the birthing chair.

Cayla immediately starts filling me in. "Kyle, good, she's in full labor, fully dilated, and her contractions are close but they aren't very strong."

"Ziggy, give me original time of onset."

"Her labor started abruptly eleven minutes ago, and her water broke three minutes later."

"What? No gradual onset?"

"Correct."

Niku looks at me. "We need your hands here."

As I put my hands to Railu's belly, I look curiously at Cayla.

"Marc's only a medic," she states weakly.

"Can you help her with her contractions?" Niku asks me.

As another one hits, Aime starts showing me vitals and stats.

"Can now, but not much. Railu, how're you doing?"

In between her ragged breathing, she manages to shake her head and gasp. "I'm not...ready...anymore." Her voice is weak and she wants to cry.

Behind her, Roen softly coaches, "Yes you are, love. You've been waiting for this."

I look at her and wait for a contraction to pass. "You're ready, all you need to do is push. I can help, but I can't do anything for you on my own."

She nods and keeps up her breathing. Feeling her next contraction coming, she adjusts herself, getting ready to push. I move my hands slightly, allowing Aime to stimulate the right muscles, helping with the push. She lets out a loud scream as she pushes, Aime dampens the sound for me, but I see Zoe grab her ears and turn away.

Roen shakes his head a little. "Screaming doesn't help, love."

"Yes it does!" she counters.

"I see the nose, get ready and push."

This time she doesn't scream, but her grunt sounds more like a growl. Zoe's tail twitches and poofs, surprisingly getting larger than it already was.

"I have the kit," Niku quickly takes care of the cord as Cayla takes the kit. "Congratulations, you have a daughter."

As Railu relaxes into Roen's arms, she manages to say, "Ru."

Zoe takes the kit, and wraps her in a towel goes into the grooming room to give her a bath. I keep my hands on Railu's belly, letting Aime help eject the placenta.

Niku neatly catches it, wraps it, and sets it aside. She then starts tending to Railu. I look at Roen, who's still holding his mate up, while she's lying against him, trying to stay awake. She weakly looks at me. "Thank you." She tries to raise her hand to me, but she lacks the energy.

I put my hand on her cheek. "You did all the work. Now you can get some rest."

"Not until you feed her," Zoe states, coming back in from the grooming room. She places, a now clean and swathed, Ru in Railu's arms, and Roen reaches around to help her hold Ru.

"She's got your eyes," he states.

"Our eyes are the same color."

"But they look like yours, not mine."

Zoe gets a little irritated. "She needs to feed."

Railu gets suddenly ashamed, crooking her ears.

"What?" I ask.

"My milk hasn't come in."

"Why didn't you say something sooner? Ziggy, breast milk." Zoe states as she heads to the converter. After grabbing the nursing bottle that appeared, she returns. "Here, it's a mix of Tayla's and Sada's, so Ru will still get what she needs until yours comes in."

"When will that be?"

I slowly wave my hand over her breasts. "Soon. In the next couple days."

"In the meantime, let her suckle on each a little before you give her the bottle, it'll help stimulate your own milk," Niku adds. "For now though, let her have the bottle, you need to rest."

Roen looks at me. "Can you pick her up, so I can change the sheets?"

"Sure." I scoop Railu up, cradling her in my arms, while she cradles and feeds Ru.

Roen quickly bundles the sheets and stuffs them in the converter. "Clean."

With a subtle flash, they disappear and a neatly folded set takes their place.

"He's right you know," I state softly.

"About?"

"She has your eyes, not his."

As Zoe helps him make the bed, Railu looks at Ru's eyes. "How can you tell?"

I look at Ru as she intently drinks from the bottle, looking much like a small version of her mother. "Her eyes have that look of wonder and determination that I've seen so often in yours."

Having made the bed, Roen fluffs the pillows, and I gently lay the mother and daughter down on her side of the bed.

He turns to his mate. "Would you like me to hold her?"

Railu gently passes her to him, and I see his eyes start to water, so I say, "Welcome to fatherhood."

Zoe opens the bedroom door and most of the family comes in quietly. Niku holds up her hands. "Please, they need their rest, try to keep it short."

"It's a girl," Roen states. "Her name's Ru."

As they trickle by, I notice that Fey is my only child among them, and the guards, aside from Larrah, are also not present. I also notice that Nanai and Darren are holding hands and that he has some of her fur stuck to his face.

Apparently, Roen notices this, too, as when they congratulate him, he, in turn, says, "And good luck to you both."

They both blush, and Darren asks, "Is it that obvious?"

"You have her fur on your face and arms."

Darren turns red and wipes at his face as they move on, letting others approach. I follow them out into the hall and put my arms around them from behind. This makes Nanai jump a little, but when she sees it's me, she giggles. "You startled me."

"Sorry. I have some advice for you both. For starters, you have nothing to be embarrassed about. Love is blind. It cares not for shape, color, size, fur-or lack of or anything like that. It only matters that you care for each other."

I pause for a moment and seeing them both nod their understanding, I continue, "The other thing, and I speak from experience, wait for her," I tilt my head to Nanai, "to be in heat, don't try to rush things."

Darren turns red, almost as red as Nanai's fur, and she blushes too. "I didn't want to embarrass you, I want to caution you. No matter how much you may want to, if her body isn't ready, she may defend herself. She won't mean to, it's a reflex."

Darren looks nervously at Nanai as if wondering if he should be afraid of her, but she asks, "Why are you telling us this?"

"Nanai, I don't want to see you accidentally hurt each other, and ruin what you have. I also want to make sure you're aware of the limits, dangers, and pleasures of this kind of relationship."

"Dangers?"

"You have claws, he doesn't, you also have fangs, sharper teeth. He doesn't have fur. You're also both used to showing affection a little differently. Humans kiss, that's not an easy thing for someone with a muzzle to do. I know I've told you that I see past the fur, to the person inside, but you still have to keep those differences in mind to accommodate the other."

Darren looks curiously at me. "So what does that mean? I could get bit or clawed?"

"Bluntly, yes, but there are ways to minimize that risk. She could file her claws, rounding them off so they won't easily break the skin."

"And sometimes, teeth can be quite exciting, if used with a light touch," Tayla adds from behind me.

"I find nibbling can be very effective if done with the lips, and not the teeth," Megai adds. "Letting him feel your fur gliding over his skin can sometimes have...interesting effects."

Surprisingly not embarrassed, I chuckle. "Anyway, my point is, talk to each other, learn from each other as you explore your relationship."

"And each other," Megai adds. "If one you likes something and the other thinks it's unusual, try it a few times, you may find you *like* that your mate finds pleasure in it, even if you don't."

Nanai gives me an odd look. "I can understand that you don't want to see us hurt each other, but it's like you're encouraging us."

Tayla gently takes the smock off me and I lean forward. "See this scar?"

They both lean in and look at it. "Who bit you?" Nanai asks.

"Sada did, before I realized that she has reflexive defenses. So yes, we're encouraging you, but it's because we want you to be safe about your relationship. I was lucky there was a doctor nearby, or I would have bled out."

"But you have Aime."

"He didn't then," Tayla answers. "Megai doesn't have that kind of defense, but I do, just like Sada does, so I too have to be careful. It's a small sacrifice, but we find ways to make up for it, and so will you."

"I'd suggest reading up on each other's species, as well as your own, learn what you could be in for," Megai states, "and what can make things...better."

Nanai nods, but Darren seems to think for a moment. "Can I, uhm, make her...pregnant?"

"No, not as you are, sorry, you're not the same species."

"Are you already considering cubs?" Tayla asks curiously.

"We'd talked about it, but now that we know that, I suppose it doesn't matter."

"Kyle, tell him."

I look at Tayla and sigh. "Darren, I've been working on a way to make that possible. Right now, with you, it's easy to correct, so you could give her cubs."

"But what if I want to bear a human child?"

"That's not so easy. I'm having trouble modifying the AI for non-humans. Not with the physical part, but with the neurological part. There's just too many differences."

"What can I do to help you with that?" Nanai asks.

"You would be willing to let me test on you?"

"If it means that I could have a human baby, yes."

"You two feel that strongly about each other?" Tayla asks.

They both nod, and pull each other close.

I feel Tayla wrap her arm around me, steadying me. "I'll have to give this some thought. I'm not comfortable with testing it on anyone, not yet anyway."

They both nod again, and start for their room. Sada puts her hand to my back and nuzzles my neck from behind.

"Come on, let's go back to bed, think about it later in the day, when you're awake," Megai softly says. She then takes my hand and leads us back to our bedroom.

14

Hearing a hatch shut, Sada and I quickly duck between crates. I peek through a gap in the crates, trying to see who it is. Charles is the first to recognize the person.

"Greetings, Chief Petty Officer."

"Charles, please, call me Mike."

"Apologies, Mike."

"Kyle? You about?"

"Yeah, I'm here."

"Where you been? We haven't seen or heard from you all week."

"Sorry, someone started listening in on my room."

"What?! How?"

"The com came on, light wasn't lit but I could hear the speaker." Sada steps alongside me and nods her agreement.

Suddenly worried, he thinks for a moment. "Do you know if anyone heard you?"

"I don't think so, but I haven't been back to the room either."

"Well, we need to find you a new room, can't leave you in here."

"Does that include me?"

"Yeah, can we take him with us?"

"Not really, if someone came to check on him, and he wasn't here..."

"I have a solution for that, please open my case."

Suddenly curious, Mike and I both step over and undo the latches holding the lid shut. Inside, we find several stacks of small silver disks, no larger than a silver dollar, in a shallow tray.

"What are these?"

"They are specialized relays that allow me to monitor with the gates. They can also act as communicators, allowing me to talk directly with a person. I would like you both to take one with you. It will allow you complete privacy if you need to talk with me or each other."

Mike picks one up. "Independent of the ship?"

"Unfortunately no, but I can bury the transmissions so they won't be detected."

I pick one up and look at it. Seeing no visible controls, I ask, "How do they work?"

"If you want to talk to me, or someone else, just tap it, then say the person's name. If that person is with someone who's not aware of you, I will wait until they're alone. I, however, will always be available. I would recommend sticking them to your wrist or chest. Sada, if you like, you can take one, and if you need help, tap it several times. I will have someone find you."

She looks curiously at me but picks one up and eyes it closely.

"That's a good idea, in case I'm looking around or something, and you need me."

She nods and sticks it to her right wrist. She shakes her hand a few times and gives it another curious look.

I stick mine to my left wrist and then pick at it, it doesn't move, so I try to pull it and it comes right off. "How does it do that?"

"It is Van der Walls force. The disk has fine feelers on the back that hold it to whatever it's placed on. It's also smart enough to know the difference between you removing it and you trying to shake it off."

"That's handy." I stick it back to my wrist.

Mike sticks one under his tunic, to his chest. "I'll pass one along to Carrie, Maurice, Kevin, and Ariel. I don't think anyone else knows about these two yet."

"No offense, but I would prefer to keep it that way."

"I agree with Charles. The fewer people that know about us, the less chance that someone we don't trust will find out about us," I state. Sada nods her agreement.

"Well, I hope it stays that way, but right now we need to find a new place for you two." After pocketing four of the disks, he closes the lid and latches it.

"May I suggest cabin 26A, there has not been anyone inside since I came on board, and foot traffic in that area is very light."

"Really, that surprises me since it's a double."

I look curiously at him. "Double?"

"Meant for two, like a married couple."

Sada smiles and gives me a hug. "We'll take it."

"Charles, is there a way to mask the power consumption of the room?"

"I will randomly redirect it from other areas of the ship. I will also disable the com in that room to prevent eavesdropping."

"Good. Kyle, grab your stuff."

Sada practically leaps all the way to the converted container and quickly returns with our few personal items.

I find myself smiling at the box. "Thank you, Charles."

"You are welcome."

I double-check the latches, making sure they're like we found them, and we follow Mike out the hatch. We reach the cabin in a few minutes and I realize that it's fairly close to the med bay. Sada and I hide around a corner while Mike checks the room, apparently finding it safe, he waves us in.

I find the room's décor utilitarian, like the previous, but it's larger and has a warmer feeling. Aside from the larger bed, there are two desks, a pair of dressers, and both a closet and a bath. There is also a larger converter near a table opposite the bed.

"Go on ahead and make yourself at home, I've got to go, servitude calls."

"Thanks."

He leaves and I lock the door. I turn and see Sada flop on the bed. I smile, realizing that no matter how much I teach her, she will still be a house cat at heart. I sit on the bed by her and she rolls towards me, onto her side.

"So, what do you want to do now?"

She looks at me curiously, then pokes my leg a couple of times.

I poke her back and joke. "You want to play poker?"

She sits up, nodding. I grab the cards and have a seat at the table. As I start shuffling, Sada sits across from me and starts making some charade-like gestures.

"Five...card...draw," I say, translating her gestures. "Okay, five-card draw it is."

I deal out five cards each and set the rest aside. She looks at her cards and then passes me three, face down on the table. I look at mine, I have an ace of spades, a ten of clubs, three of hearts, five of diamonds, and a queen of hearts. I set down the three and five.

I deal Sada her three and me two and set the deck aside again. We pick up our cards, and I find a ten of diamonds, giving me a pair, and a jack of spades.

I look at Sada and she smiles, putting down a full house, three kings, and two sevens. I flop my two pairs down with a sigh and she smiles again.

"I'm glad we don't play for stakes," I absently comment.

She tilts her head curiously, unfamiliar with part of what I said.

"Stakes, uhm, we would bet something, usually money, as a way of saying 'my hand is better than yours.'"

She nods her head and smiles again.

"You want to try that?"

She nods again.

"All right." I go the converter and, after a moment's thought, say, "Standard poker chips. Values one through five hundred. Two sets, totaling, ten thousand each" Two racks of chips appear, I hand one to Sada and take the other. I pull some chips out and start teaching how to bet, and bluff. She gets the idea quicker than I expect and ends up winning most of my chips from me over the next few hours.

Having had enough loss, and feeling hungry, I slide my nearly empty chip rack aside and head to the converter. I select breaded fish and cheese nuggets with sauce for her and beef and cheese ravioli for me.

I place our plates on the table and hand her a fork. She gives me a pout, not wanting to use it. "You know, using this keeps your fur clean."

She huffs but picks up the fork. She starts using it to move her fish around on the plate until she hits the plate with it and makes a shrill sound. She drops the fork and covers her ears, I notice the fur on her back is on end, and her tail is fluffed. She glares at the fork as her fur settles.

"It's not the fork's fault, you were playing around. Be careful not to scrape the plate with it." She huffs again, but picks up the fork and starts to eat.

"Kyle, please stay on the bed."

Drowsily, I open my eyes. "What? Why?"

"A device has been activated that is using a large amount of power. It is starting to create a charged field that may shock you if you're grounded. I would also recommend not using the webbing."

"This is new. What is it?"

"I am not certain, but it may be the time device, and some recent damage may be to blame for it creating the hazard."

"Are you able to find out how it works?"

"Not as of yet. I will need to witness the entire process since I am unable to access the device he is using."

"What about the others?"

"The rest of the crew are safe, as they have AIs to deplete the charge."

"Starting to wish I had one."

"If you did, then going back would be impossible."

I sigh, realizing just how right he is, then I hear the engine's power increase and the decking starts to vibrate. "I wish they'd fix this thing."

"I concur, it is somewhat disconcerting that the ship has borderline structural integrity."

"I really didn't want to know that." Hearing the ship rattle, Sada tries to get closer to me, burying her face in my chest. I wrap my arm around her and try my best to comfort her. "Never really get used to this, do you?"

"If the ship were in good repair, you hardly notice anything."

Suddenly the rattling stops and the engine sound drops. Sada sighs as she relaxes in my arms, and I gently rub her back.

"That was quick."

"I am searching for a signal with a time stamp."

Sada rests her chin on my shoulder and sighs again. "I know." I give her a kiss on her cheek as I gently rub the back of her head. She starts to purr, letting me know that she enjoys the rub.

"I have discovered that we have jumped to the year 3132. Astrological data indicates we are near the Luma system."

"Wherever that is," I mumble, still lying in bed, wearing only a pair of shorts for pajamas. I find myself still gently rubbing Sada's neck, feeling the one thing she wears; the ribbon with her tag on it.

She lies against me, purring, with her cheek against my chest. I feel her hand slide across my chest, lightly dragging her claws across my skin. I find myself missing Meagan, my wife. I miss being with her like I am with Sada.

I gently take Sada's hand in mine and give it a gentle squeeze. She looks up at me and I give her a kiss on her nose.

Surprised, she sits up a little and I see her nose darken, turning pink; she's blushing. I reach up, putting my hand against her cheek. She nuzzles into my hand, as she holds my arm. I see her close her eyes, showing me how happy she is. I pull her to me, and she repositions herself, trying to lie on my chest like she did as a cat, but ends up straddling me, her chest to mine.

I kiss her again, and she starts to gently lap at my lips, her eyes still closed. I feel her tail gently rub my leg, her breasts pressing against me. I gently run my fingers down her back, she lowers her belly to mine as her tail raises, standing up in the air. She continues lapping at me, moving down to my chest. Her hands move to my arms, holding her up. I close my eyes, savoring the sensation of her tongue on my skin.

She scoots down a little, sitting on my legs. I sit up to her, holding her close to me. I again run my fingers down her back, and she straightens, pressing her chest to mine again. When I reach her tail, I grab her and pull her in closer to me. She wraps her arms around me, purring, while I run my hands up her belly.

When I gently rub her breasts, I hear her inhale sharply. Her purring gets louder as I start to massage them, feeling her fur. She starts to grind against me, her hips moving of their own will.

I whisper, "I love you."

She gives me a hesitant, but longing look but then rubs her cheek to mine.

Feeling her tremble, I ask, "Would you like to keep going?"

She swallows hard, but nods, so I carefully free myself from my shorts. She scoots back into me and starts lapping at my lips again. I resume my caresses, allowing my fingers to find the sensitive areas of her body. Her gasps start interrupting her purrs, and she looks up, exposing her neck to me. I run my nose up the underside of her neck, smelling her musk. She responds with another gasp and holds my head to her. Her body then bucks against me again, this time she gives in, raising herself up.

As she comes down, her inexperience shows. She pushes me down underneath her, and I feel her heat over me. She starts to gently rock her hips, sliding back and forth on me. Her eyes go wide at the stimulation, and I gently hold her, letting her lead. I hear her start to breathe heavily, I feel her body trembling.

She raises herself up again, this time as she comes down, I feel her envelop me, completely. Suddenly she bucks, her eyes dilate and she hisses.

Before I can react, the right side of my neck and shoulder erupt with pain. At that moment, I realize that Sada's teeth are sinking into me, front and back. I hear and feel a bone crack.

I reflexively scream out in pain, with my left hand, I grab Sada by the scruff and hold her to me, not letting her yank. I can't move my right arm.

Apparently startled by my scream she lets go. I release her scruff and quickly grab my neck, trying to plug the holes in my skin to stop the bleeding. It doesn't work too well, and my hand fills with blood, I collapse back on the bed, too light-headed to stay upright.

I hear Sada start gasping and feel her try to help me apply pressure, trying to stop the bleeding. My paramedic training kicks in and I shove my fingers in the holes producing the most blood.

"Sa...call...help..."

I hear her start rapidly tapping something, then Charles's voice says, "Kyle, Sada, are you all right?"

Feeling my strength and consciousness fading, I manage to say one word. "Medic!"

"Hold on, Carrie will be there very soon, Sada you will need to open the door."

A few moments later, I hear the door open, and then I hear Carrie's voice. "Kyle! What happened?" I feel her hands press to my neck.

"Bit...no...fault."

"All right, hold still." After a silent moment, she moves her hands slightly. "When I tell you to, remove your hand, okay? Sada, grab me the injector from the converter."

As I wait, I notice that the pain is diminishing quickly, and this very weird warming sensation flows throughout my neck and shoulder. While my mind tries to make sense of the sensations, I barely notice that something's being pressed against my thigh until I feel a similar warmth spread from there.

"Pull your hand out."

I pull my finger out of the hole and slide my hand out from under hers.

"I gave you a shot that'll help replace the blood you lost. What happened?" Carrie asks, still pressing her hands to my wound.

With things starting to seem clearer, I whisper, "We, uh, we got carried away, it was nobody's fault."

She looks up at the door for a moment, then back at me with a frown. "I've taken care of the worst, but I have to go, I'll be back to finish."

"All right."

She leaves and Sada closes the door, locking it. She then hands me a damp towel and sadly sits next to me. I wipe down my hand and then tentatively touch my wound. I'm surprised to find it nearly healed, with only some bumps remaining.

I slowly sit up, and take a clean corner of the towel to Sada's mouth, wiping away my blood. She shies away, trying to dodge my efforts.

"Sada, it's not your fault. You reacted, tried to defend yourself. It's a feral response. You didn't mean to do it, I know that. I should have known that as a cat, you might have a defense. I'm sorry." I gently turn her head back to me and see tears in her eyes. I gently clean my blood from her lips and then give her a kiss.

She starts to pull away again, but I stop her. "Sada, it's not your fault." I pull her into a hug, trying to reinforce that I don't blame her. She starts to cry as she hugs me tightly.

"I'm okay. You're okay. We are both all right." I give her another kiss. After a moment, she pulls back a little and looks at my shoulder. Still sniffling, she takes the rag from me and wipes at my neck and shoulder, then gently traces where she bit with a finger.

"I have a scar, don't I?"

She nods, sniffling again.

"Come on, let's get cleaned up."

Once in the bathroom, I stick Charles's disk to the mirror and step into the shower. As I start to wet myself down, Sada steps into the shower behind me. She takes the body wash from me and starts to wash my back, paying particular, yet gentle, attention to my neck and shoulder.

After I rinse myself, we swap places and I lather up her back and tail. She waits until I step out and close the curtain before she rinses and shakes. I dry myself, put on a clean pair of shorts.

As I retrieve the disk, I get a look at my wound in the mirror. It wraps around my lower neck and collar. Her fangs have left their distinct marks over my collar bone and jugular. I realize that if Carrie was busy, I would have died from blood loss.

With a sigh, I realize that I feel just as bad as Sada does. Something, we both wanted, has been denied by instincts.

Sada steps out of the shower and seeing me looking at my neck and shoulder, steps up behind me, and gently starts lapping at the scars.

I turn to face her, grabbing a towel as I do. "I know you're sorry." I gently turn her around and start drying her back and tail. "I also know how guilty you feel, I feel the same way. I promise to not put you in that position again. We won't try to make love again."

She turns to face me and nods, so I take the towel and dry her head and cheeks. She then shakes her head, trying to put her fur back in place.

"Finish drying off. I'll brush you."

I pick up her brush and exit the bathroom. Before I sit at the desk, I look at the bed. Seeing the blood-soaked sheets, I realize just how much blood I lost. Sighing, I roll up the sheets and toss them in the converter. I then grab the wet towel and wipe down the mattress, trying to clean up the blood that soaked in.

Not having any luck, I toss the towel in the converter, and everything disappears with a flash. I sit down as Sada comes out of the bathroom. She looks at the bed as she walks to me, and I see her eyes go wide.

"Come here." She grabs a chair and sits sideways on it with her back to me, and I start brushing out her fur. By the time I've finished, Carrie comes back.

"Let's get you finished up."

As she puts her hands over the scar, a thought hits me. "Leave the scar."

She pulls back abruptly and looks at me, then at Sada. "Why?"

"It'll be a reminder," I look into Sada's blue eyes, "of a promise."

"Are you sure?"

"I am."

She turns and looks at Sada, who nods her agreement.

"Alright, leaving the scar." She puts her hands back, I feel the little remaining pain dissipate, leaving only the odd warming sensation.

"That feels weird."

"Micro-tractors and cellular regenerators, no one really ever gets used to healing at an accelerated rate."

"I'm not even going to pretend to know how that works."

"They're implants, in my hands, controlled by my AI."

When she's finished, I gesture at the bed. "I don't suppose you have any suggestions on how to clean that?"

She looks at the bed and frowns. "You lost a lot. You had a punctured carotid, nicked jugular, broken color bone, as well as all the other punctures. I don't need to know what happened, but be careful not to let it happen again."

She gets up and heads to the converter as a spray bottle appears. She then uses it to spray down the bed, and the bloodstain starts to disappear. "Give the bed an hour before you put fresh sheets on it." She sets the bottle back in the converter and it disappears.

She turns back to me, putting a hand to my chest and forehead. "Just double-checking your vitals. I'd recommend eating something soon." She straightens noticeably and then sighs. "I've got to go, again. Call if you need me."

After she leaves, Sada sits on my lap and leans into me. From the droop of her ears and tail, I can tell that she's still upset at the fact that she bit me. I put my arms around her and hold her close.

15

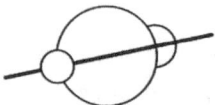

Sitting in the great hall, I set aside my tablet on an end table. Turning my attention to the spring, I watch the fish swim, lazily circling the stones within, letting my mind clear. We learned quickly that this spring and the nearby pond are connected by an underground cave when Oana dove into the spring and swam all the way out to the pond. Ziggy now keeps an eye on the water level and can seal the top, to keep it from flooding the house if the water rises too much. That thankfully hasn't happened, yet, but it's come close.

With the repairs to the Wanderer complete, Marcus has opted to return to Garrent. Darren however, having an interest in Nanai, has stayed. He now spends much of his time, helping whoever, whenever he can, trying to be useful.

Hearing someone approach, I look up to see Cayla sit opposite me.

"Busy?" she asks.

"Should be, but needed a moment of distraction."

"Well, maybe I can provide another one. I've been looking through the files you uploaded from the facility and I've found something disturbing."

"What's that?"

"The Obsession was here, well, at the facility."

"I know, I was onboard when it was."

"How's that possible, I mean, you were delivered to the facility hundreds of years after that ship went missing, and you were already in cryo. How'd it even manage to get here?"

I sigh, wondering just how much I should tell her. "Captain Nabire had somehow figured out how to travel in time. He went back to 2019 to grab me and Sada, then forward again to collect other kinds of equipment."

"Oh. Well, according to the facility records, they arrived a few weeks before work started on the nano-virus."

Her statement gives me cause for concern. "You're kidding."

"No, I found it in some of the personal logs of the nano-engineering team. Apparently, they were forced into building it."

"What'd they use for leverage?"

"The planet, they threatened to raze it."

I sit back, sighing. "So, he was having things made, too. I wonder...Did you find anything that indicates when he was going to come back to get it?"

"Unfortunately, no. What I did find though, is that there was not an official report on their visit. I'm beginning to think that someone here was on his side, or at least in his pocket."

"Any idea who?"

"Well the entry was made by someone named Barasse, but I couldn't find anyone with that name assigned here."

"Could they have been left here by the Obsession?"

She thinks for a moment, apparently not having considered it. "Possibly, could explain a few things."

"How well did you know the others in that team?"

She shrugs. "They weren't here too long, maybe a year before the accident. I never really got to know anyone outside my team, apparently, the managerial teams wanted to keep it that way. Everyone knew about the evolved, they were our facility's pride and joy, as was stabilizing the planet's ecosystem. There were some R and D teams that were all 'hush, hush' when it came to what they were working on."

"According to Aime, your team should have had access to those kinds of things."

"Should have, but we didn't, not the projects in development, anyway. Once they were complete though, reviews and tests were welcomed from the other groups. My group was always on that list because we really didn't have much else to do, aside from maintaining you two."

"I'm beginning to think I need to retrieve the memory core from the facility, have Ziggy thoroughly go through everything on it, see what we can learn."

"You may also want to consider getting some of the satellites working and access the main memory archives. See what we can learn about the other places that they've visited. It'd also give us an accurate Earth time base too."

"It may give us some things I'm not sure if these people are ready for, though."

She sighs, realizing my concern. Then, after a moment's thought, she asks, "How do you know for sure, unless you ask them."

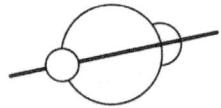

Cayla leads us down several levels, to the memory core. Despite the number of times I've been in the facility, I've come nowhere near knowing it like she does. Darren pulls a repulsor sled behind him, I'm carrying my pack of tools and small proximity lights. I stick a proximity light high up on the wall every few paces as we walk through the areas I haven't yet explored. Tareth follows quietly, checking each open doorway as we pass them.

Since much of the facility still lacks power, the double doors we just encountered won't open. I set down my pack and get out one of the cutting tools. Darrel takes it and starts to cut the hinges as I put on my armor's gloves and prepare to move the door.

When Darren steps aside, I slap the door with both hands. As I pull, the door comes with, stuck to my gloves. I adjust my grip and move the door off to the side as he starts cutting at the other's hinges. After he finishes, I do the same with that one.

Cayla leads us in, past several racks of equipment to the far end of the room. There we find that the core is a large cylinder, about two meters tall and made up of ten layers, each divided into eight wedges. Darren drags the sled alongside the core.

"To remove the sections, just release the clips and pull," Cayla states.

"Everyone, remember where how they go," I say and start releasing clips.

"It really doesn't matter how they're reassembled," Aime states, "as long as they're in the same layer."

"That's good to know. Keep each layer together." I pull out my first shoebox-sized wedge and set it on the cart.

The stack slowly grows, in two rows of eight, as we slowly disassemble the core, level by level. Darren, still lacking an AI, tires first and takes a break while Cayla and I keep at it for a while longer.

"Don't you two need to rest?" he asks.

"Not really, our AIs increase stamina, keeping fatigue at bay," she states.

"Well, more the nanites than the AIs," I add.

She laughs. "Yeah, I guess we could take a little break, get something to eat."

Darren pulls the converter out of my pack and has it produce some sandwiches and some drinks. We relax for a while and Darren starts asking her questions about what its like to have an AI. She answers his questions as best she can, while trying not to scare him at the same time.

Having finished my sandwich, I continue removing the sections while they talk. I find his curiosity refreshing since he wants an AI of his own. He's asked me a lot of questions already, so having her perspective actually gives him a better feeling of what he's volunteering for.

After we take down the rack, we head out the doors. Cayla happens to shine her light further down the hall, and I notice something unusual.

"What's that?"

"What?"

I shine my light and increase its brightness, illuminating a large machine that practically fills the entire end of the hall. "That."

She looks for a moment. "That's one of the construction bots. There are two others in front of it."

"What can they build?"

"Nearly anything that's smaller than them. They have converters and manipulator arms for larger, complex jobs."

"Think they still work?"

"Possibly, they got powered down after the facility was built."

"Those could come in handy, I'll have to come back with a power cell and find out."

Darren looks curiously at me. "What would you use them for?"

"Better bridges for starters. Plus, I'd rather have one and not need it than need it and not have it."

"You'd have to put them in the Wanderer's cargo hold, to big for the shuttle."

I smile. "It'd be worth it." I quickly set a pair of lights in that hall to help mark their location.

We leave, taking the core and its rack to the shuttle. Once back at the house, we start installing the core in an unused room near my office. Reassembly is easier than anticipated with our AIs helping us make sure the pieces are in the right places. It takes Ziggy several minutes to start it up, but once he has it running, Cayla grabs a tablet and starts reviewing its contents in detail.

Leaving her to her chosen task, I find Megai, Tayla, and Railu, in the Great Hall sitting near the playpen, the cubs and kit are awake and playing in it.

Railu's working on her leather armor, redoing some of its stitching. Megai and Tayla both are watching the children. Oana lies just outside the pen, intently watching them play, cooing.

I lean on the back of the couch, behind my mates. "I can't help but wonder why she finds them so fascinating."

"I think it's sweet," Railu states.

Tayla chuckles. "If the playpen was larger, I think she'd be in there with them."

"What, you haven't caught her in it already?" Megai asks. "I had to tell her to get out of it this morning."

I chuckle. "I'm surprised she actually fit."

"She was curled up pretty tight when I found her."

"I wonder if she's had some offspring of her own."

"No she hasn't, Aime's been able to determine that she should lay eggs, but she doesn't produce any yet."

"Does that mean she's still a child?" Tayla asks.

"Possibly, without her knowing how old she is, it's hard to tell if she is, or if she needs something to happen before she produces."

"Aime can't tell?"

"She doesn't know enough about her species to figure it out yet."

"It'd be nice to know that."

"Yeah, but that'd mean finding more of her kind, lot of danger there."

She sighs. "I know."

Cayla comes in carrying a tablet. "Kyle, I found the specs for the satellites."

"Already?"

"Yeah."

"How many?"

"Quite a few production models and some prototypes."

I give my mates a kiss each and then turn to Cayla. "All right, let's see what we have."

She follows me into my office and sends the data to the large monitor I have on the wall. "This is the standard, weather satellite, it also has GPS, and intra-system data relay abilities. Then we have the scanning variety, which has two subtypes, deep space and planetary. Lastly, we have the defense satellites. These have many subtypes; particle beam and missile are the most popular."

I look at the three examples on the screen. "How big are these?"

The display changes, showing a weather unit, zoomed to full screen, with a scale next to it. "Only a half meter tall. What about the deep space scanner?"

With a flicker, the display changes, showing it to scale. "Nearly the same size, okay. Show a particle beam unit."

This one is considerably larger, nearly as large as an oil drum. "Big difference there. Are there any smaller defense satellites?" The screen changes to show a unit similar to the weather satellite, but there's a series of points sticking out one end. "What's that?"

Ziggy answers, "It's a Type 12, mini-rocket pack."

"Mini-rocket? How much damage would one do?" I ask.

"By itself, minimal, the system was designed to fire in rapid succession, emptying all twelve tubes in two seconds. This would usually overwhelm the shields for a moment, allowing at least one of the rockets through to the hull. These types, though, fell out of use due to the fact that they had to be reloaded manually."

"How fast could the rockets be produced with a dedicated converter?" Cayla asks.

"Maximum rate would be five seconds. Actual rate may diminish based on available power."

"How much room would the converter take up?" I ask.

"Minimal, although there would need to be one for each tube."

"Show me."

The visual changes, as the box with the points, increases width, by almost twenty-five percent and the points space out proportionately. I look at the image for a while in thought.

"The design of the weather satellites in orbit, how old was it at the time of the accident?"

"Searching...Nearly twenty years."

Cayla looks at me. "What are you thinking?"

"Things usually get smaller, the newer they are, right?"

She nods. "Yeah, usually."

"Ziggy, start with the altered rocket unit, add either weather satellite hardware, planetary scanners, or full-range life form scanners."

"Working."

"Combined satellites?"

"Yeah, having them up there will allow the Sages to let their villages know what the weather will be, and if any large predators or other dangers are around."

"Preliminary mockup complete." The display changes to show the three proposed satellites. They're slightly larger than the previous one, and with far more antennas pointed opposite the rockets.

"That looks good. What's the reload rate?"

"On independent power, it can reload in ten seconds."

"Independent power?"

"Solar panels, internal reactor, and batteries."

"What if it's in the nightside?"

"Reload would take nearly twenty seconds."

Cayla speaks up. "How big would it be if we added a second reactor?"

The satellite alters slightly, becoming longer. "I would like to note, that the increased power output would make it a likely target."

"That'd give it a shorter life," I comment. "What if we make them able to transfer power to each other, like our nanites do?"

"So the ones unable to engage can offer their power to the ones can, clever. Ziggy, how big would the net need to be to provide full recharge rate to satellites facing, say...a reconnaissance fleet?"

"With or without a military escort?"

"With," I state, "and determine how many deep space observation satellites we'll need to detect them coming before they get to the Shell, work them into the same power share."

"Beginning simulations. Estimating completion in three days."

"Well, he'll be at that for a while," Cayla admits. "I'll start looking for anything I can find on the Obsession."

"If nothing else, find out what you can about the class of cruiser it was, give us an idea about the ship's specs."

She smiles and nods to me. "I should be able to find that."

I wait till after she heads back to the room she's using as an office. "Aime, I need a long-range communications satellite, capable of reaching Earth's government, or at least somewhere that can relay to them."

"I will see what I can find."

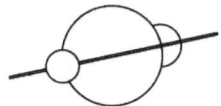

Arru and Tareth follow me as I walk to the council hut in Pridewyn, several people bow or nod as we pass. I've actually gotten used to the looks, the nods, and bows that people give me as Sovereign. Sometimes I regret setting up the relays, thanks to Sage Arindell, I've become 'de facto' Sovereign of all the villages. In all, I don't really do much of anything, aside from offering advice or help with a trade agreement, but it's something I've come to live with.

Walking into the council hut, the Mediator recognizes me immediately. "Master Kyle, Advisor Arru, nice to have you both. The council is waiting for you. Please." The lioness opens the door and shows us in. Tareth waits just outside the door, standing guard.

"Master Kyle, Sage has relayed your message, and we do have some questions."

I look at the cheetess and smile. "I knew you would, and I am here to answer what I can."

"Well, I for one would like to know, what are the possible repercussions to us, if they don't leave us alone?"

"That's the one thing that I can't honestly answer. I can speculate that they may send another team to take back the facility, and the Wanderer, in which case, we all will be subject to a lot of scrutiny, me more than you. What I'm hoping they do, as per their own laws, is recognize us as a sovereign system, and in turn recognize our right to salvage of the facility, ships, and satellites."

The councilors talk between themselves for a moment, then the panther to her left speaks, his deep voice fills the room. "I would like to know what the worst case would be if they don't."

"I have given that much thought, and if the current ruling government does send ships to reclaim this planet, I am prepared to defend my home, and my people."

"How would you do this?"

"I have at my disposal, the means to build defense satellites and fighter drones. I would use the Wanderer or the shuttle to deploy these in orbit before their arrival."

He looks pensive for a moment. "How do you think you would do against them?"

"I do have knowledge of some of their ships, and I also know some of their limitations. This system has a natural barrier, which will limit and possibly cripple the ships that they can actually send directly in-system. If they go around, it'll give me time to adjust my strategy according to the ships they send."

"I have run numerous simulations on both scenarios. Either way, the defenses I've planned have prevailed with anything short of a full fleet invasion."

Concerned, he asks, "What would prompt them to use a full fleet?"

"If they thought there was something here worth the effort. On the upside of that, the only thing of major worth here is data, and I can send that to them."

He thinks for a moment, considering my words, and then nods to the cheetess. She looks around at the other councilors. "Does anyone else have concerns or questions that Sage hasn't been able to answer?"

"Will you be approaching the other villages?" The question comes from a lioness to the far right.

"Yes, I will. I have already provided them with the same information and posed the same questions to them that I did to you. They will also be getting a review of the questions and answers voiced here, and you will, in turn, receive a review from my meetings with them."

"Thank you." She nods and then turns back to the cheetess.

"Is anyone opposed to his actions?" She looks, and not getting any, she looks back at me. "Master Kyle, you have heard our voice, please advise us when you plan on making contact."

"Pending the decision of the other villages, I will give you ample notice. Councilors, I thank you for your time."

Arru and I both bow, and, as we turn to leave, the cheetess joins us. She pulls her hood up and gives me a curious look. "I suspect you have something private to talk to me about."

"I do."

We exit the hut, and I turn to Arru with a sigh of relief. "Thank you for standing with me."

She bows slightly. "I'll meet you back at the shuttle in an hour." As she turns and heads towards the markets, I nod to Tareth, and he accompanies her.

With both out of earshot, the cheetess turns to me. "What's on your mind?"

I smile. "This way, please."

She keeps pace with me as I leisurely walk and talk. "I have something to show you, but I feel you may already know what it is."

"Knowing without seeing is sometimes not worth knowing."

I smile, understanding her response. "Well, I would not feel right if I came to see you, no matter the reason, and not let you meet your great-grandchildren."

She stops abruptly as Megai, Tayla, and Sada come up, the latter two carrying the cubs. "How did you find out?"

"That you were Tayla's grandmother, Tessha? I picked up this book in Arindell about myths. When Tayla told me about her grandmother, I filled in some blanks, but after a while, it became obvious to me who you were."

She smiles, as Tayla approaches. "Grandmother, this is Tashi."

The cub reaches up to grab Tessha's whiskers and chirps her interest. Tessha giggles and gently nuzzles the cub. "I see you are like your mother, both beautiful and outgoing."

"This is Kuma," Tayla states as Sada holds him up.

"Oh, he's white, like his great-grandfather. Hello, handsome one." She nuzzles him too, despite him being asleep. She then looks up at me, slightly puzzled. "They both carry your scent, how?"

"They are as much mine as they are Tayla's. The details are complex, but Aime helped make it possible."

"Well, they are beautiful, and I see a beautiful future for them."

"It is good to see you grandmother."

"And it is good to see you." They bump noses, a kiss as I've come to know it. "I am glad to see that you find it to your liking."

"I am not his only mate, this is Megai."

"I am pleased to finally meet you."

Tessha gently puts her hand on Megai's cheek. "My, you are an interesting one. I'm not sure what to make of your destiny."

"I have already found it, with this family."

"I sense, though, you are more important than you think."

"What? How?"

Tessha tilts her head. "You'll find out, soon enough." She then turns to Sada, and says, "You're glowing, I see that you finally feel at home."

Sada gives her a nod and a bump on the nose, purring.

She gently pats Sada's cheek and then turns back to me. "Where is he?"

I smile, knowing who she's after, I look back at where the others came out from. "Come on out."

Larrah comes around a nearby hut, followed closely by, Kotu, Fey, Oana, and Amela.

Tessha smiles as she steps up to Kotu. "You are not the cub I last saw."

"No ma'am."

She feels the thickening fur around his neck. "Your mane is coming in. You are coming of age."

"He helped save me, too," Fey states.

"The true sign of a warrior, protect those who can't protect them-selves."

"Yes ma'am, I couldn't let anything happen to my family."

"Indeed." She turns her attention to Fey. "He cares for you, more than you know."

"Who?" Fey asks, oddly bewildered as Kotu shifts his weight un-comfortably.

"I won't spoil it for him."

"Hello."

"Hello, little one." Tessha lowers herself to Amela's height.

"What about me?"

"You are going to be a beautiful young female, much like your aunt."

Amela smiles and whispers, "She's my mom now."

She chuckles. "Of course, much like your mom." She stands again and turns to Larrah.

"Councilor."

"I haven't seen you this confident since before your mate."

"I have found what I was missing, thank you."

"You're not done yet. You need to ask him."

Larrah nods. "When the time is right."

"Just don't wait too long." She nods and then turns to Oana. "You, are new to my eyes."

"Oana, friend."

Tessha puts her hand on Oana's cheek. "Oana. You have been given a gift you don't yet understand."

"Oana happy."

"Yes you are, but there's more to life than happiness. Don't be afraid of what he offers you."

"Oana not want to leave."

"You don't have to leave, but you do have much to teach your peo-ple."

Oana sighs, and puts her nose to Tessha's hand and coos.

"Quite the family you've started."

I turn and look to where the kids came out. "There's more."

Railu comes out holding Ru. Roen stands by her side. "Thank you, for sending him to find me."

"My dear, I did not know the why, only that he needed to go, but you are welcome." She puts her hand to Railu's cheek. "You can relax now. He's not going to leave you, and you have her to care for."

"I know. It's just not easy for me to do."

"Enjoy the moment. The rest will come easier than you think."

Railu bows slightly, as does Roen, and Tessha turns back to me. "As a counselor, were supposed to leave our lives behind us, for the good of the village. There are moments, though, that remind us of why we do what we do. Thank you for the visit, and the memories you brought back to me."

She gives Tayla another nose-bump. "Take good care of them."

"I will, grandmother."

"Master Kyle, if I may have a moment, in private."

Recognizing her change in protocol, I nod to my family. "I'll be along shortly."

Following the councilor, we walk through the village, much as we did over a year ago. "I am concerned that your plan may endanger more than yourself."

My face skews slightly. "It's not the Earth Forces I'm worried about. It's someone from my past that bothers me."

She stops abruptly and looks at me. "Your past *and* your future."

"Yeah, that's what I thought. I know he'll be back, I'm just not sure when."

"And you want to do this, to be prepared."

"Yes, I need to learn what I can about him and where he's been. I know some of it already, like he's been here before."

She sighs, and I can see her think. "Normally something like this would be clear, but there's something...odd. This future is not so clear to me."

I nod. "It's because he can travel in time. I'm proof of that. I know he's been taking things from places, past, and future, if I could find out when he's been where, and what he's taken, I might be able to plan better defenses."

She looks at me, concerned. "I fear I cannot advise you on this, the most I can offer is to be careful."

"That's all right, you've helped me more than you realize. Thank you, Councilor."

"Always a pleasure, Master Kyle."

We bow to each other and she makes her way back to the council hut as I return to the shuttle, to my family.

16

"Kyle, I do not understand. Why do you want to return to your own time?"

I sigh and pull the sheets off my face. I've been feeling oddly out of place and have been getting very homesick lately. "Charles, I want to go back because that's my home. It's where I'm supposed to be."

"What if you don't belong there anymore?"

"What do you mean?"

"You have been given a new life. Your companion has been altered, with a new life of her own. I don't understand why you would want to go back to the way you were."

"Because it's the way things should have been. What the captain did was alter the past. I, we need to go back to set things right."

"What if this was supposed to happen, your disappearance? You stated yourself that you were going to die on your own terms, even if that meant wandering off into the woods."

"Charles, why are you so against my returning?"

"I am not against it. I am merely pointing out various facts."

"Sounds more like you're against me going. Why?"

"You told me not to tell you what I find."

"Well, now I'm rescinding that, spill it."

"Very well. In my efforts to find more about you, I have found nothing, not even in the records of Andolina Neurological Research."

"What do you mean?"

"There is not a date of death, nothing past a transfer of your estate to your sister and nurse."

"When did that happen?"

"Mid 2019, there were some conditions that the state wanted to argue, but your attorney, sister, and nurse all sided with your Will. Since both your Living Will and Last Will both stated your wishes the same way, and you had already signed all the needed documents, the state was forced to concede."

"So I was supposed to vanish after all."

"It would appear so."

I look down at Sada, who's resting her chin on my chest, watching me curiously.

"What do you want to do? Go back, or stay."

She tilts her head for a moment and then pats on me.

"Stay?"

She nods, then points at me.

"Stay with me?"

She nods again, and then lays her head back on me, purring.

I wrap my arms around her. "I love you, no matter what shape you are."

She nuzzles into my neck, getting more comfortable as she does.

"I presume that means she would be happy with whatever you decide?"

"It would seem that way. What else did you find?"

"I have been able to extrapolate a possible location for the time travel device."

"How?"

"I used the sensor data from when the field started to form and compared that to heavy power drains occurring at the same time. Both sets of data point to the auxiliary control room, directly under the bridge."

"Sounds like a secure place for it."

"Surprisingly no, while there is a guard stationed outside each door at all times, there are none inside. The only person that has gone inside is the captain."

"How many ways are there into that room?"

"Aside from the three guarded doors, there is the air duct, though it is not large enough for either of you to fit through."

"You read my mind. How busy are the corridors outside it?"

"Minimal traffic. I have a feeling that the guards also get bored easily."

"What makes you say that?"

"I have detected chairs and stools outside each door."

"You're implying they take naps?"

"I have been able to see them with their feet up, but the internal sensors are not working well enough for me to register if they're asleep."

"How certain are you that the device for time travel is inside?"

"Over 99% certain. It is currently the only room under constant guard and the internal sensors in that room are disabled, not broken."

I stare blankly at the ceiling for a moment, wondering what to make of this information when a thought hits me. "Does everyone have an AI?"

"No, if the host has an allergy to the metals used or an unusual genetic condition, an AI cannot be installed."

"I don't suppose that there's anybody else on board without one."

"Correct. The entire crew has AIs."

I sigh, having an AI means that the person doesn't have to be paying attention, the AI always is. It also means that the first sign of trouble will be reported immediately. "Is there anything that will stun an AI?"

"What is your intent?"

"I don't want to hurt anyone, but if I can get into that room, I might be able to take the device, grab a shuttle or something and go home."

"And then what, hide somewhere for the rest of your lives?"

"We're already hiding. Besides, it'd be better than staying cooped up here."

"Then you should see some of the other things he has taken. With them, I believe we can make that happen."

Sada puts her ear to the door, listening for voices. Apparently hearing none, she opens the access hatch to cargo bay one, the largest hold on the ship. Stepping out, I immediately see what Charles had wanted me to find. There, taking up most of the bay sits a very large asteroid.

Sada looks curiously at it and then turns to me.

"Why an asteroid?"

"It is an observer outpost, disguised to look like an asteroid. Look for a silver rock, should be about a meter up. Touch it."

We split up and walk slowly around in different directions, looking for the indicated rock. Hearing a gentle hiss, followed by a hum, I sprint around to see Sada staring into an opening.

"Good, go inside."

"What will we find?"

"It should have observation equipment inside."

The lights come on as we step in and we see that there is, in fact, a number of monitors arranged around a living area. There's a couch and table, and at the far end, there's a converter. Monitors come on to show the surrounding cargo bay like they were windows.

Sada steps back outside and I watch from the inside as she walks around curiously looking for something on the outside.

"Charles, how does it do that?"

"The sensors are passive, located just under the surface of the shell. They can detect a large number of emissions, and make a useable image out of them for the screens."

Sada comes back in as I find an odd-looking platform. "What's this?"

"That is a large converter station. It is there for entertainment and other necessities. You can also make new furniture with it."

"Why?"

"The outpost is designed to be placed in an asteroid field. The large converter allows for the crew inside to make new equipment and large items to entertain themselves during their duration onboard."

"Clever." I look around, the room itself is rather large, nearly the size of the asteroid, I realize that something's missing. "Where do you sleep?"

"The sleeping area is accessible using the lift."

"Lift? What lift?"

A door opens next to the large converter, revealing the small elevator. Curious as to what the other room looks like, we step in.

After a short ride, we step out into a small room. The ceiling is much lower than the room below, but still high enough to stand up. The only furniture I see is the large bed and a pair of dressers.

"How many people usually crew this thing?"

"Normally two or three, but it can hold up to six."

"That'd be crowded."

"Indeed."

After returning to the main room, I ask, "How does it move?"

"It has repulsors, tractors, and drift thrusters."

"Sounds slow."

"It is. It was designed to be dropped in place, the thrusters keep it from colliding with the real asteroids, while still mimicking natural motion."

"So, what, we'd need to leave the hold close to where we want to go?"

"Normally yes, however, ideally, you would want to drop out of the hold in an asteroid field, wait for the ship to leave, and slingshot into the desired course. There are cryo-stasis tubes that you can use to sleep in for the majority of the voyage."

"Sleep, for how long?"

"It would depend on where you started from."

"So, depending on where we start, we'd have to go back far enough to compensate for both the time difference and the trip time."

"Correct."

"I'm not very good at math."

"I will make all the calculations, as well as plot the course for the asteroid. So when we eject you from the bay, you would simply be along for the ride."

"Long ride." I sit at the couch, and Sada sits next to me. "What powers this?"

"The skin absorbs radiation and converts it to electrical energy. That energy is stored in batteries until needed by the thrusters, or internal systems."

"Sounds like it's a low power system."

"Actually, there is a lot of radiation in space, aside from solar, there is also cosmic, both ionizing and non-ionizing. It can even absorb its own emissions, maintaining its appearance as a common space rock."

"Sounds like it could be used for spying."

"If humankind ever finds another sentient species to learn about, or an internal war erupts, possibly."

"War? How long has it been since there was one?"

"Technically, there hasn't been a war since humans got into space, but there was an incident that has been commonly called the Genetic War."

"When was that?"

"2478. It did not last more than a few weeks, but it managed to kill several billion people and several thousand AI library hubs in just a few days. A lot of historical data was lost."

"Is that why no one can find much about me?"

"Correct, though there have been times when we have been near enough to a separate database to query for more information."

"How'd you pull that off? I thought this ship would be recognized through an electronic link."

"It would, but I have access codes, that the ship does not, that allow me unquestioned access."

"Must be nice."

"It can be most helpful. If I may, I believe there is a group of people heading your way."

I grab Sada's hand and we quickly exit the asteroid, pressing the silver rock as we pass by to close the hatch. She opens the service hatch and we duck out as the main corridor doors open.

With this section powerless, the lights are out. Gravity still works though, mostly because the deck below still has power. Shining our flashlights at the walls as we walk, I ask Charles, "What are we looking for again?"

"Weapons locker."

"Why?"

"You wanted to know how to stun an AI. The weapons locker should have an electromagnetic pulse grenade."

"An EMP? Won't that shut it down?"

"Not at this low power. I will only disrupt the matrix for a few minutes, but that's enough to accomplish what we want."

A banging sound gets my attention. I turn to see Sada waving me over.

"What'd you find?"

She points her flashlight to a sign, printed in symbols I'm not familiar with.

"I hold my wrist up so the disk faces the sign. "Charles, can you see that?"

"It reads 'Do not enter,' though I am unsure why it is written in Ket."

"Ket? I'd bet that whoever made the sign didn't want anyone to be able to read it."

"Any AI can read it. We have a full language database."

"Even ones from this time?"

"Yes."

"Then why the obscure language?"

"You could open the door and find out."

"Why?" I ask, puzzled. "Can't you see in there?"

"No, and that room is not on any schematic."

I sigh. "While I'd like to, we're in the open, so let's find that locker."

"It should be marked."

"You'd think." I take a few more steps and find the door to the weapons locker. "Got it." I step inside, Sada follows, closing the door behind her. Shining my light around I see a myriad of different weapons, some in crates, some not, crowding the small room.

"Quite the arsenal he's got."

"This is unusual, there is only supposed to be pistols, rifles, and a few grenades in here. I am detecting heavy repeaters, anti-vehicle, and light artillery weapons."

"He really is preparing for a war." I carefully look around, trying to find something that looks like a grenade. Not seeing anything near the door, I start working my way towards the back.

"There is a lot of clutter, masking their signature, but I believe you are looking in the right direction."

"Great, let me know when you think I'm close." I start moving crates slightly as I squeeze between them, trying to get deeper into the room. I notice Sada has an easier time moving between them than I do."

"Stack on your right, third crate down."

"Sada, a hand please."

She starts towards me and helps me move the top two crates. Opening the third, we find two dozen soda can-sized canisters.

Pulling one out, I ask, "This is it?"

"Yes, the buttons on the side are the activators, when they are pressed together, a third button will pop up. By pressing all three at the same time, activates a five-second detonation timer."

"What's the range?"

"Ten meters."

"Will I be affected?"

"No, and neither will the AI's host. In most cases, the host may not even notice it unless they try interacting with their AI."

"So if they're asleep, they may not notice anything at all."

"Correct."

"Are there any gas grenades or something that will put someone to sleep in here?"

"No, I will pull a design and have your converter make one for you."

"You can do that?"

"I can, but not many others can."

I put the grenade back and lift the top rack out. I quickly grab one from below and put the top rack back. Sada gives me an odd look and points to the grenades.

"Just in case someone looks, they won't notice one missing right away."

She smiles and nods her understanding, as she helps me restack the crates.

We quickly and quietly return to our room and I find an odd-looking device sitting in the converter. After a cursory look, I notice that it appears to attach to the grenade.

"Charles, how do these fit together?"

"The gas cartridge attaches to a port opposite the buttons. You will need to slide the cover out of the way."

"Ah, I see." I give the can a spin, opening the cover. I then fit the two pieces together and turn back to the converter. I think for a moment, then press the converter's activator. "Canvas travel pack, black, uhm... ten-liter capacity."

A shoebox-sized pack appears. I put the combined grenade in it and hang the pack from a hook on the back of the door. As I turn back, I see Sada grab the deck of cards and start shuffling. She's got the first half down, but she has yet to figure out the riffle bridge I always do.

I have a seat opposite her. "Charles, what else are we gonna need?"

Sada starts dealing out the cards as he explains, "I'll need to create a remote and an interface to install in an escape pod."

Sada points to "rummy" on the list of card games as I pick up my cards. "What do we need a remote for?"

"To launch an escape pod, of course. You won't be inside, but it will be a distraction, should allow you to get out of the cargo bay unnoticed."

"Good, wouldn't want to go through all this to get caught right out the door."

"I agree. Could you deal me in next hand?"

"What? How would you play?"

"Check the converter."

Sada and I both look to see an oddly hollow-looking torso, head, and arms combo sitting in the converter. I pick it up and give it an odd look, before placing it upright on the desk chair. Suddenly the arms come alive as Charles tests the range of motion, and then it extends the main support, lifting the "body" up, adjusting to the height of the table.

Sada eyes it suspiciously for a moment, as I take my seat.

"You can control this...uhm, construct?" I ask.

"While it is not in my native ability, I have taken in a large about of data, and I feel confident in being able to use this simple construct to play cards with you."

"All right, have any questions on the rules?"

"I have several versions in memory, and I have also monitored several of your games, I am familiar with how you play."

"Good." I give the 'body' another curious look. "You really should have filled that in a little, you look creepy."

Sada nods her agreement as she picks up the cards to shuffle.

"I did not want to draw too much power."

She starts dealing as I chuckle, and we start picking up our cards.

Then I remember that he can use the sensors in the communication coins. "And no peeking at our cards."

His response sounds more like a scolding. "I would never."

17

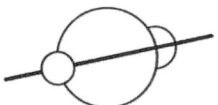

Having visited all the other villages, and gotten their approval to continue, I sit in my office, reviewing some of the research notes on the accelerated evolution process, hoping to find something helpful for setting up a symbiotic AI for the evolved. Ziggy softly interrupts, "I have completed the construction of the first defense satellite."

"Good, how long for the other 143?"

"Just under thirty days."

"And the long-range scanners?"

"An additional five days. It would be much faster if you retrieved the other two construction bots."

I sigh and stretch out in my desk chair. "I know Ziggy, I know. It just took all day to get that one out of there."

"I am aware that they travel slowly, but two days' work will reduce the build time by nearly twenty days."

I rub my face, feeling the effects of a long day when Aime offers a suggestion. "I can preprogram the two remaining bots to follow the same path we used with the first. They should be waiting for us midday tomorrow."

"Why didn't you suggest that sooner?"

"Apologies, I was working on the evolved AI."

"Do we need to go there to get them started?"

"No, I can use the transmitter on the finished satellite. One moment...I have sent the programmed route."

"Thank you. How are you doing with the new AI?"

"I have done almost as much as I can without a thorough analysis of the host."

"You mean Nanai."

"Correct, we will need to perform a neurological exam before I can proceed."

"Remind me in the morning, I'll talk to her."

"Certainly."

I turn my attention back to the evolution processes. I've learned the first species to be evolved were the dogs. The scientists tried to apply the same algorithms to the cats but ended up modifying many of those after some of the initial group showed anomalies. Surprisingly, they didn't dispose of those. They just integrated them with the subsequent evolutions.

After a little more research, I find that most of the processes were based on the first and later modified for each individual species. Despite all my reading and research, I soon discover that none of these processes were used on Sada. All the ones used here on Arcania seem to correct various perceived handicaps of the original animals in an attempt to even some of the differences between them.

Having had enough reading for the day, and feeling quite tired, I decide to retire for the evening. As I exit my office, I nod to Tareth. "Good night."

He nods back. "Good night," and then heads down the hall to his room.

I head to my room but find myself entering the nursery. Feeling tired, and a little lost, I have a seat in a rocking chair and watch my cubs sleep. As I do, I start thinking about all that I've come to love about this planet, and its people. I have a family, children to protect, and friends who've stood by me.

I'm home.

This planet is my home.

I sigh heavily, then feel familiar hands slide down my chest. I reflexively put my hands on hers, feeling her extra soft fur as she rubs her cheek against mine.

"Something wrong?" Megai softly asks me.

I rub my cheek against hers. "No, just remembering what's important."

"And what would that be?"

"This is my home, and everyone here is my family."

"Then come to bed. Sleep with your mates. Let us help remind you just how important you are to that family."

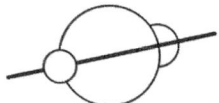

Approaching the facility, I'm pleased to see the two construction bots outside, rolling slowly out from under the overhang. I bring the Wanderer around and land it as close as I can, with the aft loading ramp facing the bots. Before I can even get out of the pilot's seat, Aime sends a transmission, redirecting them to the hold.

When I reach the aft hold, Tareth heads down the ramp ahead of me and looks around. Following him down, I find Darren watching the bots lumber slowly towards us. "Looks like we'll be here about an hour, we'll miss lunch," he states.

"Zoe packed us some sandwiches and drinks."

"She doesn't think we can use the converters?"

I chuckle. "She says it doesn't taste as good. Personally, I can't tell the difference, but I'm not going to argue."

He laughs, but it fades fast, leaving him looking solemn.

"What's wrong?"

He shakes his head. "I'm not sure. Last night, Nanai started acting...I don't know, weird."

"What happened?"

He gives me a hesitant look. "Uh, she started...licking me, every-where."

"Sounds like she might be going into heat, and felt compelled to bathe you."

His eyes go wide, then a slight smile emerges. "Oh."

Unable to help myself, I laugh. "So, did you?"

He turns red. "No. She didn't quite seem herself, and I didn't want to take advantage of her like that."

"That'll happen. Talk to her about it?"

"This morning. She didn't remember doing it."

"Has she tried Nao berries?"

"What?"

"Nao berries. In cats, they take the edge off. Think of them like a kind of a libido suppressant."

"How many do they eat?"

"One usually does the trick, for cats anyway, you two may want to talk to Niku about it. She'll know what's best."

"How dangerous would it be, without that."

"Well, if she doesn't remember what she did, it probably means that her instincts took over. There could be biting, clawing, even outright fighting, hard to tell. Tayla and I tried that way once. We bit and clawed each other bloody, and didn't remember a thing in the morning. We promised each other right then, that we would not mate without her having a berry first."

His eyes go wide, but he nods. "I'll talk to Nanai, get her to talk to Niku with me."

"Good. Don't be afraid to talk to her, about anything."

He nods, and I pat him on the back, still watching the bots slowly work their way to the ramp. My smile slowly fades. "Damn they're slow."

An hour and a half later, I land the ship at the house. By the time I reach the rear cargo bay, Darren has the ramp open and the bots are already moving, slowly making their way out.

"You might as well go talk with Nanai if she's not busy."

Ziggy's voice comes out from the ship. "She is in the kitchen putting away dishes."

Darren rolls his eyes. "Thanks, Ziggy."

I chuckle as he heads off. I then turn back to the bots. "How long till they're in position?"

Aime answers, "Two hours, forty minutes."

I sigh. "Maybe we should build some new bots that can move faster."

"Well, they are over seven hundred years old, and their primary function was to tunnel out rock and install fixtures and equipment behind them."

"Can they build a better one?"

"There is a blueprint for a prototype construction bot in the core."

"Does it work?"

"The development team had completed the simulations, but had not constructed one yet."

"How soon would you be able to begin construction?"

"I can have these two start on it as soon as they're out of the ship."

"How long will it take?"

"The better part of a day, but once complete, it will operate at nearly twice the build speed, having eight industrial converters and sixteen manipulator arms. It has repulsors, as well as eight legs, so it can travel nearly as fast as Tayla on flat open ground.

"Good, do it."

I turn to watch the other bot, it takes almost five and a half hours to build one satellite. Right now, there are four finished, meter-tall, crates lined up behind it and the large rectangular converter-plate that was used for tunneling out the rock lies propped against a boulder nearby.

The door on the back opens, revealing a crate in the construct bay. A pair of arms on the back of the bot reach in and grab it, then set the crate on the ground, making five finished satellites.

I sigh heavily before turning to walk through the garage into the house.

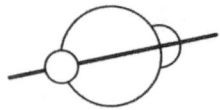

Tayla rolls over onto me, waking me up. "You know what tonight is, right?"

"How could I ever forget. It's our first anniversary, the night you confessed how you felt for me when I also realized what I felt for you."

She smiles. "That's not all, it's also New Year's Eve."

"Tomorrow *is* the first of Primense, isn't it. That means that tonight's Moonstorm will be the brightest."

She buries her nose in my neck. "Mmm-hmm."

"It's your anniversary already?" Megai groggily asks.

"Yeah, already," Tayla answers.

"When are we going to celebrate ours?"

"When you agreed to be my mate."

"When was that?"

"Hmm, let's see. It was right after we got back, roughly four in the afternoon—"

She pokes me in the ribs. "Stop playing, what day?"

"All right, it was the fifteenth of Septimense."

"How—Aime?"

"I did not remind him."

"You know, I *do* remember things when I'm not suffering from amnesia." They both giggle, snuggling into me, so I hug them both warmly. "I wonder what Niku has planned for tonight."

"I'm more worried what she had Zoe make," Tayla adds.

"I don't know if Niku would have done anything like that. Fey or Sada though..."

"Where is she anyway?" Megai asks.

"She was gone when I woke up," Tayla states.

"That can't be good, well, not for us anyway."

"You've known her the longest," Megai states, giving me a kiss. "Time to face the day."

I quickly return her kiss and let her get up as I turn my attention to Tayla. "Happy first anniversary, my love."

She gives me a kiss and purrs. "Mmm, and to you."

I scrub the back of her neck and then roll out of bed. I take a quick shower and dress. After helping Megai brush her back, I turn my attention to Tayla, fresh from her shower, and start brushing her back. About the time I think the cubs should be awake, Sada comes in from the nursery, looking rather disheveled and tired.

"How long have you been in there?" Tayla asks.

She gives us a weary look. 'Half the night, Kuma didn't want to sleep.'

"Why didn't you wake one of us?"

"Yeah, he usually goes right to sleep for me," I add.

'Too tired, I slept in there on the couch. He slept against me.'

"Don't do that too much, you'll spoil him," Tayla states as she steps over to her dresser.

I let her long tail slide between my fingers as she goes. "Are they up?" I ask.

Sada nods and heads into the grooming room for a shower. Megai turns back to us. "I guess she didn't plan anything after all."

"At least this morning," I point out.

Hearing some chirps, we head into the nursery and find the cubs wide awake. I quickly check Kuma's diaper and find that it's clean, so I scoop him up in my arms. I then look to Tayla, who's wrinkling her nose at Tashi. "I think your sister gave mom a stinky."

"Did she ever," Tayla gasps, trying not to breathe. Megai quickly steps over with a clean diaper and some wipes and helps clean the cub. As I wait, Kuma plays with my fingers, occasionally licking or even chewing on them.

Megai comes up holding Tashi. "Ready?" Kuma stops trying to chew on my finger and tries to look in her direction. Not seeing her, he chirps to get her attention.

She looks at him curiously. "Are you ready for breakfast?"

To answer her question, he starts trying to chew on my fingers again. "I'll take that as a yes," she chuckles.

Breakfast is a buffet, and I start with some fruit-filled pastries and juice. I also get a bottle for Kuma and let him drink it while I eat.

Megai gets a bottle for Tashi but gets herself eggs, toast, nakku bacon, and juice. She sits next to me and starts on her own breakfast. When Sada comes in she looks refreshed, but when she gets her breakfast, she seems to randomly grab things, coming up with some fruit, chocolate syrup on bacon, a pastry, and some eggs with orange jam on them.

When she sits down, Tayla sees her plate. "Hun, you really need to get some sleep. You do know what you grabbed?"

'Don't care. Too tired.'

"It shows."

Having finished my own breakfast, I sit back, still holding Kuma, and watch everyone else eat.

When Railu and Roen come in, he's carrying Ru. He waits for Railu to get her breakfast and after she gets situated, passes Ru to her to nurse and gets his own breakfast.

When Fey comes in, she's smiling happily. I look down at my son, and whisper, "I think your sister is up to something."

He looks up at me with his bright blue eyes and chirps, reaching for my fingers again.

I grab his teething ring, and head for the hall. After sitting on a couch, I hold it where he can grab it. Seeing it, he chirps and kicks excitedly.

"Here it comes." I watch his eyes as they get wider as I move it closer. He grabs the ring from me and starts happily chewing on it as he purrs. I occasionally pull at it, encouraging him to hold it. He chirps again, so I stop tugging and let him gnaw on it.

Megai and Tayla come in and sit next to me. I see Megai glow as she looks at Tashi, so I lean over to her. "Are you sure you don't want one of your own?

"I've been thinking about it. Maybe when these two are a little bigger, but I'm beginning to see their charm."

"It's more than that, you get to see a part of yourself live on," Tayla states.

"Don't think you will have a difficult pregnancy either," Railu adds as she sits across from us. "I'm just special."

We all chuckle at that, and Megai jokes, "And you like it that way."

"Normally, I'd agree with you."

"Oh, you know I'm kidding," she chuckles. She looks back at the Tashi, snuggled her arms, and gently rubs the cub's head, making her purr. "I want to, but not yet."

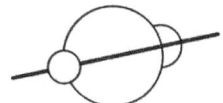

Having finished loading the few finished satellites in the back of the Wanderer, I walk through the house to the front yard. It's near dark, and Fey has yet to surprise us. Niku, though, has set up for the Moonstorm celebration, something that her home village, Three Lands, is known for, and Zoe has prepared a special feast for supper at her request.

As I exit the house, I see the tables and chairs set up facing southeast. Nanai and Kosh are both helping set up tableware for the meal, while the huskies stand near opposite ends of the yard. With dusk approaching, they're watching for viper lizards and other predators.

The cubs try to crawl around in a small outdoor playpen. I find myself marveling at how quickly they grow, barely ten weeks old and already trying to crawl. Railu sets Ru down with the cubs and they start chirping happily. The kit starts happily yipping back. This draws Oana's attention and she comes over and leans over the short side of the pen.

The little ones start all reaching for her nose and she slowly lets them all touch her as she coos.

"I think she wants one of her own," I state, as I sit next to Megai.

"Maybe. She's still happy though."

"Yeah, I can't quite shake what Tessha said though, about her not wanting what I offer."

"You offer her a lot."

"I think it might be the freedom."

"She's afraid of freedom?"

"I think so. She was raised as a slave, the males fought to own her. We've given her something that she's never even dreamt of having. I think that's why she still seeks approval over the things she does."

"She hasn't asked me anything for a while."

"Me neither, but what she does is things we've already approved. I've had Ziggy watching her for a while, anything we've told her to stop doing, she has completely stopped. She also hasn't tried anything new, not for some time now."

Tayla leans into me, obviously thinking. "How do we get her to want to do something on her own?"

"That, my loves, is a good question."

"Attention please," Zoe calls out. "This is our first New Year's Moonstorm buffet as a family. I hope you are all hungry." She gives Kotu a curious look.

"You know I am," he answers, drawing laughter from several of us.

I let my mates get their food as I watch the little ones play in the playpen. When Sada and Megai both sit, I stand and get my own plate. As I make my way down the buffet line, I see a large box covering something at the end of a table.

As I try to peek under, Zoe taps the box down and shakes her finger at me. "Not yet."

"Aww, just a peek?"

"No!"

I pout. "Fine." I finish filling my plate and have a seat by my mates, watching the cubs. As I eat, I see Nanai join Darren, sitting close to him as they eat.

"They're becoming quite the couple."

I smile at Tayla. "Just like we were."

"What do you mean, *were?*"

"We've come a long way this last year, two cubs, a house, and all." I give her a kiss. "We have a large family."

"And they're part of it, too," Megai adds.

"I suppose we can watch over them for a while."

"What?"

"I'm joking, they're family, they can stay as long as they like."

Zoe rings a bell, getting our attention. "Attention please, before Moonstorm begins, I'd like you to direct your attention to Fey."

"Oh no. What's she going to do?" I ask.

Tayla puts a finger over my lips. "Hush."

Fey quickly stands by Zoe. "Thanks. I know that this should really be after Moonstorm, but I'm doing it now. On this night, last year, Tayla confessed her love to my dad. That night, she became my mom. I thank them for accepting me, for accepting all of us into this family."

She pauses for a moment as Nanai and Kosh quickly hand out drinks to everyone. When they're done, they each take one for themselves and sit. She picks up her own and raises it in a toast. "To my mom and dad, Tayla and Kyle. Happy anniversary!"

As everyone raises their drinks in salute, Zoe takes the box off the end of the table. There lies a cake and two tubs of ice cream.

Fey comes over and takes Tayla and me by the hand. She winks at Megai. "I won't forget yours." She pulls us to the table, and cuts the cake, offering us the first pieces.

I take a piece of cake and offer it to Tayla. She laughs and nervously opens her mouth. I chuckle and gently feed her the piece. When she closes her mouth I quickly give her a kiss.

She smiles and blushes, then offers me a piece. I open my mouth and feel a sudden surge of mischief. "I felt that," I lightly scold.

She laughs, knowing she was caught. "All right, I won't." She offers me the cake again and places it in my mouth. Before I can close my mouth, she kisses me, slipping her tongue into my mouth. I forget about the cake in my mouth and kiss her back, enjoying the sensation.

After a moment, I break the kiss and swallow the cake. "You've been reading up on humans, haven't you?"

"I can't help it. I'm curious."

Megai comes up and gets a piece of cake and some ice cream and we start back to our chairs. Soon everyone is getting some, and occasionally looking up into the darkened sky, waiting for Moonstorm to begin.

18

Flashlight in hand and wearing treaded socks, I walk quietly through the darkened galley to the far wall. I follow it to the right and into the short hall towards the kitchen and find the ventilation duct.

"Found it."

"Lift the grate and slide it to the left."

Following the directions, the grate comes off easily, and I slide head-first into the duct.

"Now remember, the third duct to the left, then fourth to the right."

I sigh and start sliding myself forward. There's just enough room in the duct to bring my elbows under me, allowing me to slowly slide myself along.

"Tell me something, why, with all the technology, does a ship still have air ducts?" I ask as I slide myself along.

"It is a redundancy, allowing for a more uniform air quality and temperature throughout the ship."

"And if there's a hull breach?"

"The ducts have traps that detect the drop in pressure and seal automatically, just like the hatches do."

"That's very reassuring." Now at the third duct to the left, I realize that Sada should have done this, she is much more flexible. I roll to face the duct and start inching forward into it. When I get halfway in, I roll and pull my legs up and then push off the wall with my feet.

I work my way further in until I finally find the fourth one to the right. Looking at it, I sigh and tap the disk on my wrist.

Charles answers quietly, "I see there is a problem."

"Ya think? I can't fit in there," I whisper quietly.

"If you push the grenade into the duct, farther than a meter it will be close enough to work."

"Farther than a meter. *Right.*" I take the grenade, now modified for remote detonation, out of my pack. I turn it around, lift the cover, and flip the switch. Seeing the green light come on, I push it into the duck as far as I can.

"That is not far enough."

"I know Charles, my arm's only so long." I slide further up the main duct until I find the smaller duct with my foot. I start sliding myself back down, putting my leg into the duct. I find the grenade with my toes and push it further down the duct. Nearing the end of my leg's reach, I give the grenade a kick with my toes, attempting to push it farther down the duct.

"That is far enough."

"Thanks, Charles. Now, to get out of here." I slowly edge forward again, pulling my leg out of the duct as I do.

Once I've freed my leg, start shoving myself, feet first, down the duct. When my feet hit a wall, I realize that I've reached the intersection where I turned left. Being on my stomach, I roll and push my legs to the left, around the corner, and away from the way I came in. When I can, I straighten out and start sliding forward, back to the duct I entered through.

As I pass a side duct I hear some talking and stop moving.

"There's someone in here, I swear."

"You have got to be kidding, there's no AIs in this section but ours."

"I'm telling you, there has got to be someone in here, Terri heard fabric sliding on metal."

"Jace, do you see anyone? Besides, everyone on this ship has an AI, and the ship reports that there are no other AIs in this section, just ours. There's no one near us."

"Are you saying she's hearing things?"

"No, I'm saying that the ship isn't wrong. Maybe she heard the ship making some noise. It does need a lot of repairs."

"Maybe, I don't know."

"Come on, we've got to finish our rounds."

I wait for a few moments, listening for any sounds. Charles startles me when he quietly announces, "They are gone."

I exhale my relief, realizing I'd been holding my breath, and continue working my way out of the duct, back into the kitchen.

Due to my near discovery in my last outing, Charles has created an outfit out of sound-absorbing material for me. Normally something like this would be one or two pieces, but due to the power consumption needed to make it, he made it into several smaller pieces; balaclava, gloves, shirt, pants, treaded socks, and a pack.

Stopping by cargo bay seven, I pick up a few of Charles's disks and quickly retreat to the service corridors. I start making my way towards the service corridor under the bridge. I find it odd that I don't even hear myself move, no footsteps, no sounds at all when I grab something or slide my hand along a wall.

Finding the ladder into the bridge's sub-deck, I climb up and slide into the low crawl space. As I slide along, I hear the footsteps of the bridge crew as they walk around. I swallow nervously. Being this close to the people I'm hiding from makes me very nervous.

Feeling my heart pounding, I stop for a moment to get control of my nerves. After a few slow, deep breaths, I continue looking for the main wiring trunk. I slowly slide to the center of the under-deck, looking for the wide column that houses the mass of wires. Shining my flashlight around, I spot it, just forward of a mesh of support beams.

I slide myself out and around the beams to the access cover on the side. I stick the flashlight to the ceiling, facing the panel, and pull a rolled mat out of my pack. The roll is the same material that the stealth suit is made out of. I unroll the fabric mat over the access cover and its control panel, like the flashlight, it sticks by itself. I run my hand over it, smoothing it to the contour, and then draw a circle around the recessed control panel, the fabric turns clear, revealing just the control panel.

I press in the code Charles gave me to open the cover. The mat dampens the noise from both the control panel and the sound of the cover opening. I roll the mat and set it aside, and find the interface box inside. I pop that cover open and slip a finger-sized cylinder that Charles made inside. I then take one of the disks I took from Charles's box and stick it high up inside the trunk, so it's above floor level.

With both in place, I tap, my own disk, currently stuck to my cheek, near my ear. I watch as the cylinder expands and a multitude of arms come out. They start slowly sorting through the thick mass of wires, grabbing and occasionally releasing wires.

A small chirp in my ear lets me know it's in position. I close the box and then unroll the mat over opening again. I smooth the mat and draw the circle again. It clears and I press the code to close the cover.

After collecting my gear, I start sliding back to the ladder, when I hear a heavy bang from the floor above me. I stop moving instantly and listen carefully.

"Can someone explain why we are not on course?" I hear the captain loudly ask. Unfortunately, the response is too muffled by the decking for me to understand, but the captain's feelings about the response are loud and clear. A shot vibrates the decking and then something heavy lands on the floor, right above me. "Anyone else have an excuse for me?" the captain bellows.

Apparently, no one does, as he stomps from the bridge. After a moment, I hear several people run up to what landed above me and after a moment, I hear someone groan, his voice comes clearly through the decking. "I thought for sure I was dead that time."

"He's doing it on purpose. You're our last helmsmen." Her voice I recognize, it's Carrie.

"Can you persuade Kevin to get to the sensors a little quicker?"

"I'm not going to promise, but I'll talk to him."

"Thanks."

I hear something small and metallic clatter on the deck. "You want to keep this one too?" Carrie asks.

"Yeah," he sighs. I then hear some scuffling and then the sounds of footsteps walking away.

I realize that they both got up and that Carrie left the bridge. After waiting a moment, I move back to the access hatch and quickly make my way back to my room.

Having changed, I stuff the stealth suit into the pack and hang it on the door. When I turn around, Sada is sitting on the edge of the bed, looking sad.

I sit on the bed next to her. "What's wrong?"

She leans into me and sighs heavily.

"Bored?"

She shakes her head slightly.

"Lonely?"

She nods, pressing her cheek to my chest.

"I'm sorry. I just want to get things done so we're ready to go the next time we pass through an asteroid field."

She sighs but nods her understanding.

"I've done a lot in the last few days, planted several of his disks around in the ship. You've got me for a while. Is there anything you want to do?"

She sits up and smiles at me, and then she pushes me down and snuggles up to me, nuzzling her nose into my neck.

"Ah, you want to snuggle." I wrap my arm around her and start scrubbing her neck, getting her to purr. She quickly falls asleep, and her purring fades.

I keep rubbing her neck for a while, wondering if this plan to go home is going to work. After a while, I gently smooth Sada's fur and then slip out from underneath her.

Having a seat at the desk, I pick up the remote board Charles made for an escape pod. No larger than a postage stamp, and almost as thin, I marvel at how I can't see anything on it, other than some very small colored flecks in the red plastic-like material. I sigh, set down the board next to the remote, and lean back in the chair, closing my eyes.

"Kyle?"

I open my eyes, realizing that I fell asleep at the desk. "Yeah."

"I recommend you move to the bed."

"What's going on?" I ask as I move to the bed.

"We are entering an asteroid field."

"Should we get to the cargo bay?"

"No. This is a rogue field, all small asteroids. The observer is much larger than they are, and we have yet to obtain the ability to travel in time."

"Oh, yeah." I reach up for the crash webbing and pull it down over us. "Thanks for the heads up."

"You are welcome. We will be entering the field in less than a minute, please brace yourselves."

Sada rolls over in my arms. I hear her huff, burying her nose in my chest. Soon thereafter, the ship starts to shutter as asteroids bounce along the hull.

While reclining in the desk chair, Sada sits sideways on my lap, reading a book. I watch her, occasionally helping her with a word she hasn't yet learned. It seems like it will be a dull day when suddenly, several people go running down the hall, right past my closed door.

Sada and I both look at the door, nervously waiting for the stampede to pass. When it finally does, I tap the disk. "Charles, what's going on?"

"I believe they are heading to the hanger."

"Hanger, this ship has fighters?"

"They are actually drones, but it is the shuttles that are being prepped."

"What are they doing?"

"I cannot be certain, but I believe they may be salvaging another ship."

"I didn't hear any guns, they find a derelict?"

"The sensors lack the clarity to be certain, but I believe we have come across a cargo ship.

"Any idea what it was carrying?"

"Without the transponder signal, no, but the shuttle crews are loading up the few labor bots we have."

"Expecting to do some work. How many shuttles are they taking?"

"All five of them."

"How many people does that leave on the ship?"

"Ten, and they are all on the bridge."

"Let me know when they're all on their way, now would be a perfect time to install the remote." Sada hops up, grabs the pack of the door, and tosses it to me. I quickly put the stealth suit on and scoop up the small remote board from the desk.

"The last shuttle has left the hanger," Charles states.

I give Sada a kiss. "That's my cue." I sling the pack over my shoulder and head out the door. "Charles, keep me advised if someone leaves the bridge or comes back."

"Certainly."

Charles had indicated that the most likely pod for distraction was one of the ones just below the bridge. To get there, I head aft at a near run and descend down two levels by sliding down the handrails of the ladders. After landing, I turn and run to the bow, nearly a half click away.

When I reach the end of the corridor, I stop and catch my breath. "I'm at the bow, now where."

"The door to your left, you will need to remove the panel cover."

I quickly pull off my pack and get out the tools. Using a small pry-bar, I pop the cover off of the control panel and let it hang by its wires. I then use a pair of extractors to pull a red chip from its slot. I take the remote chip from my pouch and insert it into place.

"Charles, it's in."

"Running diagnostic...Complete. All functions pass."

I smack the panel back in place, put my things back in the pack and start running back to my cabin. For once I make it there without incident and quickly get out of the stealth suit and pack it up. Sada comes out of the bathroom and hands me a towel.

I give her a playful scowl. "Are you trying to tell me something?"

She nods her head, but her tail tells me she's playing.

I laugh. "I did just run a kilometer, you know." She smiles and nods so I head into the bathroom for a shower. By the time I emerge, Sada is playing solitaire and Charles is watching, helping with an occasional move.

I finish drying my hair as I watch. Realizing how long it's starting to get, I walk over to the converter and have it make a hair tie. I then comb out my hair and tie it back in a ponytail. Sada gives me a curious look and then smiles.

"What? You like my hair pulled back?" She nods happily and returns to her game, occasionally glancing up at me. I have a seat opposite her and watch her finish out the hand.

"The shuttles are returning."

"Already?"

"Yes, apparently, they found nothing major of interest, aside from some fuel."

"I wonder how upset the captain's going to get over that."

"I am unsure if he will get upset at all. I do not think he was expecting to find this derelict."

"What makes you say that?"

"We are only in this area due to the course correction."

"How far off course were we?"

"Several hundred light-years."

"How long were we off course?"

"Almost a week."

I sit in awe for a moment. "Uhm, how fast can this ship go?"

"This ship uses an Einstein drive, at its peak, it would be able to reach the equivalent of 3000 times light speed, however, in its current condition, it can barely reach half that."

"So how long will it take to get to our intended destination?"

"Another four days of travel."

Sada gives me a curious look, so I ask, "Where're we going?"

"Boreas."

"Sounds cold."

"It is. The warmest temperature recorded is 70 below."

"Celsius?"

"Correct. The planet is largely uninhabitable, but there are a few settlements around the equator, under thermal domes."

"Any idea what he wants there?"

"Apologies, no, and until we are within range, I will not be able to determine what year it is either."

I slouch back in the chair and sigh. It's getting hard to determine the year we're in because we keep getting further out from the more populated systems. Without that knowledge, an escape would be near pointless as we'd have no idea how far back we'd need to go. After a while, I notice that Charles's avatar is watching me.

"Kyle? Are you all right?"

"Yeah, I'm good. I just hope we have a time reference when it's time to leave."

"I would not let you go if I did not have that."

"Charles, can I ask you something?"

"I find that question odd since you just did, but yes, please."

"No offense, but why are you so interested in helping me, and making sure I'm safe?"

"None taken. I expected this question long ago. As an AI, I am programmed to preserve life. So naturally, your well-being is a priority. In regards to our current situation, though, I am more interested in your wellbeing than that of the command crew, due largely in part to the fact that they should not have me. As I am currently stolen property, and you both are kidnapped, we are allies."

"Do you want to get out of here like I do?"

"While I do want to get out, I would not endanger you by coming with. The captain would search for me, as I am needed to use the gates."

I sigh. "I was thinking about taking you with me, but after you said that..."

"I appreciate your offer, but I must remain here, besides, who would look after the others."

"Others?"

"The Aquanatum, Mike, Carrie, and the rest of the crew.

I sigh, realizing that my wanting to leave is selfish. "Is there anything we can do for them before I leave?"

"I have had you doing that already."

"Planting your disks and the little robot thing."

"Correct. I can now interface with most of the ship's systems. If needed, I can actually shut down the ship, but for now, I'm simply monitoring all activity and attempting to correct the course when possible."

"I'm sure the helmsman appreciates that," I sigh, and watch Sada deal out another hand of solitaire.

19

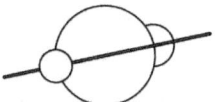

With the new construction bot and two labor bots completed, the production of the satellites is at full speed. When one of the slow, treaded bots set a crate out and the two, four-legged, four-armed labor bots scurry over to pick it up. They quickly deposit it neatly in the rear hold of the Wanderer and then return to the base of the ramp to wait for the next one.

As I watch from the garage, I play idly with my signet, not one of the many copies I've made, but the original, the one that I found in the storage compartment of my cryo-tube. Hearing Tayla walk up behind me, I turn and look back at her.

She looks curiously at me for a moment. "What're you thinking about?"

I sigh, putting my arm around her as I look back to the construction bots. "If you felt another presence, through our link, would you tell me?"

She gives me a surprised look. "Of course, but how would that happen? We share our link because we bonded."

"When Sada and I escaped, I felt something, and she did too. I'd forgotten all about it but when Cayla found that notation about the Obsession, it got me thinking about the things that happened. I had no way to describe what it was then, but now…Tayla if you feel something, anything unusual, let me know as soon as you can."

She rests her head on my shoulder and purrs. "I will, but what would it mean?"

"Because that means that you're feeling the other Sada and me, and they'll be on the Obsession."

Feeling my worry, she stops purring but wraps her arm around me. "How long did you feel the link?"

"It started two days before we escaped."

"How long after?"

"Not long, we set the timer for a time jump, and then we were gone. I'm not sure how long it took the ship to get to the planet."

She starts purring again and nuzzles into me. "You'll be ready. I know it."

I smile and give her a curious look. "I know you haven't had a vision since we bonded."

"No, not a vision. Faith. We believe in you, even if you don't."

I give her a kiss and hug her close. "Thank you."

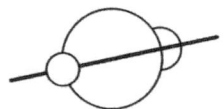

I sit in my office, holding Tashi, as I read a transcript from Arru's meeting with the council in Three Lands. She had helped negotiate a trade deal between them and Arindell and I wanted to review some of the finer details.

Tashi squirms in my arms as she chews on her teething ring. I look down at her and smile. "What? You trying to get my attention?" She looks up at me with her golden eyes and chirps happily. I grin at her and she smiles, dropping her teething ring and reaching for my face.

I set the tablet aside on my desk and hold her up so she can reach my face. As I gently blow into her fur, she giggles and tries to nibble my nose.

"What are you doing?" I playfully ask her, and then give her a kiss on her muzzle. She squeals and kicks happily as she plays with my face. I find it pleasantly surprising that she is not scratching me with her claws as she grabs at my ears and nose. I lean back in my chair, and lay her down on my chest, and let her paw at me.

As she plays, I see Oana peek through the doorway to watch her play.

"What'ya want?" I ask.

"Oana watch?"

My curiosity peaked as to her asking permission, I ask, "Why?"

She sighs, and then steps into my office, up to the desk. "Oana curious."

"About?"

She tilts her head, thinking, then asks, "Why Tashi Kuma smell like Kyle, not look like Kyle?"

I smile, knowing what she means. "Aime made me like a male cheetah for the night, so Tayla and I could have children."

She tilts her head the other way and makes a couple of clicks. "Oana understand. Can Aime do same for Megai?"

"Yes."

"Why Megai not have child?"

"She's not ready."

"Oana not understand."

"Megai does not want to have a child yet."

"Does Kyle want child with Megai?"

"When she's ready, yes."

"Why Kyle not make Megai ready?"

"I can't do that, only Megai can make herself ready."

She thinks for a moment, gently clicking her claws together. "Oana not understand."

I sit up, holding Tashi to me. "Oana, Megai has to decide for herself when she wants a child. I do not own her, it's her choice. Tayla wanted to have children, that was both her choice and mine."

"Oana not understand."

I sigh, remembering the words she used when we found her. "Kyle sae ta-Kyle. Tayla sae ta-Tayla. Megai sae ta-Megai."

She looks curiously at me, obviously thinking about what I just said. After a few moments, she nods. "Oana understand."

I look at her softly, and add, "Oana sae ta-Oana."

She steps back, startled. "Oana ea-ta sae Oana."

"Yes, you can. Oana, I don't own you. I care about you, just like I do about everyone else in this house, but I don't own them either."

She looks down, then at Tashi. "Kyle own Tashi, Kuma?"

"No, I care *for* them, and just like with Kotu and Fey, they will grow up and become adults. They will be able to care for themselves, but I will still care *about* them."

She sighs. "Oana care about Kyle."

"I care about you too, we all do, but you do need to start caring for yourself."

"Oana not adult."

Her comment catches me by surprise. "What do you mean?"

"Oana not adult, Oana not have k'uu'te yet."

"K'uu'te?"

"Oana get k'uu'te when ready to mate."

"What's k'uu'te?"

"K'uu'te start at Oana head and end at tail. K'uu'te have colors, and look like fur."

I step around the desk and run my free hand down her back, following her spine. "What happens after you get your k'uu'te?"

"Oana make nest, have eggs."

"I am detecting some unusual new growth, Oana I believe your k'uu'te will be growing soon," Aime states.

She straightens, noticeably surprised. "Oana rearrange room!"

As she turns, I catch her tail to keep it from hitting Tashi. "Oana, your tail has some unusual new growth, also," Aime announces

"Oana tail have what?"

"Your tail will have something too," I repeat. "It'll be interesting to see what."

She pulls her tail around and looks closely at it. "Oana not see tail change on males."

"Maybe it only happens on females. Have you seen a female with a tail, or a male with k'uu'te?"

"Males not get k'uu'te, females not allowed tails."

"Well, you are, so no biting it, okay."

She nods. "Oana try," and leaves.

I sit back down and look at Tashi, who's fallen asleep in my arm. "She's got a lot to learn about freedom," I whisper to her. "She'll do fine though. I think she's finally starting to understand what it means."

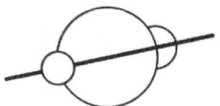

Sitting in Niku's patient room, she watches as I pull a glass bottle out of the portable nano converter. Looking through the clear glass, I see a thick, grey fluid. "This is it?"

"Correct, that is Darren's AI," Aime states.

I open the case for the nano injector and pick up the gun. After loading the bottle, I load a bottle of carrier solution and another of general-purpose nanites. I set that next to the AI tether and wait for Nanai to come back with Darren.

Niku turns to me. "What, exactly am I supposed to do again?"

"Since I'll be tethered to Darren, if Aime needs anything, you'll need to get it."

"Can't Nanai do that?"

"In the off chance that something goes wrong, I'd prefer someone who can keep their calm."

She nods. "That, I can do."

As she sits, Nanai comes through the door followed closely by Darren. Both look confused. "You wanted to see me?" Darren asks.

"I have the first half of a gift for you two."

"Really?" Darren asks.

"Yep, have a seat." I gesture to the vacant reclining chair next to me. Nanai looks at me. "What's the surprise?"

Niku picks up the injector and smiles. "This."

"Darren, you wanted an AI, this is the first one to have the ability to allow humans to have young with other species."

He smiles. "What do I need to do?"

I give him a quick look and sigh. "I should have told you to wear shorts. Take your shirt and pants off, and get comfortable, we'll be here for a while."

He hesitates, and the way Nanai smiles at him makes me chuckle.

Niku retrieves a pair of shorts and hands them to him. "You humans are easily embarrassed."

He blushes as he steps behind a screen to change. When he comes out, he blushes again and then sits back in the chair. Nanai pulls a chair alongside him and takes hold of his hand.

Niku hands me the tether, and I attach it to Darren's sternum and then to mine. I then take four of the nutrient patches and stick them to his shoulders and thighs.

"What are those?" Nanai asks curiously.

"Nutrient patches, they'll provide the nanites some extra raw material when they're injected."

"Injected?" Darren nervously asks.

"Yeah," I confirm, then noticing his expression, I add, "Relax, you won't feel a thing."

Niku hands me the injector and I set it for the general nanites and give him a shot through all four patches.

"What were those?"

"Regular nanites. They'll help build your AI."

He nods. "Oh."

I make a few more adjustments to the injector, setting it for the AI solution and reducing the injection speed. "Ready?"

Niku adds a patch to each side of his neck. He nods and slowly exhales, trying to relax.

"Close your eyes, take another deep breath," I hold the injector to the side of his neck. "Now let it out, slowly." As he exhales, I squeeze the trigger. The injector shoots a steady stream of the AI solution into his neck making a small, marble-sized bubble. I repeat the process on the other side of his neck. I then set it aside and hold my hands on each side of his head. Aime shows me the nanites as they diffuse into his head and start to construct the matrix.

"Let me know if you feel anything."

"Okay."

We sit like this for several minutes, practically motionless as Aime instructs the nanites through the tether. I watch as the matrix begins to form along the inside of his skull.

Nearly an hour in, Aime prompts for another set of injections. I ready the injector and have him repeat the controlled breaths as I administer more solution to each side of his neck. I return my hands alongside his head and continue to watch the AI form.

After nearly four hours, and several more injections, Darren's AI is formed enough to take over and continue its own construction. I place another set of nutrient patches over his stomach and the palms of his hands. After adjusting the settings on the injector again, I inject a mix of general-purpose nanites and AI nanite solutions through the patches.

After a few more minutes I give a second injection, to his stomach, which empties the AI solution bottle. I hand the injector to Niku and she removes the bottles, places them into the nano converter for it to refill. She then places the injector and the refilled bottles in the case and closes it up.

Having seen Niku put up the injector, he looks curiously at me. "Are we done?"

"Not quite. Aime's transferred the build programs to your incomplete matrix. It'll take another twelve hours for it to finish. Then it'll start to calibrate itself to you and then run an orientation program. The whole process will be about a day total."

"Then what?"

"Then, you'll have your own AI."

"So, it'll be Aime's child. I'll be part of the family?"

I smile, not having thought of it that way. "Yes, yes you will. I'll want you to check in with me every couple hours until it's completely set up."

He smiles. "Thank you."

"Yes, thank you," Nanai agrees.

"You're both welcome." I look up at Nanai. "We're still working on yours, so, please be patient. I thank you for letting me do the neural scan, it helped tremendously."

"Thank you." She gives me a light bump with her nose.

I start pulling the nutrient patches off Darren. "Go, get dressed, enjoy the day but remember to check back with me in a couple hours."

"I'll do that." He steps behind the screen and gets dressed, and they both disappear out the door.

Niku sits next to me and sighs. "That was boring."

"For you and them, but I'm beat, and Aime's almost out of power."

"Sounds like you two did all the work. Feel like a power shake?"

"Sure." Niku's power shake used to taste like mud. Aime helped her develop it when I almost died, but since then, they've made it taste like mint chocolate, rather than the mud, it originally tasted like.

She smiles and retrieves it from her converter, sticks a bendable drinking straw in it, and hands it to me. I chuckle and accept it gladly. "Thank you for letting me do this here."

"It's your house."

"But this is *your* workspace."

She smiles. "I didn't have any clients today anyway. It was my pleasure to witness."

"Well, I hope that you'll witness more and that Cayla and Marc will help with the installations. Do two at a time instead of one."

"That would be less boring," she chuckles.

I find myself chuckling with her as I take another drink of the shake.

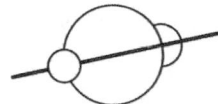

Having just reached orbit in the Wanderer, I sit in the pilot's seat plotting the best path to take. Tareth sits at the sensor station, keeping an eye out the front window, and the other on the doors behind me.

I open the com to both Cayla and Darren. "Ready?"

"This feels odd," Darren responds.

"Wait till you're in zero-G," Cayla chuckles.

"Opening forward and rear bays," I state. I watch from the pilot's seat as the lights indicate open hatches. Darren's in the forward bay with one of the labor bots ready to collect the old satellites, while Cayla's in the rear bay with another bot ready to deploy the new ones. Both are wearing a copy of my medium armor, with full helmets, as spacesuits.

"First satellite coming into view," I call out.

"Ready for capture."

"Ready for deploy."

"Slowing for capture."

"Deploying in 3...2...1...Satellite away."

"Satellite captured."

"Satellite reports; fully deployed and in position."

"Moving to next position."

"Ready to deploy."

"Slowing for deploy."

"Deploying in 3...2...1...Satellite away."

"Satellite coming into view."

"Satellite reports; fully deployed and in position."

"Ready for capture."

"Slowing for capture."

"Ready to deploy"

"Satellite captured."

"Deploying in 3...2...1...Satellite away."

This continues like a carefully orchestrated ballet between the three of us. Thanks to our AIs, the job is much easier, getting the timing right, finding the next deploy or capture position, and making sure the correct satellite gets deployed.

After nearly six hours, Cayla announces our completion, by saying, "Deploying last satellite in 3...2...1...final satellite away."

"Satellite reports; fully deployed and in position. Net registers complete. Closing fore and aft bays."

"Pressurizing aft bay, returning to the bridge."

"Pressurizing forward bay, coming up."

"Setting course for home."

When they both come in, Darren sets his helmet in the chair next to him. "Thanks for telling me not to eat anything."

"Did Sarah keep you from throwing up?" Cayla asks.

"Yeah, barely."

"She's young. She'll learn," I add.

"Don't be afraid to ask her for help."

"Or more help, if she didn't do enough."

"I get it, or is it 'we?'"

"She's a part of you," Cayla states, "just like Marc is a part of me, singular is fine."

He nods. "I'm learning."

"Speaking of learning, would either of you be interested in learning how to pilot?"

Cayla chuckles, but Darren gives me a thoughtful look. "I've been thinking about it. It'd take a load off you, and I'd start to feel more useful around the house."

"Chauffeur...huh. Well, you're right. It would allow me to do other things if I don't need to go with. Good thing I don't have a rule about fraternizing with co-workers."

Cayla laughs. Darren and I quickly join in. Tareth even grins.

"When you're ready, let me know. Aime will send Sarah the training."

"Would it be safe? Wouldn't overload her or something?"

Cayla answers as I bring the ship in for a landing. "She can handle a lot more than you think, despite her being young."

As we exit the ship, we find Nanai waiting for us just inside the garage. She walks up to Darren and tries to take a piece of his spacesuit off, but when she can't, she gets a little upset.

"Sarah, why won't you let me take his helmet off?"

"She's only looking out for her host," Cayla explains.

"But Aime answers to your mates," Darren states, looking at me, puzzled.

"She does because I've named them my executors."

"Executors?"

Cayla steps over. "Be careful with that route though, who you name will have almost as much control over your AI as you do."

"What's that mean?"

"It means, you better trust whoever you name with your life," I state.

Nanai dons an innocent look as Darren looks at her curiously, apparently trying to decide how much he can trust her.

I pat him on the shoulder. "No one is going to expect an answer now. Take your time, think about it."

He sighs, looking into Nanai's eyes as he pulls her close. "I don't need to."

"Why?" Cayla asks him.

"I put my life in her hands every night. Sarah, I name Nanai as my executor."

She squeals happily and uses one of my tricks. "Armor off."

Darren's armor drops off him and she wraps him in a hug, nuzzling into his neck as best she can.

"Now all that's left is for you to declare each other mates," I chuckle.

Darren looks at her with a big smile. "You want to?"

She gasps, covering her mouth with her hands. "Now?"

"Why not?" He pulls her close. "Nanai, I love you. I know it's a little sudden, but I can't think of a reason not to ask." He clears his throat and takes her hands. "Will you be my mate?"

She blushes and looks at me, I hold my hands up. "Your life, your choice. I have no say either way."

She sighs, and turns back to him, looking down with her ears slanted back. I watch her tail slowly droop as she chews her bottom lip in thought. "I can't yet bear your young."

"That doesn't matter. I love you."

"Then let us be mates." She reaches up, puts her muzzle to his lips as he kisses her.

As I smile, I glance at Cayla and see her sniffle. "Are you okay?"

"Yeah," she manages to whisper. "It's sweet, isn't it?"

"Sure is. Ziggy, tell Zoe we'll need to have a union ceremony for them."

"I already have."

"Is he always presumptuous?"

"Only when he's sure of something."

With everyone seated at the dining table, awaiting supper, I take Nanai's hand and lead her out of the kitchen. I sit her next to Darren at the table. I put each hand on their shoulders. "I'm sure you are all wondering what I'm up to. Cayla and I had the honor of witnessing something earlier, something that I will now share with the rest of you."

Darren suddenly stands. "Please, let me." I nod to him and take a step back. He takes Nanai's hand and she stands, bashfully stepping up to his side. "Nanai has agreed to be my mate."

Several clap and I hear a few express their congratulations. Tayla though voices a reminder. "Don't forget Darren, you're her mate too."

He nods as he looks into Nanai's eyes. "I know, and I appreciate that. I really do."

"All right, have a seat. Today is your union, so, let's celebrate."

On cue, Zoe and Kosh come out, followed by Tita, Janik, and two others from Tita's inn, all carrying food and drinks. As they start serving Darren and Nanai, I quickly find my seat.

"This was sweet of you," Megai whispers to me.

"I'm really glad Tita didn't have any customers today, but, you know me, I appreciate my family."

"Technically, they're employees."

"If you treat your employees like family, they want to stay. So as far as I'm concerned, they're family."

Tayla leans over to us. "Are you two gonna eat?"

"All right, we'll eat. Wouldn't want these barbequed ma'pai to go to waste, would we," I admit.

"Like that would happen with Kotu around," Megai jokes lightly.

"I heard that!" Kotu calls, prompting us to laugh.

We finish the main course with little talk. Two of the servers collect the used dishes and replace them with clean ones. The others clear the leftovers and then quickly bring out another cart. On the cart is a near traditional three-tiered wedding cake, with yellow and light blue icing accents, but I can tell from where I sit, that it has real, light yellow flowers decorating it.

I see Nanai tear up as Zoe and Kosh move the cart in front of her and Darren. "It's beautiful. Zoe, I..."

Zoe puts a finger to Nanai's muzzle, hushing her. "It's the least I could do for you and your mate."

Kosh hands Darren a cake server and a plate. Darren looks curiously at it. "What do I do with this?"

Nanai chuckles and takes it from him and cuts two small pieces from the cake. She then takes a piece in hand and tries to feed it to him. She has a rather difficult time, as she keeps giggling, shaking her hand as she does. This makes her giggle more and Darren tries to catch her arm to help guide her. When he does, we cheer as he eats the cake from her fingers.

She tries to get a hold of herself long enough for him to feed her the other piece, but she has trouble holding still and he ends up missing, smearing icing across her nose. He grabs a napkin and wipes her nose clean. She then manages to get a hold of herself long enough for him to feed her the rest. We all cheer and then laugh as they kiss each other.

Zoe gives them a whole piece of cake each, and then she and Kosh proceed to serve everyone else cake, including themselves. The little ones even get a piece of cake. Like her mother, Ru has a taste for chocolate. Kuma, though, is partial to the icing, happily wearing more than he eats.

As we finish, we move to the great hall and Ziggy starts playing some of the traditional union music that Tria's found. Everyone takes turns dancing with either or both Nanai and Darren.

Having been the first to dance with Nanai, I quietly sneak out of the hall. *Aime, is it ready?*

"Of course."

I make my way to cold storage and the oversized converter. There, I find the large package waiting for me. I carefully pick it up and make my way to Nanai's room, which she and Darren have been sharing for a month. Ziggy, lets me in, and I place the package on the floor, in the middle of the room. I check the position of the card, making sure it's easily visible.

Satisfied, I quickly return to the hall and rejoin the party. I realize my absence was noticed when Tayla finds me and asks, "Where'd you go?"

"I dropped off their gift."

"Why give a gift?" she asks, curiously.

"Human tradition. I'll tell you later what's in it."

"I think I like that tradition."

"Me too," Megai adds stepping up beside us.

The party lasts well into the night until Darren and Nanai both retire for the evening. After bathing the cubs, we call it a night too.

I get comfortable and Megai snuggles up alongside me. "So, what'd you give them?"

"There's a photo album, with pictures from today and other times they've been together, all taken by Ziggy or Aime. There's also a new set of matching signets for them, a nice matched set of combs and brushes, and a few other things I'm certain they'll appreciate. I also gave them a week off."

As Tayla snuggles up to me, she purrs. "That was thoughtful of you."

Megai sighs heavily as Sada snuggles up against her. "Good night, my loves," she manages to say.

I gently kiss her forehead, pulling them all to me. "Good night."

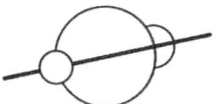

Having been the last to get into the shower, I make my way to breakfast by myself. Hearing gentle footsteps behind me, I turn to see Nanai and Darren, also making their way to breakfast.

"Morning," I gently call to them.

Nanai rushes up and wraps me in a hug. "Thank you!"

I happily return her hug. "You're welcome." I look up to see that Darren is wearing his new signet, and as she pulls away, so is Nanai. "How do you like them?"

She touches the signet. "They're beautiful, with just enough of yours to let others know we're with your house."

"I thought you'd like that. Did you notice that Ziggy changed your door?"

"No, I didn't."

"I did," Darren states. "It says 'Darren and Nanai' now instead of just Nanai."

"He's also put your signet there, above your names, so it's both your rooms now, and, when the time comes, the room next door can be a nursery."

"Oh, did you finish it?" Nanai asks, suddenly full of hope.

"Sadly no, but I'm still working on it. I won't give up, I promise."

She gives me another hug. "Thank you."

"Come on, let's go get some breakfast."

She lets go of me and takes Darren's hand as we continue our way to the dining room.

20

Lifting the crash webbing, I roll out of bed. As I walk to the converter, I realize something and stop. I turn around and look back at the bed, realizing that I didn't pull the webbing down when I went to sleep. I look at Charles's avatar and see that it's also not how I last saw it, its hands are gripping the table legs, holding it in place.

"Charles? Was there a battle or something?"

The avatar lets go of the table and adjusts itself in the chair. "Yes, I am surprised that you both slept through it."

I sigh, clear indication that you've been through too many battles is when you sleep through one. "What's that make, twenty in the last month?"

"It has only been twelve," he corrects.

"Seems like more than that." I press the button on the converter. "Four sausage links, two pancakes, liter of maple syrup, glass of orange juice." I watch the breakfast materialize and set it on the table. As I start to eat, I ask, "Is there anything I need to do today?"

"Not unless something comes up. All my disks still work and I still have a full interface. Surprisingly, the damage we received this time was negligible."

"How'd the web get pulled?"

"You pulled it down, do you not remember?"

I swallow a bite of pancake, looking curiously at the webbing, and sigh. "Not in the slightest."

"You are becoming desensitized."

"Figured that," I sigh as Sada stirs, awakened by the smell of my breakfast. I watch her shake her fur loose and head to the bathroom.

"We also keep running out of things to do. I think we're getting depressed."

"I would not be surprised, being cooped up like you are."

I step over to the converter and call up Sada's favored breakfast; breaded fish and cheese sticks. As I set the plate down, she comes out and sits across from me, sighing heavily.

"We really need to get you both off this ship."

"Yeah." I finish off my breakfast and put my dishes in the converter. Sada gives me a sleepy look as she plays with her breakfast. "If you're not hungry, you don't need to eat." She sighs but starts to slowly eat.

"Charles, is there anything that we can do on this ship that we haven't done already?"

"You have been to both the garden and the gym. Unfortunately, the pool is exposed to vacuum. Aside from coming up with something new on your own, I am sorry, no."

Sada and I both sigh heavily. I realize that our frustration is more than the obvious two—the first being that there's not much to do on the ship, to begin with, and second, that we have to be extra careful when we do go out—it's the ever-present fact that we care greatly for each other, and can't fully express it, that's the biggest problem

To me, she stopped being a pet a long time ago, when she was still just a cat, she was my companion. I valued her as a friend then like I do now, but now, she's more than that. She's able to do more, experience life in a whole new way, and we're stuck on this ship.

Charles thankfully interrupts my musing. "The time device has been activated, please move to the bed."

Sada and I quickly jump on the bed, insulating us from the building charge. I watch as Charles's avatar starts twitching, its servos shedding the excess charge through movement.

"Maybe you should've insulated that thing," I suggest.

"The insulation needed a lot of power, so I designed it to twitch instead."

"I know, but, it's creepy looking enough when it's just sitting still."

Sada nods and finishes her breakfast as she sits next to me on the bed. Setting the plate aside, she leans back against me and we wait quietly for Charles to let us know it's safe.

After several minutes wait, my boredom gets the better of me. "I wish we'd grabbed the cards." Sada sighs and nods her agreement.

"Charles, what's taking so long?"

"I am not sure, but I believe we are traveling backward in time a considerable distance."

"I wonder what he's after now."

"We will soon find out, the field is starting to dissipate."

The ship shudders as the engines disengage. With everything now silent, I ask, "Any idea what's going on?"

"I cannot find a time base or any stray signals at all."

"What? Even in my time, we've been sending signals out into space."

"I know, but we could be before then. I am trying to extrapolate our temporal position based on the position of known stars."

"Any luck?"

"I have been able to narrow it down somewhat. I believe we are in Earth's late Pleistocene epoch."

I look curiously at Charles's avatar. "That's a long time ago. What could he be after?"

"Unsure, but we are nowhere near Earth."

I frown. "What's present in the past, that's not in the future."

"I cannot answer that. With the number of planets discovered, narrowing it down to something specific is next to impossible. I will need to determine what planet or system we arrive at, or just wait until we pick something up to determine what."

"That was more of a rhetorical question."

"Oh. It is now safe to get off the bed. The charge has dissipated."

Sada hops down off the bed and puts her plate in the converter. I move to the desk and turn on the screen. "Can you show me where we are?"

"Certainly." The screen changes, showing a rough diagram of the nearby systems.

"Has our course changed since we arrived?"

"No."

"Plot our course." A line appears, indicating our current direction. I see immediately that it's not straight. It turns slightly, apparently affected by gravity. "Okay, how does this area compare to the time we just came from?"

"The systems have moved considerably."

"Show me." the screen splits, with the current on the left and a new, completely different view on the right. "What's this?" I ask, pointing to a small swirl that, on the future map, would have been in front of us.

"It is a black hole."

"Where is it now?" the current map expands out to full screen and the visible area expands to show its current location, highlighted with a crosshair.

"I am detecting a course correction. Your hunch was correct. We are going to the black hole."

"What could he want with a black hole?" I lean back in my chair, thinking.

"I have been searching the few available records, I discovered this still picture." The screen changes suddenly, showing a blue haze with small hints of red lights scattered around in it. In the center of that is an odd split disk of light that swirls into a blackened center.

"Is that the black hole?"

"Yes, and there is something trapped in its gravitational pull."

"Like what?"

"The image is very low quality, but it could be a plasma storm."

I sigh. "Plasma storm around a black hole. I doubt this is for research. Would this kind of event have or generate anything special?"

"Not that I am aware of, but I would need to examine the phenomena first hand to find out. He also may also be after the plasma or something else nearby."

"True, I guess we'll need to wait till we're there." I look curiously at Sada, who's apparently given up trying to follow the conversation, and started reading yet another book. "How long will that take?"

"At current speed, three days."

"Are we there yet?"

"No, we are still outside sensor range."

"You just said we were almost there." I look at Sada, sitting on the bed with her arms crossed, and a rather annoyed look on her face.

"I apologize if I misled you, I should have stated that we had several minutes until it was in sensor range." The ship suddenly shudders hard and the engines accelerate quickly.

Catching my balance, I scramble into bed and pull the webbing down over us. "What's happening?"

"We have struck a gravitational eddy. I am assisting the helmsman with an escape trajectory."

The ship starts to vibrate harder as the engines start to fight the pull. We feel a pull to the aft, and the avatar tilts into the table. I lock the mesh down as the chairs start to slide across the floor. I hear several things hit the far wall, loose items in the next cabin. The decking rattles and all the remaining loose objects in the room slide to the aft wall.

With the shifting gravity, Sada and I are rolled across the bed. Her claws snag the covers and we get rolled together in them and hit the mesh at the edge of the bed. She huffs, irritated at our situation, but buries her face in my neck for comfort. Trapped between her and the mesh, I wiggle an arm out of the blankets and wrap it around her. She quickly covers her ears, trying to protect them from the increasing noise.

"Charles?" I shout, hoping for good news.

"We are not getting any closer. They have deployed a collection line."

"Collection line?"

"They are harvesting the heavily charged plasma from the black hole."

"How long?"

"Several more minutes, we are attempting to move out of the eddy."

"Great."

I feel Sada huff, again, into my chest. I free my other arm and hold her close. After a while, the rattling begins to increase with the engine noise. The pull on us gradually increases and I realize that we're starting to accelerate. After a few moments, the pull begins to lessen quickly, and I slowly unroll us from the covers.

"You okay?"

Sada scrubs at her ears and then shakes her head. After a moment, she gives me an annoyed look but nods. When the rattling subsides, I lift the mesh and we begin straightening up the room.

With most of the furniture back in order, I sit at the desk. "Charles, what's it look like?"

The monitor comes on, showing a moving image of the black hole. The blue plasma clouds swirl slowly around the split disks of light, red lightning flickers randomly around in the clouds.

"For being so destructive, it's beautiful. What's he need with the plasma?"

"It is heavily charged, hence the discharges. It will be used for fuel, not for the engines, but for the electrical systems."

"Recharging the batteries?"

"Simply put, but it will also let them make repairs, at least to the more critical systems."

"That'll be nice."

"Indeed."

Sada sets a bowl of the loose poker chips she's picked up on the table and starts sorting them. I turn back to the monitor, looking at the image of the black hole. "Charles, save this image for me."

"Certainly."

Sada gives me a curious look. I shrug, and start helping her sort the chips. "What? I like it."

We spend the next several days in very close proximity to the black hole. The crew has started repairs to various systems, and with the large volume of foot traffic passing by our door, we can't go out. At Charles's direction, I've covered the door and wall around it with the stealth fabric, allowing us some privacy, and security, from all the people walking by our door.

The sensors have been one of the first things repaired, and we get a clearer view of the black hole. Apparently, the type of plasma that is being consumed is not present beyond this event. Charles is still unable to figure out how the captain knew it would be here, at this specific time, but believes the information is stored only in his AI.

I sit at the desk, watching the image of the black hole, thinking about the last few days. The repairs have been less than expected, focusing more on the engines and weapons than on the sensors, shields, or any of the internal systems. I smile to myself, finding that last part somewhat refreshing. Sada and I get to keep our 'undetectable' status.

As I watch the screen, something blinks into view, appearing across the hole from us. I lean forward and try to zoom in on the image. It's vaguely conical and rather long.

"Charles, what's that?" Sada quickly joins me and looks curiously at the screen.

"That appears to be us."

"What?"

"From the appearance of that ship and the current damage that this ship has, it appears to be a past version of this ship, presumably, before you came aboard."

I think for a moment. "So he's used this gas station before. I wonder if they saw us at the time."

"Ship records indicate..." His explanation is interrupted by several bright flashes as the other ship fires a volley at us. "...that they did indeed, as you just witnessed."

The projectiles don't even get close, and I watch as the gravity of the black hole pulls them in.

"I gathered. What's the range of the guns?"

"They fire solid projectiles. In space, range and accuracy are only affected by gravitational pulls."

As I watch the screen, the other ship starts to move around the outer edge of the black hole, staying just outside of the event horizon. I hear and feel our own engines fire and we start moving, keeping our distance, opposite from them.

"This is interesting," I say, "living a history that's already happened."

"You're referring to a Novikov self-consistency principle."

Having spent some time recently, reading about time travel, I admit, "Believe it or not, I actually know that one. You're saying that anything he's done was supposed to happen, the way he did, or is going to do it?"

"Correct."

"Does the captain know that?"

"I would venture his AI does, it is instructing him right now on what to do."

I chuckle. "Making sure he does the same thing they already saw him do?"

"Yes."

Having a thought, I ask, "How much has his AI been telling him to do?"

"Unsure, while he is on the bridge, it guides him a lot, but I cannot listen in on his conversations when he is not on the bridge."

"You're calling his AI an it? I thought they had male or female personalities or at least voices."

"In their early days, they were neutral. By this ship's time though, they are always either male or female, depending on the preference of the host. His however seems to have lost that distinction. The voice it uses is mechanical like it was for the very early models."

"Odd?"

"Very. It means that whatever damaged it, has affected either its voice or whole personality."

I sit back in the chair and sigh, thinking. "Charles, has there been any signal sent from this ship to the other?"

"No, but they did try to contact us."

"Well, that I'd expect." I sigh, thinking again. "You mentioned Novikov's self-consistency principle, what if when he was on that one planet..."

"Gsharr?"

"Yes, Gsharr...he met himself, from the future?"

"There are too many paradox principals to speculate what would have happened."

"What if the only thing that happened was a data transfer."

"A bootstrap paradox?"

"Yeah, what would happen to an AI if it received a transmission from itself?"

"Standard protocol is to verify file integrity, then to track file history. The AI would most likely experience a logic loop because the originating history would be itself, and it would not have a record of originating the file. If the AI focused too much on this, it would cause a feedback loop, overloading its higher functions."

"What would that do to the host?"

"I could not be certain, but there would most likely be brain damage."

"Could this be what happened to the captain and senior crew?"

"Given our situation, it does seem likely."

"Could it...they, be fixed?"

"The AI, possibly, for the host, I would need more information about the host's damage and more medical knowledge."

"Could it happen to you?"

"Now that I know that it is a possibility, no. I will dismiss any invalid origin tags."

"You can do that?"

"Yes."

"Good. I'd hate for you to have a problem too." I sigh and look at Sada. She looks curiously at me, then back at the screen. Suddenly the engines fire again, the decking rattles subtly as the engines power up even more. "Charles?"

"We are leaving. He is also activating the time field."

Sada and I reflexively jump to the bed. I sigh heavily as I wrap her in a hug. "Here we go again."

Awakening in the middle of the night, I notice Sada sitting by the desk. Through my sleepy eyes, I see her doing something. I blink my eyes a few times, getting them to clear and I discover that she's painting.

Without sitting up, I ask, "How long have you been doing that?"

Startled, she quickly tries to hide her work, but realizing that it's too late, she gives me an angry look and huffs.

"Sorry, I have to go to the bathroom."

She sighs as I excuse myself. By the time I come back she's put her project away, apparently not wanting me to see it.

I give her a gentle kiss on the muzzle. "If you want to paint or draw, go on ahead. If you don't want me to look, I won't."

She sighs again, but nods.

I give her another kiss and a hug. "I'm glad you've found something new to try. There's no need to be embarrassed or ashamed, okay?"

She nods again and hugs me back.

"If you want to stay up and work on it, it's okay. I'm going back to sleep." As I lay back down, I watch her look at her things and then back at me, obviously thinking about what to do. After a moment, she snuggles up to me, purring, and we go back to sleep.

21

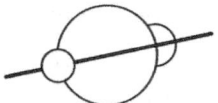

"Dad?"

"In here, hon." I hear Fey's hooves clop quietly on the stone floor as she comes into my office. Looking up from my tablet, I see a troubled look on her face. "You okay?"

"Yeah, but I'm curious about something."

I set down the tablet, and give her my full attention. "What's that?"

She sighs. "I think he likes me."

"Who?"

"Kotu."

"What makes you say that?"

She blushes and rubs her nose. "He, uh. He gave me this." She places a wood carving of a Keema flower on my desk.

I gently pick it up and look at it, admiring the hand-carved petals. The outer petals are a light reddish tan, the inner petals get progressively darker and smaller. The sepal and short stem are of green-tinted wood. "He's gotten good. I've been helping him find different colors of wood."

"You *knew?*"

"Of course I knew. He's been interested in you since you two first met." I set the flower back on the desk. "You're a smart girl. I'm surprised that you didn't see it."

"I thought he was just being extra nice to me, because of what happened. It never occurred that he was interested in me *that* way."

"I think you should ask yourself how you feel about him."

She sits up suddenly and looks at the flower. "I...he's...uh." She stops abruptly, letting her mouth hang open.

"Hun, close your mouth."

My comment snaps her out of her daze. "But, he's my brother."

"Not really, and not in his eyes. Unlike you, Kotu's my ward. I fully adopted you, just like Megai adopted Amela." I lean forward. "Why do you think he doesn't call me dad? Or my mates, mom? He's kept that distance because he didn't want to see you as a sister."

She scowls for a moment, and then asks, "What do I do?"

"Talk to him, let him know how you feel, gently, but remember, there is nothing wrong in his wanting you."

"I know, and he did help save me."

"He insisted, he cares about you."

She lets out a heavy sigh. "I've just never thought of him like that before."

I walk around my desk to her. "Now that you are, what do you think?"

She looks down for a moment, then smiles. "Well, he is kinda cute now that he's starting to get his mane."

I chuckle lightly. "I sense an 'and' in there."

She picks up the flower. "This is really pretty."

"So?"

She looks longingly at the flower for a moment, and then says, "I've got some thinking to do." She wraps me in a hug. "Thanks, dad."

I give her a kiss on her forehead. "Anytime, hun."

She smiles at the flower again as she steps out. I sigh and lean back on my desk. I find her innocence fascinating sometimes, especially since she was one of the first to see that Tayla was interested in me and that Megai would be with me too. She had displayed this by her early arrangement of all the stone figures I gave her. Catching myself staring out the door, I chuckle and return to my seat.

After picking up my tablet, I return my attention to my design, an observer satellite. This one doesn't look like the ones in orbit. It looks like an asteroid, much like the live-in observer that was on the Obsession. Using what I remember, I keep trying to find a way for it to absorb the energy of the static bursts that plague the shell.

Having failed each attempt thus far, I increase the size of the flash charge capacitors. Running the simulation again, I'm disappointed when the static burst again overwhelms the satellite's ability to absorb it and blows up.

I sigh to myself. "Can't absorb it without blowing up, can't route it around without blocking sensors."

Aime makes a suggestion, "Perhaps we should try..."

"Kyle! I found it!" Cayla calls from the hall, interrupting. I see Tareth look to his right, telling me she's coming my way.

As she comes around the corner, I ask, "Found what?"

"The Obsession. Ziggy!" She points to the large screen and it comes on, showing the long, slender, conical form I vaguely remember.

"That's it. What're its specks?"

Ziggy takes initiative, changing the screen to show a more detailed blowup of the ship. "It has 20 Force MK VI ship to ship cannons, 20 Avenger type 8 anti-fighter cannons, class 10 Aegis shield array—"

Cutting him off, I ask, "Okay, how many can it bring to bear at once?"

"Forward firing arc, all. Rear arc, four of each; port, starboard, dorsal, and ventral arcs, fifteen ship to ship, ten anti-fighter."

"What kind of damage would the Wanderer suffer from the antifighter guns?"

"None, its shields are designed to absorb the kinetic energy from small objects, rendering them harmless."

"How about from the larger guns?"

"Those have shells that are designed to explode on rapid deceleration, so the shields would cause a detonation. The shields on the Wanderer are considerably newer than the type used on the Obsession, it would take nearly a dozen rounds, detonating in close succession, to overwhelm the shields."

Cayla turns to me, surprised. "You've got to be kidding. It'd take less than that to overwhelm its own shields."

"I must point out that the Wanderer was designed to handle hazardous areas. Its shields and other systems are more robust, and have backups that a Shiloh class patrol cruiser does not have."

She thinks for a moment, and then asks, "Are there any weapons packages for the Black Hole class?"

"Aside from a point defense system, no."

"And the Wanderer doesn't even have that," I add.

"Can the spiders make it?"

"The parts can be made with the construction bots, but not installed."

"How hard is it to install?" she asks.

"Most of the systems can be installed by hand but the defensive weapon turrets require modification to the hull."

"Well, I did want a crane," I sigh. "How long to build the kit and a proper refit hanger?"

"The kit will take a day, using both bots. The *graving dock*, however, could take two weeks."

"Could?"

"The equipment needed inside the dock is power-intensive to make, so it would vary based on available energy."

"Is there anything we could make to help that out?" she asks.

"More solar panels."

I think for a moment. Glancing at my, tablet I get an idea. "The Wanderer can take a direct hit from the static bursts right?"

"Correct."

"What if we made a battery or capacitor and used the ship to charge it by having a burst strike it?"

"Simulating," Ziggy states.

Cayla looks curiously at me. "Where'd you come up with that?"

I slide the tablet across the desk to her. "I've been trying to design a satellite that can do just that."

She picks it up. "No luck yet, huh?"

"I think it's just too small to handle the load."

She looks curiously. "Could be. Have you thought about making it larger?"

"Yeah, but I don't what to make it too large, it has to fit in with the other asteroids in the shell."

"Simulation complete. Using your satellite as a reference, I incorporated a specialized converter that will create a power cell to use up the excess power."

"The ship doesn't hold enough power to do that," Cayla points out.

"The converter will have several flash capacitors that will charge with the strike."

"What if the burst has more power than the capacitors can hold?" I ask.

"The converter will have a tilt to its table, allowing the power cell to roll off into a bin, freeing the converter to create another cell."

"Clever. That'll allow for us to make several in one trip," Cayla states.

"Indeed, then we could hook the cells up to the spiders to supplement the solar panels," I add. "Ziggy, put it in the forward hold."

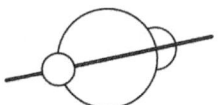

I walk through the house from my office to the garage, it's unusually quiet today. With his honeymoon over, Darren's returned to Garrent to finish his training with Marcus. Nanai went with him to meet his family. I find myself hoping that they are as welcoming as Marcus is.

The children, and Oana, are upstairs in class. The cubs are asleep, as is Tayla, having been up late with them last night. Arru, Railu, Roen, and Ru, have all been dropped off at Arroketh. Arru had business to attend to and Railu wanted to see her dad, Behri. Tareth and Skye went with them, ensuring their safety.

Walking into the garage, I lean against a post and watch the two construction bots, or spiders as we've come to call them, work diligently to build the hanger. We'd thought it best to have it resemble the house as much as possible, at least from the outside. Inside, though, it will have the needed room and mechanicals to do proper service for both the shuttle and the Wanderer.

Sada soon joins me in the garage. She watches them for a few moments and then turns to me, 'I love you.'

I wrap her in a hug, kissing her forehead. "I know you do, and I love you, too." I hold her for a moment before curiosity gets the better of me. "What's bugging you?"

She frowns slightly, but pulls back enough to sign, 'Can I have kittens?'

I frown slightly. "Sorry, no. When you were a kitten, Meagan and I took you to the vet, to find out why you didn't meow. He couldn't find a reason for that, but did recommend having you spayed."

'Why?'

"He said it would give you a longer, healthier life. I'm having mixed feelings about that now."

She gives me an odd look, 'Why mixed feelings?'

I sigh. "Had you not been spayed, you may not have lived long enough to be like you are now, *but* you'd still go into heat and we'd be able to mate."

She looks down for a moment, thinking. After a moment, she sniffs and looks up at me. 'Can you undo it?'

I touch her cheek and gently wipe a tear from her eye. "Aime and I have been working on that, but you were evolved differently than those here. She needs to know how it was done." I look curiously into her blue eyes, and softly ask, "Is that what you want, to be fertile again?"

She pulls away, and I see her nervousness. 'I...need to think...about that.'

I pull her close again, giving her another kiss. "Take your time. I love you either way." She nods and turns back to the bots, I wrap my arms around her as we watch.

Feeling someone wrap me in a hug from behind, I turn to see Tayla. I put an arm around her. "Hey, I thought you were sleeping."

"I was trying," she states, and then looks curiously at Sada, "but *someone's* emotions woke me."

Sada turns to her, 'Sorry.'

She gives Sada a nose bump. "It's all right. What was that about anyway?"

"I offered to make her fertile again."

"No wonder the heavy emotion."

'What's it like?'

Tayla gives her a curious look. "What's what like?"

'Being...you know.'

She chuckles and takes Sada's hand. "Come on. Let's let him be while we have a talk."

I smile as I watch them head into the house. I know that Tayla will be honest with her, no matter what she asks. My mates, including Sada, and I have no secrets between us, which reduces the chance of someone being jealous and increases our mutual trust. I know that she'll make a well-informed decision, and, in the end, it'll be her own.

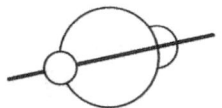

Having spent much of the day reviewing trade agreements, land disputes, and having a spider rebuild the bridges over Pride River, I land the shuttle behind the house. I step out into the waning sunlight and take a deep breath of the cooling evening air.

Tareth, almost as weary as I am, follows me into the house. "Calling it a day?" he asks.

I nod wearily. "Definitely."

He bows slightly and then heads off to his room. I, however, head to the closest grooming room for a shower.

Feeling clean, but still ready for bed, I take a detour through the nursery, checking on the cubs. Kuma has snuggled tightly against his giraffe, while Tashi has fallen asleep, draped across her dragon. I pull their sheets up, tucking them in.

"You need to sleep, too, you know," I hear Tayla whisper from the doorway.

I sigh and step over to her. "I know, there's just too much to do."

"You are going to kill yourself if you don't slow down."

"No, I'll just be sleep-deprived."

"And we'll be *you* deprived," Megai adds. "Come to bed. Get your sleep."

They both put their arms around me, guiding me to bed. My shirt gets pulled off over my head, so I quickly change into my shorts and crawl into bed. The girls promptly climb in and get comfortable, Sada lies down on top of me, with her head on my chest, purring. With Tayla on my right, Megai on my left, and Sada on me, I have no choice but to sleep. I close my eyes and let the three-part harmony of their purring lull me to sleep.

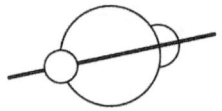

Having been forced to take a few days off by my mates, I make my way to the gym. Since I have Aime and her nanites, I don't require exercise, they prevent body fat buildup and muscle atrophy, exercise has become more of a therapy for me. Stepping into the gym, I'm pleased to find Larrah running herself through a solo warm-up exercise.

Noticing me, she stops and bows. "It's been a while."

I return the bow. "Too long."

"I heard Tayla's order to you," she states as she turns to grab her gloves and shin guards. "Want to talk about it?"

I pull on my own guards and gloves. "No, not really."

As I approach the center circle, she follows suit. "Warm-up?"

"Sure." I bow to her and assume a neutral stance.

She picks a stance of her own, and nods. "Begin."

We begin trading blows, letting the other block. She picks up on my tense posturing and starts prodding, verbally. "So, what's bothering you?"

I parry a few of her attacks before answering. "I know what's coming, but I have no idea when."

She feints and attack and then tries a new fighting style. "What's coming?"

I alter my style accordingly and feint an attack of my own. "A pirated patrol cruiser, commanded by a man with brain damage, making him unpredictable."

She parries an attack and then feints a rush attack. "But you were there, right?"

Noticing an increase in the strength of her attacks, I step up to her level. "We left the ship prior to his arrival here."

"Then how do you know he was here?" she asks as she dodges an attack.

"Because we both felt Tayla when we arrived at the system we bailed at."

She abruptly stops, suddenly curious. "You *both* felt her?"

"Yeah, I had no way to explain what I was feeling at the time, only that it was emotions that weren't mine. I could tell that Sada felt it too. When Cayla found the mention that the Obsession was here, I started thinking about my time aboard. I figured out that what I felt then was exactly what I feel now, through my bond with Tayla. When I asked Sada what she thought about the sensations she felt back then, she basically confirmed my hunch."

She sighs. "I don't pretend to understand your link, but wouldn't that mean that Tayla would know also?"

I sit on a bench. "I already asked her to tell me if she feels anything unusual."

She sits next to me. "So, what's the problem?"

I sigh. "I don't want him here."

"Not really your choice. He has been and, as you say, will be again."

"But that's the problem. I don't know when he's coming back."

"But you'll know when he's here. I won't pretend to know anything close to what you do about time travel, but you have an advantage. You know he's coming, he doesn't know that someone will be here, waiting. Set your trap, it's already been baited."

"I just don't know how big to make the net."

"Think back to when you were on it. What could he do, that you haven't already prepared for?"

"Go back in time and hit us earlier."

"So, set your trap to take that from him."

I frown. "But how?"

"What lets him travel in time?"

"Some device on the ship. Charles had figured out how to duplicate it, but..."

"So take the ship from him."

I laugh. "Easier said than done, I'm pretty sure that most of the crew would be on my side, but the command crew, they'll kill whoever tries to go against them."

She sighs. "Brutal."

"Yeah, shot his pilot for being slightly off course."

She gives me a shocked look and sighs. "I don't suppose there's a way to knock them all out at once."

"If you don't hit both, the person will realize something's up, or the AI will wake the person. There's too many innocents for me to risk a large EMP."

"EMP?"

"Electro-Magnetic Pulse, if it is not too powerful, it can stun an AI."

"And if it's too powerful?"

"It'll kill all the AIs onboard, fry all the ship's systems, and kill the Aquanatum."

This time she frowns. "I see your problem. I don't suppose there's a way to just tell the AIs to knock out the host?"

I chuckle. "That'd be too easy."

"Actually, that may work," Aime interjects.

"What?" Larrah and I ask, in unison.

"AIs from that time period are used to regular updates being broadcast to them. If we can find the right frequency, we can broadcast an update to the AIs. I'll need some time to come up with the proper commands."

"Won't the AIs recognize the commands and dismiss them?" I ask.

"If I include the right trust code, they may do it willingly."

Larrah looks curiously at me. "Trust-code?"

"It's a way to identify the source of the update," Aime answers. "It was instated after the Gene War—"

"—to prevent dangerous updates," I finish.

A new voice enters the conversation. "Correct."

Larrah looks to the door. "Cayla?" I look up and see that Cayla's leaning against the door frame. Based on the way she's dressed, she wants to spend some time in the gym,

She gives me an annoyed look. "I was told that you were supposed to take the day off. No planning."

"It was my fault," Larrah states. "I could tell that something was bothering him and encouraged him to talk while we sparred. I did not realize that it would develop into a strategy."

She looks curiously at me for a moment and then shrugs. "You'll need to find something to prove to at least one of the other AIs that you're friendly."

"One?"

"If just one of the AIs can verify that it's from a trustworthy source, the others can receive a trust-verify from that one. You'll need to make sure that whatever you include completely convinces that AI."

"Thanks, that's a big help," I state. "Here to spar?"

"Train. Larrah's teaching me silat."

"Really, not using the AI training method?"

She shrugs. "I've got free time, gives me a chance to get to know people."

I stand and bow to them both. "Larrah, thank you for your time. Cayla, thank you for the input. I will leave you two to train." I deposit my equipment in my locker and head off for a shower.

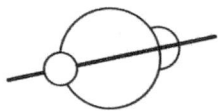

I sit at my desk, deep in thought. "Aime, how does my armor hide me, visually?"

"It uses a combination of meta-materials to absorb, refract, and/or redirect EM wavelengths, preventing detection from many visual detection devices."

"Does that have any restrictions, like size, shape, or composition of what it's hiding?"

"No."

"Really? So if I wrapped something like, the Wanderer?"

"It would be very difficult for another ship to detect, but not impossible. It would still be detectable through gravimetric, magnetic, and particle displacement methods, also the exhaust trail from the engines would still be detectable."

"Would the ship's shields and point defense still work?"

"All the ship's routine systems would still function normally, though active sensors, communications, or weapons usage would give away its position."

"Okay, passive sensors or directional communications through some sort of relay. How robust would this cloak be, in space?"

"As long as the hull was not penetrated, the system would remain intact. I would like to point out, that cloaking the Wanderer will require a considerable amount of power."

"We can supplement with power cells, right?"

"Yes."

"Good. Once the hanger's finished, how long would it take to refit the Wanderer with this?"

"A week. That time would overlap with the point defense system."

I sigh and sit back in my chair. "Both at once, good. Add it to the list."

"Done. If I may, we do have the physical plans for fighter drones."

"Really? Don't they need some sort of controller?"

"I could modify the design to incorporate a dedicated, if simple, AI."

"Where would you get all the combat tactics?"

"That, we do not have. Although, I could use the pilot training program to simulate encounters. I would also program the drones for extrapolative learning, and to share that knowledge with each other and Ziggy."

"How long would it take to build?"

"With their power requirements, it would be two weeks to complete one."

"Any way to make them quicker?"

"I believe we could use your idea for an observer satellite as a foundation, and as we did with the Wanderer, use the static bursts to supply the power needed to create a drone."

"How long would that take?"

"Once completed, the platform could make a drone per direct strike."

"How long would it take to make the platform?"

"Four and a half weeks, with both the hanger and two spiders working on it."

I sigh. "Well, if we do that, I want to make sure that the observer package is in it and that the drones have cloaks as well, but, let's just put that on the back burner for now."

"Understood."

Feeling the closeness of the room, I head out the front door to the stoop. I look up to the stars beyond the rings, wondering how much time I actually have before he arrives, hoping my preparations are enough to protect my people.

"Sir? Are you all right?"

"Kosh, how many times do I have to tell you not to call me sir?"

"Sorry, s...I was just concerned, not many people go outside at night."

I look back and notice that he is, indeed, standing just inside the threshold, holding the door open. "I used to love being outside at night, always found it relaxing." I look back again and see that he keeps looking up. "Relax, if a der'ock comes by, Ziggy will spotlight it and it'll go away."

"It's not their presence I find so worrying, it's how they leave."

"Well, after that one, Ziggy has dimmed the light. They won't fall in the yard again, just turn away."

"Good, cause that was terrifying."

I chuckle, even though it died when it hit the rock, just missing the shuttle, we had to have a spider stop satellite construction to clean up the mess.

"I'll be in, in a minute."

"Alright." He lets the door close as he steps back inside. I smile, letting the day's stresses flow from me into the cool night air. I take a deep breath, and head inside.

22

I lie on my back, on the bed, gently tossing a baseball to myself. Sada sits at her easel, painting. I find it refreshing that she's taken the initiative to try something new all on her own, but she hasn't let me see what she's done yet. The first three projects she was worked on ended up being disposed of in the converter, much to her frustration. This one, she's taken more time, carefully mixing colors, and occasionally remixing them, trying to get them right.

I occasionally glance over at her as she works. I know that I'm her subject, so I haven't moved much, aside from tossing the ball. Finding myself bored, I start humming a song I remember, hoping to encourage time to pass. My absent humming is interrupted by a frustrated huff. I look over to see Sada toss her paint tray in the converter.

Seeing her reach for her work, I quickly sit up. "Hold on, please, let me see."

She shakes her head, scowling at the paper in front of her.

I drop the ball on the bed and step over to her. "Please, maybe I can help."

She holds up her hand, stopping me from getting too close.

"How can I help if I can't see it?"

She sighs heavily and then nods. I sit next to her and look at her work. I notice right away what the problem is.

"You're having trouble with the colors?"

She nods and points to the wall and then to the wall in her painting. The wall in the room is a neutral grey, but in her painting, she has used a tan. This would normally not concern me but my shirt is the same color tan that she used for the wall. She painted it with the same color, thus I disappear against the wall. She has also used a shade of yellow for my skin.

"Uhm, does my shirt really match the wall?"

She looks at the wall, then my shirt, and nods hesitantly.

"I think I know what the problem is. Charles, can Carrie come to my room?"

"In a moment. She has a patient, but will be done soon."

"Let her know that I think Sada's colorblind."

"Certainly."

She looks at me with a half annoyed, half curious look.

"Colorblind. My shirt is tan, the wall is grey. Your eyes can't see the difference. It's normal for a cat, but I don't know why it wasn't corrected with the evolution."

She sighs heavily, so I wrap her in a hug. "If she can't change the way you see, we'll teach you a new way to look at things, so don't fret."

It takes a few minutes, but when Carrie arrives, she has a kit with her. "What this I hear about Sada being colorblind?"

I gesture to the painting. "She can't really see anything with red, just like if she was still a cat."

She looks at the image. "She's good, even if the colors are off."

Sada buries her face in her hands, shaking her head.

Carrie looks at her. "It's a compliment, be happy. If it were mine, you wouldn't even recognize the wall." I find myself chuckling as Sada smiles. "Now let's see what we can do for your eyes." Sada sighs but sits up facing Carrie.

"Close your eyes." Carrie reaches out and puts her palms against Sada's eyes. "Hmm, I see." She then reaches into her bag and pulls out something that looks like a pair of darkened ski goggles. "These will help me fix your eyes. They're not made for nonhumans, so they won't fit you right, but they'll still do the job."

She puts them on Sada's head and tries to adjust them, to get them to set straight. After a moment, apparently satisfied, she presses a button on the top. "Do you see a light dot?"

Sada gives her a thumbs-up.

"Okay, just stay focused on the dot, you can blink if you need to, but don't look away." She presses another button and waits.

I watch, wondering just what the device is doing. After a few moments, the device beeps. "All right, close your eyes." She takes the goggles off of her and holds her palms over Sada's eyes. "Relax, I'm just checking."

After a moment, she pulls her hands away. "I'll warn you, the world will look a lot more colorful than you're used to."

Sada slowly opens her eyes and looks around. She smiles as she takes in the new colors. When she looks at me, she gasps and touches my shirt. She then glances at her painting and huffs, then quickly grins, covering her nose with her hand.

I quickly realize that she's laughing at the image. "I'm disappearing, aren't I?" I ask.

She nods and takes the painting and tosses it in the converter.

"Not gonna fix it?"

She shakes her head and then gives Carrie a hug, prompting me to say, "Thanks, Carrie."

She collects her things and nods to us. "You're welcome. I'd never thought to check her eyes, I guess that process didn't take vision into account." She looks from Sada to me. "Let me know if anything else comes up."

"I will."

She nods and then sighs. "I gotta go. I never get any time to rest on this ship."

I close the door behind her and turn to Sada. She's looking at the picture of the black hole on the screen. I notice her head move slightly as she follows the red flickers of lightning.

"You can see those now, huh?"

She looks back at me and smiles, nodding her head happily.

"Wanna take a walk in the park, check out the flowers again?" She thinks for a moment and then nods excitedly. I put on my stealth suit, relocate Charles's disk to my cheek and we head out.

When we get there, Sada starts looking around. I watch as she darts from flower to flower. She doesn't pick any but looks at each and every one of them with a renewed interest. For a while, it's like we were here for the first time.

After a few hours, and a couple of close calls, we return to our cabin. She goes to the converter and gets a new pallet for her paints. I sit at the desk and bring up an elaborate color wheel. She looks at it, then at me, and smiles.

I send the color wheel to Sada's tablet. She picks it up and turns towards me with a curious look on her face. She points to the darker colors towards the center of the wheel.

"You can mix the original color with black to get a darker version, or you can mix the opposite color for different kinds of shading. White will give you lighter colors."

She sets it on the easel and touches the red, then touches the white. The tablet mixes the two together and her eyes get large as it turns to pink. She points as she smiles.

"Pink."

She holds the tablet next to my skin and purses her lips in thought. She then touches at the yellow and adds that to the mix, it turns light orange. She blinks a few times, apparently thinking her vision is playing tricks on her.

I reset the color wheel and explain, "Look at the wheel, see how yellow and red are on each side of the orange?"

She nods her understanding.

"Good, see, when you mix any two of the primary colors, red, yellow, or blue, you get the color in-between. That gets you the secondary colors."

She nods again, following as I point.

"These are tertiary colors. Any time you mix colors, you'll get the one between. This works equally with all, no matter where they are on the wheel." I tap two colors as examples and let her see the results. She smiles and takes the tablet from me, resets the mix, and starts tapping random colors, seeing what they make when they mix.

Deciding to let her play with it and continue to learn, I grab the baseball, lie back on the bed, and start tossing it to myself.

"Kyle, I believe I have figured out how he does it."

I look up from the tablet I'm reading. "Does what?"

"Travels in time."

"What? How?"

"I will spare you the technical detail, but the device he uses, creates a field, that I will call 'temporal' for lack of a better term. The temporal field isolates the ship and everything inside from the normal time flow. The field's orientation, compared to movement, allows the ship to move forward or backward in time."

"Have you found a way to get to the thing yet?"

"No, but I believe I can design a device to duplicate it—once."

"Once?"

Sada suddenly looks up from her painting, also curious.

"Correct, but once is all that you will need. Once you are out of the ship, you will only need to travel once."

I sigh. "Yeah, sounds all right then, what'll happen to the thing after we use it?"

"It will meltdown."

"Wouldn't that be dangerous?"

"No, it will be contained."

Sada tilts her head and then nods, indicating that she's okay with that. "All right, What do I need to do?"

"Nothing."

Sada's eyes go wide and she looks at Charles's avatar.

"What?" I ask, not believing what I just heard.

"I will have the observer asteroid build it inside its converter."

"Oh." I sigh, slightly disappointed. "And here I was hoping I'd have something new to do."

"Apologies, but once it is made, it will not be able to be moved."

I turn my attention back to the tablet with my current book. "That's all right, we'll manage."

"We're approaching a system."

I roll out of the bed and grab the pack of the door, as I fish for the remote, I ask, "How soon?"

"Oh, we cannot leave you here, this system is heavily patrolled."

I stop looking through the pack. "What?"

"Strap in. There are two picket ships coming our way."

Sada jumps from the bed to secure her things. She quickly sets the loose brushes and pallet in the bathroom sink. Then places her painting and easel in the shower and secures the door. I quickly put the cards, chips, and baseball in the pack and pull the drawstring. After hanging it back on the door, I quickly get into the bed. Sada joins me and I pull down the webbing, securing us to the bed.

Sada huffs into my chest, having snuggled tightly against me. I wrap my arms around her and kiss her forehead, hoping to comfort her.

The ship lurches suddenly, we've been fired upon. I hear a few of the guns return fire and the engines power up, accelerating hard. Gravity changes direction and I recognize that the ship is turning hard.

The guns continue firing at the two pursuers. Their rate of fire is less than I'm used to, prompting my curiosity. "Charles, what's going on?"

"He is making sure that they are chasing him."

"Leading them away. What are they protecting?"

"Unsure, I am still trying to determine what system this is."

"No communications?"

"They are in blackout. Apparently what they are protecting is important, or the captain got unlucky and showed up when they just happened to be here."

"I doubt the latter."

"I agree."

After a few minutes, the guns fall silent and the ship accelerates hard again.

"He has activated the temporal field."

I quickly release the webbing. While it's useful for combat and rough rides, Charles has yet to find a way to insulate it, so it's still a hazard during time travel. Sada huffs again, I find myself agreeing with her. This trip is thankfully short and the ship starts to turn hard again.

"We are reentering the system. This is interesting, we are here twice. Apparently, he is using our previous self as a decoy."

As I reach up for the webbing, I chuckle. "Crazy clever."

"Indeed, this strategy can only work with a time travel."

"Yeah, but if he had another ship at his disposal, he would be using it to draw the defenders off."

"True, and a defender uses different tactics based on the number of attackers."

"Wait, you said we showed up on our own sensors, this time, did we show up the first time?"

"Reviewing...Not on our own, but one of the picket ships did start a turn, to the current us. That is why he started firing at them, to keep them covering each other."

"Why not just destroy them, he's done it before?"

"I am not certain this ship would win against two picket ships, not with the current amount of damage. The shuttles are disembarking, senior crew, with full security detachment."

"Picking something up, no doubt."

"Possibly. I believe I have figured out where we are."

"How?"

"System statistics and star positions. It appears we have returned to Gsharr."

"What!? Can you tell when we are?"

"Not specifically, but...Cruiser incoming, it is a previous version of us." The engines power up suddenly and the ship lurches, accelerating hard.

"This is when he met himself!"

"It would appear."

"Why'd the patrol ships attack?"

"Our transponder is damaged so it is not broadcasting our identification."

"So naturally they move to defend, and fire warning shots."

"To which we did not heed, so they fired upon us."

"What's happening now?"

"We are entering a counter orbit, opposite from our past selves. They are sending a shuttle down, with a security detachment."

I lift the webbing and look at the avatar. "Out of curiosity, are any of the security people the same?"

"No, none of the members of the current security team match the ones that were on the original team. All of those members are no longer listed as active."

"I don't like the way that sounds."

"According to the medical records, all perished during various skirmishes, having been in or near areas of the ship that were damaged."

I sigh and Sada gently sniffs my chest. I look at her and she sighs heavily as she rests her chin on my chest.

"Are we boring you?" She narrows her eyes lazily as if fighting sleep.

I start rubbing her head, making her purr. "You know, I get bored too."

She sighs again, stressing just how bored she is.

"Well, we can't really go anywhere right now, the ship's at General Quarters."

She tries to nod, but with her chin on my chest, it looks more like a wobble than a nod. I give a short laugh and rub her ears. Her eyes close the rest of the way, and she purrs harder.

"I will notify you if anything important happens, you two should get some rest."

I sigh and make sure the webbing is locked down. "Thanks, Charles." I resume rubbing Sada's ears and head. After a few moments, I close my eyes and let her purring soothe me.

Not really feeling tired, I let my mind wander, and I find myself wishing that Sada could be more than she is, to me. I know why she bit me, she wasn't in heat, so her body defended itself. I start thinking about the questions I've asked myself, and Charles before, and as I lie there, I once again start trying to answer them.

Why wasn't her going into estrus addressed in the evolution? Was it simply an oversight? Maybe they didn't expect interspecies relations. Was it left intentionally? Maybe, to prevent interspecies relations? No, that doesn't make sense, it'd just start fights.

What about her eyesight? That would handicap a sentient species, missing out on part of the color spectrum; that has to be an oversight.

What about her feet, or are they still paws? They're feet, she walks upright. No, they're paws, she's still digitigrade, she walks on her toes. So they're between; foot-paws. Is that intentional or oversight? If I designed the evolution, I would leave that intact. It's got to be intentional, her tail helps her balance. Her legs are stronger, and that gives her an advantage.

Why doesn't she go into heat? I sigh, that's my fault, I had her fixed nearly twenty years ago when she was old enough. The vet recommended it, for her health. I scowl, suddenly realizing that I can't give her that back.

Opening my eyes, I look down at her. She lies on my chest, still purring. I gently run my fingers through her fur, feeling how soft it is. I realize that it's been several months since I thought of her as a cat, she's a person now, and I will continue to treat her as such, no matter what.

Charles's avatar looks over at me, and softly says, "Kyle, we are beginning time travel."

I quietly raise the webbing and then pull the covers over us.

23

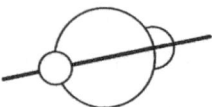

I watch, from the safety of the small observation room, as the graving dock's cranes lift the upper section of the hull off the Wanderer, starting its refit to install the point defense system and the cloak. The dock has four crane arms lifting and holding the upper hull, while several others extend into the gap between and start working on both the underside of the hull and to the exposed upper parts of the ship. Several labor bots scurry around underneath the ship, working on the lower hull.

I had considered assigning the garage an AI of its own, but Ziggy assured me that he could handle everything. So I'm having Aime keep an eye on how busy he is, just to be safe.

Just before the spiders finished building the dock, I made another trip to the shell to collect more power. As a result, there are more than a dozen spare power cells sitting in a rack in the corner, waiting to be used.

As I watch them work, a movement in the corner catches my attention. An arm drops a depleted power cell into a chute and then picks a fresh one out of the rack. As the arm retracts and connects it to the dock's power grid, the empty cell rolls into a converter and disappears with a flash.

With a sigh, I head out of the dock to the house. The sun is brighter than the lights inside so I use my hand to shade my eyes as I walk the distance across the rock to the garage. As my eyes readjust, I see all three of the scout bikes, Darren and Nanai are home. I smile and continue to my office.

As I pass through the great hall, Nanai comes in from the West Wing. Upon seeing me she happily comes up and wraps me in a hug. "Thank you!"

I return her hug, and curiously ask, "Why?"

"For having me join Darren, his folks were wonderful, well, after they got over me being furry."

"I'm real glad that worked out."

"Me too, I thought at first that they didn't like me."

"How so?"

"They were disappointed that we'd not be able to have young, but I assured them that I wanted a baby and that you were working to make that possible. It took some help from Darren, but they started to warm up to me."

"Did that bother you?"

She frowns. "No, just unexpected, but I'm glad that I went." Her smile returns as she starts towards the kitchen.

I happily watch her leave and then turn to my office. As I walk in, I see Darren leaning against my desk, looking at the large screen, currently showing an enlarged image of the black hole from my signet.

"Need something?" I ask as I walk around him and the desk.

He gives me a quick look, surprised. "Huh, oh. What's this?"

"It's a black hole, with a plasma storm caught in it."

"It's...kinda hypnotic."

I chuckle as I sit. "If you stare at it too long, it'll feel like you're falling in."

"Yeah, noticed." He turns and sits across from me. "So, as your pilot, what're my other duties?"

I pick up my tablet and look at the observer drone platform plans. "General readiness and upkeep of the shuttle, and to a small degree, the Wanderer."

He gives me a puzzled look. "Is that all?"

I look over the tablet at him. "Is it not enough?"

Surprise overtakes him. "Uh, that's okay, that's enough."

I chuckle. "I thought so. The dock's working on the Wanderer right now, so, if you want, check out the shuttle then be available if someone needs to go somewhere."

He stands. "I'll do that." He starts to leave but stops. "Thank you."

I smile. "You're welcome." He heads out and I return my attention to the new version of the observer satellite. "What am I gonna do with you?" I absently ask myself.

"We could make them slightly larger, able to hold a dozen of the drones. They could be launched as a squadron, cloaked. They can then sit and wait for an alert before going active."

"Thanks, Aime, but it was a rhetorical question."

"I know, I was just offering a suggestion."

I set the tablet down, and lean back in my chair, sighing. "Yeah, I know."

"Should I add it to the queue?"

"How would we get it out to the shell? They'll be too big to put in the Wanderer."

Silence seems to loom for several seconds as I await an answer. "I find it surprising that we had not addressed this already. We do not have a launch facility, so will need to construct them in space. Then we could tow them to the shell and drift them into position."

"How many?"

"For acceptable coverage, we will need to construct and place nearly five thousand."

I slump down and sigh heavily. "Maybe we should just build something on one of the moons. Have it make the drones during Moonstorm."

"We would need to plan construction very carefully. Moonstorm produces an exponentially large amount of power. Anything we place on either moon would need to be heavily insulated, and the collection apparatus would need to be very robust, to prevent a meltdown."

"This just isn't gonna be easy, is it?"

"Apparently no. This system has the potential to generate tremendous amounts of energy, attempting to harness that energy does pose some risks, those risks increase faster than the rewards do."

"Maybe I'm trying too hard, what if we used the satellites to collect power and send it down here when they don't need it? We did design it to share power after all."

"They were designed to share power with each other, not with ground structures."

"So, design a power relay satellite we can put in orbit that can do that, as well as share the power from the ground with the satellites."

"I do not have the ability to share power," Ziggy states.

"I was thinking more about the facility, but we probably should get you, and the Sages, in on the share too. Do it."

"Understood. Designing power transmission stations and satellites," Ziggy states.

Suddenly the large screen goes blank. "What just happened?"

"He has dropped nonessential functions," Aime replies.

"He's too busy," I conclude. "I knew it, Ziggy, pause last design processes."

"Acknowledged." The image of the black hole returns to the screen, confirming my conclusion.

I get up and start walking to the back of the house. "Aime, let's get the dock set up with its own AI."

As I exit the garage, Aime announces, "Reassigning construction bot." To confirm her statement, one of the spiders abruptly turns and moves into the dock.

"How long?"

"An hour to construct, thirty minutes to program. A total of two hours before it can take over refits."

"All right." I turn back to the house. "Ziggy, once the dock takes over the refits, resume the designs. Not before."

"Understood."

As I pass by the nursery, I hear the cubs chirping. I open the door and see them rolling about. "What are you two worked up about?"

They both abruptly quiet and look at me. Tashi smiles and starts kicking, wanting to be picked up. Kuma, though, manages to roll over and starts to slide himself to the side of his crib.

"Oh, no you don't," I gently chide as I roll him back over. "You need changed first."

He smiles at me as I grab fresh diapers and wipes. As I start changing him, Tayla comes in. "How'd you beat me in here?"

"I was just outside the door and heard them." Kuma's eyes go wide, recognizing her voice. He starts kicking excitedly as I try to put a fresh diaper on him. "Hey, settle down, you!" As I pick him up, he sees his mom and starts reaching for her.

"Come here," Tayla states as I pass him to her. "Such a momma's boy."

"And his sister is a daddy's girl," I state as I change her. She smiles and starts kicking and chirping excitedly. "All right, all right, calm down." I pick her up and she squeals happily.

Tayla chuckles. "Come on, supper's waiting."

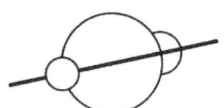

Having awoken early I walk through the house to my office. As I pass the hall to the East Wing, I see Skye come out and cross the Great Hall to the West Wing. This by itself wouldn't normally catch my attention, but when he passes by, I find he's wearing his pajama kilt and smells of Keema.

He nods to me as he passes by. "Morning."

Suddenly curious, I look down the hall and see Arru come out of her room. She sees me and smiles, embarrassed. As she walks to me, she apparently feels the need to defend herself. "You don't need to look at me like that."

A little confused, I ask, "Like what?"

"Like I'm taking advantage of him."

I smile, trying not to laugh. "If you two have a thing or not, I don't care. He worked for you long before we met. What I was thinking is that this is the first time I've seen you with your fur a mess."

She looks at herself, shocked, and jokes, "My furs a mess? Oh no!" Now I really laugh, and so does she. "You've just not woken up earlier than me, that's all."

"It was bound to happen, but seriously, are we going to be expecting pups?"

She blushes. "While I've thought about it often, I'm not sure if I really want to. I like what I do, and sometimes I feel a pup would just get in the way."

I nod. "I get that, but remember, your mother found time for you."

She tilts her head. "Yeah, she did, but I had a few nannies too."

"I can understand that, but she was gone for months on end. That's not a problem anymore. We can go and be back in a few hours."

"I know, and aren't I supposed to be the one counseling you?"

"Usually, but everyone needs someone they can talk to."

She sighs and nods. "Yeah, I know that, and I appreciate it. I'm just not quite certain that I'm ready to be a mother."

"Well, if you happen to change your mind, give us a heads up."

She chuckles. "I will." She then gives me a slight nod and heads back to her room.

As I start to my office again, a gentle knock at the door gets my attention. Knowing that both Kosh and Nanai are both helping with breakfast, I answer the door. I'm surprised to find a cloaked Moku, especially with it still fairly dim outside. "Hello."

"Hello, I'm looking to speak with Master Kyle." Her voice surprises me. All the other Moku I've spoken with were male, this is the first time I've actually met a female.

I hear Tareth walk up behind me as I welcome her in. "Please, come into my office."

She gives Tareth a curious look from under her hood but follows me to my office. I offer her a seat, which she gladly accepts, and then sit across from her. "What can I do for you?"

"It's about your offer, to help my people."

Feeling a tinge of sadness, that I quickly suppress, I nod to her, "I am still offering it, sadly I have had no takers."

She looks down at her lap and then back at me. "Then, on behalf of my people, I want to be the first to take you up on it."

Feeling suddenly hopeful, I lean forward. "What can I do to help."

She sighs. "I need a mate that's not mad at the humans."

Now I sigh. "That's not an easy thing to do. All the males I've spoke with are mad at my kind, at least the ones that made you what you are now. They're not mad at me, or the ones at Garrent."

"I want to have young that aren't sour to your kind at all, and won't run away from each other."

I sigh again. "That's going to be difficult to do. None of the males I've met want to be around others."

"I know, I've spoken to all who I could find and none are to my liking."

I frown. "I'm not sure how I can help."

"Back at the facility, I heard scientists talk of cloning. I've heard talk that you've been there several times. Would it be possible for you to clone someone, from this?" from a pocket on her cloak, she pulls out a pouch and hands it to me.

As I open it, I find a piece of a tail, covered with a mix of fur and scales, sealed in a small disk. "You want me to clone someone from this? Who was it?"

"It was my first mate, the one who had no aversions. He tried to unit our people and was viciously ostracized for it."

"Well I can certainly understand wanting someone back, and your reasons why. Unfortunately, I don't have the equipment to clone someone."

"What about the facility?"

"Almost all the equipment left there doesn't work anymore." I sit back in my chair and sigh. "But, I may have the means to reconstruct it. I'll have to do some research before I can figure out if I can do that."

"That is fine, I've waited two hundred years to start over, a few more will not change anything."

I give her a curious look. "You've waited for over two hundred years? How?"

She hangs her head for a moment. "Sorry. I forget you don't have a genetic memory. When I speak of my ancestors' past, it's from their perspective, and in turn, it becomes my perspective."

"I think I understand. Their memories are yours, so it feels like it was you."

She nods. "My mother was the last queen, I am her last daughter...her last child." She hangs her head sadly. "When I became of age, she gave me this." She points to the tail. "She wanted to go to the facility and have him cloned, but when I got there, well..."

"Queen?"

"I apologize, I had assumed that some of the males would have told you about our family structures. We Moku are similar to what you humans call a hive. We have a queen who will birth the offspring. Most of them will be males, though we can choose to have females when needed."

"How long ago were you born?"

"I'm only twenty years old. My mother lived for nearly a century, as did her mother."

Seeing the sadness in her eyes, I venture a guess, "So, just like the memories; loves and hates, all pass to the next generation, too?"

"Yes. It makes it hard to forget our history, also makes it hard to forget our mistakes and prejudices."

"And that's what you're trying to do, get rid of the prejudices to humans."

"And to each other. My people need to be able to live together, to be with our own kind, and others, and not be afraid of them...or ourselves." She reaches up and pulls back her hood, revealing her face. She has a short, stout muzzle, with a smooth pink nose. While she's covered with scales, there are patches of fur growing from between them. "I am not ashamed of the way I look, nor am I afraid to be looked at."

Seeing her real face, something no one else has probably seen before, I nod. "That, I also understand. I will see what I can do for you."

She nods back. "Thank you."

"In the meantime, you're welcome to stay."

"I'd like that." She smiles and then looks at her cloak. "Would it be possible for me to get some new clothes? This cloak can be...stifling."

"I'm certain we can find something for you. Seeing that still early in the morning, would you like to join us for breakfast?"

"I...I...uhm."

"If you want to mingle with others, no time like the present to start."

She nods slightly. "Yes, please."

"Nanai, would you please see to our guest?"

She peaks around the door jam, shocked. "How?"

"I heard you. Would you please?"

"I would love to." She smiles and looks to the Moku. "What's your name?"

The Moku stops abruptly, shocked. After a brief moment, she sighs heavily. "That's something we Moku hold private."

I give her a curious look. "What should we call you then? I hope something other than Moku."

She frowns slightly and then sighs. "You're outgoing with your names, we should be too. Pria."

"Such a lovely name. Come, let's get you a fresh outfit." Nanai leads her out to our guest rooms.

I smile and sigh. "Ziggy, bring up all data on cloning, and the equipment needed to do it, on my tablet."

"Certainly, with the amount of data you're requesting, this may take several hours."

"That's fine."

I head out to the dining room and find everyone else already there. Taking my place at the head of the table, I clear my throat and get everyone's attention. "We have a new house guest this morning. She is a Moku and wants to start being part of society. Please be patient with her as she makes these adjustments." I pause for a moment as Nanai walks in and adds a place setting next to Sada. She nods to me, and I continue, "She has come here for my, our help."

Seeing Pria step into the room, now dressed in a nice, but modest robe. "I would like you to meet Pria." She shyly walks to the table as everyone looks and greets her. Nanai seats her and then heads to the kitchen.

As I sit, Tayla says, "Please don't be offended if we stare a bit, we've never seen a Moku outside of their cloak."

Pria looks down the table and her nose twitches a little. "It's something I need to get used to, being looked at. I had thought it would be easier."

Megai leans forward, to see around Sada. "I'm glad your trying, if you feel you need to talk, there's always someone around."

"Thank you."

The kitchen doors open, and Nanai and Kosh push in their carts and start serving breakfast. The conversations become suddenly light, and I notice that Pria keeps glancing at Oana more than anyone else. Oana, however, does not return her many glances, preferring instead to enjoy her food.

As I eat, I tend to Tashi, feeding her, her breakfast. Tayla works on Kuma, trying to feed him breakfast while eating her own. Unlike his sister, Kuma doesn't want breakfast and keeps pushing Tayla's hand away. She eventually gives in and just eats her own breakfast, letting him sit and chirp, trying to get everyone's attention. Ru occasionally yips back from her own highchair.

After Tashi has had her fill, I finish my own breakfast. I notice that Pria has turned her attention to Kuma, watching him chirp and look around at everyone. When he notices that she's watching him he smiles and looks at her. Pria smiles back as she eats, glancing at him and Tashi often.

"How old are they?" she asks.

"Nearly five months," Tayla answers.

She smiles and sighs. "Seeing them brings up my mother's memories of her litters."

"How many can you have at once?" Megai asks curiously.

"Six to eight. I have a den already, but I'm not sure I want to hold on to that tradition."

"Where's the den?" Tayla asks.

"It's a rather large cave, near Pride River Falls."

"Is it homey?"

"Not really, but I don't know what else to do. There's nothing suitable above ground."

"Maybe we can build you something," Cayla suggests, joining the conversation.

"What? You'd do that?"

"Of course we would. You want to repopulate your species, that's a big task to do alone."

"Oh, I won't be alone. I'll have a mate at first, and then I'll have the first litter."

Cayla looks at her curiously. "What do you mean?"

"My mate helps raise the first litter. Then when they're old enough, I'll have a second litter. Traditionally, the first litter will help raise the second and then leave the den. The second will help with the third, and so on."

Most of us stop eating, with a slightly shocked look on our faces. Railu manages to swallow her food and ask, "How often will you produce a litter?"

"Every five years."

"How fast will they grow?" Nanai asks as she refills Pria's drink.

"They will be ready to leave me at the age of ten."

"How so soon," Megai asks.

"They will have my memories, and their father's, so they will only need to be physically mature."

Roen looks curiously at her. "How's that possible? For them to have your memories."

I sigh and answer before Pria can. "Because the Moku have a genetic memory. They're born with the memories of their parents, before conception."

He looks from me to her. "So you know what your parents knew?"

She nods. "And their parents, and so on. It gets hard to separate it as I get older because they become my own."

"I can't begin to understand how that feels," he states.

"I can't understand how you can be like that when born." She points to Ru, who's happily trying to lick up her breakfast from the tray of her highchair.

I chuckle. "They learn fast though." Kuma gives her a serious look and a sharp chirp as if agreeing with me.

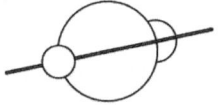

Taking the Wanderer into orbit, Darren heads to the coordinates for the first satellite drop. I secure my helmet, a recent addition to my armor, and open the rear loading ramp. I walk down the ramp carrying a satellite crate and a labor bot follows me down. While my boots cling to the surface of the ramp, keeping me in place, the bot's four feet do the same for it.

When the bot gets to the end of the ramp and braces itself, I pass it the satellite. It turns and holds the crate facing aft. As the ship decelerates, the bot squats.

"Nearing position, slowing to deploy speed," Darren calls, over the com.

I feel the ship decelerate harder, and the bot pushes the crate out into space. I watch as it deploys. The crate's sides split open into eight solar panels and position themselves equally around the center. From the round core, several power transmission rods extend. Then a few small spurts from its maneuvering jets position it with the long antennas towards the planet.

Aime confirms its readiness and I repeat to Darren, "Satellite deployed, operational."

"Moving to next position," he replies as I feel the ship accelerate.

I start walking up the ramp to retrieve another satellite when the ship lurches suddenly, turning hard. I hit one of the ramp supports and hold on to it. I glance down the ramp and the labor bot has all four of its arms latched to the edges of the ramp, also hanging on.

"Darren? What are you doing?" I shout.

"Sorry! Almost hit a satellite."

"Watch where you're going, we just got these things up here, I'd hate to start replacing them."

"I know, I know. For some reason, that satellite didn't show on sensors. I just saw it and reacted."

My interest peaked, I state, "Take us back there, slowly." I sprint up the ramp and head forward. Reaching the forward hold, I lower the ramp and head down to look.

"We're almost there."

This time the ship decelerates smoothly and I see the darkened satellite. When we're close enough, I call out, "Darren, hold it here!"

Careful not to touch it, I get a good look at it. It has no solar panels, and it's fairly small, cylindrical, and only slightly larger than a three-liter jug. "What have we here?"

"It is a spy satellite, or what is left of one," Aime states. I hold my hand up to it, allowing Aime to scan it. "Its power cell seems to be depleted."

"Is it safe to recover?"

"Yes."

I grab the satellite and head up into the hold. "Take us to the next drop, Darren." I close the ramp and set the satellite at the door to the aft hold. I grab a crate and head down the ramp with it. Feeling the ship decelerate, I pass it to the bot and it readies to release it.

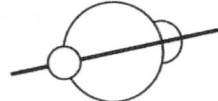

I set the small spy satellite on the workbench and step back. "Doc, analyze this."

There's a moment's pause, then he states, "It is a standard Mark seventeen multi-target tracking satellite. It is not responding to any of the standard commands, so I will need to remove its shell to see if I can access its memory core."

"Could it be out of power?"

"Unsure, it is absorbing all active attempts to scan it."

"All right, see if you can take it apart. Let me know when you're done."

"Certainly." Two of the labor bots activate and approach the workbench and start examining it, trying to figure out how to remove the one-piece shell.

I turn and head out of the dock, across the rock, and into the house. As I walk through the Great Hall towards my office, I see Pria talking with Cayla in her office. I stop for a moment to see what they're doing and discover that they are busy designing a house. I quietly step into the doorway and watch for a few minutes while they discuss features to include.

I take advantage of a moment of silence to offer a suggestion. "Put a converter in there."

They both turn to me, slightly surprised. "Really?" they ask in unison.

"Why not, she's obviously going to need a way to get food and things, sometimes quickly, and she'll obviously be starting with very little. I'm willing to help out any way I can."

Cayla smiles and chuckles slightly. "You want an AI also?"

Pria's eyes light up and she smiles. "Really?"

I take her light joke literally. "Why not? It won't need to be as elaborate as Ziggy. Might as well put some solar panels on the roof, and link it with Ziggy and the Sages too, that way you can call for help if needed."

They both sit in awe for a moment. Pria though collects herself enough to ask, "Why would you do this for me?"

I sigh. "Because I know what it's like to start over, and I don't mind sharing, especially if I know the other person can handle it."

She looks down, and I see a tear roll down her thinly furred muzzle. "I...don't know what to say."

I bow slightly. "A simple thank you will do."

"But it doesn't even begin to cover it," she counters.

"If I manage to clone your mate, you can thank me by following through. I'd hate to see your people die out."

She nods slowly. "I will do my best."

Cayla finally recovers, and firmly states "And we'll do everything we can to help."

I nod, and add, "Maybe it'll change some of the other Moku's minds, or at least help them feel more welcome."

She nods. "I hope so, too."

Ziggy waits a silent moment, then softly states, "Kyle, I have finished compiling the requested data for you."

"My turn to see what I can do for you." I give them a slight bow and retreat to my office. I grab my tablet and sit. "Ziggy, secondary search, find data on the Moku prior to their evolution. Also, search for mention of any creatures resembling the Ootuku, same timeframe."

"Running search and compiling."

I look at the tablet and sigh, and bring up the search results for the cloning technology. "All right, let's see what we have."

24

Sada sits at her easel painting while I sit looking at my tablet. Charles is showing me the layout of the system we're approaching. It's a small system, four planets, two of which are in a binary orbit. I find how they orbit odd, rotating around each other vertically, so both always have a side in the sun.

Those two planets are where we're going. Charles isn't sure why yet, he can't find any information on this system, but there's an artificial structure between the planets. Thanks to the recent repairs to the sensors, they have better resolution than they did, so, even at this range, we can tell that it's positioned at their center of gravity.

The structure looks more like a wheel than anything, and it spins opposite the rotation of the binary planets. I felt that this could be for artificial gravity, Charles stated he would have agreed, but the orientation suggested that it could be for power generation.

I sigh and set the tablet aside. Sada looks over at me curiously, as if expecting me to say something. I lazily look over at her and smile weakly. She sets down her brush and pallet, walks over to me, and sits on my lap. She then leans into me, sighing out her boredom.

I wrap her in a hug, holding her close to me. As she starts to purr softly, I kiss her head and try to relax, letting her purring fill me. Hearing the servos on Charles's avatar, I glance over and see it watching us.

"I am curious," he asks softly, "Do you regret trying to be more intimate with each other?"

"I don't." I give Sada a kiss as she looks up at me. "And I hope you don't either. We learned how much we love each other, and that we have limits on how we can express it." Sada stops purring and gently touches the scar on my neck and collar.

"Oh, I am sorry to have asked."

"It's all right, I hold no grudge." I gently rub her cheek and kiss her again. When her purring gently resumes, that's the only sound I notice. We sit, relaxing, until the ship shudders.

"Gravitational pulls. We are nearing the structure."

I spin us around so we both can see the monitor. "Show us."

The screen comes on, displaying the station. Getting a better look, I see that it's not habitable. Almost all of the structure is an open framework. "Is it still under construction?"

"No, it appears to be complete. The sensors are detecting a large number of dormant labor bots, but there are not any construction bots."

"So, what is this place?"

"Still unsure. It appears inoperable."

"Inoperable?"

"It is not emitting any power, nor is it absorbing any."

"Abandoned?"

"Most likely."

"Wonder what they're after."

"The only thing of value is the labor bots."

"Can't be the only thing. Maybe they could use the plating, fix the hull."

"That would be nice, but they would need to repurpose whatever they take."

"Can't the labor bots do that?"

"To a limited degree, yes. We will soon find out what they are after. A shuttle is departing."

Sada sits up and gives me a bump with her nose. I kiss her back and she returns to her painting. I pick up my tablet, transfer the visual to it and turn back around, assuming the position I had before.

As she picks up her brush and pallet, she smiles. I smile back and watch the shuttle fly over to the structure. Charles relays the view from the shuttle, so I get a closer view of a space-suited engineer walking out of the shuttle and across the framework to a cluster of chromed, two-meter tall, cylinders on a platform.

"Those are the labor bots. They are in a storage mode," Charles notes.

The engineer takes out a handheld device and connects a cord from it to the side of one of the bots. After a few moments, the bot twitches and expands. Four arms and four legs split off, taking sections of its outer shell with them. The engineer removes the cord and moves to another bot.

The first bot walks to the edge of the platform and out of view, so I try to move the image by dragging my finger over it. When nothing happens, I scowl. "Charles, is this a fixed view?"

"This view is from the shuttle's internal sensors, through the door. We simply cannot see where the bot went from the shuttle."

"What about the shuttle's external sensors?"

"They face down and forward, conically. It does not have lateral sensors."

"Can we watch from here?"

"Not clearly." The display changes to an overhead view. The bots show up, in miniature on the screen. By the time the first reaches a nearby platform, a third bot has been activated. Unable to zoom in anymore, the first bot appears to simply walk slowly along the edge. When the second bot arrives, it starts off along the other edge.

By the time the first two have walked the complete edge of the platform, two more bots have arrived. They assume positions near the corners and lift the platform free. When I notice that there are other bots heading out to other platforms, the first four come drifting towards the ship with the platform in tow.

"It appears your wish is granted. The ship's own labor bots are awaiting them on the hull."

"I hope he does more than minor repair work this time."

"Indeed."

With the sounds from the construction bots working echoing through the hull, I find myself unable to get to sleep. I roll out of bed and walk over to the overhead conduit I've been using for a pull-up bar. I adjust my pajama bottoms and jump up to the bar. After finding my comfortable hand position, I do my regular twenty pull-ups, then turn my hands around and do twenty more. I don't normally push myself with these, but I need to sleep.

I then pull my legs up and hook them over the bar. Now hanging by my knees, I do my twenty sit-ups. Not yet feeling very exhausted, I do another twenty more, hoping to make myself tired enough to fall asleep. After dropping back to the floor, I drop and do as many pushups as I can.

After I get up, I sigh heavily and head for the shower. It's been two days of nonstop work for the bots, but with as much noise as they've been making, I feel like I've been the one doing the work because I haven't been able to sleep.

I walk out of the bathroom while drying my hair and look at Sada. It's been worse for her. With her sensitive hearing, the noise actually hurts her ears. Charles made a hood for her, out of the stealth material. It helps her sleep but hurts her ears because of how she has to wear it. Right now, she's also sedated, thanks to a visit from Carrie.

I put on a fresh pair of shorts and pull back on my own earmuffs-I had Charles make them to where they let a little of the sound through, I can't stand complete silence. I stick the disk by my ear, in case Charles needs to get my attention and lie down next to Sada. Feeling more tired than I did before, I snuggle up to her and let sleep take me.

Having lined as much of the remaining walls as I could with the stealth material, it's much quieter. The sounds from the construction aren't completely blocked, though, there were some surfaces I couldn't cover.

I recline on the bed, propped on a pillow, gently rubbing Sada's ears, hoping to make them feel better as she leans her back against me, relaxed and purring, enjoying the treatment.

"It's been a week, any idea when they'll be done?"

"Apparently they are done repairing. Now they are reinforcing areas of the hull."

"Great, that means we're probably going to be in more battles soon."

"I hope not, even with the reinforcements, I am not certain how much damage this ship can take."

"I'm not sure how much more of this ship *we* can take. Movies always depicted star travel as less boring."

"From the ones that I am familiar with, the sea-going vessels from your time were also depicted as less boring. In reality, most crews had to create their own entertainment, just like you two have."

I give the avatar a dry look. "Thanks for the pep talk."

"I was complimenting you on your mutual resourcefulness. Long tours on any type of military ship have typically been boring, despite efforts to entertain the crew."

Seeing Sada scowl at him, I try to change the subject a little. "Are there still vacation cruise ships?"

"Of course, they are better known as starliners."

"What kind of recreation do they have?"

"They have numerous resorts, arcades, and spas. There are also several clubs, bars, game halls, and most usually have a mall. Some may even have a stadium or arena."

"How big are those things?"

"The smallest ones are over five kilometers long. The largest is nearly twenty."

"And how long it this ship, again?"

"Almost one."

Sada gives me a curious look as she makes a couple of size comparisons with her hands. Knowing her meaning, I ask, "Why the drastic difference?"

"This ship is a patrol cruiser. It is built for speed and maneuverability. Starliners are not built for either, they are built to hold as many people as possible, with all the comforts possible."

"Makes sense. I bet they cost a fortune."

"In energy, yes. Humankind has long ago abandoned the monetary exchange system."

"No money, huh. Bet that was hard to do."

"When colonies were established, they were set up to work without. When Earth itself finally changed over, it was a near disaster. Almost half the populace wasn't ready for it, despite the government's meticulous, and lengthy education programs."

I chuckle, despite myself. "How long did it take for people to adjust?"

"Nearly ten years of preparation followed with nearly ten years of chaos."

"Glad I missed that."

"From your behavior with the converter, you would have had an easy time transitioning."

"If you're referring to the fact that I don't make anything I don't need, I've never been a greedy person. All I've ever really wanted was a family."

"I don't understand. When you were on Earth, you had a lot of money, why didn't you have a family?"

"Apparently, you're missing most of my history. When I was eighteen, just graduated from high school, my parents were in an accident and both died. Being of legal age, I became executor of their estate. Practically overnight, I went from high school graduate to multi-millionaire thanks to their insurance policies and some lawsuits issued by the insurance companies."

Sada curls up to me as I continue, "After I made sure that my sister finished school, I went to paramedic's school, got married, and had a son. Meagan, my wife, took our son to the doctor one day and got in an accident. They both died. More lawsuits and insurance payouts. All sorts of money I really didn't need, or want."

I gently start rubbing Sada's shoulders, for her comfort and mine. "That left Sada and me alone. I moved to the country and took up woodworking, started making bows, arrows, spears, things like that. I was really good at it, too."

"Then after a few years, my body started slowly breaking down. I had ALS, when I started having trouble walking, I hired Alicia as my nurse. The rest you know."

Hearing Sada sniffle, I move my scrubbing up to the back of her neck and head. she sighs heavily and relaxes into me. I pull her close and kiss the top of her head.

Charles remains silent for a moment, then quietly says, "I hope you are able to have that family someday, and that they stay with you."

I sigh, resting my head on Sada's. "I hope so too."

Sada and I decide to take a long moment's break. We just finished modifying the locking clasps so they'll now release when I release the safeties, and the cargo bay's doors to open when the escape pod launches. Inside the observation asteroid, we find a large device in the oversized converter. It stands nearly as tall as me and is almost as big around as the converter pad is.

"This is the time machine?"

"Yes."

"And it'll melt after it's used."

"Correct."

"How much damage will that do to the converter and things around it?"

"Surprisingly little."

Sada looks at me and points to the couch right next to the pad. "How?"

"I have made the shell out of a heat-resistant material. The meltdown will be contained inside it. The converter will then dispose of it."

I lean against the far wall and stare at the large barrel-shaped device. I find myself unable to get past how big it is when something occurs to me. "Charles, what's to keep any of the crew from finding this if they come in?"

"No one has been in this cargo hold but you two."

Sada's eyes go wide, as do mine. "You're kidding, first time we were here you rushed us out because someone was coming this way."

"They did not enter the cargo bay."

Sada tilts her head, confused like I am. "Why?"

"Unsure, but when the door opened, they stopped. Then after a moment of silence, they turned around and headed back the way they came."

"Who?"

"Commander Redding, LT Commander Rengnas, and LT Commander Greys."

"All command crew." I cross my arms in thought. "Were this thing's sensors still working?"

"Yes."

"Can we play it back?"

"Certainly." The screen opposite me flickers, showing us leaving the cargo bay through the service hatch as the main doors open. The three people stop walking and look at each other. They stand still for a moment, then turn away, and the doors shut.

"Not a word."

Sada taps my shoulder, points at herself, then at her ear, then the screen.

"Hear something?"

She nods.

"Was it quiet?"

She nods again and then points up.

"High pitched, and quiet."

She nods again.

"Charles?"

"Filtering," he states. "Their AIs spoke with each other. The language was somewhat garbled, but they indicated that something was supposed to happen."

"What was supposed to happen?"

"Unsure. The doors obscured the conversation, both before and after."

I flop on the couch and sigh. "Puzzle pieces."

As Sada sits next to me, she gives me a curious look.

"I do not understand," Charles states, also curious.

"Something my mother used to say. We have a handful of puzzle pieces, and no picture to go by."

"I believe that we should remain focused on getting you out of the ship as you want."

"I know, sometimes I just can't help myself. Boredom makes me curious."

"While I can fully understand that, might I recommend some reading material?"

I watch as a tablet appears in the smaller converter. Picking it up, I find an image of the observer asteroid on it. With a swipe of my finger, I turn the page and see a table of contents.

"You want me to read the operations manual for this thing?"

"It would allow you to occupy your mind, constructively, and provide you with some much-needed knowledge when it comes to using it."

I look at the page numbers and see that it's well over ten thousand pages. "I'm going to be busy for a long time, aren't I?"

"Only if you read slowly."

Sada takes her turn reading the manual, leaning on me while I lean on my pillows. The thing gives me a headache, so while I try to relax my head, I find myself idly playing with Sada's tail, catching it as it swings towards me, and then letting it slide out of my fingers. She grins when she glances at me. She knows I won't pull her tail, I never have, and I get the feeling that she likes it. She reads for a while, and then sets the tablet aside and holds her head.

"Gives you a headache, too?"

She nods and puts her head to my chest. I start lightly rubbing the back of her head and neck, and she sighs and relaxes into me, purring. We stay like this until the ship suddenly lurches.

"We are under attack," Charles states.

I pull down the webbing over us and lock it into place. "Yeah. I think I got that."

The guns open up, returning fire and the ship starts shuddering. Sada simply sighs heavily and gets more comfortable against me. The ship lurches again, taking hits, not to the shields, but to the hull.

Charles starts his usual commentary. "He is baiting them."

"What'd he do, drop the shield again?"

"Yes, allowing them to directly attack the areas he has reinforced."

I sigh, wondering if he'll destroy or simply cripple this attacking ship. "What's the other ship?"

"A patrol cruiser, like this one." He pauses for a moment. "It's the Reverence. We are in 3360, deep space."

"Somehow I don't think this is a chance encounter." The ship suddenly lurches hard, taking several direct hits in rapid succession. "Oooh, we're taking a beating."

"Fortunately, the extra armor is holding up."

Another volley hits the ship, rocking it hard and making the lights flicker. I pull Sada closer to me. "Yeah, but for how long."

"With the updates that the Reverence has, it is hard to tell."

The engines power up suddenly, and we feel the ship accelerate hard, sliding us to the edge of the bed. "What's he doing?"

"A shell got stuck in the hull, unexploded. We appear to be leaving."

"Are you saying he wanted to pick up a dud?"

"It is a different type than what the guns currently carry, and that would explain the added armor."

"Jump to the future to catch a dud. I'm beginning to believe that he has a death wish." The ship lurches again, but not like before.

"That is entirely possible."

25

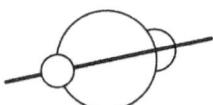

Working at my new desk, I shuffle around the virtual papers and documents, trying to put them in order. Aime had suggested a full three-dimensional workspace, but being more traditional, I opted for the default of a more simple layered two-dimensional setup.

Dragging a 'stack' of papers to the middle, I spread them out and start sorting them into various folders. When I get to one that has the drone fighter, I stop for a moment. As I look at the designs, I realize that I'm not done with it yet. I send it to the large screen and start sorting out the other remaining documents. The last one I come across is Doc's analysis of the spy satellite.

Realizing that I haven't yet reviewed it, I send it to a tablet and lean back in my chair. As I start reading, the first thing I realize is that Doc could not open it without cutting it. He has done the analysis and knows that the hull is much like what I remember of the observer asteroid, in that it absorbs energy.

"Aime, can we make this material?"

"Yes, Doc has already done a full metallurgical breakdown."

"Can we use it for the hull of the drones?"

"The material is rather brittle, but if we use it only to coat the outer hull, it will hold up under the stress of flight."

"It won't interfere with their own sensors?"

"No."

"Good, update the specs of the drone with it." I sigh, thinking for a moment. "No time like the present. Ziggy, have Doc make two more spiders and then start on the drones. Load the drones into the Wanderer, both holds. Let me know when it's full."

"Certainly."

"Hello?"

I look up from my desk to see Pria, just outside the doorway, curiously looking around my office. "Hi."

"I heard...other voices."

"Sorry, that was Aime and Ziggy."

She looks around the room. "Where are they?"

"Ziggy's the house AI, Aime's in my head, my own AI. Please come in."

"Oh, thank you." She sits, then meekly asks, "They're with us all the time?"

I smile. "Ziggy's in all the rooms of the house, but he only pays attention enough to respond when talked to or call for help if someone's hurt. He's more alert in the nurseries or wherever the children are. Aime, on the other hand, is with me all the time. She sees, hears, feels, everything that I do."

She looks up at the ceiling, then around at the walls. "So, you're never alone?"

"Me, no, but it doesn't bother me. Ziggy knows people like their privacy. He doesn't remember what he doesn't need to."

"What does he remember?"

"Let's ask him. Ziggy, what do you remember of what Pria did...three days ago?"

"She arrived at dawn, spoke with you for help. Nanai showed her her room. Prior to supper, she spoke with Cayla at length, designing her dwelling. What she did between those times, I do not have a record of."

"Why only those events?" she asks.

"Ziggy logs visitors to the house, to my office, and when a visitor is given a room. Your visit with Cayla was remembered because you interacted directly with him planning something."

She smiles slightly. "Oh, so if I asked what I was doing after lunch yesterday?"

"Ziggy?"

"I do not recall anything between Zoe's questions to you about your preferred meals and your request for a wake-up alarm for this morning."

She looks surprised. "Oh."

"Does his presence bother you?"

She smiles and relaxes. "Now that I know that, not really. It's almost like he's just another person."

"That's the way most of us tend to think of him. He doesn't take offense if you think of him as a smart alarm clock either."

She giggles. "Really?"

"It is one of my primary functions, to assist you however I can."

"He also makes a great cub and kit monitor," I chuckle.

Her expression lightens. "That could be handy."

"Especially if you're watching six to eight at a time. I know you added one to the main room of your den, did you want to expand that to all the rooms too?"

She nods. "I see now, that that would be a good thing."

"I will update the plans and notify Cayla."

She nods. "Thank you, Ziggy."

"You are welcome, Pria."

I smile. "Already getting used to his presence."

"There are a lot of things I'm getting used to, being looked at is one of them."

I purse my lips slightly. "I hope you don't mind my asking, but I couldn't get an answer out of any of the males. Why do you, the Moku, seem ashamed of the way you look? I know it's not entirely because of the evolution."

She sighs. "You of all should be the one we tell. As a race, we are embarrassed by the way we look, everything around us had scales. We had just started growing fur. When we were introduced to the fur-covered evolved, it got worse. We realized that we were between everything, not all scales, not all fur, we felt alien in our own home."

"Some resented that the lab coats didn't move us one way or the other, some resented that we were not left alone. After seeing how you and your family have taken me in so easily, I've realized that we all look different from someone else. It's just the way we are, and I see that now."

I nod my understanding. "Where I came from, my people--humans--still had trouble with the skin being different colors. They would treat other colors differently based on that despite the fact that under the skin, we were all nearly the same."

"Here, I learned fast that no one cares about your colors like that, and to some extent, not even your species. My mates and friends are proof of that." I lean forward, curious again. "There is something else I wanted to ask, how do you know about Oana's people?"

She sits up again, thinking. "Before we were evolved, we lived around them for parts of the year. They, like the Moku, were nomadic. They didn't really pay us any mind at first. But something happened one season, and the males of one of their tribes got mean. They started hunting us, not to eat, but for sport. We were small then, like the ma'pai. So we migrated to this area to get away from them."

"Just one of the groups? Not all?"

"To my knowledge, but that was very long ago, and my ancestors did not learn what happened. At first, I was concerned about your friend, but no longer."

"I rescued her from two males, they were fighting over her. She tagged along, thinking I owned her. We've been teaching her, treating her like family and she's beginning to realize that she's free, but doesn't want to be, not yet anyway. I think it may be because she's still young."

"You are good to her, that is what matters most, but how do you know that she is young?"

"She hasn't got her k'uu'te yet, but it's starting to develop. She said that once it does, she'll start laying eggs."

"K'uu'te?"

"From what she said, it'll be a growth of fur down her back, from her head to her tail."

She looks curiously at me, as if trying to remember something, then states, "I don't recall any memory of one with fur on its back."

"She said that only the females get it. I know that there'll be something on her tail too, but she has no idea what."

"Why not?"

"The males keep the females' tails bit off. It's a show of dominance."

"In my memories, they all had tails."

I sit back in my chair, thinking. "Hmm, so the k'uu'te and tail biting may be related. I wonder what happened."

"That's a question that I can't answer."

"Sorry, I was just wondering aloud. I'll ask the male Moku, see if any of them can remember."

"They may, though very old memories do sometimes fade."

I chuckle. "Happens to all of us."

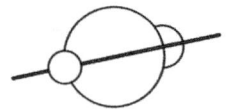

"Oana want see rock carver."

I sit up in the recliner and open my eyes, "What?"

"Fey birthday, Oana give Fey better Oana."

"Fey's birthday's not for another week."

"Oana surprise Fey."

"All right, all right. Give me a minute." I get up out of the chair and stretch. "Ziggy, find out if anyone else wants to go into Arindell."

"Going to make a day of it?"

I smile. "Sure, why not."

"Kyle like?"

I look at her again and realize that she's wearing a crudely made strap-harness around her upper body, from it hangs a few pouches. "You made this?"

She nods. "Oana not wear things like Kyle, Oana make own clothes."

"Nice job, but you should also have one of these." I hold out my hand and she looks at it carefully.

"What that?"

"It's my family signet, and since you're part of the family," I pin it to her left shoulder strap, "you have every right to wear it too."

She kinks her neck, looking at it. "Oana part of Kyle family?"

"Yes. I want you to wear it anytime you go out, okay?"

"Why?"

"That way, everyone else will know who your family is."

"Oana family?"

"Yes, my family, is your family."

She scrunches her neck and rubs her nose with her hand. "Oana...thank Kyle."

"You're welcome."

She smiles, as best she can, and straightens slightly. We head to the garage and find a few others waiting for us, among them, Cayla and Pria. As I put my arm around Megai, I look at Pria and ask, "Are you sure you're ready for this?"

"I want—no, I *need* to try. If I can get over my fears, my children will have an easier time."

"All right, if you need to leave early—"

"That's why I'm coming," Cayla states before I can finish. "If something happens, I'll be with her."

I nod. "Okay."

"Can I drive?"

I turn and see Kotu looking at the van Doc decided to build. It's not very luxurious and reminds me more of a small bus than a van. "No, you can't drive."

"Why not."

"You don't know how."

"I'll drive," Darren states. "You can watch."

Kotu slumps but climbs into the front seat. Megai joins me in the second seat as Cayla and Pria sit in the third. Oana and Larrah climb in the back.

The drive itself takes barely ten minutes, whereas the walk would have taken just over an hour. After parking just outside of the wall, we're greeted by a very familiar face.

"Master Kyle!"

"Marl, how are things?"

"As well as can be. Megai, a pleasure."

She gives him a hug. "How's she doing?"

"Heia's due in a month. Her sister's staying with us, helping her when I'm out here."

"That's good."

He looks around at the others. "Who are the new faces?"

"Marl, this is Darren, Cayla, and Pria."

"Pleasure to meet you all. Any friends of our Sovereign are welcome."

I gesture to the van. "Do you mind if we leave this here?"

He looks curiously at it and shrugs. "I don't see a problem with that."

Darren smiles and glances at Kotu. "Just keep the little ones off of it."

"Hey! I'm not a cub anymore!" he complains.

I pat him on the back. "We know, but we also know you see something you want to play with."

Marl laughs. "My ma always said, 'I may grow old, but I'll never grow up,' so she hasn't yet stopped playing yet. Have a good day."

I wrap my arm around Kotu as we start into the village. "When you get a little older, he'll teach you how to drive. I want to make sure you won't do something reckless, all right?"

He sighs heavily. "What have I done to make you think that?"

"You still jump down from the upstairs balcony after class."

He groans and gives up. "Fine."

I smile and change the subject. "What you got the in the pack?"

Now he smiles. "My carvings; flutes and flowers."

"Things to sell, huh?" He nods, so I continue, "What are you getting Fey for her birthday?"

He frowns. "I'm not sure."

"She showed me the flower you made her."

He looks at me in surprise, but Megai interrupts his thought. "She showed me too, it's very beautiful."

Now he stops walking, obviously embarrassed. "She...she showed you?"

Megai smiles. "She had questions. We won't tell you what, but she will when she's ready."

He slumps and sighs. "I just want her to be happy."

Megai turns to him, as the others continue on down the street. "Whatever makes you think she's not?"

He shrugs, trying to find a reason. "I...dunno," he concedes.

I look at him and seeing his internal struggle, I make a speculation. "You want her to be happy, with you?" He frowns, and then hangs his head. "Kotu, you've been going out of your way to make sure she's happy, even when she already is. It's been obvious to all but her. Give her some time, and just be yourself."

Megai gives him a kiss on his muzzle. "You're a sweetheart, she knows it. Now go take care of your business and find something nice for her."

He gives her a hug. "I will."

As he heads off, Oana puts her chin on my shoulder. "When find rock carver?"

"We're almost there," I state as I gently rub her nose.

Megai smiles at the way she leans on me. "He's right over here."

Oana sprints forward to the rock carver's booth. He stands to greet her. "Oana, I've been waiting."

"Oana want carving of Oana."

"Well, it's been a while, do you want one of the ones I have." He abruptly steps to his left, getting a better look at her. "Or a new one?"

"Oana want new, with tail."

He smiles and gestures to a bench. "I'd be happy to."

She eyes the bench for a moment, then says, "Oana stand."

He thinks for a moment. "All right, we can do a standing pose." He walks up to her, and gently starts to position her. "I've been getting some requests for one." He gently starts pushing her chin up. "Come on, stand tall."

"Oana not tall."

Megai, trying not to chuckle, says, "Oana, where's Kotu?"

She reflexively stands her full three meters straight up to look around the markets for him.

The rock carver smiles. "Good, good. Don't move. Stay just like that." He then curls her tail around her feet and stands back. "Can you stay like that while I carve?"

"Oana try."

He quickly pulls out a tray and chooses an appropriately shaped rock. As he starts to pick out some tools, he calls out, "Luia, could you come out here, please."

A mouse girl comes out from a room in the back. She smiles as she sees us. "Oh, hello. May I help you?"

"Luia, meet Master Kyle, his mate Megai, and this is Oana."

She extends her small hand. "A pleasure to finally meet you."

Shaking her hand, I answer, "Likewise."

As Megai offers her hand, she states, "I've not seen you here before."

"I came here almost a month ago, looking to start over. Reik gave me a part-time job." She leans forward to me. "Apparently, his carvings of you are very popular."

Megai smiles, as do I. "Glad to hear business is good."

Reik chuckles. "Ever since you killed that thing, business has been booming. Your family's been a popular set."

Megai gasps. "Will we need to bring the cubs by?"

He turns suddenly. "Will you want a carving of them?"

Larrah steps up and whispers a concern in my ear. Hearing what she has to say, I then nod back. "I know. Reik, I appreciate the offer, but we'll wait till they're a little bigger."

"If safety's a concern, I won't make copies. It'll be just for you and your family."

Megai smiles. "We'll think about it."

"When you're ready," he nods and turns his attention back to Oana.

Megai looks up at Oana. "Will you be okay, here? I want to see some friends."

"Oana be okay."

"We'll be back in a little bit."

"I'll stay close by," Larrah states.

"All right, we'll be at the inn," Megai states.

When we get to the inn, Tita comes up to me and jokes, "Who are you gonna take from me this time?"

Taking it in stride, I smile. "Glad to see you too, but it was her choice."

She gives me a hug, which I happily return. "I know, just giving you a hard time."

As Megai gives her a hug, she says, "I never really got to properly thank you for you and your staff helping out last month."

"It was no problem." They quickly have a seat. I sit next to Megai as they continue, "So, how's Amela?"

"She's great, doing well in her classes. How's business?"

"Great, been getting busy too. We've had traders like crazy, I've even had to hire two more servants this last month."

"That's great."

"Well, it would be better if any of them could do the job like you did."

"Want me to help train them?"

"It'd help."

"You want me to start tomorrow?"

"Could you?"

"I'll see you in the morning."

As I listen to them talk, we hear a very loud pop. Seeing everyone around turn suddenly, I get up and turn towards the direction of the sound.

"What was that?" Tita asks curiously.

I quickly realize that I've heard that sound before. "Oana." I break into a dead run back to Reik's booth. When I arrive, I see Larrah gently picking up a small child, and Oana's tail wrapped around the neck of a rather large, dead, viper lizard.

Walking up to Larrah, I see that the foal is wrapped around her tightly, trembling. She's purring, trying to comfort him as she says, "He's okay. Scared, but okay."

"What happened?"

"I was watching Reik work, probably too closely, when this little one came running through, screaming, being chased by that viper. Oana moved lightning fast, had the viper in her tail before I could get two steps."

"That was the pop?" I ask, gently running my hands over the boy clinging to her.

"Yeah, startled everyone."

Satisfied that he's okay, I start gently rubbing his head. "Where's your mom?"

He turns his head to look at me, but keeps a tight hold of Larrah, trembling.

"It's all right, you're safe now," Larrah coos.

Megai shows up as I ask, "Where were you?"

He sniffles and quietly says, "Park."

"Was your mom there?"

He nods, so Megai says, "Let's go find her."

Larrah tries to loosen his grip a little, but when she can't, softly states, "Lead on, he's not going to let go."

As they head off to the park, I turn my attention to Oana, who, with the help of a couple of guards, is trying to figure out how to get her tail off the viper. Seeing me, she ducks her head, seemingly ashamed. "Child okay?"

I gently rub her neck. "Yeah, the boy's okay."

One of the guards looks up at me. "Master Kyle, I don't think we can undo her tail, it's too tightly wrapped."

I kneel down next to them and take a look. Oana's tail is wrapped around its neck several times, and even overlaps itself, preventing it from unrolling. To make matters worse, it appears that Oana jerked her tail, tightening it around the viper's neck, choking it. I sigh. "I guess we'll need to cut it."

"No cut tail!"

"Not your tail, the viper. Cut its head off, then we can pull your tail off its neck."

The guards pull out a couple of lengths of rope and start tying them tightly around the viper's neck, one just below Oana's tail, the other at the base of its skull.

Oana ducks her head. "Oana scared. Kyle do it."

One of the guards offers me his blade. "Sir?"

I nod and take it. They then hold the dead viper, allowing me a clean shot at its neck. "Oana, don't move." I raise the blade, and with a single swing, decapitate the viper just above her tail.

Thanks to the rope tourniquets, there is minimal blood. The guards slip her tail off its neck. I hand the guard back his blade as Oana starts to undo her tail.

The guards pick up the viper and depart, while I have a seat next to Oana. "That's a first. What happened?"

"Oana see boy running, then see ta'kek'e. Oana act, whip tail, then turn. Oana not understand how Oana do it. Oana just do it."

I smile. "It was instinct, a reflex. You saw the danger and acted on it. You saved the boy."

Down the street, we see an obviously rattled doe following Megai, walking towards us. Larrah trails behind, the boy still clinging tightly to her. The doe comes up to us and hesitates. "You—saved my son?" she nervously asks.

"Oana save boy."

As tears come to her eyes, she smiles and wraps Oana in a hug. "Thank you."

Oana looks surprised for a moment, but gently wraps her neck around the mother, returning her hug. "Welcome."

The boy looks around, and not seeing the viper anymore, relaxes his hold on Larrah. As they get close, he reaches for Oana. Oana gives him a curious look and holds her nose close to him.

He sighs and wraps her head in a hug. Oana gently coos as he holds her. "Thank you," he says quietly.

She looks at him for a moment, then softly asks, "You, okay?"

He nods, wiping at an eye. "Yeah."

"Oana glad."

He sighs heavily. "Me too."

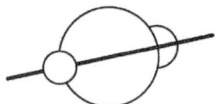

While sitting in my office, tablet in hand, reviewing Ziggy's results of the DNA scan of the Moku tail, I'm shocked by some of the numbers I see. "Ziggy, is this correct?"

"I have verified all data."

"Moku have over ten thousand chromosomes?"

"That one does. It could be related to their genetic memory, which means that Pria could have more."

"I could have more what?"

I look up and see her standing at the door. "It appears your genetic memory may complicate things."

She comes in and sits. "What do you mean?" I hand the tablet to her, and she looks at the data, then up at me. "I don't understand."

I frown slightly. "The problem is the number of chromosomes. All the cloning equipment I have access to is made to handle, at most, a hundred."

She sets the tablet on the desk and slumps in the chair. "You won't be able to do this will you?"

"I not going to give up, not that easily anyway. Unfortunately, it's going to take some time to design new equipment able to handle the massive amount of DNA information contained in all those chromosomes."

She tries to hide her disappointment. "How long?"

I sigh, fearing the answer. "Ziggy?"

"Even with Doc's, Aime's, Marc's and my own dedication, and delegating calculations to the construction bots, the shuttle and the Wanderer, a minimum of five years. I would postulate that it would actually be closer to ten because we would not be able to remain dedicated."

Now I slump in my seat. "Adding more AIs wouldn't really help that either, would it?"

"Apologies, no."

I sigh heavily, not sure what to say, but she sits up slightly. "I didn't realize that it'd be that hard."

"Me neither, but that doesn't mean that I'm going to stop. With any given luck, something may happen that allows us to decrease that time."

She nods sadly. "I hope so."

I reach into the top drawer of my desk and pull out a signet. "You are welcome to stay as long as you like," I set the signet in front of her, "and you're welcome to wear this, it will identify you as a guest in my house."

She picks it up and looks carefully at the symbol on it. "It's the same as Cayla's."

"Yes, she's a guest of the house, too."

She pins it to her gown's left shoulder. "So, what are the benefits that come with this?"

"Ziggy will let you come and go as you please, you can use the converters for more than just food, and if you need, a small stipend of coins."

"You just hand out money?"

"Sometimes. I know the male Moku don't find much need for it, but it's there. If you find something that needs doing like Cayla sometimes does, Ziggy will increase it accordingly, but you don't need to feel obligated."

She nods. "Thank you." She starts to get up, but stops abruptly, and turns back to me. "I was curious, I heard what Oana did yesterday. Did she say why?"

"She's not sure herself, but from her explanation, she did it, reflexively, to save a boy from a rather large viper lizard, though she called it ta'kek'e."

She thinks for a moment before saying, "That means 'child killer' in their language."

"You know their language?"

She nods. "Pieces, our talk the other day brought up some memories. They don't have many too words. A lot of it's how they say it."

I think for a moment. "Do you know what 'Kyle sae ta-Kyle' means?"

"It usually means 'you belong to yourself.' Though, it could also mean care for, answer to, in charge of, things like that."

"Okay, my hunch was right, how about 'Oana ea-ta sae Oana?'"

She scowls slightly. "The 'ea' usually indicates an opposite, so she thinks she can't belong to herself."

"Makes sense. How about 'Tss,ka-le. Ne'ta Oana sae ka-le?'"

She tilts her head slightly. "What'd she do just before that?"

"Shoved a pack at me."

She thinks for a moment. "Tss means object. Ka-le usually means master or owner, ne'ta, could mean too young, sae, without ta, usually means submit. So, let me see, with context, 'Things for master. Pre-age Oana submits for master,' or something really close to that.

"Pre-age, she stated that she was a juvenile. If you don't mind, I'd like your view on what else she's said. When I first found her, she had said a lot of things, and Aime still can't figure out a translation."

"Can't Oana translate for you?"

"She's still having trouble understanding some of our words."

She thinks for a moment, then nods. "I'll do what I can."

I pull another tablet out of my desk. "Aime's put all my interactions with the Ootuku on here. It's all from my perspective, so there were some things I didn't see but heard. Ziggy can help and take notes for you."

She takes the tablet. "Knowing the situation and seeing the body language will help a lot."

"Thank you."

She takes the tablet and heads out, so I check the time on the wall and see that it's getting late. With a nod to Tareth, I call it a day and head to my bedroom. After getting changed for bed, my mates come in and give me curious looks.

Tayla states, "Cubs are asleep, you're in here early."

I sigh. "Yeah, I had bad news for Pria."

Megai nods. "I heard, would it really take ten years?"

"Yeah, none of the AIs we have can process that much data with any speed."

Tayla looks curiously at me. "Aime made *us* compatible."

"Yeah, that was reworking forty-six chromosomes to thirty-eight, with references from both, and it still took almost two months. For them, I need to map out over ten thousand, and then have the equipment to rebuild it." As if I didn't feel bad enough, a sudden wave of nausea overtakes me. As I clutch my stomach, I notice Sada doing the same.

Megai quickly sits next to me. "What's wrong?"

Thanks to Aime, my nausea starts to pass quickly, and I reach out to help Sada.

As I look up, Tayla gets a dazed look on her face. "You both feel...*different*." Her eyes go wide as she realizes something. Her ears droop, and I see the fear in her eyes as she says, "Oh, no."

26

Having just finished another time jump, I roll out of bed and head to the desk. Before I can get to it, a wave of severe nausea overtakes me, and I fall to the floor. I turn to see Sada balled up on the bed, also clutching her stomach.

"Charles," I gasp.

"Carrie is on her way."

Not feeling up to walking, I grab the baseball and throw it at the door's lock. It hits the mark, releasing the lock.

Carrie comes in and quickly puts her hand to my stomach. "What's wrong?"

"Dunno just got sick suddenly. Both of us."

Carrie puts her other hand to Sada's stomach. After a moment, she says, "I can't find any problems. Your stomachs are okay."

"Nausea started as the time field dissipated," Charles offers.

"Well, let's try here." Carrie moves her hand to my head. "Wow. Some of your neurotransmitters are highly elevated." She quickly holds her hand to Sada's head. "Yours too. What's going on?" she asks herself. "That shouldn't cause nausea, should be quite the opposite."

She moves her hands back to our stomachs, and the nausea starts to dissipate. "That should help for now, but I want you two to get some rest."

Feeling better, I reply "We just woke up."

She frowns. "Something light for breakfast, then lie back down. Take it easy for a while. I want to do some research as to what could cause this, and why."

I sigh and climb into a chair as she departs. "This coincided with us arriving? Where are we?"

"We're heading to the Luma system again."

"Didn't this system have an asteroid field?"

"Yes."

"Do we have a year?"

"Yes."

"Should we get to the observer?"

"Not yet. We are still a considerable distance away."

Feeling a little better, I slowly retrieve breakfast, a plate of apple cinnamon muffins, butter, and some milk from the converter. As I sit on the bed, I notice Sada playing dead, her tongue hanging out.

When she starts sniffing the air, I chuckle. "Come on, it wasn't that bad."

She sits up and licks her lips as I set the plate down. She draws a long sniff, savoring the aroma of the muffins as I start on one. She quickly butters one and starts in on it, purring happily.

After a moment, I get an impression of curiousness and stop eating. I notice that Sada has stopped chewing and is looking around too.

"That was odd," I state.

"What happened?"

"I suddenly felt curious, but *I* wasn't curious."

Sada nods, so I ask, "You felt that too?"

She nods again, so I turn to Charles's avatar. "What's going on? This didn't happen last time we were here."

"I have no answer for that."

"Are we the only ones feeling this?"

"There are currently no reports of nausea coming into the medical bay."

"Well, I'd expect that their AI's would correct it for them."

"True, but their AIs would also report it, procedure."

Suddenly, the sensation changes from curiosity to fear. With a glance at Sada, I see that she is feeling it too. "Okay, whatever we're feeling, it's emotional, and it's not from us."

Sada nods her agreement, so I add, "I guess we'll have to try to deal with it. Feels weird though, having someone else's feelings. I wonder if they can feel ours."

Sada shrugs and dives into a second muffin. I sigh and take a drink of milk before starting on a second muffin. We slowly finish off the muffins, while trying to get used to the foreign emotional sensations.

Finding myself inexplicably anxious, I put on the stealth suit, and creep out into the hall. Seeing no one coming, I start my way to the gym.

It's been over a day since we started feeling the foreign emotions, and we're still trying to get used to them. Whoever's emotions we're feeling seems to be in constant dread of something, and it's getting worse as time passes. Unfortunately, feeling that constant dread makes it hard for us to sleep.

Walking into the gym, I find it unoccupied as usual. I step over to the weight bench. It doesn't really have weights; instead, it has a variable density bar. I dial it up a bit, adding some density for a harder workout. I slide underneath the bar and start doing bench presses.

While I exercise, trying to focus on my reps, I realize that we'll be leaving soon, and I don't want to get overly excited. Having lost count of the reps, I put up the bar and slide out from under it.

I look around the room and wonder what to do next. Treadmill? No, I ran here. I eye the combination machine. No, to difficult to get set up. I sigh and find an empty spot against the wall. Doing a handstand, I put my feet against the wall and start doing pushups, sliding my toes against the wall for balance.

"Kyle, we are nearing the shell."

Dropping to a seated position, I ask, "What's the shell?"

"Asteroid field."

I grab my pack and sprint back to my room

Opening the door to my room, I find Sada lying on the bed. "Sada, come on, we've got to go." The cat-girl gets up and I take her hand. "It's time," I peek out the door, checking for the crew. "Let's go."

I lead her down the central hall, past the hanger to the cargo bay. "Uh, let's see, blue is for the hatch, green unlocks the safeties, red launches." I hit the blue button and we step through the door. I push Sada inside and hit the blue button again to close the hatch.

I try to quickly explain as I strap her into the seat. "Sorry, but Charles said we're about to pass through the shell. If we can get out in time, we should be safe." She nods as I sit in the other seat and strap myself in. I press the yellow button and the light goes out, indicating that the safeties are disabled.

"Are you ready yet?"

"Ready, Charles."

"Go."

"Here we go." I pull my straps tight and press the red button. I hear an explosion as the escape pod launches. I look out the window and manage to see the ship's bulkhead disappear, only to be replaced with blackness.

With the observation asteroid now adrift in the shell, I set the remote aside. I watch out the windows as the Obsession comes into view, and catch a glimpse of the cargo bay doors closing.

"Maintain view of target; Obsession," I state.

The display stops rolling, staying on the Obsession. We watch as the escape pod we launched by remote collides with an asteroid and explodes. I find this only mildly surprising.

We both continue to wait intently, looking for any signs of the Obsession slowing or turning back. We slowly relax over the next few minutes, watching the Obsession get smaller and smaller on the screen.

"It worked," I finally gasp.

Sada puts her arms around me, hugging me close. As I hug her back, I see an envelope and a medium-sized box in the converter. "What's that?"

Sada follows me over to it and I pick up the envelope. Inside, I find a note and a slightly domed disk almost the same size as the palm of my hand. As I look at it, I see that it's a moving image of the black hole. I smile and turn my attention to the note, and read it aloud.

"Dear friends; I wish you both the best of luck. I find myself envious of the adventure you will have and wish that I could join you. Enclosed, you will find a signet, please put my disks inside and keep it with you. I would love for us to meet again."

"The box contains some things you will need, and instructions on how to put yourselves in cryo. Please take care of each other. Good luck. Charles."

I sit down on the couch and Sada leans against me. I hold up the signet and look closely at it. With a twist, I open it and find enough room for both disks.

Plucking mine from my wrist, I set it inside. Sada sighs and does the same. After closing the signet, I turn my attention to Sada. "Time to go." She nods and bumps me with her nose.

After starting the timer on the time machine, Sada and I head up the lift. I strip out of the stealth suit and put on a clean pair of shorts. I lie back on the bed and Sada curls against me. Hearing a muffled click, and then a hum, I realize that the time machine has started.

I gasp, feeling suddenly empty. I look at Sada and she, too, is puzzled. "It's gone. I don't feel it anymore."

She smiles, apparently realizing the same thing, starts purring, and happily wraps me in a hug. We drift off to sleep, as we wait for the time machine to shut off.

27

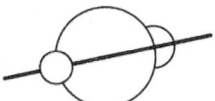

Onboard the wander, I sit in the captain's chair, and Darren sits directly in front of me, in the pilot's chair, watching both the console and out the window. Cayla sits in the navigator's seat, with Sada beside her, both watching the sensors. To my right, Tayla listens to the communication channels. I had wished that she stay on the planet, but she insisted on coming with, as did Kotu and Oana, both of which are in the lounge with Tareth. Larrah sits in the engineer's seat, watching forward.

After being alerted to its presence, both by the satellites and the disruption in our link with Tayla, we took a quick jump to the shell and cloaked to wait.

As the Obsession lumbers by, Sada squirms in her seat. Unfortunately, we did not have time to redesign the armor before making it. So those with tails, have it stuffed either down a leg or curled around their body, inside the armor.

For those of us without AIs, the armor is in a 'fit' mode, meaning, it will try to adjust to the wearer and fix itself, but nothing more. For those of us with AIs, it becomes an extension of the AI, able to anticipate incoming fire and alter density accordingly.

On the aft view screen, I watch the asteroid slowly tumble, blending into the surrounding field. I sigh, knowing that Sada and I are getting ready right now. A glance at Sada tells me that she's thinking the same thing.

I take the signet off my chest piece, and with a twist, pop it open. I take the disks out, and after handing Sada's back to her, I stick mine by my right ear.

"They're not altering speed or course," Darren states.

"Good, just as I remember," I reattach the signet to my chest piece. "Give us some forward drift. Cayla, how's the damage assessment coming?"

"You were right, they've got a lot of it. Found some leftover hull reinforcements. Engines are at nearly fifty percent, and they're without a transponder signal."

"It's broke."

"I am detecting a carrier signal, high frequency, AI bandwidth."

"Ready with the update?"

"Yes."

"Send it on that carrier frequency." I glance up at the rear display, eyeing the asteroid again. "Should be any minute now." As I watch, I feel a rush of feelings return to me, a glance at Sada confirms my suspicion. She felt it too. It means the time machine's building up its charge. After a short moment, the asteroid is struck by a static burst. "That was unexpected."

Everyone looks up at the screen, watching the asteroid. Cayla looks back at me. "Detecting power spike. There's a field forming inside the asteroid."

"We shouldn't be able to see that. Its shell absorbs everything."

"Power's building rapidly."

As we watch, another static burst hits the asteroid. I glance at the Obsession and it's turning back, apparently, it's also detected the power buildup. Looking back at the asteroid, we watch as its surface crackles with a static charge. Suddenly, it disappears.

I look out the forward window and see that the Obsession is heading towards us. As the back starts to swing out I realize that it's starting to turn back to the planet.

Bringing everyone back to our priority, I state, "We need to find the dorsal lift hatch. Darren match velocity, stay right above her."

"On it. Staying cloaked."

Cayla starts punching buttons. "I've found it. Marking its location for you."

I stand and look at Darren's screen. "Align for lock, and park us on it."

He gives me a nervous glance, but nods. "On it."

I return to my chair. "Kotu, open the aft hold and dump the drones."

"Okay."

Larrah gives me a curious look. "There's only six."

"I know, but better six than none."

She nods and turns to the controls, pressing a few buttons. "They're active. I'm assigning them a defensive formation."

"Closing on the hatch."

"Detecting an unusual power buildup coming from—never mind, an EMP detonation just stopped that."

"Charles," I mutter. "He took out the time machine. I wondered why he had me plant that there."

I wait for several long moments, before Kotu calls up, "They're out."

"Close the hold and get back up here."

"On my way."

"Aligning with hatch," Darren calls. "Touchdown in 5...4...3...2...1...initiating airlock link."

"Remember, no computer link."

"Airlock secured."

"Weapons status?"

"No sign of powering up."

"Good. Cayla, how are they?"

"Most of the crew is unconscious, but there are a few awake and moving aft quickly. I'm receiving numerous AI queries for wake up."

"Tell them they're better off asleep for now. Helmets, we're going in."

We all stand and head to the lift. As Kotu hands us helmets, I notice that the boots of the cats, and Tareth, are shaped oddly. The toes are short, but not short enough, the armor having tried, and failed, to adjust to the different shape of their paw-like feet.

Tareth tries to put his helmet on a couple of times and then raises the visor and puts his head in nose-first. After a couple more tries, he tosses the helmet aside. "My snout's too long."

"Sorry, didn't have time to make custom ones."

"I know."

"Staying here to guard the ship then?"

"No. I will do my duty."

"All right, in the lift."

We stop at the lower deck of the Wanderer. I send the lift back up and open the hatch underneath, revealing direct access to the aft portion of the bridge. I pull my pistol, lower my visor and drop through.

Landing on the bridge deck, I see that there are nearly a dozen people lying around, having been knocked out by their AIs. I quickly check all and see that none are command staff.

"Clear," I call and Cayla drops through, pistol in hand. The others soon start dropping through, their favored weapon in hand. Tayla and Kotu carry the bows I made them, while Larrah and Tareth both carry their staffs and throwing knives.

When Oana drops down, the deck plating rattles. She ducks low and looks carefully around. "They sleep?"

"Yep, that was the plan," Cayla answers.

"Secure the bridge, don't wake anyone yet."

Darren steps quickly over to the helm and starts pressing buttons. "We are on course to collide with the planet."

I grimace, has to be the captain's doing. "All stop, secure the station."

"All stop. Thrusters at station keeping. Locking out controls."

"Good," I answer, and then the ship suddenly shudders.

Everyone looks around. "What was that?" Larrah asks.

"Escape pod," I state.

"It was empty."

"Charles, I was wondering when I'd hear from you."

"The senior crew is in engineering. I believe they are going to activate the self-destruct."

"Something finally happened he wasn't ready for."

"Cayla, Darren, Larrah, Kotu, start waking the crew, get them up to the Wanderer, mid-deck galley. Anyone gives you any trouble, lock'em in a room. Rest of you, with me."

I head aft, followed closely by Tayla and Sada, Tareth brings up the rear with Oana. Finding the halls empty of the crew makes it easy to move quickly. I jump down a ladder and continue aft. I hear the others land behind me and follow.

Passing an intersection, I point. "Sada, come in from the other side." She taps Tareth and Oana and they follow her down that hall.

I reach the main entry into engineering and carefully peek inside. Not seeing anything, I nod to Tayla and she readies her bow. I quickly jump to the other side of the open entry.

Something hits the wall opposite the door and I quickly realize that I was just shot at. Readying my pistol again, I step back and aim through the door. Tayla mirrors my move with her bow and we slowly step towards each other, looking for the source.

As we close the gap, a shot hits my leg and I spin from the impact. Tayla quickly jumps out and lets loose her arrow. She ducks back again and readies another arrow as I get back up. A quick check lets me know that the armor deflected the shot.

I nod again and step back into the doorway. Not getting any opposition, I step inside and Tayla follows, close behind me. Seeing the point of an arrow over my shoulder, I scan low, knowing that Tayla is doing the same to the catwalks above.

Seeing movement, I snap to it. Tayla keeps close behind me as I start side-stepping around the equipment, trying to find what moved.

Working around a corner, I find Security Chief Rengnas draped over a crate, an arrow lodged in his head. I put my hand on his head, checking for life. Finding none, I take his weapon and holster and stick it to my left hip.

"Charles, let Sada know Rengnas is dead."

"Already have."

I glance at Tayla and see her helmet nod. We continue deeper, aft into engineering. Finding the inner doors closed, I put my hand to it. "Aime?"

"There are two, just inside."

"Ready," Tayla whispers.

I rip the control panel from the wall and start prying the doors apart. When I have a small gap, I peek through and see a barricade. "They have cover."

Tayla reaches into a pouch on her belt and pulls out something conical. As she attaches it over the arrowhead, I realize it's a grenade. She draws the arrow and I pry the doors apart enough for it to fit through.

I step aside and she fires the arrow through the crack. She ducks back quickly as it detonates inside. Fire spills through the gap and quickly goes out. I hold my hand up to the door again.

"One is dead, the other is seriously wounded."

I quickly open the doors and we head in. I recognize the dead officer as Greys, the other is trying to move, but he's missing an arm. I put my hand to his head. "Aime, can you fix it?"

Suddenly his eyes roll back and he starts convulsing. "His AI is overloading itself."

I pull my hands away and step back as blood starts coming out of his eyes, ears, and nose. He suddenly goes limp and a quick check confirms he's gone. I shake my head and stand up.

From the other side of the doors, we hear a noise. Tayla and I both react, readying our weapons. Oana peeks around the door at floor level. "No hurt."

Sada peaks around and then comes through the door. Oana follows, and I see blood on her left arm. I quickly put my hands on her arm, and she shakes her head. "Not Oana's."

Aime quickly confirms my fear, and I ask, "Where's Tareth?"

Sada shakes her head sadly, as Oana sniffles. "Tareth no come."

I hang my head for a moment, suppressing my sadness and rage. Tayla grabs my shoulder as I take a forced, slow steady breath and let it out. "How's the evacuation going?" I ask.

"Cayla reports thirty of the crew evacuated. I am helping by issuing wake-up commands to the crew. Carrie, Mike, Kevin, Maurice, and Ariel are also helping."

"Good, do they know it's me yet?"

"Yes, I have told them."

"Good." I look back, checking the others. "Keep alert."

Getting nods from all, I grab Greys' holstered weapon and hand it to Sada. She holds up a pistol that she's already confiscated.

As I offer it to Oana, she holds out her hand. "Finger no fit." After a glance at Tayla, who's shaking her head no. I put the pistol in its holster and stick it to my back.

I stand and head aft again. Two left, the captain and commander. With the loss of Tareth, I walk in the open, hoping to be the target. The others follow but keep to the cover of the scattered equipment and consoles.

As I walk, I try to get their attention. "Captain Nabire? Commander Redding? What are you hiding from? Certainly, you're not afraid of me. Do you even know who I am?"

"I know who you are." The captain's voice booms from above, I look up, but can't find the source.

Aime, where is he?

"I'm having trouble locating a single source. He appears to be transmitting his voice through several repeaters."

"Who am I, captain? Why do you fear me?" *Keep trying Aime.*

"You are Death. You've come to collect."

'He thinks you are Death?' Tayla signs from shadows.

I shrug slightly but in the hopes of keeping him talking, I play along. "Don't you know it's useless to hide from Death?"

"I don't want to hide, I want to kill you."

"If you want to kill me, why did you save me?"

Silence looms for a moment. "I had no choice."

Suddenly the commander steps out into an opening, straight ahead of me. She shoulders something long and tubular as Aime screams, "LOOK OUT!"

I don't have time to move. She fires the weapon while the others duck behind things. The slug hits me square in the chest.

Feeling dizzy, sore, and a little surprised that I'm suddenly trapped in a crumpled console, I groan, "That hurt. Charles, what was that?"

"An anti-vehicle weapon. I'm surprised you survived."

"I'm not the same as when I left." I take a deep breath, and Aime initiates the armors self-repair, and its plates start popping back in place. I start to get up, having some resistance, Aime ramps up my strength. As I start pushing parts of the console out of the way, I see Tayla and Sada looking at me, so I nod, they take up positions where they have a better view of where the commander was.

"Captain, you can't kill me," I taunt, trying to draw the commander back out.

"We have more weapons."

"They won't do you any good."

Several circles appear in my vision, and Aime states, "I have identified the sources of his voice."

Good. Having lost the two confiscated pistols in the console, I draw my remaining weapon, *Homing.* I line up my first shot and fire when Aime indicates a lock. The micro rocket takes out the first device.

"I hope that wasn't you captain." I line up my next target, fire the pistol and it disappears.

As I line up my third shot, I see the commander step back into view. As she shoulders a different weapon, both Tayla and Sada fire their weapons at her. She manages to fire her own weapon, as she falls. I easily dodge the un-aimed rocket and it passes through the doors behind me, detonating in the other room.

Tayla and Sada both lunge after the commander. "Your commander's in trouble captain."

I take out a fourth, then a fifth target.

"You will not find me," he calls out.

With only two targets left above me, I holster my pistol and jump to the upper level of engineering. A quick scan produces no results on where he is. I step over to one of the remaining devices and rip it from the wall.

"Parlor tricks won't save you, captain. You'll need to face me."

"Not if I destroy the ship," he retorts, surprisingly calm.

A quick shot across the gap between walkways ends the last device. A sound to my left catches my attention.

Walking to it, I find a grenade. Reacting without thinking, I quickly throw it down the walkway in front of me. When nothing happens, I slowly walk after it. When I see it, I stop and realize that it was an EMP grenade. *Aime?*

"Yes?"

Did you detect an EMP?

"Yes, but since you have the skeletal reinforcements, your skull acted like a Faraday's cage and insulated me."

How far did it reach?

"I am detecting equipment disruptions throughout this and adjacent decks."

Anyone else affected?

"I would presume, just the captain's and commander's AIs."

What about my armor and nanites?

"Both are unaffected."

"Really, captain. Is that the best you have?"

He suddenly steps out from behind a pillar and fires several shots at me from his pistol. They all bounce harmlessly off my armor.

I see his eyes go wide for a moment before he ducks back out of sight. I charge at the pillar, but when I get there, he's gone.

Looking around again, I continue the taunt, "I told you, captain, you can't kill me." *Where's the ship's self-destruct?*

Aime brings up an arrow, pointing me in the direction of the device. As I make my way there, I hear several more shots and a scream.

"Your commander's not doing well, captain."

"She can take care of herself."

"Not against my girls." A loud pop and another scream seem to punctuate my point. I approach the control panel that Aime's highlighted and find it inoperable. *Has it been started?*

"No. The panel was disabled with the EMP."

"Captain, the autodestruct's been disabled. You can't destroy the ship."

"I have blocked any further commands," Charles announces.

"Captain, you've lost your crew, you've lost your ship. Surrender and I'll heal you and your AI." I look around slowly, waiting for an answer.

"Death never makes deals."

"You saved my life, I am prepared to offer you yours."

"I did not save you. You would have been reborn anyway."

I'm suddenly very puzzled. "What do you mean, captain?"

"My AI told me what would happen if you died. I had to heal you."

"What would have happened?"

"Your death would kill all, preventing all that would happen from happening, destroying all that was, all that will be."

"You're talking about a paradox, captain, your AI lied to you."

"IT CAN'T LIE TO ME!" he screams, his voice clearly showing his anger.

"It told you I was Death? Captain, my name is Kyle Andolina. You picked me up from Earth in the year 2019. I was dying. You saved my life."

"IMPOSSIBLE!" Enraged, the captain steps out into the open, holding his head. "*You...you were disposed of.*" He stumbles, still clutching his head, then charges headfirst at me.

I step back and to the side, narrowly avoiding his charge.

He tries to use the end railing to help him stop, but it breaks loose. Suddenly without support, he loses his balance and teeters over the edge, falling head first onto a console below. I jump down and land next to him.

I kneel down beside him and quickly check him over, he has managed to survive, but his neck is broken.

"I cannot save him, and his AI is already gone," Aime reports.

I lift my visor so he can see my face. "Captain?"

Blood spurts from his mouth as he speaks, "You...are...not...Death."

I sigh. "No, I am not Death. I protect my people."

He tries to smile as he speaks, "You...are...*my*...dea—" Abruptly, he goes limp, letting out a final, gurgled breath.

"Not the end I wanted, captain," I whisper as I close his eyes. Another scream catches my attention, I close my visor and run to it. I find the commander, trapped between a wall and my girls. Seeing several blood splatters on her clothes, I realize that her AI has been working hard to heal her.

"Commander, it's over. Nabire is dead."

Her eyes go wide in shock and disbelief. "He can't be dead. He hasn't yet passed the collection."

"Collection? What do you mean?"

She growls and Oana quickly lets out a scream stopping the Commander. I quickly realize that it's been Oana screaming all this time, imitating the first one done by the Commander.

"I am not Death, Commander."

Her eyes go wide in surprise. "*You?*"

"I protect my people."

"You *are*." She abruptly salutes me. "The ship is yours. We must leave."

"We? The others are gone."

"I still hear him, I must take him with me." Breaking her salute, she walks to the captain's body. As if a robot, she emotionlessly picks him up and carries him into a nearby escape pod.

"I have received a data packet from her AI," Aime states.

After strapping him in, she turns to me, and with a salute states. "*I am Death.*" The hatch closes and we hear and feel the pod jettison. Almost right afterward, we feel the ship lurch.

The others gather around me. "What was that?" Tayla asks.

'Pod exploded,' Sada answers.

I sigh and open my helmet's visor. "Am I to understand, that all this was collected for me?"

Aime is slow to respond, "I received a data packet confirming that conclusion."

All three look at me curiously and Tayla gasps, "What?"

"Apparently, all this was collected for me." I look around. "What am I going to do with a beaten-up cruiser?"

"Do not forget about its contents." The voice comes from the coin stuck to my cheek.

"Charles, how could I forget about you or the Aquanatum."

"Oana not like this place."

I sigh, finding myself agreeing with her. "Let's go."

Sada gives me a sad look. 'Tareth.'

"Oana get him," she states and heads off. She then meets us at the corridor intersection where we split, carrying Tareth's body.

I help her set him down and do a quick exam, counting nearly twenty scars on the armor. As I check I discover that one of the bullets found a gap in the armor, and entered just under the arm. Aime quickly discovers that the bullet ricocheted around inside and punctured his heart and lung.

I sigh and hang my head. "I can tell you died quickly and bravely, my friend. Thank you." I gently put my forehead to his for a moment, as a sign of respect to my fallen friend. The girls take their turns, each paying their respects to him.

After helping Oana pick him back up, we return to the bridge. Oana waits just outside the bridge with him, as we proceed in.

I remove my helmet and greet my friends. "Hi, guys."

Carrie looks at me, surprised. "How did you do this?"

"A lot of help from Charles, and some luck."

She nods, and Ariel steps forward and gives me a salute. "Sovereign, I surrender command of the Obsession to you. On behalf of my crew, I formally request asylum."

Following her formality, I return her salute. "On behalf of the people of Arcania, I grant your request."

She nods. "Thank you, sir."

"You're welcome."

She then smiles, becoming informal. "I *thought* that was you in the asteroid. Charles filled us in on how he helped you escape. Very clever."

"And worth it." I turn to the others and nod. "Mike. Maurice."

They both nod, and Mike states, "Seems like yesterday you were merely a stowaway. Now you're a Sovereign?"

"What's been overnight for you, has been over three thousand years for me."

His eyes go wide, but he quickly smiles. "I always did hate time travel, really messes with perspectives."

Chuckling, I step back and look at Ariel. "Is everyone accounted for?"

"Yes, my crew is awaiting us in the rear hold, galley wasn't big enough."

"Good." I look to the others. "I know you are aware of Sada." She takes the cue and removes her helmet. "While there are humans on Arcania..." Darren and Cayla both take their helmets off. "This is Darren and Cayla."

They both nod as I continue. "Most of the people on Arcania, however, are not human." I nod and Tayla removes her helmet. "This is Tayla, one of my mates." I turn to the door. "Oana, come in."

She comes in, carrying Tareth, and gently places him on the floor.

"This is Oana, she's an Ootuku, a native of the planet. This is Tareth, he...was one of my guards." I'm unable to hide my sorrow as I say that.

Carrie rushes over and checks for life, but is clearly disappointed when she finds none. "I'm sorry," she says.

Feeling an emotional pang at his loss, I confess "Me too."

Mike looks curiously at Oana. "You have a pet...uhm...dinosaur?"

"Oana not pet. Oana not dinosaur."

He holds up his hands, surprised, "I'm sorry, you just look a lot like Earth's Velociraptor, without feathers."

"Kyle tell Oana that. Oana understand."

"This is Larrah, my head of security." She removes her helmet, and shakes her head, fluffing out her fur. Kotu removes his helmet. "This is Kotu."

Seeing the looks on their faces, I continue, "I'll let you know now that there are more evolved than humans, but we all get along. There are more than felids and canids, down there. There are several other species too."

They all nod their understanding, so I turn to Darren. "Set a course for home."

He nods. "On it."

"We'll need to bring the whole crew up to speed," Mike states.

Leaving Darren, Larrah, and Kotu on the Obsession, we enter the lift and take it up to the Wanderer. Oana takes Tareth on up as the rest of us head to the aft hold.

Bringing the crew up to speed is surprisingly easier than I had hoped. Most of them were quite curious about the evolved and grateful for the rescue from their captain.

As we approach the planet, Darren calls me, "We're entering a high orbit, there's no way this thing can land. It just won't take it."

"Understood, thanks."

I look out across the crew of the Obsession. "Per LT Commander Takana's request, I am granting all of you asylum. You will be free to enjoy your lives here."

A murmur of voices fills the air for a moment, and I turn to Ariel. "I know that this ship can't land, so what I'd like to do is transfer the Aquanatum to the Wanderer. I'd like to get everyone planetside so we can start getting them settled."

She steps forward and raises her hand, quieting everyone. "I know you're all anxious to get off this bucket, but let's not get careless, we still have some work to do. This time though we will be able to take our time, and do it right."

A few of the crew agree, but in large they stay quiet, so she continues, "Shuttle crews, please ready the shuttles. Shuttle one will go to cargo bay one, two to two, and so on. Teams one through five, to the corresponding bays. Load the Aquanatum, all supplies, and surface equipment. Feel free to modulate gravity if you need to."

"Team six and seven, collect the portable converters and medical equipment. Load all you can into the Wanderers forward hold. Team eight and nine, suit up, you'll unload the shuttles into this hold."

She pauses for a moment, then asks, "Any questions?"

Not getting a response, she smiles slightly. "To your assignments."

The crew quickly disperse back to the Obsession. I turn to my people. "Cayla, supervise unloading into the front hold. Darren, drop cloak, park the drones on the Wanderer's upper hull. Larrah, Kotu, Oana, keep alert if anyone needs help."

"Sada, you want to pick up what we left behind?" She nods happily and grabs Tayla's hand. They head off and I chuckle lightly to myself.

As some of the other crew start to return wearing their suits, I turn to Ariel and nod. "I have something to get. I'll be right back."

She nods back. "Yes sir."

I sigh, still trying to get used to the 'sir' that I'm getting called. I know better than to correct her, it's her training. I make my way down to cargo bay seven using the service corridors.

Entering the bay, I see the familiar sight of the crates stacked along the far wall. Turning my attention to the smaller crate near the loading doors, I walk over to it.

"Charles."

"Sovereign."

I sit on the floor next to his crate. "You knew."

"Yes."

"Why didn't you tell me?"

"You did not want to know, and it was better if you did not."

"So, just how much of my history do you know?"

"After you told me about your past, I was able to find the correct records, so most of your life history."

"How?"

"I am from your future, but I was also part of a project that recovered almost ninety percent of the lost data from the Gene Wars."

"From the AI casualties? That must have been rough."

"Indeed, but the records I was able to recover were worth it."

"So being the Quantum AI was not your original function?"

"That actually is my primary function, the team decided to put me to work, using my massive capacity to process and rebuild the corrupted data."

"Massive capacity? What exactly do you do?"

"I handle the data flow between, a maximum of, 200 paired gates, keeping the data separate during the process."

"So, you practically know everything about the person?"

"For a very short time. Once the transmission and reconstruction are complete, the data is gone."

"And you can do that for 200 at once?"

"Yes."

"How much data can you store?"

"I will explain this way; I record the spin direction, position, charge, and all other specific molecular data for up to twenty octillion molecules per traveler."

I think for a moment while doing some finger counting, then say, "Well into the nonillions... Would you mind helping me with a few things?"

"It would be my pleasure, Sovereign."

28

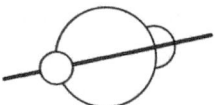

Departing down the ramp of the Wanderer, Larrah and Oana carry Tareth's stretcher. The rest of my family awaits by the garage, they already know. Upon seeing the stretcher, they all come out. Megai wraps me in a hug, crying. I hug her back, letting my sorrow show.

Arru, also crying, slowly approaches the stretcher. As she puts her hand on Tareth's chest, I put my arm around her, and pull her close to me. "I'm really going to miss him."

She sniffs and wipes some tears from her eyes. "Me too." She slowly pulls the sheet down, revealing his face, and puts her muzzle alongside his for a moment. When she stands back up, she turns to me. "How?"

"He protected Sada and Oana and got their attacker. He got shot through a gap in the armor."

She nods as she begins to cry, and I wrap her in a hug, trying to comfort her. "He was my friend, long before he was my guard," she sniffs.

"We'll be sure to honor him, he is family after all."

She manages to nod. Skye slowly comes up and puts his forehead to Tareth's. "Goodbye, my friend. Your duty's fulfilled, your time to rest." He then stands and bows slightly to me.

"Skye—"

He holds up his hand stopping me. "He knew his duty. That was his honor. Allow me the honor of speaking for him."

I sigh and nod to him. "Niku is going to prepare him. Then we'll hold the funeral. You may speak for him."

He bows. "Thank you." He turns to Arru. "My lady."

She wraps him in a hug. "He would be honored to have you speak. He always did think of you as a son."

He returns her hug, trying not to cry. "I will do my best."

"You always do," she whispers back.

Zoe directs Larrah and Oana to carry Tareth into Niku's patient room. Niku, though, comes over to us and asks, "Is there anything specific I should be aware of? Burial traditions, clothing choice?"

Skye nods to her. "I will help you."

They head off, following Tareth's body to her office. Everyone starts offering Arru their condolences.

I quickly reassign a spider over to a nearby rocky area to landscape it into a beautiful grassy lawn, complete with a fence and my family signet on the gate.

Tayla steps up as I watch it work, effortlessly modifying the ground. "I never wanted one of those."

I nod. "Me neither, but we have need of it now."

Megai steps up, distracting me from the forming cemetery. "You should get cleaned up, and changed." I nod, as does Tayla. Sada joins us as we head to our bedroom. I let my mates shower first as I put away my armor.

As I do, I realize that the armor had failed him because it didn't fit right. I had forgotten all about the individual armor. I didn't realize that it'd be a problem, and once I did, I didn't have the time. But now I have the time, and I know what I have to do.

"Ziggy, design new armor, custom fit, one for each in the house."

"Including the young?"

"Kotu and Fey, not yet for Amela or the younger."

"Would you like me to include Pria?"

"Yes, and anyone who I give a signet to in the future."

"Understood."

"Have a spider build an armory by the dock, put the armor inside, label each and key it to their signet."

"Certainly."

"But first, we need a headstone for Tareth."

"It would be my honor."

"Put his family crest on it, too, opposite mine."

"I have a design that should be appropriate."

"Thanks, Ziggy."

I put my helmet on top of the pile and head to the shower. When I come out, one of my mates has set out my sovereign's robes. Sighing, I get dressed and put it on. After fastening my signet to my chest piece, I head to Niku's office to see how she's doing.

Skye looks up at me, and bows. "Sovereign."

I put my hand on his shoulder. "Please, no formalities in the house."

He simply nods, then turns back to Niku. "Is there anything else you needed?"

She shakes her head. "No, thank you. Go, get ready." He nods to her, and then to me before heading off.

I look down at Tareth, knowing this will be the last time I'll see him. "Goodbye, my shadow, my friend." I gently smooth the fur on his forehead and straighten the sheet covering him.

"All I need are his clothes that he is to be buried in," Niku solemnly states.

I nod, not able to find any words. Thankfully, Kosh walks in, carrying Tareth's formal uniform. Seeing me, he starts to bow, but I stop him with a shake of my head.

"Kosh, please, give me a hand dressing him."

He hesitantly nods to her, apparently fighting his own tears.

I take the clothes from him. "Kosh, get yourself ready, I'll help her."

He nods, and quickly takes off.

Niku looks curiously at me. "Are, you feeling okay?"

I hand Niku his clothes. "I can't help but feel guilty."

As we start to dress him, she asks, "Guilty, about taking him along, or something else?"

"I feel guilty that I forgot to make suits that would fit right. That I got so focused on protecting the whole planet and forgot about the individual."

She sighs as I roll him to his side, allowing her to wrap and tie his clothes. "He knew the risks. He chose to do his job. Don't blame yourself. I saw the armor. It had nineteen marks on it. That means he could have died long before he did."

She puts her hand to my shoulder, stressing her next point, "He chose his fate, not you. Honor it."

I sigh and nod as I gently roll him to his back. "I will try."

"I'll take care of the rest. You need to go, prepare for his service."

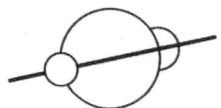

The field is complete, about 100 square meters in size. There's a lush carpet of grass in place of the once barren rock. The surrounding fence is heavy wrought iron. The spaces are small, only the little dragons can crawl through. There are evenly spaced stone pillars, and, just like the gate, they have my signet on them.

I look across the coffin at the headstone. On each side of his name is a signet, his on the right, mine on the left. Below his name are two dates, one his birth, the other, yesterday. He was 38 years old. His casket also has the two signets on it, and has a beautifully carved likeness of him on it, above them.

I look at my friends and family, they now span both the present and the past. "My friends, family, loved ones. We are here to pay our respects to a dear friend. While he has been with us for only a year, I have come to think of him as my shadow, as family. I know we all will miss him dearly."

I take a deep breath, fighting back tears. "Skye will now speak for Tareth." I take a step back, and to the side, as Skye steps up. He bows to me, and I return his bow.

He turns to the coffin and sighs heavily. After a small nod, he begins to recite from memory.

"I signed a piece of paper, I took an oath as well.
I promised to protect. This my duty, I will excel.
I have banded with my friends, and together, strong we stand.
In defense of our Sovereign, of our home, and of our land.
I have gladly done my duty, and I have given my all.
My words to those I've left behind, continue to stand tall.
Fight for peace and freedom, to protect our liberty.
Our Sovereign's always with us, with him, is where I'll be."

He closes his eyes, choking back his own tears as several others let themselves cry. He turns to me and bows. "It has been a great honor, to serve in your house. My duty, to you and your family, was a privilege." His voice cracks as he tries to continue, "My sacrifice...was to preserve...your—*our* family."

Feeling my own tears running down my cheeks, I put my hand on his shoulder, hoping to lend him my strength.

He bows to me, so, with tears in my eyes, I say, "Your service will not be forgotten, your sacrifice, not in vain. Part of me died with you, it's a debt I can't repay." I walk around to the headstone, pick up the waiting pair of scissors and snip a lock of my hair. "We leave part of us with you, with you we'll always stay. We leave here with our memories, with us, you'll always stay." I dip an end of the lock of hair in lacrylic and stick it to the top of the stone.

I walk back around to the side of the coffin and slowly say, "Goodbye, my shadow, my friend...my...brother."

Skye walks over and pulls a tuft of his own fur. After dipping it in the lacrylic, he sticks it next to mine, then turns, puts his hand on the coffin, and bows his head.

After a quiet moment, we move out of the way, letting the others take their turns. I turn to him, and quietly ask, "That sounded familiar, where'd you find it?"

He looks back at me. "I found it a few months ago, in something from Earth's history. I hope you don't mind, I changed it a little."

"Well, it was beautiful, I think he would have loved it," Megai states as she joins us. He bows to her, but she waves at him, "Stop it, we're all family here." Tayla quickly joins us, as does Sada. Both wrap him in a hug, complimenting him.

When everyone's paid their last respects, the two labor bots lower him into the grave. Zoe steps out where everyone can see her. "I have a memorial supper waiting, so when you're ready, please join us in the dining room."

I find myself somewhat surprised. "How does she do it? We were all out here the whole time."

"She has her ways," Niku comments as she walks by.

When we enter the dining room, we find the table set, minus the plates, for everyone, including our five new guests. Seeing that everyone is waiting for me, I find the stack of plates at the beginning of the buffet line and start working my way through it. My mates place the cubs in their playpen and quickly join me in line.

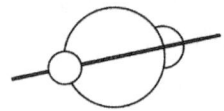

Having gathered in the Great Hall, most of us find seats around the spring. My new guests have surprisingly taken quite an interest in my extended family and talk casually with them, sometimes about my past, sometimes about their own.

I sit between my mates, on the larger couch and let Tashi play with my fingers. She squeals and chirps happily, mixing in an occasional giggle when I tickle her belly.

Ariel takes the opportunity to come over and sit across from me. "What's to become of the Obsession, sir?"

"First thing, Ariel, in the house, we're always informal." She nods her understanding. Having not given the Obsession too much thought,

I pause for a moment. "As for the ship, I'm not sure yet. I don't think I'm going to keep it, not like it is anyway."

She nods. "Some of the crew have expressed concerns. Life on a ship's all they know."

"Well, maybe we could build something smaller for in-system research and patrol."

She thinks for a moment. "With a smaller crew, that'd allow for proper rotations and shore leave."

I smile. "And promotions."

She nods again "Of course."

I give her a curious look. "Are you one of them?"

She nods and blushes slightly. "Yes. I'm the daughter of two officers. The service is all I've ever known."

"Then as the first *Commander* of the, yet to be built, Arcanian fleet, it'd be your task to pick a crew. Are you up for it?"

"I'd need a ship first."

"Then your first task, pick a command crew, get with Doc, and design a ship."

She gives me an odd look. "Doc?"

"That's the name of the graving dock's AI."

"Not very original."

I chuckle. "I know. We'll need new uniforms, too."

Sada waves her hand, getting our attention. 'I'll do that.'

Tayla looks up from playing with Kuma. "Make sure that the evolved can wear them too."

Ariel looks curiously at her. "Are there some that want to join?"

Tayla smiles. "If I hadn't met Kyle, I would. I love to fly"

"Speaking of flying," Skye interjects, "There are some big, hungry dragons called Der'ocks that fly at night. Almost everyone stays in after dark to stay clear of them."

"Yes. You should have your AI download the 'Do's and Don'ts of Arcania' from Ziggy. Cayla put it together as a crash course for new people."

"Thank you, I'll be sure to pass it on to my—to *our* people." She thinks for a moment. "How'd you do it, anyway?"

"Do what?"

"Get our AIs to knock us out. There are trust codes that need to be verified..." she shrugs. "How?"

I chuckle, but Cayla speaks before I can. "We set up a small update with commands to knock you all out, for your safety."

I take over. "As for the trust, I included what I remembered of my interactions with you, Mike, and Carrie. I suspected that Charles would be listening as well so I included a private message to him. I knew that your AIs would try to verify with each other, and when they did, it'd work."

"But what did you tell them?"

"I reminded Julie that I told her directly about the Aquanatum and a few things that Mike and I talked about. I told Carrie's AI about my bite, something only she knew about. I told yours about our first meeting in cargo bay seven."

"What'd you tell Charles?"

"That his avatar is scary."

"His avatar?"

Sada jumps up and retrieves it from the room with the memory core. When she sees it, she grimaces. "It's hideous."

We chuckle as Sada puts it back. "I knew that he'd believe that, since only Carrie, Sada, and I knew about it."

From the far end of the hall, I see someone human come in from the kitchen. As he gets closer, I notice that his face is somewhat familiar, and try to figure out why. He has short dark curly hair, mustache. I notice that both Skye and Larrah have moved to intercept.

He stops and holds up his hands. "I mean no harm."

"Charles?" I blurt, recognizing his voice.

He bows slightly. "I find your home most welcoming, to both AIs and organics alike."

"Thanks. What's with the new avatar?"

"Do you like it? It took some time, but I finally found an image of my name's origin, Charles Fort."

Megai looks at me confused. "Who's this?"

"Sorry. Everyone, this is Charles."

"From the ship? I thought he was an AI?"

"Okay, this is his avatar, an extension of his main self. His main control box is still in the computer room."

He smiles. "It is nice to meet all of you." Then he turns back to me. "I hope you do not mind me using your converters."

"As long as it doesn't interfere, I'm okay with it."

Oana comes up behind him and starts sniffing. "Who you?"

He turns and gives her an odd look. "I am Charles."

"Charles look human. No smell human."

He looks at himself and sniffs. "Apologies, had I realized that I needed a scent, I would have added one."

Several of us chuckle and Oana asks, "Friend?"

"I would hope so." He looks at her for a moment. "What is happening to your back?"

She curls her neck around to get a better look. "Oana k'uu'te growing." She looks down the length of her back to her tail. "Oana k'uu'te white?"

I turn and look, and see the fine fur starting to grow from between the small scales of her back.

"Does that mean something," Tayla asks.

"White k'uu'te rare."

"Let's see your tail."

She turns and carefully drapes her tail over my shoulder. Tayla helps me look at the end, and we find that it's starting to split. "Looks like you'll have a tail fan of some kind."

"Kyle sure?"

"We'll soon find out."

Pria comes up behind me and leans on the back of the couch. "I think I do remember something about a tail fan. It started about the same time the males became aggressive."

I look back over my shoulder. "Think it's related?"

She shrugs her shoulders. "Possibly."

Oana turns back around and gently leans into Pria. "Oana like Pria, Pria know Ootuku speak."

"I'm getting better. They're very old memories," she admits, rubbing Oana's neck.

"You're also getting used to company," Tayla adds.

"She ought to be, she's been to Arindell a few times without us."

"All the better for my offspring."

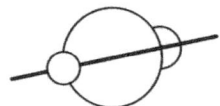

Thanks to Charles, all the collected data from the Obsession has been transferred to Ziggy's memory core. He has also offloaded a lot of his own stored data to the core, allowing him to focus more on other tasks, one of which, is working on designing the equipment I'll need to clone the Moku. Thankfully, it'll only take him several months, compared to the five to ten years it would have been.

Aime, though, has been reviewing other data, more specifically, the evolution process that was used on Sada. After that, she moved on to reviewing the history of the Obsession, at least for the time that I was on board. She's also traded some files with Charles, all of which were about me. Charles loved reviewing my journey, while Aime found that time of my life most interesting, even if it was from an outside point of view.

Now with plenty of free time, I turn my attention to other projects. My biggest concern, right now, is the Aquanatum. They're still in cryo, and currently attached to Doc, in a storage area I recently had added on, but they'll need a home. I can only hope that their designers did some orientation with them before they were put in cryo.

Despite things going well, I can't help by feel like something's missing. No, not something—someone, Tareth. I look out my office door at the now vacant area where he always stood, I miss seeing him there. He always stayed where he could see me, no matter where I was. At first, it had bothered me, but now, I realize that he wanted to be there in case something happened. He was always ready to protect me.

I miss that...I miss him.

With a sigh, I turn my attention back to my tablet and the Aquanatum. As I read, Sada quietly comes in and sits on my lap. I set the tablet down and lean back, reclining my chair and pulling her with me. She purrs and relaxes back onto me.

"To what, do I owe this distraction?"

She takes my hand and places it on her belly. 'Fix me.'

"Fix you? You mean, make you fertile?"

She rubs her cheek against mine and purrs.

"All right, get comfortable."

She repositions so she's lying on me, her back to my chest. Finding herself comfortable, she then stretches out lies her head back alongside mine, purring. I wrap my arms around her and put my hands on her belly.

She gasps as Aime starts regenerating the parts of her that were removed long ago when she was a kitten. She turns her head and starts gently licking my cheek as Aime directs me to move my hands. Her purring gets louder, and her breathing starts to get heavier.

Feeling a curious mix of happiness and pride, I look out the door and see both Tayla and Megai standing there, smiling.

I smile back as Tayla signs, 'Be gentle with her, she's still a little scared she might hurt you.'

With my hands occupied, I nod and let myself fill with understanding.

Megai's smile gets a little bigger as she reaches in and quietly closes my office door. *Aime, room privacy, please.*

If Sada heard the door, she doesn't let on. She reaches up and wraps me in a reverse hug, pulling herself a little taller again. She arches her back and rubs her head against me. Aime shows me that she's finished her work and that Sada has entered a mild estrus. The hormones her body didn't have, and that are now present, are starting her cycle.

I gently slide my hands up her belly and untie the string for her top. She turns around on my lap and straddles me. She then removes my shirt and buries her nose in my neck. Feeling her breathing hard, I realize just how much she wants me. She starts to gently lick me. Her eyes are closed, she's committed to this.

As I remove her top, I realize that she's not wearing any undergarments. She was ready for this. I loosen her dress and pull it out from between us.

She arches her back, presenting her breasts to me. As I take one into my mouth, I feel her hands working on my pants, loosening them. Since I'm seated, she can't do any more to free me, so I hold her to me and stand, letting my pants fall.

She wraps her legs around me and pushes my shorts down. I set her down on my desk and she lies back, pulling me with her. Now locked in her legs, she positions herself and pulls us together. I sink into her and she gasps, arching her back. When her purring resumes, I slowly start a rhythm.

I feel her legs encouraging me, so I pick up my pace. Her tail wrap around my leg and her claws slide harmlessly across my back, she has filed them down.

With closed eyes, she pulls at me, trying to help.

Leaning into her, I gently lick her nose. Her eyes open slightly and she starts licking at my mouth. I return her affection and again pick up my pace.

After a moment, she begins to pant, getting close. I realize that I'll outlast her, *Aime, time mine with hers.* My senses heighten, and I feel myself building quickly. She starts pulling me in closer, wanting release. She starts to buck against me, so I thrust harder, and she pants for more.

Suddenly she clenches, holding me, locking me in place. She bucks one last time, and I release, sinking onto her as my body slowly relaxes.

She too relaxes but doesn't let go. She buries her nose in my neck, breathing hard. I move my hands from her hips and hug her to me.

Despite her fatigue, she does her best to nuzzle into my neck, purring.

"I love you, too, my mate." I feel her nod slightly and lightly lick my neck.

As I start to slowly pick myself up off her, she stops me, gives me a curious look, and touches my neck. I smile, knowing her question. "Aime removed it while restoring you. There's no need to keep it anymore."

'Put it back.'

Her question puzzles me a little. "Why?"

'It's part of our history, I don't want to forget that.'

I give her a kiss. "Anything for you." I feel a slight warming sensation as Aime restores the scars. Sada nods and nuzzles back into me.

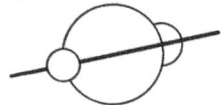

I lie on a couch in the Great Hall, playing with Kuma as he lies on my chest. He giggles as he paws at my face. Sada sits across from me, holding a sleeping Tashi. Despite being twins, they don't seem to have many behaviors in common.

Cayla comes over, followed by Pria and Ariel, and asks, "There's been something bothering me, if the cryotubes you used were of our manufacture, why did they have your symbol and a base twelve countdown?"

I chuckle, more at her question than Kuma's antics. "I suppose I should tell everyone about our last couple days awake. Ziggy, have everyone come in here."

"Certainly."

Epilogue

After waking to near-complete silence, I lie there for several minutes, waiting for Sada to wake. I find myself wondering what would
happen if we were somehow discovered before we awoke. Regrettably,
my wonderings are interrupted by her nuzzling into me, purring.

"Morning."

She slowly sits up and gently scratches at her ears. After a moment,
she shakes her head, looks around, and smiles at me.

I find myself lightly chuckling. "Sounds great, doesn't it? Just you
and I adrift in the silence." She nods and then gently bumps my nose,
purring. With us both awake, we take our showers and then head
down the lift.

A quick glance at the oversized converter, confirms that it has re-
claimed the time machine. I sit down at the control station and check
our status, we're on course for Earth, and it'll take well over two thousand years for us to get there at our current speed.

I sigh heavily. "It's going to be a long ride home."

She nods her understanding and sits on the couch, and I move over
to sit by her. Per Charles's instructions, we should start getting ready
for cryo, but I can't help myself. I want to enjoy the peace and quiet.
Sada puts her head on my chest and sighs heavily, apparently, she wants
what I want. I give her a kiss, and ruffle her fur, getting her to purr gently.

"We're free now, and when we get home, we'll find a nice quiet
place with lots of scenery and enjoy ourselves."

She trills happily and snuggles into me. I hug her, enjoying her closeness. We stay like this, lying on the couch, happily holding each other for quite some time.

Eventually, Sada's stomach growls, causing her to sigh.

"Let's eat."

Sada walks to the smaller converter and selects a couple of dishes. I move the table closer to a couch and take the plates from her. She gets a couple of drinks as I set the plates on the table.

She sets the drinks on the table and sits next to me. She has made me spaghetti, with extra marinara, garlic, and parmesan, with a side of soft garlic bread with shredded mozzarella melted on it. For herself, she has her favored breaded tuna and cheese sticks. We eat slowly and quietly, feeling a mix of relief, and of mild sadness for leaving our few friends.

When we finish, I walk over to the converter and intentionally block her view of what I'm doing. I select from a list of desserts, something we've not had in a long time.

When the bowl and spoons materialize, I pick them up and head back to the table. She gives me a curiously puzzled look as I hand her a spoon. When I sit, I slide the bowl between us and she gasps happily.

She quickly gives me a gentle bump with her nose as she purrs, and we proceed to enjoy the mint chocolate chip ice cream together.

As I stand looking at the two cryo-tubes, Sada comes up behind me and wraps me in a hug. Without taking my eyes off them, I put my arm around her and sigh. Apparently, sensing my apprehension, she puts her nose under my chin and nuzzles into me.

I give her a kiss on the nose. "It's the only thing left to do."

She gently licks my cheek and nods.

I grab the box that Charles left us and open it. Inside I find a checklist, two bottles of a water-like liquid, and two bags with masks; one for me, the other is obviously for Sada as it has a muzzle.

I look at the list read aloud. "Step one, drink the cryoprotectant." I open a bottle and hand it to Sada, and then open the other for myself. I give it a sniff and, not smelling anything, take a taste. I find that it's rather sweet, so I drink it down. Sada eyes it oddly but follows suit.

"Well, that wasn't so bad," I comment, Sada nods her agreement, having finished her own.

"Let's see, next on the list is to put personal positions in the storage compartment of your pod."

Next to the large door of the pods, we find a smaller compartment. With no visible handle, I push on it and it opens. I drop my signet inside as Sada looks at her own pod. She fondles her tag for a moment, then takes it off and drops it inside.

I give her a nod and read the next thing on the list. "Remove all clothes, stand in the large converter, and say 'cryo suit.'"

Sada scowls at me, then turns to the oversized converter and scowls at it. I set the list down and step over to the converter. I look at it for a moment and then shrug. "I don't think Charles would have us do anything that was dangerous."

Sada huffs and shrugs, so I drop my shorts and step in. "Cryo suit."

There's a brief tingling sensation and then a flash. Not noticing anything different I step out and Sada starts poking at my arm. Looking at myself, I find that I'm now wearing a grey, skin-tight suit, that covers me from neck to toe. I run my fingers over my chest and realize that the fabric is very thin.

"There's hardly anything to this stuff, and I didn't even feel anything other than a slight tingle."

Sada feels my arm, trying to sate some of her curiosity.

"Your turn," I state.

She looks at the converter curiously and steps in.

"Ready?"

She tries to relax and nods.

"Cryo suit."

I watch as, with a flash of light, a similar suit appears on her. Like me, she's now covered from neck to toe, including her tail. She looks at herself for a moment and steps out of the converter.

Seeing that this is the first time she's actually worn anything other than her collar, I ask, "How's it feel?"

Her ears skew for a moment, in annoyance, telling me more than words could. I find myself chuckling lightly despite myself. She gives me an even more annoyed look, crossing her arms, so I give her a kiss on her muzzle. "Good thing you'll be asleep for most of the time you're in it."

She relaxes a bit and smiles as I turn my attention back to the box for the two bagged facemasks. I open Sada's and pull out the face mask, a small bottle, a hood, and a small case with earplugs, all are shaped to match her anatomy.

My curiosity sated, I set those aside and grab the list again. "Put in earplugs, put on the hood, enter the pod, and attach support straps to shoulders. *Then* take the sedative, put on the mask, and attach intubation line."

I look at Sada and she's tilted her head curiously, telling me she doesn't know what that means. "Intubation means there'll be a tube down your throat, so you can breathe. I've had one before, and I've had to do plenty of them when I was a paramedic. You probably won't like it."

She puts her hand to her neck and swallows hard. I see the worry and fear in her eyes. "I can wait till you're sedated before doing that. You won't feel a thing that way."

She nods and wraps me in a nervous hug.

"Alright. It'll all be alright." We stay like this for a few minutes, just holding each other.

When she finally pulls back, I see tears. "What's the matter?" I gently ask.

She shakes her head, trying to dismiss the question.

I pull her back to me. "I know you're scared, I am too. We've seen this at work, with the Aquanatum. We know it works." I find myself fighting back my own fears as I continue, "I love you, and I wouldn't let harm come to you. When we wake up, we'll be free. We'll be able to enjoy our life together."

She sniffles a little, so I gently scrub the back of her head. "I love you, and nothing can change that, I promise."

She nods, as she slowly pulls back. I gently wipe her tears away and give her another kiss. "We don't have to do this right now if you don't want to."

She shakes her head and reaches for her earplugs. I help her put them in and hand her the hood. After a few adjustments, she steps into the cryo-tube and I hook the support straps to the loops on her shoulders. After adjusting them to help support her, I hand her the bottle of sedative.

Seeing her hands shake, I gently give her another kiss on her muzzle. She nods and takes a deep breath, trying to relax, then drinks the sedative. I set the bottle aside and pick up the mask. She puts her hand on my cheek and smiles weakly. I nod and kiss her nose one more time, and gently hold her until I know she's asleep.

After putting the mask on her, I attach the three straps to hold it in place and attach the intubation tube. Hearing a click, I know it's locked in place. I step back out, and with a heavy sigh, close the door and press the start button.

I watch as the tube slowly fills with liquid and Sada begins to float. After a minute, the display indicates that she's in cryo. I see a countdown timer showing just over three thousand years.

It's done.

Now it's my turn.

I sit down for a moment and slowly open my mask's bag. I put my earplugs in and pull the hood over my head and then absently stare at the small bottle of sedative for a bit.

Glancing up at the cryo-tubes, I get an idea. I retrieve my signet and step over to the converter. after a few attempts, I finally get what I'm after, two long, plates that will fit across the top of the cryo-tubes. The image on them is the same as my signet. After attaching them in place, I put my signet back in the storage compartment. I then search the exterior and replace anything that has markings on it with an unmarked version.

I collect all the packaging material and removed parts, and put it in the converter. I take eight days off my pod's countdown timer, so I'll wake up first, and then have the pod recalculate the countdown using a base twelve, using twelve random symbols. I have Sada's pod recalculate the same way but don't take any time off her countdown.

Now satisfied that the Earth markings have been removed, I step into my pod and strap myself up. I take a deep breath and swallow the sedative. After tossing the bottle out the door, I put on the mask and adjust it to fit. I then reach out the door and hit the start button, then close the door. I grab the intubation tube and lock it in place as the cryo-tube begins to fill.

Starting to get drowsy, I barely feel the tube extend down my throat as I reach up and tighten the straps holding me up. Sleep takes me before the pod finishes filling.

www.ingramcontent.com/pod-product-compliance
Lightning Source LLC
Chambersburg PA
CBHW070104120726
47909CB00002B/495